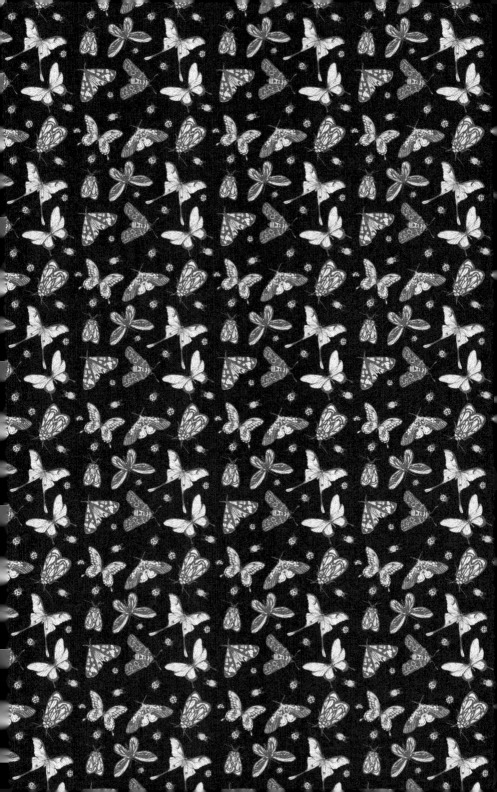

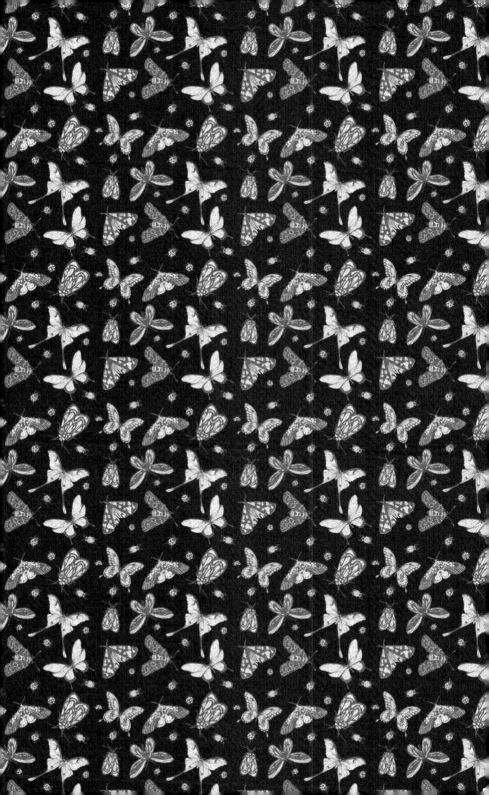

ZELDA FRENCH

3

COLETTE INTERNATIONAL

The International Edition

ISBN: 9781739686475

COVER DESIGNED BY MIBLART
COVER PORTRAITS BY KOMIKLY
INTERIOR GRAPHICS: ISEN ALEJO
INTERIOR ILLUSTRATIONS: JESSYM.

SUBSCRIBE TO ZELDA'S MAILING LIST AT:
WWW.ZELDAFRENCH.COM

BEFORE YOU READ

Content warnings:

This book is not intended for readers under the age of 18.
The subjects treated as well as the various occurrences of violence, profanity and sex may make some readers uncomfortable.

Go to page **403** to find the full list of possibly triggering content.
(The list may contain spoilers.)

Fair warning:

The following story is unapologetically slow-paced, angsty, and aimed at readers who enjoy long and tortuous narratives.

Language:

The different languages spoken throughout the book have been adapted/stylised to ease the reader's experience.
You will find **footnotes** where needed.
Alberto learned English in the U.K, whereas Mathias was taught American English. Their chapters reflect that.

·𝕭·

FICTION IS NOT REALITY.
THE CHARACTERS IN THIS SERIES SOMETIMES ACT IN AN OVER-THE-TOP FASHION THAT WOULDN'T BE APPROPRIATE IN THE REAL WORLD.
YOU ARE **NOT** ENCOURAGED TO REPRODUCE SOME OF THE THINGS YOU'LL READ HERE.

A WORD FROM THE AUTHOR

This narrative wasn't written as a novel, but as a serial,
with chapters grouped together as *arcs*.

There are seven arcs in total.

The book you're holding now contains arcs 1 to 3 pertaining to
Alberto and Mathias's story.

It is recommended to take a short break between each arc.

*"We don't know what secrets hide in the hearts of people,
what wound lurks and festers in the darkest corner of their soul.
If we did, we would all go insane."*

Book of Rain.

Fall

"My body's a temple.
My body's a prison
from which there is no escape."

Strangers

1

A BEAUTIFUL BOY

ALBERTO WAS A BEAUTIFUL BOY.

From the moment of his birth, it was settled. His appearance was a constant cause of wonder, one he was well aware of. In fact, he had known since he was old enough to understand words.

From dawn to dusk, friends, co-workers, and relatives of his parents would come forward, one after the other, to pay homage to his mother and father. Old men grinned, ladies swooned, and wave after wave of faceless strangers marvelled at his features, all of them with the same words on their lips.

"My God. What a beautiful boy."

So much like his mother.

When Alberto was a young child, Mamma used to comb his hair in front of the large, gilded mirror of her antique dressing table. With the open French windows welcoming the Neapolitan Sea breeze inside, Alberto would lose himself to the delicate motions of the curtains stirred by the wind, and to the floral scent of Mamma's long black locks. Amidst the distant sound of waves breaking against the rocks, she would whisper in his ear praises of his ethereal beauty, thanking the gods for his good luck, making wishful promises that everyone in the world could only love him simply because they would love looking at him.

She used to say, most people wouldn't understand, but it didn't matter as long as they couldn't look away. Unadulterated beauty, Mamma insisted, was outside the realm of control. Few people had it. It was how it was. Nothing fair about it.

Alberto didn't understand fairness then, but he got a better grasp of it later. Life wasn't fair. Some had it all. Some had nothing. Some had just enough, and perhaps they were happy. What Alberto had, he saw every time he faced the same old mirror, until the day his gaze was forced away.

A decade later, Alberto wasn't a boy anymore, but he was still beautiful. Years had taught him some, and yet they had taught him nothing, but nothing was ever required of him, anyway. He could simply stand motionless in a room, not even necessarily awake, and he would receive the world's boundless adoration. He had learned he didn't even need to be nice, he would still be the brightest star in the room, a blazing light, impossible to ignore.

History proved it time and time again. From athletes to movie stars and even the most powerful emperors, no one was impervious to beauty. At the age of seventeen, Alberto was more than ever, the recipient of infinite gazes of admiration, of yearning, of love.

But Alberto didn't feel much loved that day.

He stood in tailored clothes in the middle of a cluttered office, succeeding one pose after another, stifling yawn after yawn. His cool-grey eyes cast longing glances at the small window overlooking a trio of waste bins, and out of nowhere, the thought popped into his head and lingered, relentless; he started daydreaming about a train.

Facing him was the unrelenting eye of a camera. Through the lens, the stern-looking woman standing on his left had claimed, his truth would be revealed. Alberto stared into that lens at length and wondered what the photographer would see in there.

Her truth, maybe.

His truth…? Maybe not.

With expert eyes that had seen their fair share of beauty — *the best in the world* — she observed him for a long time, and she could still eye him with interest. She stared as she worked her camera, producing clicks at the speed of a machine gun, until Alberto felt she could see everything, from the inexistent layer of fat around his muscles to the extent of the damage that had taken root in his heart.

After a long time, she turned to the side. "Can he smile?"

She was asking Josephine, Alberto's prospective new agent and an old friend of Mamma's. Friendly enough to accept seeing him anyway. The stern-looking woman arched an eyebrow at him.

"Can you?"

Alberto didn't smile. He threw a hesitant look at his mother. Josephine then turned to her. "Can he?"

"Does he have to?" Mamma didn't smile either. "Smiling gives you wrinkles."

"Mm." Alberto agreed.

The photographer looked at her boss who shook her head. She took a few more shots then relaxed her stance on her stool. "You were right about those eyes. He's a natural."

Alberto wanted to yawn, but he didn't dare in front of Mamma. He scratched his cheek, and the photographer frowned.

"Don't touch your face. Look at me. There. That's good."

"So?" Mamma uncrossed her legs and crossed them again. "What do you think?"

Josephine went to her assistant and took a look at the pictures on her camera. "How tall is he again?"

"One-ninety-one[1]."

Josephine hummed appreciatively. "He's beautiful, for sure."

Ten minutes later, they were all sitting in her office, and Alberto was signing documents with a blotchy fountain pen. When he was done, Josephine gathered the pile of papers and flashed him a polished smile.

"You know, Alberto, I was so glad when Olympia called and said you're finally ready to take modelling seriously."

"Mm."

"She told me you tried it a few years ago, but you didn't like it."

Alberto shrugged and glanced at his mother who was hovering

---

1. Almost 6'3".

nervously in the back. Josephine let out an amused laugh. "He's a quiet one, for sure."

Mamma took a step toward them. "He's a bit shy, that's all."

Josephine and her assistant exchanged a brief look. "So, what made you decide to try again?"

The rusty gears of Alberto's mind started playing *ka-ching, ka-ching, ka-ching*.

"I don't know," he said. Remembering Mamma's words, he added, "It's an exciting career," and he said it convincingly enough that nobody noticed the flat tone of his voice.

"Look at him." Josephine let out a sigh. "Absolutely gorgeous."

Mamma put her hand on his shoulder.

"Thank you," he said politely.

"You're welcome, sweetheart." Josephine and her assistant got up in a loud scrape of chairs. "We're very happy to have you."

"Thank you," he said again, but in the bustle, his voice was lost anyway.

"—and this is just the beginning."

The sound of his mother's voice tore Alberto from this somewhat uneventful memory. Her cool-blue eyes, grey in a certain light, were fixed on him and filled with a certain pride.

Alberto yawned in response. Watching him caused Mamma to helplessly start yawning as well. Her husband, Dimitri, affectionately brushed his thumb against her cheek as she did, and she blushed a little. Alberto lowered his gaze.

"I can't get him to do anything this morning." She sighed. "Here. Have more coffee."

"What did he do this time?" Dimitri's gaze was soft as it fell on Mamma, but when he glanced at him, all warmth was gone.

Alberto ignored him. He murmured his thanks to Dina, their maid, when she placed a cup of coffee in front of him, and he drank it in silence.

Mamma never noticed these things. She put her chin in her hand and chuckled. "He's getting worse and worse. I had to pull his leg to get him out of bed this morning."

Alberto didn't care for the irritated look on Dimitri's tanned face, but he knew what his mother said was the truth. Alberto didn't like being awake as much as he liked *not* being awake. Today was the first day of class since the *Toussaint* holidays. He'd had an excellent break, filled with peaceful naps in an almost empty house. Of course, he'd rather stay in bed instead of going back to school and dealing with all that rabble.

"Alberto…" Mamma knocked on the breakfast table to get his attention.

"Yes?"

"Look at it."

"I've seen it already."

"Look at it again."

Mamma handed him the *Paris Monthly*, which was distributed to hundreds of thousands of Parisians and tourists on the subway. It was open to that double picture of Alberto posing for the *Oɔcult* brand of clothing.

It was the first contract Josephine had gotten him and, in her words, "not the last". He had two more shootings scheduled this month alone.

Ka-ching, ka-ching, ka-ching.

Alberto tossed his airbrushed face an indifferent look. Not the shadow of a smile, but that's what the client had wanted anyway.

Mamma packed the magazine in Alberto's backpack to show all his friends. He slowly pushed his long arms into the sleeves of his black kimono jacket and pretended not to notice Dimitri's meaty hand on her waist. She wished him a good day, and he shuffled toward the gate without a look back.

"Don't eat trash!" Mamma called after him.

As if he ever did.

The gate creaked faintly as it swung closed. The security camera's buzzing was faint but still discernible in the quiet, leafy street. Imposing houses stood on both sides of the road behind sturdy gates, but Alberto didn't pay them any attention. He soon reached a busier intersection where the noise of the city assailed him properly. Cars honked, scooters zoomed by, and pedestrians flocked the pavement, their racket slowly pulling him out of his drowsy state.

When he reached the tube, he realised he'd left his *Navigo* pass at home, and he had to stand in line for a few minutes to purchase a ticket. As he waited, he picked up a discarded flyer about an exhibition at Centre Pompidou, and he put it in the front pocket of his backpack with the others. Once he reached the platform, Alberto positioned himself strategically so that he would enter the coach closest to his future exit, found a seat by the window, and stretched his long legs. Pulling his hood over his head, he switched on the alarm on his phone for exactly eighteen minutes later.

It was neither warm nor cold on this second day of November. Thick clouds blanketed the sky, promising drizzle, but for now, it was dry. A small mercy.

Alberto reunited with the white buildings of Colette International High School for Bilingual Students without emotion. He didn't care much for school in general, but he didn't mind being back. What he didn't like was how short the days had become since they'd turned back the clocks last weekend. He didn't like getting up in the cold and the dark and going home the same way, with the autumnal rain seeping into his clothes. He always forgot his umbrellas everywhere.

Feeling sleepy already, he dragged his feet past the gate and toward the main building, but he paused when someone called his name.

It was the girls. Since he couldn't tell them apart, he didn't know who spoke at first, but it made no difference. The tallest one's hand was still up, so it had to have been her. She and her friends had been following him around for about a year now. Like every morning, he did not respond to her greeting. Like every morning, she giggled when they made eye contact while her friends' mouths hung open in suspense.

No one else tried to get Alberto's attention that morning. He was the first to arrive in the English Literature classroom, and he reluctantly took the seat assigned to him. This bad seat was a consequence of an even worse idea of his. Now, he had to remain seated here until the end of the school year, way too close to the annoying Mrs Paquin, and even closer to the only person he ever dated, whom he wasn't dating any longer.

And that person arrived a breath later.

Zak took his seat with a bright smile, chirpy as usual now that he'd found love — again, not with Alberto, who was ditched before the one-month mark — and his smile vanished at the sight of him, so Alberto made sure to face the opposite side.

It was only eight a.m. when Paquin began screeching about *Sense and Sensibility*. Alberto was already dozing off, his head resting in his hand. Life was just as it ever was: a succession of indistinguishable days, nothing worth staying awake for.

2

PARENTS VS TEACHERS

It felt like only a minute had passed before he woke to general laughter and the sound of knuckles rapping against wood. Paquin was leaning on her desk, her hawk eyes peering at him.

"Mr Gazza, what's your answer?"

After being woken so harshly, Alberto looked around the room in confusion and met Zak's eager expression. He would rather face Paquin.

"I don't know." He yawned. "Sorry. What was the question?"

It didn't take long. Spitting and screaming, Paquin slammed her book on the desk without much sense or sensibility, and she kicked him out while the others looked at him with either compassionate or gleeful expressions.

It wasn't the first time his English Literature teacher kicked him out. It was, however, the first time he was kicked out during the first period of the first day back from the holidays. He had accidentally broken his own record, and Paquin felt they should celebrate by sending him to the headmaster. She ran after him, her eyes glinting maliciously, slapped a note in his hand, and sent him on his way.

It wasn't even nine a.m. yet, and he sat for the first time in Van Bergen's legendary steel-blue office, a place both revered and feared by Colette students. Alberto had heard all sorts of things about the headmaster. People said he was both insanely arrogant and arrogantly insane. The rumours could have very well been true, but Alberto didn't believe in gossip, despite how many pictures of greyhounds were hanging on the office walls in their expensive frames.

Facing him was the man himself. He was staring at him while playing with the wedding ring around his finger, an amused smile curling his lip. As he waited for the storm, Alberto absently admired the way his dress shirt stretched over his muscles. Part of him thought he should feel honoured to have been sent here so early this morning — and in the term — but of course, he felt nothing.

"You like dogs?" Van Bergen asked when Alberto's attention returned to the pair of greyhounds hanging above his head.

"Not as much as you do, apparently."

Van Bergen gave a chuckle, and his gaze finally moved from his face to Paquin's note. His fingers, however, didn't leave his wedding ring.

"So…" He glanced from the note back to Alberto. "Falling asleep again?"

"Yes."

"First day. Not bad."

"Thank you."

Van Bergen's eyes narrowed. "You're welcome." He abruptly got up, startling Alberto, and walked to a cabinet on the side. Sliding it open, he flicked through a few files before finding the thing he was looking for. He skimmed through a series of documents, his expression unfathomable. "Apparently, you fall asleep all the time. Not getting any sleep at night?"

"I'm naturally sleepy."

Van Bergen's eyebrows rose as he returned to his seat. "Naturally sleepy. Fancy that." He said it in a tone that suggested what he thought of his excuse.

The file he dropped on the desk had Alberto's name on it. *Seriously*. Van Bergen drummed his fingers on its cover. "You have shit grades, too."

Alberto peered through the window into the grim playground.

"Why do you have shit grades?" Van Bergen insisted. "Is it because you're naturally sleepy?"

Alberto stifled a yawn. "Yes."

Van Bergen slammed his foot against the bottom drawer of his desk. "Good God, can you at least control yourself for a minute?"

Alberto nodded with difficulty.

"You're almost eighteen. Wouldn't want to spend another year at Colette, I assume."

No, he wouldn't.

"At least your Italian's flawless. Top grades. I guess you're taking full advantage of the options here."

Alberto shrugged. Being Italian himself, it would have been stupid not to jump on that opportunity for easy grades.

Van Bergen tapped on the file's cover again. "Why did you drop Drama Club?"

"I thought I didn't need it anymore."

"I see…" Van Bergen leaned back in his chair with a sigh. "I don't know what to do with you. Complaints about you are always the same: you're sleeping through lessons, but you don't have a bad attitude beyond that. So, what am I supposed to do? If I give you detention, you'll just sleep through it, and you won't learn a thing."

Alberto pinched his lips. He really didn't want to do detention. He would never live it down at home. The headmaster stared at him for some time. Alberto let him, staring right back at him. Van Bergen had frank eyes, bold and inquisitive, like a photographer's eyes. Alberto looked into the man's face the same way he did at the objective: full-on dead eyes.

"You look familiar, kid. Why do you look familiar?"

Alberto sniffed and scanned around the room for a certain magazine. The *Paris Monthly* was there on his desk, between two folders. Alberto picked it up and placed it in front of the headmaster. He tapped it with his fingertip, trying his best not to yawn again.

"In here?" Van Bergen asked. "You're in here?"

Alberto nodded.

The headmaster, with a little derisive snort, opened the magazine and flipped through it until he got to the *Occult* campaign he did six weeks ago. It was everywhere now. His face was even plastered on a bus stop not five minutes from here. Alberto's expression right now was the same as in the picture: full-on dead eyes, that look which somehow made people yearn for something they didn't know they were yearning for.

The headmaster's eyes narrowed slightly as they slid from the picture to the real Alberto.

"Is that why you're tired? You're a model?"

"It's a job like any other."

"Fair enough." Van Bergen flipped the magazine closed and linked his fingers together. "Is your mother coming tonight?"

"What? Why?"

The headmaster arched a teasing eyebrow. "The Pa—"

"Parents-Teachers meeting."

"There you go."

Oh no. Alberto had completely forgotten about that cursed meeting. Today was not even Monday, but it felt like a Monday. Like a really shitty Monday.

Alberto didn't know what to say. Mamma said she was coming, but that was weeks ago. She had probably forgotten all about it by now, and Alberto was fine with that.

"I don't think she'll be there," he mumbled.

"Let's hope she will be." Van Bergen got up and gestured for him to do the same. "I can at least tell your mother to watch over your sleep pattern or something."

Alberto almost laughed, but he decided it would be foolish. He hadn't expected Van Bergen to let him go so easily, but perhaps even the formidable Colette headmaster didn't want to bother with students so early on the first day.

Good for him.

To Alberto's surprise, his mother had not forgotten, and she hadn't driven herself either. She told her driver, Oleg, to come back in an hour, and she sent him away. Alberto anxiously watched her approach. This was the first time she came to one of these meetings. Mamma didn't storm the schoolyard, but she wandered nonchalantly as if she owned the place. The moment she passed the gate, all eyes were on her.

But, like always, Mamma only had eyes for him. She clattered toward him in her favourite *Louboutin* — the ones with the red soles — which made her eyes twinkle when she received them from her ex, Martin. Perched on these, she was slightly taller than him.

"Where are your friends?" She left a kiss on his cheek then wiped a trace of her lipstick away with a long finger.

"I told you, they're in other classes. You won't see them tonight."

"Why don't you have friends in this class? It's been two months."

"What are you talking about? I have plenty of friends."

His mother looked unconvinced, but she gave up the subject. She shivered in her trench coat. Mamma hated the cold, but she loved that coat too much to wear something warmer.

"Take me inside, *Tesoro*[1]."

Alberto led his mother toward the front doors to the main building, his heart in his throat. He felt like he could hear every sharp intake of air and every surprised or lewd comment. From the corner of his eye, he noticed Kayvin's group. Bunch of losers. When he heard their cavemen laughs, he threw a dark look over his shoulder.

Mamma didn't notice anything off. She was struggling with her phone and not paying attention to what was in front of her.

"Dimitri says we have a special guest for dinner."

"Great," Alberto said without enthusiasm, and he quickly stepped up before Mamma walked straight into the front door. Mostly made of glass, it wasn't always easy to discern, in his opinion, and he heard more guffaws. Mamma put her phone back in her pocket without realising she had caused a mini storm out there.

Alberto let out a sigh of relief when she found a seat at the very back of Paquin's classroom. While the place filled up with parents and their offspring, he kept his head down.

Van Bergen came in his tight suit, his perfect smile not completely masking the deranged glint in his eye. He introduced

---

1. Affectionate pet name similar to "Honey", it literally means "treasure". (Italian)

himself, and after promising a short speech, he started blabbering nonsense about Alberto and the other students' futures.

"What a handsome man," Mamma said. She looked surprised.

"You think?" Alberto might dislike Dimitri more than his morning alarm, but he wouldn't want his mother to elope with the headmaster either. "He's too big," he said in a cold tone.

"Look at that confidence." She chortled. "*È magnifico.*"

Alberto squinted and attempted to calculate how old Van Bergen could be. He was probably in his late thirties, around the same age as his mother, and Alberto was about to panic when his mother added with a sigh, "He's gay, though. The best ones always are."

She started messing with her phone again, leaving Alberto to ponder her words. After half a minute, he gave in and asked, "How do you know?"

"Hm?" Mamma had already moved on. "What?"

"How do you know Van Bergen is gay?"

She gave a half-shrug. "I have an eye for these things."

Did she really? As she yawned, Alberto observed the side of her face for a moment, perplexed. Then, he returned his attention to Van Bergen and decided he was, in fact, quite handsome, even if he *could* lay off the lifting for a bit. Or at least wear shirts of the right size.

As he promised, Van Bergen left four minutes later, leaving the stage for the other teachers to continue. Neither Alberto nor his mother would remember who said what during this tedious meeting, as Mamma almost fell asleep on Alberto's shoulder. She sprung to her feet when they were all dismissed. Someone's father tried to introduce himself to her, and he was beautifully — and unintentionally — ignored. Alberto assumed the murderous-looking woman at his side was his soon-to-be ex-wife.

Wishing he were taller and as big as Van Bergen so that he could conceal her from all the unwanted glances, Alberto trotted after his mother. But Mamma didn't mind being stared at. She had accepted her extraordinary beauty. Only an idiot would reject such a great gift.

Van Bergen's annoying frame proved useful when he used it to block the way out. He flashed an absolutely devilish smile at Alberto's mother. "Would you spare one minute for poor old me?" He sounded like a kiss-ass, but they were just talking among divine-looking people. They recognised each other as being above the others, so they didn't mind weird familiarities like that. Mamma slowly blinked at him in acknowledgement.

"Lead the way," she said.

Alberto couldn't glare at Van Bergen; he was domineering and hot, and he was even hotter since Mamma had declared he was gay. Weird how that stuff worked. He let Van Bergen take his mother back to his office while he hung out in the corridor like a lost kid in a supermarket.

At some point, Zak walked by with his mother. She was dressed like a rainbow of sorts, an explosion of colour, and Alberto thought, *There you go; that explains Eric.* He leaned against the wall and spaced out.

Mamma wasn't happy on the ride home.

"If you can't keep up, you'll be homeschooled."

Alberto didn't want to have this conversation in front of the driver, whom he suspected could understand Italian, but he didn't have a choice.

"I just fell asleep once… maybe twice… There's no need to—"

"But I think it's best for you. I can watch over you at home. I don't know anything about what's happening to you over there."

"Nothing's happening to me over there."

Truer words were never spoken. Alberto mentally patted himself on the back, but his mother, upset at his absence of good grades, was getting restless.

"And how come you don't have any friends?"

"I told you. They were in other classes. You left so quickly, you didn't get to see them; it's not my fault."

Mamma sighed. "You really have to try to stop sleeping in class."

"I'll try."

"I'm serious. For me."

Alberto took her arm. "For you, I promise."

Her shoulder relaxed when he laid his head upon it. "Van

Bergen said he'd call me the next time this happens. I don't want him to call me."

"Oh? I thought he was *magnifico*."

"He is, bless him, but I don't want to go back there unless I have to. It's too cold outside. Do me a favour and wait until summer before you start acting up."

Alberto snorted, Mamma answered in kind, and before he knew it, she had pulled him into a hug.

Hand in hand, they reached home in higher spirits. Alberto was so relieved his mother had dropped the idea of homeschooling him, that he failed to pay close enough attention to his surroundings, so he didn't notice the blonde flash of lightning on his left until it tore into him with a shriek.

"Surprise!"

Alberto's heart jumped into his throat, and he inadvertently took a step back. While he stood there in shock, Dimitri tore Mamma away from him. She gave his only daughter a rare smile, going as far as holding her hands and kissing her cheek.

"Welcome back, Stasia. It's good to see you."

"You too, Olympia, you too!" The girl turned to Alberto. "So… did you miss me?"

Using his generous reserves of self-control, but with a bitter taste filling his mouth due to the effort, Alberto stared at the smiling face before him with a blank expression.

3

EVIL SPAWN

Alberto was an atheist, but that never stopped him from believing one thing: Stasia was the Devil.

That was the most plausible explanation. If she weren't the Devil, she was working for Him. She was a harpy, one of Satan's minions. If she weren't any of that, then Alberto would have to worry again about having been born under the wrong star, and that sounded even more outrageous and mystical. He was an atheist, after all, who didn't believe in gods or angels and definitely not in astrology. Now... inner demons and ghosts from the past, that was another subject, but right now, he couldn't let his imagination run amok because the Devil was standing in front of him.

"Albertino, come here, come here."

Alberto glanced at her from his spot by the front door, but he didn't move.

Stasia wasn't as tall as him, but she was athletic, and her vicious nature gave her almost supernatural strength. She moved so fast that it sometimes felt like she was in two spots at once. One moment, she would be jumping him outside the bathroom, the next, she'd be throwing food at him in the kitchen. Maybe it only felt like this because she was well-practised in the art of bullying, and when he met her, she was taller than him by half a head. But despite her smaller stature, Alberto had always felt she was towering over him. That's because there was no balance between them. She was almighty; he was not.

Perhaps it also had to do with the fact that she somehow felt allowed to put her hands on him, and he, of course, was absolutely not allowed to touch her for one simple reason: that evil spawn wore the skin of a woman, and Alberto was naturally raised never, *ever* to put his hands on a woman, whatever she may say or do. And Alberto really, *really* wanted to live by his mother's rules, because in his heart, no one could best Mamma, and he truly wanted to be a better man than the ones he'd had the misfortune to meet in his life.

Stasia was cunning, and she knew of this rule, so she was certain Alberto would never fight back. Turned on by weakness — he had learned to assume — she had grown fond of tormenting him, and she was creative. From the moment he first saw her at the age of fourteen, she had made his life a living hell.

Alberto had never complained to anyone about this, and as a result, no one knew. If he spoke up, it would only drive a wedge between his mother and Dimitri, and they would be forced to move again. Mamma would get sad, and Alberto had had enough of making his mother's life difficult and watching her weep because of him.

So, he had to endure Stasia.

At first, she was just a bully. She would chase him around the pool with her friends, steal his things and hide them, add salt to his juice, and stuff like that. Back then, she was a spoiled brat, but she was bearable. However, she left for the university over a year ago, and just when Alberto had begun to relax, she returned from the grave like a monster from a horror movie, freshly dropped out of school. After taking a long look at her Albertino, all grown up, as she said, her bullying had faintly changed in flavour. She would still try to toss him into the pool if he was stupid enough to approach her, but she was doing weirder things now, like trying to sneak into his bed, rub her foot against his leg under the table, and consistently touch him in all sorts of places without a care for his dignity at all.

Any time he would use words in an attempt to defend himself, she'd only get more aggressive, confident in the knowledge he'd never lay a finger on her. He'd usually put up with it to a degree, sometimes slapping her hands away or wriggling out of her grip, which she enjoyed tremendously, but sometimes, he'd manage to run away altogether, and she'd end up empty-handed. Usually, she settled those accounts by being extra cruel the next time she had him cornered.

Thankfully, Stasia was living a pretty hectic life. Between the endless parties, which she called *networking*, and her bottomless appetite for finding rich fools to date and drain financially and emotionally, she was sometimes gone for days, even weeks, and he could focus on living a normal life. Those were the days.

Today was not such a day.

She was supposed to be in Costa Rica with a group of friends — people he was grateful he had never met — but instead, she was here, stalking toward him.

Mamma and Dimitri had withdrawn to the lounge for a glass of wine. Alberto could hear his voice, adoration for his mother palpable in the timbre of his laughter. Meanwhile, his evil spawn stood before Alberto, barely bothering to pretend to be human.

"I heard you were at a parents-teachers meeting?" she asked, fingers trailing across the wall. "How did it go?"

"Great." Alberto rapidly kicked off his shoes. If he got upstairs fast enough, she may lose interest. It all depended on how bored she was today.

"Did they kick you out yet?"

He rolled his eyes behind her back. "Why would they kick me out?"

"Once they notice you're brain dead, of course."

Alberto ignored her jab — it was an easy one; she had just gotten back, after all — and started climbing up the stairs. Then, he turned around, unable to stop himself.

"What happened to Costa Rica?"

"Ah!" Her face split into a wicked grin. "So you did miss me. I was heartbroken by your earlier reaction. So cold." When Alberto didn't react, her mean smile widened. "Fine. If you really want to know, I broke up with Romaric." Stasia spun around and ran her hand through her bleached-blonde mane. "But you should rejoice. I'm thinking of getting a dog again."

With a last wink, she walked out, leaving Alberto frozen in the middle of the stairs.

Whenever she was staying here, Stasia lived in the dependence at the end of the garden, a luxurious one-bedroom unit with all possible comfort and a view of the pool. If Alberto was grateful for anything, it would be for that. She used to sleep in the room across from his when he first moved in. At that time, she also had a dog, a Pomeranian named Georgie. Her pets were always named after her last boyfriend victim, and they never lasted. In less than four years, she'd buried three of them already.

Alberto thought of them as he got up the next morning. He could see the lawn from his window, and he could pinpoint the exact location of the tombs he had seen the gardener dig up, Stasia's fake tears rolling down her cheeks as she watched. As for how they died, Alberto didn't want to guess. That was one of the many doors he refused to open. Repressing a shudder, he put on the clothes neatly laid out for him.

At seven a.m., it was too early to catch a glimpse of the Devil. Alberto drank his breakfast under the sleepy gaze of his mother before he left for school. This time, he had his pass, so the journey happened without hurdles.

Above the white Colette buildings, the same lid of low grey clouds was threatening everyone with a good shower, and yet, nothing was happening. Sitting on his lonely bench, Alberto lost himself to the sight, his cigarette smoke reaching toward the sky like an outstretched hand.

Stasia was back. That meant he had to plan for his evenings and his weekends again. He couldn't rely on the Drama Club to save him from her clutches once a week as before, but he still had the option of exploring Paris's infinite number of museums. Alberto opened the front pocket of his backpack and examined a few flyers, stopping at the one advertising the exhibition at Centre Pompidou.

Someone called his name, forcing him to look up. Alberto was surprised to see his one time friend, Sander, ambling toward him, flanked by his classmate, Arthur, a skinny and dishevelled guy. Following them with a frown was Zak, who was close friends with Arthur. Sander stopped in front of Alberto with an awkward smile.

"Hey, man. How are you?"

Once, he and Alberto were inseparable, but now they had nothing to say to each other, so Alberto immediately became suspicious. At least Sander didn't waste time and went straight to the point.

"So... was that your mum we saw last night?"

Alberto's lip curled into a derisive smile. "What if I told you she wasn't?"

"No way." Sander's eyes shone as he spoke. "You look so similar."

"Then why do you ask?"

He hesitated. "You talked so much about her. It was weird to finally see her in person, after all... you know... after all this time."

Zak glanced curiously from him to Alberto and back, his friend Arthur doing the same. No one understood how Sander and Alberto went from being besties in *Seconde*[1] to not speaking at all over the course of a few months.

It was pretty simple, actually. Sander was a boring person, with little to no personality. He was also sweet and gentle, despite his frosty manners. A perfect companion for a guy like Alberto.

Well, almost perfect.

Sander was obsessed with girls, unfortunately, and they were the sort of girls who were obsessed with guys who looked like Alberto.

At first, Alberto and Sander had the perfect partnership. They used each other for company, and their mutual temperaments were such that they got along quite well, but, eventually, even Sander grew tired of Alberto. He once hoped hanging out with him would put him in the path of countless girls, but all he got for his efforts was the unpleasant feeling of living in some zombie's shadow, a guy so out of touch he never spared a glance at any girl who wasn't his mother.

---

1. The first year out of three in French high schools.

Alberto got it. He was a walking disappointment. When he returned from the summer holidays with Zak as his boyfriend, something clicked within Sander at last. He saw no reason to force himself to remain by Alberto's side. He and their mutual friend, Oliver, rapidly used the excuse of not being in the same class anymore to distance themselves from him, and Alberto was left with Zak, but, eventually, even his biggest fan had had enough and broke up with him.

Sander found Alberto on the playground afterwards and tried to talk to him about it. He couldn't believe Zak would ditch him after months of cult-like adoration. Alberto told him Zak was in love with someone else. Sander retorted it was more likely that he left because Alberto was "shit at making people feel special". That wasn't untrue, so he let Sander go, too. That week, he was dumped twice.

Alberto remembered staring at his large shoulders as he walked away and thinking, *Meh… Whatever.*

Behind Sander, Zak felt the atmosphere was too uncomfortable and changed the subject. "What's that? A new exhibition at Pompidou?"

"Hm?" Alberto looked down at the flyer in his hand. "Yes."

"Can I see?" He handed over the thing. Zak stared at it intently. Then, he suddenly asked, "How about going together?"

Alberto's eyes widened. He had no clue how to answer that, but thankfully, Arthur coughed in his fist, jolting Zak back to reality.

"That's fine," Zak said with a laugh, but he still threw a quick look over his shoulder. "I just… I'd love to see this one."

Alberto spoke fast for once, "Sorry, I'm not going this weekend."

"But isn't it the last weekend? Look at the dates."

"Zak!" Arthur called. He jerked his chin toward the other side of the playground. Zak's expression went from mild and friendly to almost demented with joy. His dumb boyfriend had just walked through the front gate.

It was clear now nothing else mattered for Zak but to close the distance between him and Eric. He absently gave Alberto his flyer back and darted off, leaving Arthur and Sander in the dust.

Alberto followed him with his eyes, but just as Zak and Eric were about to jump into each other's arms, Sander blocked his view, pointing at the cigarette in Alberto's hand. "And you're smoking now?"

"... Yes."

He really didn't like it when people stated the obvious.

"Won't it damage your skin? Your mum will flip when she finds out."

Alberto sighed. It pained him to have to lie to his mother about having friends, but really, he didn't miss Sander at all.

The arrival of Eric had made Zak forget all about going to the museum with Alberto, which was a good thing. He was riding on a cloud too high to notice his existence, and Alberto happily returned to pretending that he didn't exist, as he always did with people and things that reminded him of particularly distasteful moments of his existence.

But the problem with Zak and Eric was that they really liked to make their presence known. As Alberto stepped outside at the end of this interminable day, his gaze accidentally fell upon them, and he found himself stuck in place, unable to look away.

There are some who clearly don't fear a punch in the face.

Eric had no shame, and surprisingly, Zak turned out to be similar. Granted, they had found a somewhat isolated spot on the playground, but by stretching one's neck, anyone could see it.

And everybody was staring.

Alberto was staring, too. It was almost mesmerising, this show of abandon between two guys in broad daylight. In fact, it was something that had probably never been witnessed at a school like Colette before. Some talked about how Michael and Louis had been a hot couple a few years back, but no one had ever caught them doing this, though this schoolmate, Xavier, swore he saw them in the men's room once, and it looked like they had been making out — he still obsessed about it.

Eric had enveloped Zak in his arms and was apparently determined to explore every corner of his mouth. Zak seemed intent on doing the same to him. They had moved to another plane and cast aside all other concerns. From the look of it, if one even dared, one wouldn't stand a chance of smashing their perfect little bubble. Each time they briefly parted to get some air, Eric would shower Zak with featherlight kisses on the corners of his mouth, his expression faintly astonished, as though part of him still couldn't believe he had him in his grasp. As for Zak, he had become completely limp. Liquid. A puddle.

Alberto *despised* them.

It was a good thing Eric was already really popular before he turned out to enjoy little twinks because, otherwise, he and his lover would have been cornered into an empty classroom and beaten into submission a long time ago.

Alberto *really* despised them.

Ah, well. How bitter he sounded. Why? He couldn't put his finger on it. He wasn't even interested in Zak. Or in dating. Still, he couldn't stand it.

The way they felt about each other.

The way they *felt*.

Alberto tore his gaze away from the lovebirds and glanced up. So many types of clouds inhabited the skies, but he had to be born under a dull, grey one.

Never mind them. Alberto needed to go home and sleep. Thinking too much only gave him headaches. Then, his mother would worry. Now that he had started modelling again, it wouldn't be good to think, worry, and grow wrinkles on his forehead.

Pulling his hood over his head, he set off along the side wall of the school where the least amount of people were likely to see him. He was struggling to recall whether or not Stasia was home tonight when someone crashed into him, knocking the breath out of him.

For a second or two, his mind went blank.

When he came to, he found himself slammed against the wall, staring at a face full of anger. Blinking in confusion, he looked down at the person who hit him. Apart from the height difference, the most notable thing about that stranger was his buzz cut hairstyle and the unusual set of hazel eyes currently burning holes into him.

Did he know him? No. Should he ask? Alberto seriously had no clue what he could have done to warrant this. It could just be a mistake.

"Hello," he said in an attempt to remind this guy that he was a living person.

The grip on his sweater tightened before the stranger spoke to him in a low but sharp voice. "Tell your mother to stay away from my dad."

Alberto blinked some more. He turned and turned the words in his head, but he decided they really didn't make any sense, so he snorted. "What?"

"Do I sound funny to you?" The guy pressed him deeper into the wall.

Alberto tried to think, but the short trip from the playground to a concrete wall — unsurprisingly — did not help with his mental faculties.

His mother… His mother…

His mother was home with his arse of a stepfather, waiting for Alberto to return. His mother was definitely not shagging this angry… buzz cut's dad, whoever that was.

"I think you have me confused with someone else."

"Like hell I have," the guy said, but Alberto felt he somewhat relaxed his grip around his sweater. "It's not like your mother isn't memorable."

Touché, Alberto thought. He shrugged. "How do you know she's my mother?"

Angry Buzzcut frowned. "I'm talking. You're not talking."

"*O-kay.*"

Now he seemed disoriented by Alberto's lukewarm reaction. Perhaps he had expected him to fight back? What a joke. Alberto could only look down at him just as he looked at anyone who interrupted the course of his life: mildly, indifferently, and thinking of his next nap.

Clearly, it was enough for this guy to reconsider his actions. His face slowly relaxed, the fire in his eyes dimming to embers.

"Just… tell her to stay away from him. She'll know." With a last skewering glance, he released him and walked away.

Stiff and still against the wall, Alberto stared after him. He seemed athletic, like Eric, but stronger. There was something dangerous about him, even in the way he held himself, slightly hunched over. What did he expect from him, coming at him out of nowhere like that? Fear?

But, disappointing as always, Alberto felt no fear. What he felt was... curiosity. He went to put a cigarette between his lips, and only then did he notice his mouth had been hanging open.

4

A PRIVATE GUY

MATHIAS WAS A PRIVATE GUY.

He was no stranger to secrets. If cornered, he'd confess that, yes, Cyril Rodin, the math teacher freshly hired here at Colette, was indeed his father, but all the same, he preferred it if nobody found out.

His kid sister attended Colette as well, and she was eager to conceal their kinship, too. Not because she worried about what things people would say about him, but because she seriously believed that their connection put her principles of objectivity and fairness at risk.

Mathias respected her choice, even if he doubted any fifteen-year-old was capable of flawless objectivity and fairness. He'd let her do as she pleased since she was a bawling baby. That wasn't about to change now. If anything, he was relieved he had to pretend not to know her. He hung out with a crowd of idiots, save one or two, and they would have made lewd comments about her. Then, he'd have had to do something about it.

Mathias's well of patience tended to dry quickly, so stupid comments and other bullying antics usually had the effect of making him throw his fists at people's faces, and that's how he got in trouble at his former high school.

Silver lining, getting kicked out made him conscious of his

anger problem, so he signed up for a boxing class, which had proven a wise decision, but in the end, he still had to abandon his town and most of his friends to come here to this alien institution in which he was certain he'd never fit.

Here, for the sake of his family, he was determined to adopt a different attitude. After all, he only had to survive until the end of the school year, and then he'd be free to enter culinary school as he always wanted. So, even if he appeared unfriendly, at least he was calm, and he was satisfied to stand in his new friend's shadow.

Eric loved the spotlight, being everyone's favorite. When he and Mathias first met, he was like a superstar, a promising football talent already signed with one of the biggest clubs in the country. Nowadays, Mathias had noticed his popularity had waned, but Eric didn't care about trashy people or their trashy views. His fists never left his pockets, and he could take a few slurs with a smile on his friendly face.

Mathias was different. His own fists always itched to break free from their confines, the front pockets of his faithful gray hoodie. That was the thing with his hands: they seemed to have a life of their own. Every day, Mathias forced himself not to feel much, but his hands, they did all the processing for him, and if he didn't bury them in his clothes, he was worried they would be the end of him.

That particular day, Mathias was exiting class at Eric's heel when, all of a sudden, a horrible blaring sound exploded in the corridor. He jumped and moved in front of his friend. "What the fuck was that?"

Eric hadn't moved nor did he look surprised. "Don't worry about that. It's just the headmaster."

Rubbing his ears in pain, Mathias twisted his neck to confirm his words. Indeed, Van Bergen was standing at the end of the corridor, an air horn in his hand and a smile on his smug face. "Quiet in the corridors!" he bellowed dramatically.

"Yeah…" Eric sighed. "He does that sometimes."

"Because walking around with a riding crop wasn't enough,"

Mathias said with a grimace. "Psychopath. Why is everybody so weird and noisy in here?"

"Huh? We're not noisy." Eric's lips pursed childishly. "Oh, look, it's Xavier!" He cupped his hands and shouted right by Mathias's ear, "Buddy, we're here!"

Mathias rolled his eyes as he opened his locker. Eric had long lost the key to his own, so they shared it together. It was easy to see which part of the locker belonged to whom. Eric was easily distracted—think "puppy spotting a butterfly"—but he was weirdly anal about neatness, while Mathias treated his belongings just as he treated unimportant people: getting them out of sight and closing the door in their faces.

Eric perked up when he spotted the apple he left in there yesterday, and he almost decked Mathias in the face in his haste to reach it.

"You're the noisiest of them all," Mathias mumbled.

"What? What did you say?"

Mathias kicked him. "And you're fucking deaf, too!"

"Language," a smooth voice said behind him.

Eric glanced up and choked on a piece of apple, making Mathias whirl around. The headmaster had somehow teleported from the end of the corridor to their locker. He leaned against the wall and lazily scratched his temple with the butt of his air horn.

"For fuck's sake…" Mathias muttered.

Eric yelped and tugged his sleeve.

"Ho-ho!" Van Bergen smirked. "Who taught you how to swear like that?"

Mathias didn't flinch. "My mom."

The headmaster hummed, and his eyes narrowed into slits. "Alright. Piss off, then."

He turned around and strolled toward Xavier, who appeared to have accidentally gotten his hand stuck in his locker. Mathias watched Van Bergen make fun of him without lifting a finger to help.

Eric tapped his shoulder to get his attention.

"Matt!" Eric's eager expression made him take a step back. "How come you can speak to the headmaster like that? If it were me, I'd be suspended from the ceiling right now." Mathias snorted, making Eric laugh in turn. "Seriously! And the headmaster likes me! He likes football, so of course he likes me."

"Great."

"I play football pretty well—"

"Show off."

"—and I'm cute, so he likes me."

"Again. Show off."

"But, but… why does he like you so much?"

Mathias quirked an eyebrow. "Are you saying I'm not a good goalkeeper?"

"No! You're great."

"So you're saying I'm not cute."

"God, no!"

Mathias evaded his attempt at a hug. "Back off."

"But seriously. Is it because your dad works here?"

Mathias almost punched Eric in the shoulder but instead hissed, "I told you to keep quiet about this."

"Sorry, sorry."

His puppy eyes were unbearable. Mathias shook his head. "You like sticking your nose into other people's business too much."

"Only people I really like."

"Thanks, I'm touched."

"Could you say that without rolling your ey—ah! Zak's here! Zak! Move, buddy. ZAK!"

Eric's howls were twice as loud as the headmaster's air horn; Mathias had to rub his ears again.

Emerging from a classroom, Eric's boyfriend, Zak, flinched at the sound of his name. Short, skinny, and with his irritated expression and his crazy nest of hair, he always looked like he was forced out of his bed at gunpoint, but he was all right. He did speak like an old man, but he didn't talk much compared to Eric, and he had a good head on his shoulders. At least most of the time. The rest of the time, he was completely obsessed with Eric, and the two of them were disgusting to watch.

Eric was on his toes, waving at him frantically, and Zak's face darkened a bit when he saw him. Mathias instinctively looked around for the nearest exit.

He had only been here two months. At first, everything was pretty normal. Average school for average privileged asses. Chances of surviving the school year: about 95%. But about four weeks ago, Eric, who was what you could call a chick magnet, showed up at school with the largest smile and another guy in his arms. He introduced Zak to Mathias as his boyfriend, as well as the most amazing human being on the planet.

Mathias could only blink in shock and disbelief. Even today, he wasn't sure how it happened, but, apparently, Eric turned gay from one weekend to the next. His mom had often warned him that the world was filled with inexplicable things, but this still came out of nowhere.

And Mathias wasn't the only one to be stunned. Everyone on the football team started looking at him differently. After a few days, one of the defense players, Xavier, couldn't hold it in anymore. Because everyone was a little worried about Eric, during practice, Xavier asked him, "Have you noticed that Zak is *not* a girl?" But Eric replied his eyesight was still the best on the team, and Xavier should focus on the ball instead of thinking about Zak. Mathias was sure Xavier was trying, since he never mentioned it again in front of Eric. He still missed the ball during practice, though.

It wasn't that Mathias was embarrassed to be seen with them, but he was uncomfortable. It's just that these two were constantly on top of each other, while Mathias couldn't remember the last time he'd held someone's hand, to say nothing of Eric's smugness every time he succeeded in isolating his target during breaks. If he made out with Zak at lunchtime, he had to brag about it all afternoon. Mathias had yet to learn how to tune him out.

Despite all of this, Eric was Eric, and without him, Mathias would have had an even tougher time adapting to this school and to these people who couldn't be more different than himself.

Unlike so many of his schoolmates, Eric didn't have a mean bone in his body. He was always in a good mood, and he didn't mind Mathias's lack of interest in the others. He would talk and talk about stupid shit at length with everybody, and Mathias could sit back and observe without worrying about losing his temper.

Despite appearances, Mathias wasn't an asshole who couldn't stand most students for no reason. It's just that he had to become an adult at a pretty young age. When one's forced to age that fast, they often find it difficult to relate to the problems of spoiled and entitled little shits. That's how he saw it, at least, and it's not like Eric gave him a choice either. On the first day of school, Mathias was calmly settled at the back of the class, when he showed up, pointed at the empty seat next to him, and went, "Hey! Wanna sit next to me?" Before Mathias could protest or agree, that bastard had already dumped his ass on the chair and made it look like Mathias had been the one asking for it.

After that, Eric started following him around like a shadow, dragging him into one scheme after the other. Mathias had always been good at sports, and his dad wanted him to participate in extracurricular stuff, so less than a week later, he was named goalkeeper for the school's football team, and Eric, their best striker, had almost passed out from excitement.

So, yeah, they were sort of friends now, and it would be a bit awkward to ditch him because he was obsessed with another boy, right? But he'd prefer if they could turn it down a notch. Like, seriously.

Zak stopped in front of them, his dark eyes glinting. "So… Alberto got kicked out less than an hour into class!"

"Yeah, I know," Eric said. "You posted it on Facebook. I even commented." He looked crestfallen. "Don't you read my comments?"

Mathias shook his head. "Do any of you ever do any studying at this school?"

"Sometimes," they answered at the same time, grinning at each other.

They were interrupted by a line of half a dozen girls who forced their way between them, throwing avid looks around. When they failed to find what they were looking for, they let out a sigh of disappointment. Eric stared after them with a puzzled look.

"Did someone die?"

Zak shrugged. "They were waiting for Alberto outside the classroom, but no one knows where he is."

"Did *he* die?" Eric asked.

"Eric!" Zak adopted a stern expression.

"Sorry…" Eric lowered his head. "I'm sorry."

Mathias stared after the girls with a frown. "Do they really follow him around all day?"

"Not all day," Zak said. "Sometimes, he's nowhere to be found. Anyway, I wonder what Van Bergen did with him."

"You mean *to* him," Mathias muttered.

"Maybe he was expelled," Eric said, and Mathias noted he sounded almost hopeful.

Eric rarely sounded unfriendly except when it came to this Alberto. Mathias was aware that his nemesis was Zak's ex-boyfriend, but apart from Eric and Zak themselves, no one at school actually believed those two were really dating. Even Zak himself doubted it, going as far as claiming Alberto was not gay after all, but it didn't matter to Eric, who was on an imaginary warpath with this guy.

Mathias's friend had reached the end of his patience, and he was now staring at Zak like a ravenous beast ogling a piece of juicy red meat. Mathias shuddered, but Xavier had finally freed himself from his locker, and he came to stand between them. For once, Mathias was happy to see him. He was dumb but mostly harmless.

"Xavier, my man!" Eric was always glad to see him. "Is the baronet coming tonight?"

"Which one?" Xavier asked with a blank look.

"The… hang on."

"How many are there?" Zak asked.

Xavier would tell everyone that his father was a baronet. Mathias had no idea what a baronet was. From the sound of it, it sounded like his father was a small baron. What the fuck was a small baron, then? Not that it mattered.

"There's my dad, and there's my eldest brother," Xavier said proudly. "But he's only just the heir."

Eric stretched out his arm and ruffled Xavier's hair. "Why would he come to the parents-teachers meeting anyway?"

"Huh? Oh, crap!" Xavier guffawed. "Completely forgot about that. No, Father's not coming. He's not even in the country."

"Your mom, then?"

"No, she's with him."

"Who's taking care of you then?" Mathias asked without thinking.

Truthfully, Xavier really looked like the type who'd set the house on fire trying to make toast. Still, as soon as the words left his lips, Mathias regretted them, but Xavier was too air-headed to even register any attempt at sarcasm. He laughed and patted Mathias's shoulder. "Don't worry about me, mate. I have a maid."

Mathias moved out of his reach.

A maid? Seriously?

These fucking people.

5

FAMILIAR FACES

MATHIAS DIDN'T HAVE to worry about the parents-teachers meeting. His dad already knew everything that was wrong or amazing about him from his coworkers. Mostly, what was wrong. Mathias wasn't amazing at many things anymore. He'd lost interest in school when he lost interest in everything else, but Dad couldn't say anything because Mathias was still better at keeping his shit together than him by far; he didn't waste time trying to micromanage Mathias. He went with the flow, and Mathias was grateful enough to try to stay out of trouble.

Most of the main players from the Colette football team were hanging out in a corner of the playground after class, some smoking cigarettes, others just chatting idly. That jerk, Kayvin, was captain now, and as a result, he spoke loudly and with authority about everything, from passes to cars to "handling chicks". Mathias was bored and lighting smoke after smoke, his other hand flexing inside his pocket. Eric looked completely frozen, but the moment he spotted Zak lumbering out of the building, half-smothered under thick layers of clothing, his face split open with a smile, and he pretended not to feel the cold at all.

Hopeless.

Mathias turned his head away when they reunited and kissed,

but he also ignored the jeers and the nasty comments from some of the other members of the team.

"Aren't you going in?" Eric asked.

"It hasn't started yet. I wanted to see you."

Eric smiled, too happy that Zak would brave the arctic winds and half a dozen idiots just to be near him. Eric had told Mathias his boyfriend wasn't particularly a fan of his friends. Mathias didn't have to wonder why.

All of a sudden, Kayvin went into a violent fit of coughing. "What the fuck is that?" he spluttered, hitting his chest.

The others drew their attention to the place he was pointing at. Voices rose amidst the group, full of shock and admiration.

"Is that…? No way…"

"Shit…"

"Is that Alberto's mom?"

It was nighttime, but the playground at Colette was always well lit. Mathias glanced toward the front gate then did a double-take.

Perched on black stilettos, the woman appeared just as tall as her son. She had long, glossy, dark hair that flowed elegantly with the wind, a fitted dress cut at the knee, revealing a pair of perfect legs, and a red leather coat fastened around her slim waist. There were no other words for it: she looked out of this world. Mathias's breath caught, his throat constricted, and he barely paid attention to the surrounding prattle.

Zak sounded astonished. "She must be a supermodel like him…"

"That guy's a supermodel?" someone asked.

Eric cleared his throat. "Just a model."

"What's the difference?"

"Well, he's not super!"

"I think he is," Xavier mumbled.

"Who gives a fuck?" Kayvin sniggered. "But the mom… she's something, I admit."

Mathias blinked furiously. He could hear his heart pounding in his ears, hard, fast, and unforgiving. An angry drum that rooted him to the spot, unable to tear his gaze away.

All this noise coming from their group got the son's attention.

His head snapped back, and even from his spot, Mathias noticed how cold his eyes looked. It really was Eric's nemesis, Alberto. Falling a step behind, he put himself between their group and his mother.

Kayvin clapped his hands, jubilant. "Look, he's vexed now!"

"This guy? Vexed?" his friend Steph said. "That would be a first."

Xavier spoke up, "But he is— I've never seen him look so… so…"

"Show any expression, you mean?"

"It's his mom, what do you expect?" Eric snapped, looking angry. "Could you back off?"

He rarely raised his voice, and tonight was proof that when it mattered, most still listened to him. After all, he was the best football player here, and that mattered to some. He'd probably be famous one day, and that mattered to them even more. Kayvin snorted and made a show of holding his gaze, but Eric had already returned his attention to Zak, who looked dumbfounded.

"She's so beautiful," he kept repeating.

There was a brief moment of silence during which everyone was forced to agree.

"Damn…" Steph said. "I'm moving to Italy if all women there look like that."

"Don't be stupid," Kayvin said. "Most women don't look like that. Alberto's dad is probably one of the richest guys in the world, considering how hot chicks are all gold-diggers."

"I think they look the same," Xavier said.

"What did you say?"

"I think Alberto and his mum, they sort of look the same. Their faces—"

"Who cares about her face? Have you seen her ass?" Steph roared. "Can someone tell me if Alberto's got an ass like that? Zak, anything?"

Zak ignored the laughs but clicked his tongue in annoyance. Eric was probably red from head to toe with rage right now, but it was too dark for Mathias to know for sure. Everyone kept staring as Alberto and his mother walked toward the building, but then, instead of opening the door, that woman walked straight toward it, and she would have smashed her head against it if her son hadn't stopped her in the nick of time.

"Did she just walk into the door?" Eric asked faintly.

"She did..." Zak said in awe.

Eric pulled him closer and they watched, transfixed, while Kayvin turned to his friends with a laugh. "Didn't that fuckhead do the same once this summer?"

"He did," Xavier said.

"I guess looks aren't the only thing they have in common."

Xavier watched his friend with a complicated expression. Mathias could see that he was deliberating whether or not to say something. Finally, he steeled himself. "I thought you liked him."

Kayvin's lip curled in disgust. "I never said I liked him." His tone was scathing, but at this point, Mathias had never seen him act nice to anyone but Xavier and his two other midfielder pals, so he brushed it aside.

Eric was looking at him with strange eyes, eyes that begged, *Please don't do this now.* Kayvin noticed and forcibly looked away. "I tolerated his ass for two and a half weeks this summer. Doesn't mean we're friends or anything. The mom sure is hot, though; I wouldn't mind hitting that."

"Didn't you just say they look exactly the same?" Zak said with a shrug.

Kayvin threw him a dark look. "I never said that. It was Xavier. What? Do we all look the same to *you?*"

Zak's eyes bulged. "What the fuck?!"

Eric opened his mouth, but Mathias cut right across him. "I think she's way out of your league."

Since he didn't speak very often, was good at his job on the football pitch, and, at this exact moment, looked like he was about to stab someone in the dick, no one dared speak for a few interminable seconds until Steph broke the silence with a heartfelt sigh.

"She's the ultimate milf, bro." He bumped his fist against Kayvin's.

Zak looked like he was about to puke. Looking torn, Eric buried his teeth in his bottom lip.

"But Zak's right," Steph added. "Alberto looks kind of the same." He burst into a laugh which didn't amuse Kayvin at all. "You should hit on him, Kev. I'm sure he'd be grateful, too."

"Why?" Mathias asked, unable to stop his heart from thumping.

"He's gay, everyone knows it."

"Not everyone knows it," Zak said darkly.

"Just because he didn't want to touch you doesn't mean he's not gay," Kayvin said with a sneer. "He just didn't like you."

Subsequent laughter forced Zak into an awkward silence. Mathias felt bad for him and even worse that Eric wasn't defending him. Eric was always going on and on about his Zak. Why couldn't he punch everyone here to defend him? But he was, in fact, forbidden to do stupid shit like that by contract. His football club had no tolerance for scandals of any sort, and players were told anybody with a reputation for violence was easily replaceable.

Mathias wasn't tied to any contract, and after what he just saw, he wouldn't mind a live punching ball right now. He thought maybe next time Kayvin spoke about Zak, he'd get him, but maybe not. He didn't want to be accused of fancying Zak.

"He asked *me* out," Zak mumbled sheepishly.

"After you embarrassed yourself at that party," Kayvin said without mercy. "He pitied you, that's all."

"Or he's not that gay," Eric cut in, his tone sharp.

"Oh, he sucks dicks all right," Kayvin said, and there was resentment in his voice. "Every hot girl at school has tried to get his attention, and… nothing. It pisses me off. He's not even that good looking." A few of the guys exchanged disagreeing looks, but no one ever dared contradict Kayvin.

"The guy's dead inside," Steph said with a shrug. "I met this girl at Xavier's a few weeks ago who had *the. Best. Lips.* She was rubbing herself against him in her mini dress and even offered to suck him off right there at the party, and do you know what he said?"

Xavier whimpered, looking like he didn't want to hear about this at all. Mathias started to feel bad for him too, but Kayvin looked curious.

"What?"

"He asked the girl if she was on catnip and told her there was a scratching post in the corner with her fucking name on it."

Zak tried his best to smother a burst of laughter, but everyone heard it anyway. Even Mathias's lip inadvertently twitched.

"So he doesn't like hot chicks," Kayvin's other friend said. "Means gay."

"But what happens if you send him a hot guy?" Steph asked. His jab was followed by general laughter.

Mathias thought of that unreal woman from earlier. Smashing his own head against a door didn't sound too much like a bad idea after all.

"Xavier, you go get him," Steph said, and Kayvin snarled at him.

"No!" He grabbed Xavier and pulled him to his side. "Leave him alone."

Eric seemed to take exception to that, because he finally started pushing Zak toward the building.

"Cam isn't here yet," Zak said, talking about his best friend.

"Let's get you inside. I can't take any more of this."

They walked a few steps, and there was an unpleasantness weighing in the air. Some of the team didn't care that Eric preferred guys now, and they never liked to see him leave, while others found it too much to bear and were glad to see them both gone. Mathias didn't bother thinking too hard about this. All he knew was that Eric pretty much adopted him since day one, so his feet had started moving instinctively. When Eric threw a hesitant look over his shoulder, he smiled with relief when he found Mathias right behind him.

Mathias had other concerns in his mind anyway. Who cared whether that long-legged creature liked dicks or not? Now, he understood why Alberto's face looked so damn familiar. This woman, this tall, freakish woman, wasn't she the same one who gave his dad a ride home that time?

His *married* dad?

He was certain it was her. You didn't—you *couldn't*—forget looks like that once you'd seen them. No way. Her and her long dark hair, her thin fingers clutched around the wheel of her fancy car.

The way she didn't smile when he accidentally caught her eye.

No. Fucking. Way.

There was no way he could let this happen.

No way he would let this creature worm her way into his house, into his family, and steal his mother's spot. There was nothing he wouldn't do to keep his family intact. Nothing at all. No one he wasn't willing to threaten, frighten, or eradicate. His blood boiling, Mathias hadn't even reached the building door when he already knew what to do.

He didn't care for waiting. He acted the next day.

He had to make sure this Alberto guy was on his own, and he had to make sure Eric wasn't anywhere near, but that was easily settled.

On Wednesdays after class, Eric always picked up Zak from Drama Club. At the time, the school grounds weren't crowded. Once Eric got Zak to himself, he would forget all about Mathias. Then, he would only have to catch Alberto as he made his way out.

How did he know that Alberto left school at the same time? He had to maneuver a bit to find out this piece of information. He did it without feeling proud or embarrassed, more like it was something he had to do for the sake of his family. A short conversation with Zak—while he was being distracted by Eric's relentless pawing—had informed Mathias, Alberto was no longer part of this drama thingy, but Zak had noticed he still left school at the same time as him on Wednesdays.

That could only mean he attended another club or advanced class.

Mathias thought about it for a second. Which class would he take if he were in his shoes? Just like Mathias chose Spanish to get easy grades, he tried his luck with Italian, spotted the attendance list pinned on the classroom door, and found that lazy bastard had had the same idea as him.

After that, it was just a matter of stalking him and waiting, a bit like in those movies where the cops are doing surveillance, usually in pairs, and they eat greasy food while complaining about their marriage. Well, this time, Mathias was on his own, his stomach was growling, and he had no marriage to complain about, but he still patiently watched Alberto as he came out of the building and paused to stare indifferently at Eric and Zak's make out session.

Fuck me if Kayvin was right, Mathias thought with a grimace, but this guy really did look dead inside.

Alberto tossed his cigarette to the ground and pulled his hood over his head, and Mathias sprung to his feet.

There it is, there it is.

Without hesitation, he went after him. His pulse quickened, and his whole body tensed up as the distance between them shortened.

Ten steps, five steps, two steps.

No going back.

A PARTY

RAIN HAD BEEN FALLING for the past two days, and, at last, it had stopped, and students could venture outside.

Sitting on his favourite bench in the back of the playground, Alberto was minding his own business, tightly wrapped inside his coat over his sweater, the hood pulled over his head. Enjoying his peace and quiet, he was failing at *Fruit Ninja* on his phone when a third of the Colette football team, clad in their matching uniforms, stopped at his feet. Alberto reluctantly looked up.

He vaguely knew them from an old Drama Club project dating a few months back. Some football players got to participate in the making of their short film, for reasons he couldn't care to remember. As a result, he had gotten acquainted with Xavier, a clueless guy with a "baronet" for a father, another student — Charles-Edouard maybe? — who had such little presence, Alberto kept misremembering his name, Kayvin, a vicious walking time bomb, and of course, Eric.

Zak's Eric.

He and Alberto weren't on friendly terms. After all, Zak had ditched him for Eric. Alberto wasn't stupid; he knew he wasn't suited for Zak and Eric was, but there was still a sting, and the less they saw of each other, the better for everyone. As for him, Eric had never forgiven Alberto for rejecting then dating Zak while he

56

was desperately pining for him. Alberto knew that because Eric was warm to everybody — warm to an annoying and gross extent — but he never was with Alberto. It was dumb and immature, but Eric was a dumb and immature guy, too frustrating to even think about. It wasn't even like Alberto got to Zak first! Eric was his first kiss, not himself. Alberto barely touched Zak, *barely*, but Eric took it as a capital offence anyway.

"Albertooo! My Alberto!" Xavier jumped to his side, swung his arm over his shoulder, and squeezed him until pain exploded in his bicep. "Why are you always hiding your face?"

Xavier tried to push his hood down to expose his face, but he jerked away.

"I look like shit today."

Xavier laughed, joined by Charles... Was it Charles-David? Alberto couldn't remember, really.

"He says he looks like shit. Thanks for the rest of us. My Alberto, you couldn't look like shit even if you tried."

Alberto glanced at him. "Did you come all this way to suck my—"

"Ha!" Xavier drowned the rest of his sentence in a laugh. "Alberto!"

Alberto knew Xavier didn't like this kind of joke unless he was the one proffering them. He was one of those sexually confused homophobes who were only homophobic because they thought that it was what society — i.e., Daddy — expected of them. Alberto always thought it would take less than a bottle of cheap vodka to get him to make out with a guy. Any guy.

"I'm not... no. I am..." Xavier was making wild gestures with his hands. "I mean, I never—" Everyone was staring at him. Alberto waited for him to collect himself with a blank look. After a while, Xavier wiped his forehead and started again, "Ah! Alberto, you're so funny! Anyway, I wanted to invite you to my party tomorrow."

"No." Alberto returned his attention to his phone.

"Alberto, come on." Xavier seized his arm. "For me, please!"

As a general rule, Alberto avoided parties. He found them exhausting. They mostly consisted of staying away from alcohol he didn't want to drink and hiding from people he didn't want to date. He was already forced to attend countless tedious social gatherings under his own roof. Why would he drag himself out into the cold when he could be buried under a thick comforter, propped on six fluffy pillows, away from this hostile world?

Since Xavier wouldn't let go of his arm, he heaved a small sigh. Kayvin noticed and wrinkled his forehead.

"Why do you keep inviting him to your parties? He never comes."

"Yeah, why?" Eric asked.

Xavier grinned. "Every time I say he'll be there, I get more girls to come."

Eric looked dubitative. Alberto ignored him and freed himself from Xavier's hold. "That doesn't sound like my problem at all."

"Please! When they realise you're not coming, they'll leave. Come on, Alberto." He scooted closer and whispered a few words in his ear.

Now, it was Kayvin's turn to stare with cold eyes.

"Not this time, thank you," Alberto said.

Xavier wasn't one to give up so easily. He thought for a second then said, "Lots of hot guys will be there. The whole Colette football team!" He pointed in their direction. "And even those who didn't make the team."

Alberto didn't care about that. He didn't want to date anyone, especially not a football player.

But just as he thought this up, the angry stranger from last time appeared on the other side of the playground in full Colette football gear, carrying a pair of gloves. Alberto stared briefly at his legs, at the way his right fist was punching his left as he talked. He remembered how easily that guy squashed him against the wall, the furious sparks in his eyes, and the powerful grip of his hands around his sweater.

Alberto bit into his lower lip. "Alright. Maybe I'll come."

"Seriously?" Xavier's face brightened.

Eric looked down at Alberto in surprise, then, spotting his other teammates in the distance, he turned on his heel and set off in their direction. Grinning, Xavier leaned forward in an attempt to kiss Alberto, but he was pushed away.

"I said maybe."

"Alberto, you're the man! If I score with that girl I like, maybe I'll suck your dick after all!"

Alberto couldn't help feeling amused. He always felt that when it came to himself, it wouldn't even take Xavier a drop of vodka to get down to business.

Kayvin seemed to agree; he glared at Xavier with a murderous expression. "You're such a moron."

Xavier laughed but didn't add another word, and, just as quickly as they arrived, the whole group walked away; Alberto could finally enjoy his peace and quiet again.

When Alberto came home the following evening, Dimitri was already there, standing in the middle of the dining room and shouting in Russian at some poor guy on the other side of the phone. His mind set, Alberto slunk past him without acknowledging him.

Alberto wanted to tell Mamma he was going to a party on his own, but he knew she'd worry, so he'd said nothing last night, putting it off until the last minute. He was thinking that Angry Buzzcut better be coming tonight, or he'd be responsible for making his mother sad. Unacceptable.

Mamma was seated at the large table, making a dress. She was quite good at making clothes, she was just really slow. She'd made Alberto's favourite kimono jacket, and even if she didn't like it at first, she got used to it as long as he agreed not to wear it often. He wore it all the time, but she didn't know that.

Tonight, she was even slower than usual, struggling to cut a piece of dark-green velvet. When she saw Alberto, she surrendered with a sigh. "I give up. They're pretty much useless now." She was pointing at her pair of silver scissors. Alberto knew they were older than him.

"I'll get you another pair," Dimitri said before Alberto could open his mouth. He was still on the phone, but he never missed a single word that came out of his wife's mouth. She didn't notice or ignored the hostile look they exchanged, and she caressed the edge of the scissors with her long finger.

"It was a gift from my mother. One of the only things I took when I left."

Alberto rushed to her side, knocking his knee into the table leg as he went, to take them away. "No one is saying you should get rid of them. Just put them away. You might hurt yourself if you keep using them." He glanced down at the scissors. Even if they were useless at cutting fabric, one could still stab a bitch with these.

"I'll get you another pair," Dimitri repeated, cutting his call short and covering her hand with his own.

"Hi-hi everyone!"

There she was. Stasia and her irritating voice. Alberto's fingers clenched around the scissors, while Dimitri's face split into a smile. He went to kiss his evil spawn's forehead.

"Guess who's staying for dinner?" Stasia sang, her washed-out blue eyes sweeping over Alberto.

"That's lovely," Mamma said without enthusiasm, her attention still on her scissors.

Stasia barely managed to conceal her loathing. She forced a smile, hugging her daddy tightly. "What about you, Alberto? Any plans tonight?"

She loved to ask because she knew he didn't have anyone, like she always seemed to know everything about him. Another sign that she wasn't human.

"I'm going to a party tonight," he said.

His mother wrenched her attention away from the scissors. Even Dimitri couldn't suppress a look of surprise.

"Where?" Mamma asked immediately. "Who with?"

"My friends," he said slowly, and he slipped a glance at Stasia. "It's not far. I'll be home early."

"But what are you going to eat over there?" Mamma gasped. "Or drink?"

Dimitri uncharacteristically rushed to support him, no doubt delighted to have him out of the way for one evening. "Let him have a slice of pizza or a beer once in a while. He's a man, after all! Not a little boy."

Mamma grunted her disapproval and started rambling in Italian. "Don't take the tube at night. Or the bus. No pizza. No beer. In fact, no junk food or alcohol, period. Call me when you arrive." She absently switched back to English. "Call me when you arrive. Oh, and please, stay away from coke."

Alberto thought she was talking about sodas. Probably. But after that, she gave in with a sigh. Dimitri rubbed her shoulders affectionately.

"Look at you, living the life," Stasia said with a fake smile.

Alberto could hear in the tremolo of her voice that she hated not to have him at her mercy this evening. For that alone, Alberto felt it was all worth it. Worth dragging himself from photoshoot to photoshoot, worth selling his image to strangers at the cost of his soul. Every euro he earned was another brick in that wall he'd erect between the two of them. With enough money, he'd be able to move out of there, and that was worth a few heartaches.

He left five minutes later with an inexplicable feeling of anticipation, and he was already halfway through the interminable lawn when he heard his mother running after him. He immediately turned around to meet her.

"Remember, *Tesoro*," she said breathlessly. "Don't—"

"I know, Mamma. I won't throw myself away to the first one who asks."

7

INVALIDES

A GRINNING XAVIER LET Alberto inside his immense but garish Haussmannian flat, going on and on about how excited he was to see him.

"You don't need to tell me," Alberto said mildly. He could feel it from the way he was groping him.

Xavier burst into a laugh, clapped his large hand on his shoulder, possibly breaking it, then completely abandoned him to chase after some brunette with big breasts. Alberto was on his own.

Perfect.

He wasn't worried at all. He did a quick tour around the flat, recognising a few familiar faces here and there, such as Zak and Eric, and his old friends, Sander and Oliver. A horrid girl with ruby-red puffed-up lips tried to jump him on her way out of the bathroom, but he expertly tossed her into somebody else's arms and retraced his steps to the living room. Evidently, Angry Buzzcut wasn't here.

Alberto felt irritated for some reason.

He thought perhaps he was on his way and would arrive shortly. Leaning against a console table clearly designed by a madman, Alberto pulled out his phone and programmed an alarm to set off in thirty minutes. Angry Buzzcut was intriguing, but not enough to make him wait longer than that. Alberto lit a cigarette, opened a random Wikipedia page to discourage randos to start a conversation, and spaced out while others around him were getting trashed to the pounding beat of some cheap electro.

Some minutes later, he was brought back to reality by someone trying to get his attention. *What now?* He looked up to see some guy with a blond ponytail handing him a beer.

Alberto scratched his brow with the back of his thumb and, after a brief hesitation, he accepted the drink. "Thanks."

Ponytail Guy eyed him strangely. Alberto vaguely wondered what he was about. The guy was slightly older than him, with large rings on his fingers and an angular jaw... He was handsome.

"How old are you exactly?" Ponytail Guy asked out of the blue.

Alberto met his gaze this time. Was he some kind of creep? He didn't look the part, but you never knew. Wouldn't be the first time. Just last week, he was waiting for his mother to drive around the corner to pick him up after a shoot, and some guy in an overpriced Mercedes stopped to ask him if he wanted to get in, so Alberto asked, "... What?" The guy realised his mistake and burned a red light in his haste to sod off.

Anyway, Alberto had had his fair share of creeps. He blew cigarette smoke out of the corner of his lip. "Almost eighteen."

"Almost?" The guy stared to his heart's content, up and down, down and up, then his lip twitched a little, and he took a swig of beer. "And you're a model?"

While Alberto's expression didn't change, he surreptitiously glanced around the room for someone — anyone — to talk to, but he didn't really know anyone here but Zak, who had resumed his favourite stance, which was tongue-deep in Eric's mouth. Xavier was somewhere in the back, hunting his future ex. Sander was here, too, but he was with his girlfriend, and he didn't like Alberto anymore. With an inaudible sigh, Alberto returned his attention to Creepy Ponytail Guy.

"Yeah, sort of."

He expected some kind of reaction, but not the resigned little smirk he saw on Ponytail Guy's face. Now a bit perplexed, Alberto focused as hard as he could on his features. He was a little short, compared to him, but he could be a model, too. In fact, he might be just that. Alberto couldn't tell. He rarely bothered looking at people twice. After a while, everybody started to look the same to him.

"Are you a model?" Alberto asked.

Ponytail Guy laughed dryly. "Nope. I'm Louis."

Well, that settled it, then, since Alberto had no clue who Louis was. Xavier did, probably, since he invited him, but it's not like guests were announced by footmen like in the good old days. Alberto gave a curt nod in acknowledgement and returned to his cigarette.

"Michael's boyfriend," Louis added, pointing toward the fireplace at the other end of the room. Alberto followed his gaze and blinked twice.

Oh. *That* Michael.

He realised his movements had stopped, and his cigarette hung in midair, abandoned. He quickly stuck it back into his mouth. Another nod, then.

Louis gave him a stern look. A worried look. Did he know? No way. He couldn't know. If he knew, he would have punched him in the face. Alberto had noticed the way he was fidgeting, twisting the large rings on his fingers, and struggling not to grind his teeth. This guy was the anxious type. He could throw a punch if he wanted to, but he didn't want to, apparently. He just wanted to look at him, and now he had.

Alberto blew a thin cloud of smoke. "Cool," he said, noncommittal.

Louis made a little scoffing sound, stuck one hand in his pocket, and raised his beer to him with the other. "Nice talking to you."

"Thanks for the beer," Alberto said, trying to sound kind, but his voice sounded flat, as usual.

"You didn't even drink it."

"Sorry. I guess I'm not thirsty."

Muttering something under his breath about subtext, Louis left with his ponytail and his angular jaw and returned to his Michael. And Alberto returned to his cigarette, relieved, but also disappointed.

He would have preferred a punch in the face.

Exhaling a large puff of smoke, he once again scanned his surroundings just in time to see Angry Buzzcut walk into the room. His pulse quickened. Alberto's pulse hadn't quickened since 2007. He consciously straightened up to make himself taller.

Angry Buzzcut had such presence that Charles-Something stepped aside to let him stand between himself and Eric. Even more surprising, Eric slipped his tongue out of Zak's mouth to shake his hand, which Angry Buzzcut didn't even take. He fist-bumped him with a disgruntled expression that made Alberto's lip twitch upward just a little.

Alberto thought it was dumb to call him Angry Buzzcut when he was clearly so much more than that, and tonight, he'd learn two things: his name and the real reason why he attacked him the other day.

Being that tall had its advantages. After a few minutes, Angry Buzzcut couldn't pretend to not see Alberto leaning against the console, but there was nothing friendly in the way he watched him. This guy was all edges, the sort that breaks rather than bends. He was possibly an idiot, but it's not like Alberto had anything else going for him at the moment, so, at least for tonight, he would do.

Alberto left his spot and tentatively strolled around the room to gauge his reaction. He looked pissed off; nothing new there. But his gaze was focused on him, anchored to his every step, and after only a minute, he left his friends and disappeared into the long corridor.

Ignoring two girls who were asking him if he wanted another drink, Alberto took a swig of bitter-tasting beer and went chasing after him. What was the worst that could happen? What could life possibly throw at him now? Apart from a train, he considered, peeking into every room, but that guy had felt just like that, the moment he squashed him against the wall.

He found the stranger standing in the middle of a tacky home office, possibly the only room so tragically decorated that it scared even the horniest kids away, so he probably wasn't an idiot after all. There he was, staring at the books sitting on the shelves, a frown on his face.

"Looking for a book?" Alberto asked, closing the door behind himself.

Angry Buzzcut slowly turned around. "Looking for trouble?"

Well, yes, possibly, Alberto thought with a start. Probably? There was even a — small but real — chance that if this guy hit him right now, he'd love him forever.

Obviously, he couldn't say that. There was always an appropriate time for exposing one's weirdness, and now was not the time. Alberto approached the stranger cautiously, as one would a wild animal, knowing it'd be safer to let the beast come his way. He leaned against the wall farthest from him and racked his head for something to say to break the ice.

With a teasing half-smile, he went with, "Alone at last."

Angry Buzzcut's mouth twisted in disdain. Yeah, yeah, Alberto agreed. It sounded stupid. Angry Buzzcut even took an extra step to the side, his gaze flickering toward the door.

"Let's make this quick."

Alberto snorted. While others out there were trying so hard to get his attention, this one didn't even want to be found in a room alone with him. It was a little bit annoying, to be honest. Never, *never* had he felt obligated to learn any of those so-called social skills. He was so handsome, it wasn't required of him. That, or any other skill, for that matter. So why wasn't this guy swooning over him like all the others? Alberto showed none of his irritation and merely shook his hair back into place. "At least you know why I'm here."

"I guess."

"So… what the hell happened the other day?"

Angry Buzzcut gritted his teeth. "What do you think?"

Oh, that scathing tone! Hell hath no fury like an Angry Buzzcut. His fingertips tingling, Alberto smoothed his hands against the wall.

Faced with Alberto's disinterest in answering pointless questions, Angry Buzzcut blinked several times, shoved his hands in the pockets of his hoodie, and approached with a sigh. "It's as I said before. Your mother and my dad. They're having a thing."

He was enunciating everything carefully as though he was talking to a slow-witted child, but it still made no sense to Alberto.

"That's really… That's not possible." He scratched his eyebrow. "Who's your dad?"

Angry Buzzcut's expression turned uncomfortable, and Alberto felt oddly tempted to press his finger between his wrinkled brow to relax the visible knot there.

"My dad's Mr. Rodin."

"Oh." Alberto clasped his hands behind his back. "Who's Mr Rodin?" He received a look of surprise.

"The new math teacher?"

"I don't have him."

Angry Buzzcut actually looked relieved.

"Wait." Alberto realised something. "Your dad's a Maths teacher?"

"Yeah."

Alberto shook his head. "My mother's not doing him."

"You think I'm lying?" Angry Buzzcut's peculiar eyes shone with defiance. "I'm telling you, I saw her. Twice. Get it?"

This guy looked tempted to slam him against the wall again, so Alberto took his time to choose his next words. "How did you know she was my mother?"

"Your mother isn't a giant woman with a long, blood-red leather jacket who drives a black Jaguar Cabriolet?"

A giant woman? Poor Mamma. Alberto let out a sigh in his heart. "Actually, it's a Burberry trench coat."

"See? That's her!"

It was her. Then… Alberto spaced out for a moment, trying to make sense of it all before he snapped back to reality. "But how did you know she was my mother?"

Angry Buzzcut's mouth fell open. "Christ! Are you stupid or something? I just said it!"

Alberto looked at him, unfazed. "But that she was *my* mother. *Mine.* That we're related. That's why you went to find me, didn't you?" He was thinking, *Do I really look like a giant woman wearing a blood-red leather trench coat?* He already knew the answer, but he still wanted to ask.

Angry Buzzcut was scowling at him like he was deranged. "Seriously…? You look exactly the same."

Alberto dug his nails into his palms. Exactly the same? Despite the claims, it wasn't even true.

"And…" Angry Buzzcut seemed to hesitate. "I saw you together at the parents-teachers meeting."

Of course. That made more sense.

Alberto didn't like people comparing him to his mother, but he couldn't help it, so he shook it off. "So, what's your name?"

Angry Buzzcut furrowed his brow, opened his mouth, closed it, and opened it again. "Mathias."

Mathias. *Ma-tyas*. Alberto wanted to say the name out loud a few times to check how it sounded, how well it rolled off his tongue, but he didn't dare. He retreated against the wall. "In which class are you?"

Ma-tyas rolled his eyes. "Same as Eric. Are you stupid *and* blind? I'm always with Eric."

"Whatever you say." Alberto wasn't irritated by his harsh words. In fact, he felt entertained. "But how would I know? Why would I be looking at Eric?"

Mathias seemed thrown by the question. "I don't know… I guess I'm used to people paying attention to him."

"Oh, really?" Alberto bit back his urge to smirk.

For a few seconds, they were silent. Staring at the wall, Mathias seemed absorbed by his own thoughts. Alberto realised he wasn't going to ask, so he offered the information himself.

"Alberto. That's my name."

"Yeah, I know."

"How do you know?"

Now he seemed pissed off again. "I told you I—"

"Oh, yes. Eric."

"Mm."

"I'm sure he has many nice things to say about me."

Mathias gave him a bewildered look. "He really hasn't." He took a step toward Alberto. "Look, I admit what I say sounds crazy, but I don't need to convince you. I've seen them together. Twice. So, you can just come with me next time, and I'll show you. Yes? No? Yes? Yes." He even accompanied his words with an impatient "let's go" gesture.

Alberto had no clue what he was saying, even less so what he was offering. He could only look at him blankly, which was enough to set him on edge.

"Come on! I don't have all day!"

Alberto ignored him and allowed his gaze to drift toward the only window in the room. Outside, the rooftops of Paris were lit by moonlight and not much else. He realised with disappointment that he was tired already. Just then, his alarm rang.

"Time's up." He straightened up. "The thing is, no offence, but I already don't have much energy. I'd rather not waste it."

Mathias took on a puzzled expression, as though he wasn't sure he heard right. "What?"

"I mean it." Alberto dragged his feet toward the exit. "But let me know how it goes." He left the office before Mathias could think or retort, and didn't even bother stopping by the living room, walking straight to the front door instead.

In the backseat of the cab driving him home, Alberto noted that the evening had only been a partial success. Indeed, he'd survived another party, learned Angry Buzzcut's name and the reason why he ended up against a wall, but after this encounter, Alberto's interest was already fizzling out. One meeting, and it was clear that Mathias was just like everyone else. Just another person spouting nonsense to get his attention. Alberto's mother didn't do Maths teachers, as bad as it sounded, so that story sounded like a load of crap. Whatever happened, either he'd fantasised it, or there was a perfectly sound explanation. Nothing to lose sleep over.

Alberto really didn't feel it was worth making an effort. If this guy wanted his help, he'd have to ask again and better than that.

BAD PEOPLE

NOT TWO DAYS LATER, Alberto stood motionless in the middle of the morning room as a trio of witches looked him up and down and showered him with compliments. *Com'è bello!* this and *Stupendo!* that. Alberto tuned them out, and his mother flashed them all half-smiles on his behalf until one of them had too much white wine and said, "He looks nothing like his father." Mamma's eyelid twitched, and she shook Alberto's sleeve.

"Manners," she said.

He started and forced another faint smile. "Thank you."

Mamma took him to the side and fixed his lapel. "What's happening to you? Since when do you not thank people when they give you a compliment? I taught you better than that."

"I know."

"That's common courtesy." She brushed imaginary dirt off his cheek. "Do you know how many people would kill to look like you?"

Alberto had a dark joke on the tip of his tongue, so he bit it to keep silent. Mamma hated this sort of joke. In fact, she usually didn't get humour at all, so she didn't notice that the real jest was that she considered this group of harpies her friends. They were not her friends. They should have been, but despite his mother's wild attempts at justifying their behaviour, Alberto knew they were only visiting Paris for another one of those women's wedding, to which Mamma was not invited, of course. Alberto knew they came to visit her for two reasons only: to get a good look at Dimitri, especially his house, his cars, his bank account if he'd let them, and to inspect Alberto as well, if only to verify if he really was worth all this trouble after all.

As he stood dutifully under their expert — but inebriated — gazes, Alberto was well aware he wasn't grateful for his gift. These three women in front of him, former models and coworkers of Mamma from back home, they were the grateful ones, even if some had spent so much money on cosmetic surgery, their original gift was long stitched over. The most beautiful one, Chiara, was still nonchalant enough, but she was lazy and uninterested. The other ones, Cristina and Antonia, were barely able to contain the scorn and jealousy in their eyes as they realised former teen model superstar, Olympia Gazza, was not as miserable as they expected her to be. In fact, she and her son appeared to be doing just as well as she'd claimed.

Alberto pretended to have to use the bathroom and excused himself. His mother fell on a chair with a disappointed look. Alberto said he'd be right back, but she rightfully doubted it. In reality, he'd only turned around the corner to catch his breath and gather the courage to return. Mamma was probably as nervous as she was happy that her friends came over. No one ever visited. She had told them about the *Oscult* campaign and how proud she was of him. He had to help her.

On the other side of the wall, his absence triggered an avalanche of compliments.

"You did so well, Olympia. He's a beautiful boy."

"Hush, Cristina. He's a man now!"

"Right, right, he's a man."

Mamma took the compliments one after the other, proffering her thanks every time. In her mouth, the words sounded sincere.

"That's true, he's a man," Chiara said. "He'll leave the house soon."

"I…" Olympia's voice cracked. "I hope not too soon."

"Don't let him fall into the grip of some nasty little French freak!" Antonia, the drunkest, never cared for tact. Alberto would have admired her if she didn't make his skin crawl. "Tell him only to date Italians. Only Italians know class."

Alberto recognised the way his mother tapped her index finger against the rim of a Champagne glass, a sign she was frustrated by the turn of the conversation. "I… I don't think he's interested in dating."

Antonia snorted, and some other woman seemed to have slapped her on the shoulder, because she swore.

Mamma ignored her and went on. "I've always told him to be careful and not to throw himself away to the first one who asks him out."

"Of course you would tell him that."

There was a brief silence after Antonia's outburst, but then Olympia's soft voice filled the room again. "It's true. I don't want him to make the same mistakes."

But mistakes were already made, Alberto thought without emotion. Despite her best intentions, his mother couldn't save Alberto from making them or even from being a living, walking one.

For instance, ever since he returned to school, Alberto couldn't help but gain a nasty reputation. Though he felt it pointless to justify himself to people he didn't know, it wasn't like he felt absolutely nothing when he heard some of the things people said about him. He'd just learn to float above it like he'd learn to float above everything else; it was still better than to trudge through dark waters as he used to attempt to.

Antonia barked for more wine, and Mamma seemed to take this as an excuse to hide from her friends in the kitchen. The moment she was gone, they all lowered their voices.

"He really is gorgeous," Chiara said.

"Just like his mother," Cristina added in a bitter tone.

"Poor thing."

"That's a shame, isn't it?" Antonia asked.

"Why? Why is it a shame?"

"He's not interested in modelling, but, apparently, he's got literally no other talent, no other skill of any kind."

"Just like his mother," Cristina said.

"Ah!"

The wine glasses clinked, and Chiara heaved a loud sigh. "It is a shame. I think he better make the most of his beauty before it's too late."

"She made that mistake," Antonia said haughtily. "Married too young. Look where that got her."

"Different times."

"Different times, yes," Cristina agreed.

Antonia let out an impatient groan. "This one won't get married! He's queer."

"How do you know?"

She hissed, "He hasn't even looked at us twice."

There was a murmur of agreement. Then, Cristina's voice fell to a whisper, "He's bizarre, isn't he?"

"I know!" Antonia sounded excited. "Have you seen his eyes? Cold and hard."

"You think? You think he's like—"

"Probably. He makes my blood curdle, really."

"Shh…" Chiara paused for a beat before speaking, "Maybe he just came back different, you know… from…"

"From Italy," Cristina whispered.

"That's what I said. Poor thing."

Antonia slammed her glass of wine on the table. "Oh poor thing this, poor thing that. Is he a man or is he not?" She clicked her tongue disapprovingly. "We all have to make the most of life using what assets we've been given. This one, he's been blessed! If he were smart, he'd use that face of his to get as far as he could. Save some money. He can go to school later, find a job, do whatever he wants, but one thing is certain: he'll never be that beautiful for long."

"Men age well," Chiara said. "He could—"

"Stop it. He won't get far in this job, and you know it."

As he listened, Alberto's lips stretched, and he almost let out a laugh. After all, Antonia wasn't wrong at all.

"Why are you saying that?" Chiara asked.

"I'll tell you why. He doesn't have the backbone for it!"

"Antonia…"

"Don't 'Antonia' me! I know all about it! Years ago, his mom crawled on her hands and knees to get him a photoshoot with Philip Hellsinger in London, and what do you think? Philip said he doesn't have what it takes."

All traces of amusement vanished from Alberto's face.

"He just didn't have the grit, you know?" Antonia lowered her voice. "He said he's too weak, can't take the pressure. At his age, he would have fallen apart immediately. The kid wasn't even able to handle three banal photoshoots, so never mind the runway. Olympia was heartbroken, I'm telling you."

"Pff!" Chiara snorted. "Phil is full of shit, too."

"Maybe. He's a bald asshole, but he's the best. He's photographed some of the most beautiful people on the planet, and he's scouted a lot of them, too. He's always had an eye for talent."

"For sure."

"If he says this one can't do it, then he's right."

"I heard about this, too," Cristina said. "I heard Olympia had begged him to take pictures of her boy. She was desperate."

"That's because she knows, like us, he doesn't have any other talent. What else is he supposed to do? She's just trying to help him out. She's alone, and it's difficult. Do you know how many people turned her back on her when she left Italy?"

"But not us, of course."

"Of course not. We're not like that. We…"

Alberto didn't hear the rest of the conversation because he'd put on his coat and left the house without a word.

He stood for a long time outside the Boulogne-Jean Jaurès tube station, racking his brain for somewhere to go. Then, he remembered the Pompidou Exhibition ended today, and he decided to go there. Art exhibitions were great because they could take all day, and no one would ever bother him there. They also gradually improved his culture, a skill Mamma thought indispensable to secure decent connections in life. He hoped he wouldn't run into

Zak, but he thought the chance was slim, if not inexistent. It was a Sunday, so he was probably in bed with his stupid boyfriend where he should be. No one in their right mind would spend their weekends dragging their carcass from museum to museum when they had someone to snuggle under the blankets with.

The journey felt interminable. He almost missed his stop, and then he almost got out at the wrong exit. He thought about how he could be happily buried under pillows and blankets instead of stranded out here in the cold... Still, it beat being with those harpies. Eventually, he reached the museum, the fierce autumn wind slashing at his face. He was counting how many days were separating him from spring when he once again came very close to making out with a glass door. Some blurry person held it for him at the last second, so he assumed no one noticed. Not that he cared.

He stood in the special line for Museum Passes carriers, yawning the whole time. He wondered if he couldn't catch a nap somewhere in the back of the museum until his turn came, and he couldn't find his pass. It wasn't in his wallet where it was supposed to be. Alberto looked up at the ceiling, cursing everyone around him, especially himself, when the young woman waiting behind him giggled and told the receptionist behind the desk, "Let him in! He's a work of art himself, come on!"

She and her friends started to laugh. The receptionist blushed as she smiled, and Alberto went still. He knew he was supposed to say thank you, but the words were stuck in his throat.

"Oh-oh," another girl said after a moment. "Seems like you put him in a bad mood."

Alberto turned around to face them. Naturally, he towered over them. The three girls, probably art students, judging from the look of them, went quiet when they saw his eyes. He should have said thank you.

"Not today," he said instead.

He just left it there, already feeling sort of guilty, and he simply walked out of the building only to be almost knocked over by a gust of wind.

Seriously, what a shit day. What was he supposed to do now? He could either calm down, return inside, and purchase a full ticket, or he could give up and go to the nearest train station. The thought made him snort, and he had begun to walk away when a mocking voice rang behind him.

"Does it make you happy to be a dick to people?"

Alberto froze. That voice...

"No," he said, facing Mathias cautiously. "I get a bit of a rush, though. It's something."

Mathias, eyes narrowed and hands in the front pocket of his grey hoodie, took his time to close the distance between them. Alberto hadn't expected to see him so soon, but it seemed like life was trying to teach him happy accidents do happen, too. He slowly reached for a cigarette in his pocket and said, "Did you come all this way to let me know how much better you think you are?"

Mathias snorted, but he didn't look amused. "No. I'm a piece of shit."

Alberto's movements paused. *Go on, tell me how horrible you are. I'll tell you if you're on the right track.* But Mathias didn't do anything. He stood there, looking at him. With his hoodie up, presumably to protect himself from the wind, he looked even more murderous. Alberto licked his lips before pressing the cigarette between them.

"What are you doing here?" Alberto asked. "I didn't take you for a museum guy."

"I came here with Eric."

His words sent Alberto into a coughing fit. If this day kept getting more absurd, Alberto would seriously start believing he was dreaming all this. While recovering, he tossed Mathias a resentful glare.

"Zak's idea," Mathias added with indifference.

Okay, that made more sense. So, it appeared that Zak had dragged Eric here instead of spending the day making out with him, and Eric had brought Mathias along.

People were really beyond his understanding.

"So..." Mathias said, the hands in his pockets moving back and forth.

"So what?"

"About what I said to you at the party. Have you thought about it?"

Alberto wanted to laugh, but he didn't know why. "I have."

"And?"

He said nothing. In truth, he couldn't remember which conclusion he had reached. Mathias's nose wrinkled. His hands came out of his pocket and balled into fists.

"Can I get an answer today or do I have to wait until the next fucking eclipse?"

In response, Alberto tilted his head and slowly blew a cloud of cigarette smoke.

Mathias averted his eyes. "You're weird."

"Yes. But, no. There's no way my mother's doing your dad."

Mathias's expression went from annoyed to outraged in less than a second. "There is… way. There's way, way."

"Your English sucks."

"Fuck you." Anger lit Mathias's hazel eyes, turning them into glowing amber.

Nice.

Alberto no longer felt cold, so he pushed his luck. "I was just saying, my mother and your dad, they don't… how can I put it… operate in the same world. No offence, I'm sure he has many impressive… assets, but that won't be enough for my mother. Do you know what I mean?"

From the way his face darkened, Mathias seemed to have taken offence anyway. "I know what you mean, and I'm saying it's bullshit. We need to tail them and get to the bottom of this."

Alberto shrugged. "And then what?"

"Then we confront them and tell them to stop!"

"But why? If my mother wants to do your dad, as far as I'm concerned, she's welcome to it."

Mathias gave him a look that promised trouble. "Say that again and see what happens."

There was a silence. They held each other's gaze, neither of them willing to give ground.

"You know I have to do it now," Alberto said, breaking their stance. "I have to say that again because I really want to know what's going to happen."

Mathias threw a quick look around him before coming closer. "You… Are you stupid or something?"

Alberto enjoyed the sight of his confused expression and wondered—no, impossible. Things were never as good as they first appeared to be.

"I'm going home," he said flatly.

"Hey!" Mathias followed after him. "I'm not done talking. My dad's married, you piece of shit."

Mathias roughly grabbed him by the arm and pulled him away from the front doors out of earshot. Amused, Alberto allowed himself to be dragged along. "I thought you were the piece of shit, and, honestly…" He shook his wrist in an attempt to break free. "… what do your parents put in your food for you to be so aggressive? Batteries? Rat poison?"

Mathias let go of him with a disgusted expression. Alberto missed the pressure on his arm as soon as it was gone. He pressed on, "In fact, even if my mother becomes your new stepmum, it has nothing to do with me. Perhaps I'll even encourage her, considering."

Mathias's face turned ashen. "I'll break your fucking legs before you try."

"Won't stop me from opening my mouth."

"Then I'll break your mouth or whatever."

Alberto quirked an eyebrow, thoroughly entertained now. Mathias's eyes appeared alight with fire. *Nice.* But then he started to backtrack. Perhaps he really was afraid to punch Alberto in the face and preferred to leave after all. Alberto didn't want things to get to that point. He gave in and tossed his cigarette.

"Okay, fine, I'll go with you. You can just… defuse yourself or whatever. You look like you're about to pop a vein."

Only then did Mathias appear to calm down. His hands returned to the front pocket of his hoodie.

"Okay, Tuesday evening, then. Don't be late."

"Fine."

Mathias frowned. "Yes?"

"I said I'll be there."

Alberto watched Mathias retrace his steps back into the

museum with a blank expression, but there was a smile in his heart. Angry Buzzcut — no, Mathias — was much more interesting than he appeared at Xavier's party. Alberto was a simple guy, after all. All he knew was that he was having a really bad day earlier, and now, he was not.

And that's all that mattered in the end.

9

SPIES

MATHIAS KNEW how to bark orders, but logistics wasn't his thing, so he was nervous when the time came to take Alberto to his residence to spy on his father. He was nervous because he'd never told that arrogant prick where they were supposed to meet and because he didn't know how to let him know. He couldn't exactly go and meet him in front of everyone, or they would assume they knew each other, and Mathias really didn't want anyone to think they had some sort of relationship.

It was already difficult to pretend not to know him on Saturday. When Zak came up with the idea of going to the museum and let it slip that Alberto would probably be there, Mathias accepted Eric's panicked offer to accompany them. Luckily enough, Alberto showed up right when they'd received their tickets. Despite being sort of moved by Eric's despair, Mathias urgently excused himself, pretending he needed a cigarette, just to talk to his mortal enemy. What else was he supposed to do? The moment he saw Alberto's face—and he had his eye on the doors—his heart rate went up just like that.

So, Mathias could only stalk Alberto again, feeling a bit shitty about it and wanting to just go home and forget about the whole thing. He kept repeating to himself, *Do this for your family. Do this for your family. Do it for mom.*

In the end, he waited by the library and knocked into Alberto as he was coming out of the nearby men's room. Not only that, he forced him back inside, twisted them both around, and used his body to keep the door shut.

"Seriously?" Alberto looked more irritated than shocked at finding himself slammed against another flat surface.

"Sorry." Mathias let go of him and wiped his hands on his trousers. "I didn't have your number."

"There are other ways. Ever heard of Facebook? Instagram?"

"Oh." Mathias really hadn't thought about that at all. In his defense, he had Facebook and Instagram because everyone else did, but he didn't spend much time on them.

"Anyway..." he said, quickly making sure no one else was around. "It's now or never."

"Okay. How——"

Mathias shushed him. "We can leave together now. Eric and Zak have gone home already. So has everyone else. In fact, it's so late, I think even Van Bergen is gone, and you, me, and the janitors are the only ones left. What the fuck were you doing in here?" He gave a subconscious look toward the blue stalls in the back. "Jerking off?"

"I was just killing time, waiting for you to find me. I didn't forget we had a thing today."

"We don't have a thing." Mathias noted Alberto didn't deny jerking off at all. He shoved him aside so he could open the door, and he stretched out his hand to invite him to go first.

He had lied. It wasn't that late. He just really didn't like waiting, especially for somebody like Alberto. People like him, they made everybody bow and scrape for them. Mathias felt nothing but contempt for such assholes, so he was almost smiling when he dragged that posh bastard into the parking lot of his building on Rousselet Street. He told Alberto not to move and to watch out for his father's blue Toyota. Alberto looked almost... disappointed, and he took in his surroundings and leaned against the wall to light a cigarette without a word.

The parking lot under Mathias's building was not under-ground, so they could see the narrow one-way street outside while being well-concealed themselves, but it didn't stop the place from being drafty and overall unpleasant. Ten minutes in, Alberto, an obvious lightweight, was already looking half-dead, but Mathias couldn't know if it was because of the cold or because he was, well… Alberto.

He'd heard all sorts of things about the guy; some people even went as far as calling him a zombie or a vampire. Mathias slipped him furtive looks here and there, and all he saw was a privileged brat who acted bored with life. However, as time went on, and despite Mathias's expectations, he'd yet to complain. He kept to himself, seemingly uninterested in talking to him. Mathias didn't like having him standing at his back so much, but he also didn't want to be the one starting a conversation, so he kept his eye on the road, hoping his dad or Alberto's mom would show up sooner rather than later.

When Alberto finally spoke after the thirty-minute mark, he had been so quiet this whole time that Mathias's entire body jerked forward when he felt his breath upon his ear. "Should I have worn a trench coat like in the movies?"

Mathias glared at him. "Excuse you?"

He didn't appreciate the way Alberto had suddenly appeared behind him. Worse, he leaned into his personal space, his voice lowering to a whisper, "Have you done this before?"

"What?"

"Playing detectives. Spying on your own dad."

"No, of course not." Mathias wasn't a psychopath. The circumstances were complicated. However, why should he explain it to this guy? "Look, I just have to do it." He had almost said "we," but he didn't like the sound of it at all.

That asshole snorted quietly, but he retreated at least.

Mathias observed him from head to toe, his mouth twisted. "We're not here to fuck around. This is serious!"

"Fine, fine."

Alberto yawned at length and leaned back against the wall, his arms folded over his chest. Mathias felt irritated, but he couldn't pinpoint the reason why. All he knew was that with each of Alberto's yawns, he felt an irrepressible need to gnash his teeth.

Approximately fifteen minutes and three hundred yawns later, just as Mathias was about to lose his temper, Alberto opened his mouth again.

"Serious's not the word I'd use to describe this. Boring. Boring's the word."

Mathias wanted to choke him. "Could you shut up? Do you really think I want to be stuck here with you?"

Alberto glanced at him with indifference. Mathias expected him to ask why, so he was thrown off by his apparent lack of curiosity. Just like Eric and the others had warned, it was like staring at a blank canvas.

"So, what's your deal?" Mathias asked in a sharp tone. "Hm? Why are you so fucking weird?"

Alberto's cold gaze didn't flinch, but his lips remained closed.

"You're not gonna answer me?"

"What's the point?" He threw a vague look at the line of passing cars. Mathias stared at the side of his face with growing listlessness.

"Great talking to you."

"I know. Aren't I just a treat?"

"And you talk weird." Mathias shoved his hands in his pockets. His gaze slipped back to the road, only for his heart to stop when he thought he'd spotted his father's car, but this one kept driving without slowing down.

Mathias shivered. It was starting to get cold out here. "Why does it look like you don't care about my dad and your mom being together?"

"Maybe because I don't?"

"Really? You expect me to believe that?"

"I don't expect you to believe anything, honestly."

Fuck. He was infuriating. He was the most freakishly annoying bastard on the planet, and he had to be the one Mathias had no choice but to get stuck with, because for once, his dad decided to take action in his life, and it had to be *this.*

Fuck, fuck, fuck!

Alberto acted like a conversation with Mathias was beneath him. Like standing next to him was beneath him. Even like moving and breathing near him was beneath him. And yet, they were both here. Together. The most unlikely pair.

"Guess we should call it a night," Mathias muttered.

"Oh?"

"Yep. I have to be somewhere." If he didn't get his ass to the boxing gym soon, Mathias wasn't sure his hands wouldn't end up on this guy. He knew the signs. He had to be smart. "Wait here a second. I've got to get my bag upstairs. Keep an eye on the road. Remember, it's a blue Toyota. My dad, my dad looks like—"

"I'm only here to check if my mother will show up. I know how to recognise my own mother, thanks."

Asshole. Mathias's hands balled into fists in his pockets. His heart pounding in his ears, he went upstairs to get his boxing gloves and his duffel bag.

He'd never been very good at analyzing his own feelings. To him, they came and went in waves of colors. Blue when he couldn't hold back his tears, red when he was choked up by rage, yellow when Eric laughed at one of his own jokes. Around Alberto, he felt different. Everything blurred, and nothing made sense. He could feel the rage, see it swirl around, red and hot like magma in his gut, in his lungs. But it wasn't just that. He was murky waters, he was black, he was gray. He felt completely unknown.

He couldn't possibly be afraid of that prick, so why was he feeling so unsettled every time they were near each other? Mathias had first attributed it to the fact that he knew his hands were capable of punching any idiot in the vicinity, and Alberto was obviously very punchable. Then, just as he rode the elevator back downstairs, he finally understood. He was envious of him. Of his ability not to feel. That was it. Envy. Not great, but nothing to panic over. Anyway, in a week or two, they'd never see each other again.

In the parking lot, Alberto was staring at the buzzing light overhead and not at the road at all. Mathias could safely say he had never met anyone who appeared so useless in his entire life.

"Seen anything?"

He had to ask twice because Alberto didn't even notice he had returned the first time.

"Ah? No. Nothing."

Mathias sighed and put the gloves down. Alberto glanced down at them then back at him.

"You're a boxer."

Mathias shrugged. "I'm not very good at it. I just like to punch things."

Alberto turned his back to the road and came closer. "Really…?" He bent down to brush a finger along the curve of a shiny red glove. "Do you like punching people?"

"I said things. Not people."

"But isn't boxing about punching people in the face?"

"I guess, but they're not like… innocent people."

Alberto blinked slowly. "You've never wanted to punch innocent people?"

"What?"

"Never thought of strangling a puppy or drowning a kitten?"

Mathias's eyes widened. "What the fuck?!"

Alberto backed away with a lazy flick of his wrist. "Nothing, nothing."

Of course Mathias couldn't drop it. "What the fuck are you saying? Do you do this sort of thing?"

"Me? I've never hurt a fly."

The lack of expression on his face made Mathias doubt that statement very much.

"Sure."

"Promise." Alberto crossed his fingers and frowned at them before hiding them in his pocket.

"Eric's right," Mathias said slowly. "There's something wrong with you."

Another car was approaching, so Mathias went to check it out. He heard Alberto's mocking voice behind him.

"So that's it, then. I agree, it's smart to take Eric's word for everything. He's known to be the wisest guy ever."

Mathias didn't bother turning around. "He's not dumb."

"He's not smart."

Now he did turn around, his teeth gritted. "Don't you hang out with fucking Xavier?"

Something flashed in Alberto's eyes. "First, no, I don't. Second, how would you know who I hang out with?"

"Pff." Mathias returned his attention to the road, but the car was gone. It hadn't looked like a Jaguar or a Toyota anyway. "Only because Zak obsesses about it."

"Really? Cute." Alberto made a sound that vaguely resembled a laugh, his gaze softening for a second. "What? Why are you looking at me like that?"

Mathias sneered. "Looking at you just pisses me off. I don't know why."

"Don't look at me, then."

As if it were that easy.

It wasn't. In fact, it was impossible not to look at him. Mathias knew he wasn't sophisticated, not into finer things, not at all like the people Alberto most likely hung out with, but he could recognize when someone was unusually good looking.

This guy really had it all. His giant of a mom and her sleek Jaguar, they probably lived in a castle somewhere that Mathias imagined was like *The Rocky Horror Picture Show*. Alberto was tall and rich, and he looked like this, and yet, it seemed he felt not even one ounce of gratitude. Even accusing his mom of being a cheater didn't bother him in the slightest. It was unbearable. It made Mathias want to grab him and shake him. In fact, if he didn't leave now…

"Will you fuck off now?" Mathias asked abruptly.

"Oh…" Alberto looked around in confusion. "Are we done?"

"Yes." Mathias pushed him aside to pick up his bags and his gloves. "I have punching bags to deal with. Unless you want to replace one of them."

He could have sworn Alberto looked tempted. Mathias bit the inside of his cheek to stop himself from making any comments.

Alberto picked up the gloves before he could and handed them over. "So, how long do we have to do this?"

"Until we catch them together." Mathias hoisted his bag over his shoulder. "We finish school at the same times on Tuesdays and Thursdays."

"How do you know?"

"*Shh*, I'm talking. Let's just meet here next Tuesday." He noticed Alberto's frown and added, "We don't have school this Thursday, remember?"

"We don't?"

"No. We have a four-day weekend. How can you not know?"

"I'd forgotten."

Mathias took a deep breath. "Then meet me here next Tuesday. Don't let anyone see you. And hey! Wait." He waited for Alberto to turn back. "You can't tell anyone we... we know each other."

"Oh." Alberto arched an eyebrow. "Are you... embarrassed of me?"

"Fuck yeah, I'm embarrassed of you."

"Is it because of Eric?"

Mathias didn't see the need to answer. Alberto snorted loudly, and Mathias's hands grew still in the pockets of his hoodie.

"What's so funny?" he mumbled, vexed.

"You. You make it sound like I'm your dirty little secret."

And before Mathias could hurl insults at him, Alberto had disappeared into the night.

10

GARDEN PARTY

Alberto worried about Mamma.

It was a constant in his existence, worrying about his mother. He couldn't remember a time when he wasn't watching her back, making sure she was fine, she was safe, that she was around and close by.

Her husband couldn't stand it. Everyone knew Dimitri Ribakov was head over heels for his wife. He was even creepy at times. His adoration was visible, even inside the house, in which he had dedicated entire rooms to her beauty. He worshipped her like she was a goddess.

Alberto was the thorn in Dimitri's side, his only rival for Mamma's undivided attention. He only had to breathe a little louder than usual, and she would drop everything to be at his side. He and his stepfather tolerated each other for her sake, but Alberto knew that, were they characters from one of those tragedies, they'd already have been at each other's throats, and judging from Dimitri's aura as compared to his own, Mamma would have been mourning the loss of her son long ago.

So, was it possible that she was seeing someone behind Dimitri's back? Would she even dare? Why would she leave the safety and comfort of a life of riches with an adoring husband for a Maths teacher with a wife and a bad-tempered son? She had been married before, and she'd never been so at ease but with that overly tanned thug. Nothing made sense at all.

But Mathias knew she was driving a black Jaguar even though she showed up at the parents-teachers meeting in the SUV. Mamma was not a good driver, and Dimitri — as well as Alberto, to be honest — preferred when her driver, Oleg, took her around town. What if she really wanted to leave Dimitri to be with Mr Rodin? Then… Alberto and Mathias would become half brothers by marriage. The thought was laughable. At least, to him. Alberto was certain Mathias wouldn't laugh at that idea at all, so he decided to bring it up the next time they met.

If Mathias clearly didn't loath Alberto so much, the latter would have been certain he had lied to get close to him. After all, how hard could it be to find out his mother had a Jaguar? You never know, these days. If Mamma didn't know Rodin — and it was way more probable than the idea of her cheating on her husband with a teacher — then there was only one explanation: Mathias made it all up.

But why? It made no sense at all because the loathing was real; Alberto could feel it like endless pinpricks of electric currents crawling under his skin whenever Mathias glared at him. It amused him almost as much as it didn't. He wondered about the scathing looks, the disgusted grimaces, the bitter notes in his voice when he addressed him. If he'd done or said something wrong, fair enough, but it was most likely because of some other thing, something beyond his control, as usual. Eric, Zak, Michael… The list of people thinking less of him was probably getting longer day after day.

Alberto was used to the lack of agency in his life, but it didn't mean he didn't find it as unpleasant as ever. He didn't choose what he ate or what he wore, but that didn't really matter to him. Not choosing where he lived was harder. Not choosing the company around him, who got to be close, was even worse. Being at the mercy of others, their words, and their actions, that's what he disliked the most.

He preferred to keep his distance from people, and he usually couldn't care less about being disliked. He even preferred it at times. But when it came to Mathias, he felt a twinge of impatience at being loathed for some nebulous reason. On the other hand, Mathias was really easy to manipulate and enrage, and his spontaneous bouts of anger were greatly amusing. Pushing his buttons gave Alberto that much-needed illusion of control. After a lifetime of the opposite, it was kind of addictive.

Why are you so weird? He'd asked. *Why are you so weird?*

It brought a faint smile to Alberto's heart. Mathias was handsome when he was angry, wasn't he? A few sparks, and his eyes went from brown to amber. And he was a boxer. How charming was that? That meant he could fight. Mamma would say to stay away from his kind of people, but he said it himself, he'd never hurt innocent people, and his overreaction was proof he wasn't into tormenting pets either.

No, Mathias really was handsome. Handsome enough to produce little sighs, Alberto reflected, sliding down in his lounge chair. He was so absorbed by his own thoughts that he hadn't noticed the person approaching him in the dark, and he blinked in surprise when a glass of red wine magically appeared before him.

"Here," the man said. "For you."

Alberto knew better than to accept drinks from strangers, especially drunk old men, but his mother and Dimitri's guests were all important people, and Alberto had been instructed never to be rude to them. Tonight was another one of these tedious parties including an unsavoury bunch of politicians and equally uninteresting businessmen, as well as a few once-in-a-lifetime artists whom Dimitri liked to invite for his mother's sake. Alberto had already made an appearance in an expensive suit bought and tailored by Mamma herself, had shaken hands and answered questions as requested of him, and made her so proud she'd produced a half-smile behind her glass of alcohol-free Champagne, wrinkles be damned.

Alberto glanced up at the man and recognised him from earlier. He was a fashion and jewellery designer, and he was exactly the sort of person Mamma wanted him to be especially nice to. After all, this sort of celebrity had the power to launch his career, advance it, destroy it, whatever… and Mamma really wished for Alberto to have a modelling career.

Before it was too late.

The conversation from the other day was still fresh in Alberto's mind, and he took the glass of wine from the man's hands. "Thank you," he said in a polite tone, putting it away on the small table at his side.

"Aren't you cold out here?"

Feeling temperatures was the prerogative of living people. The dead don't feel the cold, didn't you know?

"I'm fine," Alberto said, but he subconsciously tightened the lapels of his jacket around him.

He had escaped into the garden some time ago, unable to fake interest in the conversations around him and even more exhausted by the looks Dimitri gave him every time his mother stood too close to him. He didn't mind the dark nor the cold, but he was surprised this man had found him in his hiding place. Perhaps he'd noticed the glow of his cigarette and was drawn to the light like some kind of moth.

"Do you remember me?" The man sat and laid his arm on the back of his chair. Alberto naturally tensed, glancing down at the hand resting by his shoulder. It held a glass containing a dark liquor, and on one of his fingers, an enormous ring reflected the cold light of the moon.

"Sorry, I don't."

"That's okay. I'm Jean-Pierre. I used to work with your mother a long time ago."

You and a million others, Alberto thought. He'd met so many of them over the years.

"Oh."

"We've met before. In fact, the first time I saw you, you were just a baby."

He laughed. Alberto didn't. The whiff of whisky he caught on Jean-Pierre's breath made him turn his head away.

"I haven't seen you in years," the designer went on. "How much you've changed… You're a man now."

Alberto knocked his heels together. "Yep."

"And you are… Can I say it?" He chuckled like an embarrassed teenage boy. "Irresistible."

The wind rustled in the thickets of rose bushes on the side. Alberto's gaze lingered on the dead canes.

"Thank you," he murmured.

"I was just talking to your mother, and I agree with her. You would go so, *so* far in this career, if only you'd really get into it. You want to know why?"

Alberto didn't really care, but Mamma would be having kittens if she found out he was rude to a famous designer like Jean-Pierre Denizon, so he nodded absently. The guy didn't notice his discomfort. He was drunk. He saw what he wanted to see.

"You really are the epitome of ravishing beauty… and the cruelty that goes with it."

Alberto glanced up. Cruelty? But the man only laughed when he read his expression.

"I'm joking. I'm joking. But… it's true that cruelty is the gift of the truly beautiful."

Jean-Pierre finally withdrew his arm and raked his hand through his hair. Alberto caught sight of the ring. It was the silver head of a monstrous wolf, its expression fixed in a savage snarl. The eyes were made of two glowing fire opals. Once he saw it, Alberto couldn't look away. It was ugly, and yet…

"You like this ring?" Jean-Pierre spoke in a soft, coaxing voice.

"Mm." Alberto nodded. "Reminds me of someone."

"I designed it."

That explained why it was so ugly.

"I could give it to you," Jean-Pierre purred.

"I don't have any money."

"I don't want money."

"What do you want, then?" Alberto discreetly rolled his eyes, knowing full well where this was going.

"Just one thing." Jean-Pierre leaned into his space. "Just one kiss."

With a sigh, Alberto knocked his heels together again. "I'm seventeen."

The man came even closer, the smell of whisky wafting into Alberto's nostrils, sweet and acrid. "I won't tell if you don't."

Alberto stared at his own feet for a while, thoughts swirling aimlessly in the fog of his brain, before snapping back to Mathias's angry scowl. What would he do in this situation? Laugh in this old man's face? Swing his fists at him? Not that it mattered. Alberto could bet guys like Mathias never ended up in such situations. Only wimps like him did.

"No thank you," he said. He put the effort into trying to sound cold, and he forced himself to look straight into this old man's eyes.

For a second, he thought had been successful, because the guy blinked and backed away, but then, without warning, Jean-Pierre attempted to kiss him. Alberto abruptly got to his feet, and he watched Jean-Pierre lose his balance and nearly fall nose-first against Alberto's now empty chair. Bleary-eyed, he used his hand to push himself up, and the moonlight once again shone over the vicious head of the wolf.

"Thank you for the wine," Alberto said.

He didn't wait for Jean-Pierre's reaction before he slunk back inside. With no intention of returning to the party, he crept back to his room, silent as a cat, and shut the door behind him. He sat with his back against it, in the dark, for a long time.

Tonight, he particularly wished he could lock the door and everyone out and hide in here forever where only Mamma could find him, but Stasia had stolen his bedroom key a long time ago, and he had yet to get it back. So, he sat against the door until the party was over, and everyone had returned to whatever hell they'd come from.

11

TELL-TALE SIGNS

ALBERTO SLIPPED against the wall with a groan.

"I want to go home."

"No."

"Nothing's going to happen. She won't come."

It was the next Tuesday after school. Mathias had rushed home to meet Alberto under his building. All day, the weather had been good, only for an annoying drizzle to start falling as the sun set, darkening his mood. Mathias became certain he wouldn't find Alberto here, but he had showed up despite the rain dampening his hair and the strange oversized jacket he wore all the time.

"Complaining isn't gonna make this any easier."

"She's not going to come," Alberto repeated, articulating the words for emphasis. "We both know it."

"Hey!" Mathias charged toward him with the intention of telling him to shut the hell up or something equally bad, but he stopped at the sight of Alberto's face. His eyes heavy with sleep, his mouth slightly open, he was looking at Mathias curiously.

Alberto had distracting lips. They were, like the rest of his features, well-defined. Full but unwelcoming, they never parted for a kind word, and they certainly didn't stretch into smiles of the genuine kind. Mathias stared at them, lost his footing, and what came out instead surprised the hell out of both of them.

"... What did you do this weekend?"

Alberto's eyebrows rose to his hairline, and the corners of his treacherous lips curled. "I almost got eaten by a wolf. You?"

Mathias gritted his teeth. He really wished he'd gone with *shut the hell up* instead. "If you're gonna tell me a load of crap, then don't bother talking, really."

"You asked for it."

"I asked what you did this weekend, I didn't ask for a serving of bullshit." His words were met with dry laughter, irritating him further. "And I was only asking because I wanted to know if your mother was around the whole time. I personally don't care what you do on the weekends."

"Okay, okay."

Mathias had spent the whole four-day weekend keeping an eye on his father, going as far as following him to his favorite bar. Meanwhile, Alberto had probably spent his weekend admiring himself in the mirror and taking selfies. From the way he kept yawning and rubbing his face with both hands, he was clearly tired.

Maybe Mathias was wrong about the selfies. Maybe Alberto spent the weekend in bed with someone doing all sorts of things. His eyes narrowed as he spoke, "Would you even have noticed if she was around?"

"Why?"

"You look like you didn't get much sleep this weekend."

"Oh, I slept. I don't have any problems sleeping." He shot Mathias a quick look. "In fact, I probably sleep better than you."

Mathias felt annoyed at that statement, knowing it was true. He hadn't had a good night's sleep in years, but it got worse since he'd gotten into that school. He sneered, defensive. "Are you some kind of narcoleptic?"

Alberto puffed out a laugh but didn't answer.

"Seriously. Why do you always look on the brink of death? I'm curious."

"Why, why, why. You're the Why Guy. Always asking questions."

Mathias scoffed. "Are we calling each other names already?"

Alberto shrugged.

"So, should I call you the Narcoleptic Guy, then?"

"It doesn't sound as good."

"No, it doesn't," Mathias admitted.

Don't you worry, he thought. *I'll find an appropriate name for you soon enough.*

Now exasperated, Mathias dropped the subject and Alberto altogether, and he went to stand by the gate as far as possible from him.

"Am I annoying you?" Alberto asked, a teasing note in his voice, unwilling to give him any ounce of peace.

"Yes."

"Why?"

"You talk too much."

"If I talk, I annoy you, but if I don't talk, I'll fall asleep, and then you'll be mad anyway."

"Probably."

Alberto swiped his tongue across his lip. "Are you always this pissed off?"

"No. Sometimes, I'm even worse."

He laughed again, but there wasn't any trace of humor on his face. Mathias turned his attention back to the road.

"I can't help being curious," Alberto went on.

Mathias tried to, but in the end, he couldn't resist asking, "About what?"

"What is it about me that annoys you so much?"

Words failed Mathias for a second or two. He took a deep breath and said, "Don't bother talking to me. We're never gonna be friends, and if you can't keep yourself awake on your own, then I'm sorry to tell you, you won't amount to much in this life."

Behind him, he heard Alberto chuckle and light up a cigarette. Silence descended upon them. Neither one talked or moved for over ten minutes. Then thirty.

And Mathias was getting nervous.

His dad should have been home by now unless he'd gone to the bar first. Then, he wouldn't reappear for hours, but generally, he drove home to leave the car in the parking lot before heading out.

Mathias could read in Alberto's attitude the tell-tale signs of his mounting lassitude. He was slowly reaching the conclusion that he'd been dragged here based on nothing, that they were wasting their time. Mathias felt he had every right to believe that, and he was annoyed.

And so they waited and waited until the rain died down. Then, it got warmer, so much so, Mathias had started feeling uncomfortable wrapped in so many layers. He heard some rustling behind him and tossed a look over his shoulder. Alberto had opened the top buttons of his expensive-looking shirt, revealing his long and slender neck. With his indifferent expression, he looked like nothing in this world could bother him enough to make him stumble.

Alberto noticed him staring, and Mathias jerked his head to the side. It felt awkward, as if he'd been caught in the act of something shameful. He resented the silence now just as much as he welcomed it. And his dad still wasn't here.

"Where were you before?" Alberto's voice rang behind him.

Mathias was surprised to hear him ask a personal question. He found himself annoyed and perhaps a bit flattered. Mostly annoyed to be flattered.

"Why are you asking?"

"Why not?"

Mathias couldn't deny that they had nothing else to do. There was no harm in answering that question. It wasn't too private. He checked his phone for the time and decided to humor him.

"I used to go to a public school. In Essonne. That's… farther south. In the suburbs."

Alberto was lighting another cigarette, but he looked up at the sound of the word suburbs.

"I don't live there anymore," Mathias added, and he hated himself for it. What was he trying to prove? "I… I live here now."

Alberto half-lifted his shoulder. "I live in the suburbs."

"The rich ones, I assume."

Alberto didn't reply.

Mathias went on, "My dad was offered this job; he couldn't refuse it. We got help finding the apartment, too."

"But you didn't want to come."

At first, not really, no, but he had to toughen up and take care of his family, and that included leaving some people behind. He stared down at his feet. "It's just... it's not convenient, that's all."

"I get it."

Like hell you do, Mr. Fancy Pants.

How could he, with his supermodel job and his probable mansion in the rich suburbs? He looked like he was styled by a professional every morning. Shit, he probably had a valet just to make sure his hair looked that amount of stupid.

"Do you miss your old school?" Alberto asked after a long drag.

Mathias shrugged. "Not really." He hesitated before adding, "I got expelled anyway." He thought he saw a flash of curiosity in Alberto's eyes.

"Why?"

"For hitting somebody."

"Someone innocent?" Alberto teased.

"There were no innocent people in that case."

"What happened?"

"He made one too many jokes, and I'd left my sense of humor at home."

It was one thing to call him a stupid name like *Period Master* because he punched a bully once, resulting in his girlfriend sticking a tampon up his nose, but when his friend used the same nickname to make fun of his relationship with Daphnée, Mathias saw, well... red. She was off-limits. His people, in general, were off-limits. Cross that line, and Mathias would forget all about keeping his hands in his pockets.

"So, if I make a bad joke," Alberto asked his cigarette, "are you going to hit me?"

Mathias looked closely at him. "I started boxing so I wouldn't do that sort of shit anymore."

"Never ever?"

"I'm not as angry as I used to be."

Alberto's lip curled into a mocking smirk. "I wonder how you were before, then."

Mathias had no clue how to answer that. His gaze flickered toward Alberto's cigarette and remained there, fixed on the burning end and the long fingers holding it, until Alberto tossed it away with a sigh.

"Do you have a girlfriend?"

Mathias flinched. "Why?" he barked more than he asked.

That wasn't any of his business. Though, Mathias didn't understand why he would be so rattled by such a simple question. Eric had pretty much given him an interrogation in the first hours of their initial meeting, and it hadn't bothered him that much. Well, except, it kinda did, when Mathias realized his friend was bi. But nothing weird happened since, and Mathias quickly relaxed around him.

He now realized he was being aggressive for no reason and that Alberto was still watching him, his lips slightly parted, waiting for an answer. He felt like a dumbass.

"I did," he said in a quiet voice. "I don't anymore."

He felt a bit cheap saying that. He could say he had to leave her behind, too, but first, he hadn't had a girlfriend in over two years, and second, he was never into her in the first place. He got together with someone he knew he shouldn't have and then went with the flow, but his flow was perturbed. He was never the same, and still, they clung to each other because no one wants to break the heart of someone who's lost everything. And so he kept her around because she was familiar and because she was there.

Anyway, since her, he'd been single. He'd fooled around some —too much, even, in his opinion—but he was never a good boyfriend. No girl at this age, or no girl at all, would want a boyfriend who never had the time nor the patience to be around her. Everyone deserved better than that.

Mathias had watched Alberto's face attentively as he answered, and he noted no particular reaction. He thought perhaps he should ask him the same. He'd heard all sorts of things about this guy. They all sounded like bullshit and, yes, a part of him was curious, so why not ask him? He lightly cleared his throat, his foot grinding the pavement. "And you? Do you have a girlfriend?"

Alberto met his eyes. "I don't like girls."

Mathias's heart thumped. "You mean you're gay?"

"That too."

A long silence followed, and Mathias furrowed his brow.

That easy? He'd heard Alberto had a habit of telling girls he was gay and telling guys he was straight. Eric's friend, Joy, commented about it all the time at school. Why was he giving Mathias a different answer?

But if he'd just told the actual truth... then Mathias would have received confirmation about something many people at school were currently betting on. He could share that information with Eric and earn himself some money. Wait... maybe not Eric... he was the one betting on Alberto not being gay and Zak being *his little mistake*. But from what Alberto just said, then he really was gay, and he really was with Zak two months ago... but it never showed. Mathias had seen more physical signs of affection from Eric inexplicably flushing every time Zak drew near than from Alberto who was dating the guy himself.

But, of course, he wouldn't repeat that information to anyone. It was nobody's business what Alberto did and with whom. The only problem was now they'd have to be extra careful not to be caught together. What would it look like if someone from school were to see them hanging out? They really might get the wrong impression. Mathias's best friend at school was already gay-ish, now this motherfucker coming along made it look like Mathias only hung out with gays.

Damn it, damn it, damn it.

Mathias bit his lip, annoyed because of that. He was also a bit annoyed because he suspected Alberto to be gay from the start, and it bothered him less when he wasn't so sure. He glanced back toward the road, and that's when he saw it: his father's car. He jerked back.

"Fuck! That's him!"

The blue Toyota made its way into the parking lot. To avoid being seen, Alberto flattened himself against the wall. Mathias flew near him and pressed himself into his space. They both held their breath as the car maneuvered into its spot. Mathias's nose was basically against Alberto's throat. He stared, unblinking, at the way it shifted every time he swallowed. His own throat constricted when he realized his heartbeat had turned abnormally fast.

The car engine was cut, the driver's door opened, and there he was, Mathias's father, getting out of his car.

Alone.

Alberto let out a groan of frustration, oblivious or indifferent to the lack of space between them that had Mathias boiling inside. "So much for nap time."

Mathias squeezed his eyes shut and inhaled the scent of Alberto's skin. He didn't wear cologne or aftershave of any kind. Only the faint traces of a minty yet flowery soap lingered on his skin, and nothing else.

With the help of a sharp intake of breath, Mathias pulled himself together. What the fuck was he thinking, sniffing that guy in the dark corner of a parking lot? What the hell was he up to?

He waited until his father had crossed the lot and disappeared through the exit door to jump a good meter back.

"Let's call it a day, then," he said quickly, eager to retreat to the privacy of his room, away from Alberto.

He was worried Alberto had noticed his discomfort, but when he finally met his eyes, he only found an empty void, and he almost shivered.

"This isn't working," Alberto said flatly.

Mathias agreed, and, yet, he had to convince him. He had to convince him to try again one more time. He felt it would all work out if only they had more time.

"One last time. Come back on Thursday. If they don't show up then, we'll go our own ways and never see each other again."

Alberto looked around the damp and cold parking lot, and his lips pursed. Mathias stared fixedly at them, anxious about what sentence they'd deliver whenever they would part.

Alberto took a long time to speak. His voice was softer when he said, "*O-kay.*"

HEAD-ON

On the following Thursday, Mathias surrendered a sigh. The ugly truth was that he didn't expect his dad to show up with Alberto's mom either—not that he'd admit it, not even at gunpoint—but he really didn't.

In fact, he had started to think he was going a bit crazy. It was to be expected. No one would give him a hard time if they knew, but they'd never know because he never shared anything with anyone.

Alberto, smoking cigarette after cigarette a few meters away under the yellow lights, didn't help with his feeling of helplessness. He watched from the corner of his eye as the cloud of smoke swirled around his face, blurring his features. He watched, and he felt tired.

"Can I have one of those?"

Alberto obliged without a word, stretched his fingers to pluck a cigarette out of the pack, then changed his mind and handed the whole thing over instead. Mathias thanked him, partly grateful, partly frustrated. Everything felt wrong today, like the roof of the parking lot was pressing down on him, and he had a bit of trouble breathing.

"Fuck." He leaned against the wall and lit up. "You win. I give up."

Alberto gave him a quick sideways glance. "It's boring, isn't it? A complete waste of time."

Mathias nodded, thinking, *Yes, it's boring. You win. Whatever.* Alberto came to stand against the wall near him, but not too near.

"Let's give it another fifteen minutes, all right?" Mathias offered. "Then, we can forget about the whole thing."

Alberto gave him a long look. "Okay." He propped himself against the wall as well, and in the dim light of the parking lot, he suddenly looked older than he was.

"Why are you named Alberto?" Mathias asked suddenly. The question had occurred to him before, but he had no reason to ask. Now he felt he was running out of time.

"Why?" Alberto quirked an eyebrow. "You don't like it?"

"Sounds old."

"It was my grandfather's name."

"Ah. Your mom kept it traditional, then."

Alberto shook his head. "My dad chose it. My mother wanted to call me something else. Something French."

"Why something French?"

"Her favourite movie's French. She's been obsessed with France ever since she saw it, and she always wanted to live here."

"Which movie?"

"*An Impudent Girl.*"

"I don't know it."

"The French name is *L'Effrontée.*"

"Oh, right. I've seen it. That's the one with that Italian song."

"Yes." Alberto's tone had grown cold. He switched his phone on and stepped away. "And you? Why Mathias?"

"My mom read it somewhere, and she loved it. She said it sounds good in every language."

Alberto replied with a noncommittal "Mm," which somehow irritated Mathias. He quickly glanced at Alberto's phone to see what he was doing and saw with surprise he was looking at himself on Instagram. Alberto noticed his judgmental scowl and said, "I'm not in love with myself. That's my professional profile."

Not quite believing him, Mathias took another reluctant look. He noted that Alberto's iPhone wasn't very well cared for, compared to his own older model. The screen was cracked in two places. His gaze slipped across the screen and stopped abruptly. "Shit! You have thousands of followers!"

"Yes."

"… How?"

Alberto shrugged. "They're good pictures."

Mathias guessed he was right. They were professional pictures, after all. "How long have you been on it?"

"A few months."

"And you've already got so many followers doing… nothing?"

"I guess." He met Mathias's eyes. "That's the job."

"Do you like doing it?"

"I like getting paid for it."

Mathias snorted. "Does it pay well?"

"Sometimes. I got paid really well for the *Occult* one, and it opened some doors. Now, I'm gonna get paid even more, as long as I do what I'm told."

Weird way of saying it. Mathias gazed absently at all the square pictures of Alberto appearing on the cracked screen. He spotted one or two really good ones.

"All these people on Instagram… do they hit on you?"

Alberto's lip curled just enough to annoy him. "Maybe."

"Do you get creepy messages?"

He shrugged. "I never read them."

"Never?"

"Ever since the first dick pic, no."

Mathias frowned. "People really do that?"

"Yes. People are weird."

"You're weird."

"True, but I keep my dick in my pants."

Mathias fell silent. He studied the side of Alberto's face for a long time until the other noticed, and he had to turn his head away. "You don't even bother reading the compliments, then?"

"Why bother? I don't care."

"Sure, you don't care."

Alberto seemed bored and amused at the same time. "They don't know me, and I don't know them. Why should I care what they think? Whether they find me hot or not is beyond my control, and it's not going to change my life."

"If people didn't find you hot, you wouldn't have a fucking job."

Alberto pondered his words with a small frown. "Still, that doesn't mean they own me, or that I owe them anything. I really couldn't care less whether they hate me or love me."

"Really?" Mathias sneered. "If the perfect guy on Instagram tried to hit on you, telling you you're gorgeous, you're still going to pretend like you don't care what they think?"

Alberto gave him a thoughtful look. "How would I know he's perfect for me?"

"I don't know. Imagine he's super hot."

"How would I know? I don't even look at their pictures."

"You don't?"

Alberto shook his head and put the phone back in his pocket. Mathias was surprised, but he recovered quickly.

"Okay," he said, "so if the hottest guy ever was in front of you and tried to hit on you, then...?"

"Like, right now?"

Once again, Mathias found the wording weird and stopped talking altogether.

"Obviously..." Alberto ran his hand through his hair. "There's a difference between online strangers and people in real life."

"So, you'd date him?"

Alberto grimaced. "I don't date."

"Liar. I know you dated Zak."

"Everyone knows that. It wasn't a secret."

"Then why did you just say you don't date?"

"Because I don't."

"But—"

"Maybe he broke my heart, and now I'm traumatised."

"Bull... shit." Mathias puffed out a laugh. "It didn't even look like you were together."

Alberto took a moment to speak. "How do you know? Were you watching me?"

"We both know a certain someone who spent a lot of time watching you."

"Eric told you Zak and I weren't really dating?"

"He was hoping for it." Mathias looked away. "He was hoping you kept your dick in your pants, too."

Alberto let out a dry laugh. "What about you?"

"What about me?"

"Do you keep your—"

"I'm not a stupid supermodel with thousands of followers."

"So? There aren't any girls at school trying to get your attention?"

"Don't think so. Don't care."

"Why not?"

Mathias scowled. "Why are you so talkative suddenly? My life's none of your business."

"You ask questions but you don't want to make conversation." Alberto lightly shook his head. "Let me know when you're ready to make sense."

Mathias didn't want to look at him. He turned his head away and jerked back in shock. "Wait!"

His father's car was slowing down in the middle of the street.

Mathias held his breath as the blue Toyota turned into the parking lot, and even Alberto lazily bent his neck to get a better look, a strand of hair falling into his eye. But it was all for nothing. Even from here, they could both see Mathias's father was the only one in the car.

Ever so quiet, Alberto slid along the wall to stand in the shadows. Mathias tossed the butt of his cigarette and begrudgingly followed, making sure to not find himself too close to the jut of Alberto's throat. The strange flowery notes of his soap hit him anyway, and this time, Mathias recognized them: lavender embraced by a subtle hint of mint.

His scent.

His jaw clenched, and Mathias forced his attention back to the Toyota. His old man got out of the car, unaware he was being watched, and stood awkwardly with his keys in his hand, his gaze fixed on the exit door in the back.

106

"What is he doing?" Alberto asked, this simple action triggering a yawn. His elbow brushed against Mathias's chest when he raised his hand to his mouth.

"Hm?" Mathias blinked. "What?"

"What's he doing?"

Mathias's mouth was dry, and he didn't want to answer. He observed as his dad, his eyes shut and his head low, made his decision before he turned on his heel and walked back out into the street.

"Where is he going?" Alberto asked.

Mathias knew but said nothing.

"Should we follow him?"

"What?" Mathias snapped. "You think you can tail someone? You're as tall as a giraffe with none of the stamina. So, what do you think you can achieve?"

To his surprise, his outburst was met with a laugh. "Okay, but now you can't say I didn't try to make an effort."

Whatever. That was better than telling him his dad was going to his favorite bar to get drunk with a bunch of other sad fucks.

"I know where he's going," Mathias muttered. "Don't you worry about it."

"As long as you're sure he's not sneaking out to meet my mother." Alberto teasingly arched his eyebrow. Mathias felt like grabbing him and turned away, ashamed.

"You think I'm full of shit."

Alberto didn't reply, giving him confirmation, which made him even more frustrated. Perhaps he could tell him the truth… or perhaps he should just shut that whole operation down and return upstairs to make dinner. That was something he was good at, at least.

"We could text her," he offered without enthusiasm.

"What?"

"Text your mom. Ask her where she is."

Alberto's brow furrowed. "No."

"Why not?"

"She won't answer."

"Why not? What kind of mom doesn't answer her son's messages?"

Alberto shook his head. "She's probably asleep."

Mathias gave him a bewildered look. He shoved his own phone under Alberto's nose.

"It's not even five p.m. Why would she be asleep?"

"Maybe wait until after five, then."

"Text her, now!"

What sort of bullshit was this? Mathias, suspicious that Alberto really was treating him like an idiot, glared at him until he clicked his tongue and did as he was told. Using his long fingers, he fished around in his pocket and retrieved his iPhone.

"Show me the text," Mathias said, reaching for the device.

Alberto infuriatingly held it over his head, out of his reach, almost asking for a punch in the gut. "Do you speak Italian?"

Mathias suspected he could, in fact, at least a little bit, since he spoke Spanish relatively well, but he didn't want to start debating with that prick.

"Then write to her in English."

"Uh-uh. If I do that, she'll think I've been kidnapped."

Mathias rolled his eyes. "Who would want to kidnap a guy like you?"

Alberto sent the text, and, as Mathias suspected, not twenty seconds later, he got an answer.

"Oh, she's awake," Alberto said, looking surprised, while Mathias grimaced in disbelief. "And she's home." He turned off the screen and put the phone back into his breast pocket. "Happy?"

"Means nothing." But he knew how unconvincing he had started to sound. Alberto noticed it and put a finger on his chin.

"Why, exactly, are you so convinced about this? Is your dad a cheater? Has this happened before?"

"Shut up. My dad is not a cheater."

"Then why—"

"It's your mom," Mathias hissed. "That sort of person, they always get what they want, don't they? And whoever they want. Why are you making that face? Am I wrong?"

108

Alberto blinked, looking unconvinced. "Okay, let's see. Assuming they do… hang out… how did they meet each other?"

Mathias turned his back to him with a scowl. "I don't know. One day, I saw her drop him off, right here. The other time, she was in his car. I freaked out and ran upstairs so they wouldn't see me. I don't know what happened, then. When I looked out my bedroom window, they were both gone. My dad returned two hours later." He paused. Then, he added darkly, "That's how I knew."

"Knew what?"

"That she was a home-wrecker."

"A home-wrecker…" Alberto snorted and lit another cigarette. He looked bored to death. "Assuming you're right, and you really saw them together—"

"I did, you—"

"Then what?" Alberto exhaled a puff of smoke. "People are lonely. My mother is lonely, and your dad looks lonely as hell. So what if they decide to spend time together? It's none of our business."

Was he kidding or was he completely dumb? Of course it was their business! It was their parents!

"It's totally our business!"

"You're worried that they might decide to marry?" Alberto went on. "So what? My mother likes getting married. If she wants to get married, then let her. It would only be the fourth time." He quirked an eyebrow at the sight of Mathias's murderous expression. "Don't worry, my mother's great at many things but not at matrimony. They'll be divorced within a year."

"No!" Mathias shoved him abruptly. "My mom— My mom's great. Your mom, she's just some… woman. My mom— My mom's the best!" His voice started trembling despite his efforts. "I don't want your mom, I want *my* mom, mine! But guess what? I can't. I can't have her because she's fucking dead, okay?"

The words had poured out of him really fast, and now he found himself staring into Alberto's eyes, breathless, waiting for a reaction. He didn't know whether he was surprised or not when he saw nothing. Mathias flexed his hands in his pockets, focusing on his breathing, and he didn't even register that Alberto was speaking to him at first.

"Sorry, what? What did you say?"

Alberto shuffled his feet. "You seem angry."

"Of course I'm fucking angry. My mom's dead, yours is alive, and she's messing around with my dad. I'm pissed off, okay?"

"Okay."

"Okay?" With a clenched jaw, Mathias watched the young man in front of him. "That's all you have to say to me? Okay?"

Alberto lowered his eyes with a shrug.

"You don't care?" The frayed ropes that held Mathias's self-control together were beginning to snap one by one. "You don't care at all?"

All he got for an answer was a blank look. Mathias pushed him away, and Alberto had the gall to snort in his face. "Care? About what, you? You want me to care about you?"

That line made Mathias see red. "My mom's dead."

"I heard you."

"And you don't even show an ounce of compassion. What are you, a fucking robot?"

"No, I asked what happened. You're the one who didn't answer."

Mathias frowned. He didn't recall him asking anything. Alberto was totally bullshitting him. Mathias shoved him again, and Alberto's back hit the wall.

"Ouch."

"You don't care. You just— You don't care."

"Seriously…" Alberto said, undeterred. "What's your problem with me today?"

"Today?" Mathias held his head in his hands. "*Today?*"

"I'm sorry your mum is dead, Mathias. I am."

"No, you're not."

"Okay."

Mathias glanced up at him, his whole body taut with anger. "You wanted to know why you annoy me so much."

"Yes, please."

Mathias's breath caught in his throat. "Everything I heard about you. Everything people say… They were right."

Now Alberto looked like he was watching the rerun of an unexciting old movie. "Let me guess… I'm bland. I'm boring."

"Right."

"I don't have a soul."

"You don't." Mathias met his eyes and held them. Mirth shone faintly in Alberto's gray irises, and Mathias could feel himself starting to ignite.

"What else do they say about me?" Alberto whispered, taunting.

"You're entitled."

"Oh?"

"And selfish."

"How so?"

"What you did to Eric."

"Is he complaining a lot about me to you, then?"

"You took Zak away from him."

Alberto's faint amusement vanished in a blink. "Did he say that?"

"And this summer, you went after his friend, Michael, when you knew he had a boyfriend."

Alberto rose his eyebrows, but he didn't deny it. Mathias's outrage burned through his veins.

"And that arrogance…" Mathias choked out a laugh. "People told me about you." He lowered his voice. "You're a fake."

Finally, a mocking smile curled Alberto's lips. "And you're quite something, you know that?"

"Didn't I tell you? I'm a piece of shit."

"And you're trying so hard to prove it." He let out a dramatic sigh. "Look. I didn't ask for any of this. You came to me, remember? For help?" He emphasised the words to enrage Mathias further.

"Who asked you for help? I was only trying to prove to you that what I saw was real so you'd believe me and then—"

"And then what? Break them off for you?" His derisive laugh was like a poisonous needle pricking Mathias's stomach. "Please."

He flicked his wrist, his cigarette smoke coiling like a snake toward his face.

"I just can't stand people like you…" Mathias murmured, his eyes not leaving Alberto's face.

"People like me? What *people like me?*"

"You take, and you take, and you take…"

Alberto huffed. "You're the one who sought me out."

"I didn't seek you out!"

"But you did. You literally pinned me against a wall. Just like you're doing now." He bent his neck to be at eye-level with Mathias. His voice was low and teasing, "You're so pissed off, and you don't even know why. You don't have a clue, do you?"

And then, he laughed again.

What a sight.

Mathias took in the curled lips and the taunting gaze, his heart thumping in his chest. Something snapped in the confines of his mind. He grabbed that rich fucker by the front of his sweater and pressed him hard against the wall, and, still, Alberto wouldn't stop laughing.

"What the fuck are you trying to say?" Mathias asked, his voice hoarse.

Alberto unexpectedly pinched his lips together.

Oh, *now* he wouldn't speak. Mathias gave him a shake. Alberto tossed his cigarette butt on the ground, cool-gray eyes fixed on him. Mathias noticed his own hands were shaking. He couldn't believe how incensed he became, all from a few simple words from this asshole. He stared at the face before him in anguish.

Could anything, anyone, be more maddening, more infuriating than this smirking poser? He had him between his hands. Literally. The lapels of his fancy jacket crumpled in his fists. His back was crushed against the wall, probably screaming in pain, and yet, Alberto was staring down at him. Mocking him. Daring him.

So, without knowing how it happened, Mathias met his challenge head-on.

He kissed him.

13

SIMPLE PLAN

ALBERTO WOULD SAY SO HIMSELF: there were few things more unpleasant than an unwanted kiss.

The opposite was just as true.

Their lips had met and clashed like the charge of two enemy armies. Alberto had wanted Mathias to lose control, and once it was done, only then did he understand how much *he* had been wanting *this*. He'd watched Mathias this whole time, noting his furious stance, the strong curve of his eyebrow, the flame in his eye —and he kept pushing.

Alberto could almost taste his shame.

He chased after Mathias's lips every time they withdrew, urging him for more. Every time, Mathias relented. He kissed him until he drew blood and then pulled away.

When Mathias's hands released his coat, Alberto noticed they were shaking a little. Mathias, panting, used them to smooth the creased sides of his jacket, then he gave the whole thing a harsh tug. His eyes, brighter than fire-lit ambers, never left him.

"Happy?" Alberto whispered.

Mathias exhaled a long breath. He was clearly so mad at him and himself, and his anger was like a fuel Alberto needed to douse himself in.

Alberto had won a battle. *He* had won a battle. He wanted to laugh, and he wanted to cry. Of course, he did none of that. His head swimming, he waited for Mathias's reaction, and, once again, he didn't disappoint.

Without a look back, the enemy retreated. Mathias had chosen to run away.

Alberto played and replayed the memory in his head on the way home so much that, if not for the alarm on his phone, he would have missed his stop again.

He got off that night. He sneaked into the storage room behind the kitchen where Dina kept the cleaning supplies, and from the top shelf, which only he could reach, he retrieved a lock box.

Dina's supply room was the only place where Stasia wouldn't be caught dead, even to torment him, so it was the best spot to conceal personal items. Only once she had been furious enough to go in there when he was hiding from her, and after the beating she gave him, she squealed in horror to find herself surrounded by mops and brooms. She was so furious, she kicked him in the face while he was down. Alberto remembered that one because he had to make up a story about some robber to explain the mark on his face. His mother lost it, and he was lucky Dimitri didn't care for him or she'd have convinced him to find that imaginary thief and bury him six feet under.

None of that mattered now. Alberto took his treasure back to his room, and from the box, he retrieved three little friends, though the biggest one was nothing small at all. He went to bed feeling satisfied, for once, and one of his three friends received a new name.

The next week, Alberto returned to school, his head filled with thoughts of the past Thursday. Of all the things Mathias had called him, fake was the only one that had stung. To quote Salinger, he didn't like phonies. That was the only thing he could quote, since he never finished the book. That wasn't his fault. He could never finish any book, unless he was forced by his teachers under the threat of repeating another year.

Yes, Alberto was very much aware what people said about him

within the school walls. Soulless, arrogant Alberto. Cruel Alberto. Beautiful Alberto. There were all lies.

They were all true, also.

And so, the second time they kissed, it was naturally Alberto's fault. A whole weekend and a day had passed, and they both knew what the other tasted like. Alberto was thinking of nothing else. It had felt so good when their tongues first entwined, good enough for the hair on his arms and nape to rise in ecstasy.

Alberto had felt something, and now he wanted to feel it again.

But since they'd never agreed to meet the following week, how could he make it happen? He had never really tried to hit on anyone, he definitely couldn't rely on what he'd learned over the years, and, of course, he wanted to avoid a repeat of that Michael thing at all costs.

How did any of this work? Not only was he lacking in skills, most flirting was boring anyway. Dull serenades from wingless birds. Mathias didn't bother with that stuff and just went ahead and kissed him. Now Alberto's blood thrummed with the memory of that kiss.

The answer had been before him since he came across Mathias the morning after, and the bastard pretended not to know him.

Make him furious again.

Never mind flirting with a lost cause like him. Just push his buttons, get thrown against a wall, and reap the benefits.

Simple plan. Great results.

Nothing to fear.

Alberto observed Mathias from a distance for the better part of the day. It was a Tuesday, and he knew they finished at the same time, which meant Eric, his shadow, would be out of the picture the moment Zak was free. Their classrooms had to be close to their own since Eric always waited for Zak at the door, panting with anticipation like the dumb dog he was.

To save precious time, Alberto didn't even bother getting his notebook and pens out of his bag during the history lesson, and he left the classroom first and with a warning from the teacher. He didn't care. He lived his weekends at the museum, and despite having an undeniably poor memory, he knew he would both nail the test and the teacher's mouth shut when the time came. He couldn't be bad at everything now, could he?

Alberto hummed in satisfaction when he spotted Mathias slip into the bathroom near the library. It was the best place for unlawful business, and since it was far away from most classrooms, it was likely to be empty.

While the library was close by, most guys avoided that place like the plague except nerds like Zak — and now his boyfriend. Eric most likely didn't read any books without pictures in them; he only used the library to make out with Zak since they'd found out the librarian never patrolled the tech section.

Finally, most students at Colette didn't nurture thoughts of cornering other guys for some illicit kissing, so Alberto wasn't worried about finding it crowded.

He quietly snuck inside and hoisted himself up between two sinks, but when he heard the sound of flushing, he slid down and adopted a nonchalant pose.

Mathias got out of the middle stall and recoiled when he saw Alberto standing there. He clicked his tongue in annoyance. "Get away from the good sink."

Alberto moved aside. "Not a fan of urinals?"

"… I'm not gonna answer that."

"What is it?" Alberto's eyes narrowed. "You have a small dick or something?"

Mathias took a deep breath and slowly, *very slowly*, shook his head. Alberto's stomach did a little somersault.

"Are we—"

"There's no *we*."

"—spying tonight?"

Mathias kept his eyes on his hands while washing them. "I thought it was a waste of time."

"Maybe I was wrong."

Despite his apparent foul mood, Mathias shot him a quick glance before turning to the good hand-dryer. That thing worked, but it was so loud, no one could speak while it was in use. Alberto drew closer as he waited for him to be done.

"Fuck!" Mathias flinched again when he turned round and saw him so close. "Why are you still here?" He shoved him aside.

"You didn't answer me."

"I can't tonight."

"Why not?"

"I have boxing."

"Today? So early?"

Mathias didn't answer.

"Need to relieve some tension, maybe?"

That earned him a warning look. Alberto decided to go all in. "You know… because you're gay?"

The next second, he was slammed against the wall, and he was trying really hard not to laugh while simultaneously fending off the little black dots filling his vision.

"You got something you want to say?" Mathias pressed him into the wall. "Go ahead, say it."

"Hold on, hold on." Alberto forced his eyes open. "One second."

As expected, Mathias released him with a resentful scowl.

When he told him about his mother, his voice cracking, Alberto felt his fear and resentment, and he wanted to take it from him. He wanted to say, *Give it to me. I can handle your grief better than you.* He got a bit drunk on Mathias's anger, and he knew that he would either get punched or kissed. He was seriously hoping for the latter, but the former would have been fine, too. God knows he deserved it and more.

But now that Mathias's eyes were burning into him, he wasn't sure whether he found him really hot or really frightening. Maybe a bit of both.

"What?" Mathias breathed. "Nothing to say?"

Alberto didn't dare move anything but his lips. "You kissed me. I didn't. You did."

"And?"

Ouch. Alberto shook himself free with a grimace. "I'm a guy, am I not?" When he received no answer, he felt somewhat confused. "So, what's your excuse, then? You're lonely?"

Mathias smirked. "Don't you know? You look just like your mother."

Alberto didn't have to look in the mirror to know his expression had probably turned frighteningly cold. Mathias met his gaze without fear, and Alberto was the one who wanted to avert his eyes. He tried to turn his head away, but Mathias grabbed his chin and forced him to face him.

"Don't believe for a second that I'm like the others."

A subtle twitch occurred down below, and Alberto received another confirmation that he was not and would never be normal.

"The others?" he asked, his voice weak.

"Bowing down to you because you won the genetic lottery. It's not gonna happen."

"What are you complaining about? You're good looking yourself."

Mathias frowned. "We can't even begin to compare."

I beg to differ, Alberto thought, but it would sound desperate to say so. Alberto didn't do desperate... at least, not in public.

"You can't let that go, can you?" he asked with a note of defiance.

"Can't let what go?"

"Yes, I'm a model. So what? It's not all it's cracked up to be, you know."

"*Sure,* enlighten me."

"Honestly?"

"Poor Alberto..." Mathias released his chin. "Tell me how horrible it must be to be the next supermodel, to have legions of fans who'd do anything for a minute alone with you. I can't wait to hear it."

Alberto could still feel the searing imprints of Mathias's fingers on his face. "You spend most of the time waiting for the others to do their job. People dress you like a doll, and some of them don't even spare you a look. You don't matter. The clothes do. That's the job. It's true that outsiders — fans, as you call them — think you've solved world hunger or something, but, in reality, your job is to sit down, shut up, and avoid creeps and pedos. Sorry, but it really is that boring."

Mathias swept his gaze over Alberto's face. "You're so weird…"

"You know what else is weird?"

"What?"

Alberto offered him a teasing half-smile. "Creeps and pedos."

To his surprise, Mathias let out a little laugh, his eyes igniting like bonfires. Alberto's fingertips tingled against the wall. He took a page from Mathias's book and shoved them into the pockets of his jacket.

"You've got a weird sense of humor, too," Mathias added, almost to himself.

"Made you smile…"

All warmth in his eyes vanished instantly, replaced by something darker and even more alluring. Alberto felt a sudden pang of fear, fear that he'd never get to kiss that guy again.

"That's okay," Alberto said, raising his hands. "In truth, I really don't care what you are."

He meant it. Whether Mathias was into guys, girls, dragons, mermaids, blasted unicorns, unless it was dogs, none of that mattered to him. Alberto just wanted to feel Mathias's tongue against his own one more time. Seriously, what was the point of looking like he did if he couldn't make out with anyone he chose?

Mathias fidgeted, seemingly torn. Then, he threw a look over his shoulder and forced Alberto into the nearest stall. He slammed the door shut with one hand, the other gripped tight around Alberto's sweater.

"About your mother…" His expression twisted. "I shouldn't have said that."

Alberto nodded a bit too eagerly, and Mathias yanked him closer. He inadvertently held up his hands in defence, and he immediately felt stupid about it. But Mathias didn't pay attention. He slid his own burning hands around his neck and tugged down. Understanding the invitation, Alberto obediently lowered his head. Mathias pressed their lips together, and as he did so, he plunged his hands into his hair and slowly but mercilessly pulled his head back.

"Is this what you want?" he whispered against his throat.

Alberto nodded, feeling himself relax all over when he brought their mouths together again, but he immediately yelped in pain when Mathias viciously bit into his lower lip.

"And I want to go boxing," Mathias said, pushing him away.

14

GOING UNDER

NO MATTER how much Alberto willed Mathias to catch him and kiss him again, nothing happened until two days later.

Alberto had felt a thrill earlier this morning when Mathias found a way to speak to him in the corridor between classes. Eric had successfully trapped Zak against the wall to steal a kiss. He was being so gentle with him, Alberto couldn't help thinking they were doing it wrong. Suddenly, he heard Mathias's low voice speaking right behind his ear.

"Do you—"

"Yes."

He may have said that a little fast, but Mathias replied, "Parking lot. Tonight." Then, he was gone.

In the tumult, no one had seen anything. Zak had a different hairdo when Eric released him. As Alberto was poking at his own burning cheeks with a puzzled expression, their eyes accidentally met. Zak flashed an awkward smile that Alberto pretended not to see.

After class, he went to the rendezvous point in the parking lot under Mathias's building. He was first. Mathias arrived ten minutes later, his hands shoved in his pockets and his demeanour surly. He barked at him to keep his eyes on the road, that they had to catch their parents in the act or die trying... In short, nothing had changed, and Alberto immediately knew he'd get kissed again.

Therefore, he was a little disappointed when nothing had happened twenty minutes later. Perhaps Mathias needed to be nudged a little. Slowly and silently, Alberto drew closer and closer. Mathias was staring at the road with a closed-up expression. His eyes narrowed when he finally spotted him.

"What are you doing?"

"Nothing."

"Keep an eye on the road."

"Wait..." Alberto gave him a startled look. "You were serious?"

"Of course I'm serious. What? You think this is a date?"

"Tsk. Of course not."

Mathias watched him closely. "I'm dead serious when it comes to my family, buddy."

Buddy. *Buddy.* He sounded like Eric now. Alberto thought he'd better kiss him real good tonight to make him forget that offence.

Mathias didn't notice his cold glare and continued, "I still saw what I saw, and you still need to see what I saw. Okay?"

"Yeah, *o-kay.*"

That tongue of his was better at kissing than talking for sure. Alberto decided that if he pretended to behave then became annoying, he'd probably get the same results as before. Therefore, he didn't mind going along with Mathias's bullshit for a while.

But if Alberto liked to get on Mathias's nerves, the latter was incredibly good at wasting time, and he really seemed determined to go ahead with his lie and catch their parents together. At first, it was fun, but Alberto's thirty-minute bout of energy was about drained, and Mathias still hadn't shown any signs of wanting to kiss him. He had to focus his eyes somewhere or he'd close them alto-gether, and the clouds, drifting fast as the sky gradually darkened, were as good a distraction as any.

"What is it about the clouds that you find so fucking interesting?"

Alberto hadn't paid attention to Mathias for exactly two minutes, and there he was, pissed off again. How did this happen?

It was like there was a fire constantly burning under his arse or something.

"I don't know. Clouds are nice."

"Clouds are nice." Mathias balled his hands into fists in his pockets. "Clouds are nice. Well, I'm glad I came out to hear such bullshit."

Hey, you're the one who said this wasn't a date, Alberto thought resentfully. He wisely kept that thought to himself.

"You could always make conversation instead of glaring at cars. Then, maybe I'd stop staring at the clouds." He pouted, feigning innocence. "Since it bothers you so much."

"I'm not— What bothers me is to be the only one looking out for their cars. You never help me out. What's the point of having you around, seriously?"

Good question. Alberto didn't see the need to answer, casting his eyes down instead. Mathias seemed even more annoyed at his lack of reaction, and he turned away. Only then did Alberto return his gaze overhead. After a short while, he noticed Mathias was looking up, too. An aeroplane was crossing the sky, probably headed for Roissy. Alberto watched it without interest until Mathias spoke, his voice softer than usual.

"When I was a kid, I—" He interrupted himself and shook his head.

"What?"

"It's dumb."

"Okay."

Mathias clicked his tongue. "You…"

"What?"

"Nothing."

"Go on, I want to hear it."

"Then why don't you just say it?"

Alberto frowned. "I did."

"What? When?"

"Are you going to say it or not?"

Mathias stared into his face, and his lips tightened in an invisible line. He was so red, he looked like he was close to a nosebleed. "It's nothing," he grumbled eventually. "I just— I used to imagine

124

planes could go into the future. It was dumb kid stuff." He shook himself as if he were suddenly cold. "Now I… I'd rather go back to the past."

Alberto returned his gaze to the clouds. The plane was long gone. For him, it was the other way around. He wished he could let go of the past and focus on the future.

"I don't get it. What's so good about the past?"

Mathias shrugged. "Good memories."

"You can always make good memories in the future, but you can't change the past."

"So? You don't know if horrible things wait for you in the future."

"But if you can't go forward, then…"

"You stand st—"

"… you go under."

Mathias furrowed his brow. "What do you know about going under?"

Alberto's lip curled. He knew all about going under. In fact, he hadn't been above the surface in years now, but he doubted Mathias would want to hear such rubbish. Not that he had any intention of oversharing anyway. He kept his eyes on the side of Mathias's face, who was still looking up as if he was hoping the long-gone aeroplane would make an unexpected comeback.

"What happened to your mum?" Alberto asked in a muted tone.

Mathias glanced at him, at his own shoes, then back at him. "She… hum… Cancer."

"Oh." Alberto wasn't sure what to say after that. He scratched his eyebrow with his thumb. "When did it happen?"

"Three years ago."

"2007… Shit year, it was."

"Yes," Mathias agreed absently. "Yes, it was."

Alberto recalled what people usually said on these occasions. "I'm sorry. About your mum, I mean."

Mathias had trouble meeting his eyes. "There's… like— It's not like there's anything anyone can do about it."

Silence settled between them. Alberto really had no clue what the next step was after that. He hoped Mathias knew better, but the perplexed frown on his face told a different story.

"So, you said your mom is married?" Mathias asked, the frown deepening.

"Yeah."

"But not to your dad."

"No."

"Where's your dad, then?"

"Not with my mother." Alberto almost smiled.

Mathias's gaze hardened, making Alberto feel a little exposed. They returned to their silent stance, Mathias springing up every time a blue car drove down the street.

"It's getting late," he mumbled.

"Yes, it is."

Alberto actually disagreed. After all, the sky wasn't dark yet, but he wasn't so tempted to annoy Mathias anymore.

What would he do if Mamma got cancer? He'd rather not know. Or perhaps he knew already, and it was too upsetting to contemplate. Hopefully, his mother would never get sick. Hopefully, she'd always be around.

Alberto briefly fell into a well of worry, forgetting all about watching the cars. When he came to, Mathias stood before him with a strange expression, staring into his face as though he was some kind of maths equation. Alberto didn't move, but in his chest, his heart gave a thump.

Mathias spoke in a strained, controlled voice. "I've seen dead bodies that looked more alive than you."

"You've seen dead bodies?"

Mathias gave a long sigh.

Before they knew it, they were kissing again.

With his back against the wall and rough hands gripping his hair, Alberto, out of breath, let Mathias do as he pleased until the latter tugged his hair hard enough to tear it from his scalp. Alberto's hands fumbled and found the sides of Mathias's jacket, but this simple touch only made him more aggressive. Pain flared across his scalp; he let out an inadvertent moan.

The sound reached Mathias's consciousness. Without breaking

their frantic kiss, his hands finally left Alberto's hair and groped clumsily down his chest and abdomen until they found the hem of his sweater and snuck crudely inside. His cool palms against Alberto's skin forced a gasp out of him. Mathias's grip tightened, turning painful even, like he wanted to dig his nails into his flesh and pluck out his ribs.

Alberto could feel Mathias's fear blending with his rage. It felt raw, hot, powerful. A sense of exhilaration engulfed him, starting from the roots of his hair to his perplexed prick below. Then, it suddenly made sense.

For the first time in his life, he was being touched by someone and he found himself wanting more. And for the first time in his life, he made the first move. Without hesitation, he stuck his hand to Mathias's crotch.

Upon hearing his huff of surprise, and with the way he jerked his head back, Alberto half expected to feel Mathias's fist on his jaw, but it didn't come. He was only faced with two bright eyes, lit up by desire and resentment. And he heard two words, spoken in a hushed and yet hoarse voice.

"Not here."

Alberto was way too dizzy by then to remember how it happened exactly, but soon enough, they were inside the building, flying up the stairs. Mathias was pulling him by the lapel of his coat, and Alberto was tripping on every other step, too dazed to protest, but he was mildly amused by Mathias's unwillingness to touch his hand itself.

They reached a landing at last, and Mathias flung the door open, his face set, and Alberto tried to catch his breath while the other was fidgeting with the keys to his flat. A loud slam rang in his ears, and he was dragged along a seemingly interminable corridor. Finally, a door opened on the left, and he was pushed unceremoniously against another wall, his neck pulled down.

Before he could utter a word, Mathias was kissing him again. Alberto wanted to laugh, but he knew if he dared, Mathias would stop at once and kick him out without hesitation. Now that he was finally having fun, he really didn't want that. With his head buzzing and a familiar heat simmering in the pit of his stomach, he focused on Mathias's breathing, the feeling of his tongue against his.

Before long, his fingers curled, and the rest turned kind of blurry. He recalled rough hands feeling him from his waist all the way down to his arse, and this is how his own palm once again ended up on Mathias's dick.

They looked at each other. Alberto's cold gaze, an eyebrow vaguely quirked, was asking, "Yes? No? What's it going to be?" Mathias's wide stare was full of, "Fuck, are we doing this? Never mind him, *am I* doing this?"

Alberto rubbed him through his jeans to make his intentions clear. Mathias closed his eyes and brought their lips back together, thus giving Alberto permission to make short work of his belt and slide his hand into his pants.

He made a funny sound upon their skin making contact, but it didn't make Alberto want to laugh. It made him want him to do it again, and again, and again. While that didn't happen, it was nice for a while, until Alberto caught Mathias's hand and put it on his own dick. That's when Mathias jerked away, a look of panic in his eyes.

"No," he said, wrenching his head back as though Alberto's cock bit him.

O-kay, I get it, Alberto thought. *I get it, I get it.*

He repeated the words to himself, his hand moving methodically, earning himself a kiss that split skin. Suddenly, he tasted copper. He only got more excited after that, his own jeans stretching taut, and he didn't even mind that the guy he was getting off slapped his hand over his eyes, forcing him to work in the dark, or that he ground Alberto's cheek against the wall as he came. He didn't even mind the fact that Mathias couldn't look at him afterwards, going so far as leaving the room altogether and slamming the door behind him.

A faint smile on his lips, Alberto stood against the wall, his hair a mess, his clothes dishevelled, and his hand sticky. He looked down at his own dick, pressed uncomfortably against his thigh. He thought about invoking Stasia's name until it did the trick, but he opted to relieve himself instead. It didn't take long, not with the memory of Mathias's muffled groans and rough fingers still so fresh in his mind.

When he was done, Mathias was still hiding God knows where. Alberto left his spot against the wall to look around the room. It was nothing new. Peacock-blue and grey walls, a queen-size bed with sheets a rich crimson shade — not a very high thread count — cheap carpeted floors, also grey, a cluttered desk... The door to the large fitted wardrobe was slightly open, revealing the mess inside.

Even though the blinds to the windows were open, the room was still sort of dark. Alberto liked it. He favoured the darkness. *Al buio, tutti i gatti sono grigi.*[1] The walls were bare, save a poster for a Garbage concert from over a decade ago. Bright orange against the deep blue of the wall, it almost looked like a target.

Garbage.

On tour.

Garbage.

Alberto reluctantly tore his gaze away and found a box of tissues by the bed, next to the picture of a younger Mathias in the arms of a laughing woman. He carefully wiped himself and his fingers. The lust that animated him a minute ago had already vanished, replaced by the usual light-headedness.

He strolled around the room and tried to learn something about Mathias by flicking through his book and music collection. He possessed no notable books, save a large cooking manual oddly left open in the middle of the desk, but he really was a Garbage fan. In fact, his large collection of music was all from the nineties and early 2000s. Alberto spotted a series of Bloodhound Gang albums on the top shelf and couldn't help chortling.

When Mathias returned, he was wearing different clothes, and he hovered by the door like an idiot. "Sorry," he said, not meeting Alberto's eyes.

Alberto shrugged, uninterested now that he got what he wanted. *I get it, I get it, you're not gay. Who cares....?*

"It's just that…" Mathias hesitated.

---

1. "At night, all cats are grey." (Italian)

We get it already!

"I'm gonna go," Alberto said.

"Oh?"

"Yeah."

The least he could do was spare them both this insanely boring conversation. Alberto took a cigarette from his pocket and put it between his lips only for Mathias to charge at him.

"Hey! You can't smoke in here!"

Alberto extended his arm in defence with a click of his tongue. "Can't smoke in here, can't get off, can't even look at you… what exactly can I do in here?"

The snap of a lock down the corridor interrupted them, and Mathias's face turned green from shock.

"Fuck!" He mouthed.

Oh yes, his dad. They had forgotten all about him.

"You need to leave," Mathias said, fingers curling around Alberto's shoulders, his mouth twisted in anguish.

"Do you have a back door or should I throw myself out of the window?" Alberto joked. He even tossed a look over his shoulder toward said window. "Are we on the top floor? Sounds doable."

"Shut your face!" Mathias gripped him and pushed him onto the bed.

Alberto snorted. As usual, the more Mathias resented him, the more he wanted to fuck with him. Alberto was the same with everyone. The only difference was that rattling Mathias also made him want to… *fuck* with him.

"Can I please go wash my hands before you kill me?"

Mathias harrumphed. "Forget it."

"Now that is so unkind, especially after what I did for you."

Mathias's fingers dug into his shoulders, terror clear in his eyes.

Alberto sighed. "There's really no need to panic, Mathias."

"Who's panicking?"

Huh… the nerve on this one. Alberto blinked slowly. "Let me wash my hands. When I come out, I'll thank you for your help with my homework, and I'll go home."

"Homework?"

"Yes."

Mathias relaxed, as though he wished he'd thought about something like that before. He released Alberto.

"Okay, you can go. It's right across the corridor."

"Thank you," Alberto said in a fake voice, wondering if that bastard would have had the guile to kick him out with his hands covered in his spunk. Alberto had values. Not many, but still.

Just as planned, it went without problems. Alberto washed his hands, met Mr Rodin in the hallway, and they exchanged pleasantries. Alberto stared at his tired face, not believing for a second that his mother would be messing around with that man.

"What's your name?" the Maths teacher asked, eyeing him curiously.

"Alfred," Mathias blurted out of nowhere.

Alberto speared him with a glare behind his father's back.

"Oh, right. And what subject did you help him with?"

Alberto's lip twitched. "Spanish," he said before Mathias could answer.

He knew Mathias had taken an elective Spanish class, and even if Alberto hadn't, Mathias's father wasn't aware of that. Alberto watched Mathias's throat bob as he swallowed nervously and almost smiled.

"It was nice to meet you," Alberto told Mr Rodin, extending a hand politely as he was taught. His handshake was a little stiff, however, and he made sure to offer the same hand he just used on Mathias, just in case, just in case it was true, and this guy had laid his hands on his beloved mother.

Mathias held the door open for him and called out his name when he was already across the hall.

"There's an elevator," he said, pointing at it.

Alberto stared at it, dumbfounded, then back at Mathias. His mouth fell open in outrage. "Then why the hell did you make me climb up those stairs?"

Mathias shrugged. "Was busy. Couldn't wait."

And ignoring the flutter in his chest, Alberto thought, *Game on.*

15

FROM HELL

THE FIRST TIME THEY KISSED, Mathias felt like he'd rediscovered flavor after years of tasting ashes. What did Alberto taste like? Danger, yes, but also life, like newfound expanses of lush green fields stretched before him after a lifetime of wandering the desert. That's what Alberto felt like.

His manners, his arrogance, even his mind-boggling beauty, Mathias despised all of it. He couldn't help hating the guy. He couldn't help wanting to devour him, too.

Mathias knew he shouldn't have kissed him, that this moment of weakness had started a chain of events he had no confidence he could keep under control. He was worried. He wanted nothing from him. He also wanted more. He couldn't know for sure.

It was all because of his lips. Those fucking lips. Mathias suspected them to be carrying a curse. It felt like they parted only to push the wrong or, let's say, *right* buttons. One misplaced word, one over-pronounced "*p*," one little half smirk, and Mathias couldn't be certain he wouldn't lose control and damage him, *really* damage him. He couldn't understand that feeling.

He really didn't want him.

He *couldn't* want him.

And yet—

"Best buddy is on the moon again."

Mathias started and dropped his gloves at his feet.

"*Dans la lune*[1]," Eric added, poking Mathias's forehead with a smile.

Mathias looked around the football pitch and realized he hadn't paid attention to what was going on. It was clear because Kayvin, his eyes as dark as the swirling clouds overhead, was glaring at him as if they'd just lost the finale of the Champions' League because of his inattention.

"I'm sorry," he told his friend.

But, no, he wasn't on the moon, and he wasn't on earth either, unless they started digging and went deeper and deeper until they reached hell.

Mathias was in *Alberto Hell*.

Eric led him to the side, unconcerned by Kayvin's increasingly purple tinge, and took his wrist in his hand. "What's up with you? Does it still hurt?"

Mathias followed his gaze absently. He was a little behind during his last save—*Alberto Hell*—and landed badly. And it did hurt, actually. He was about to use this excuse to bullshit his friend, but Kayvin smacked into him, breaking them apart.

"Hey! Would it kill you to listen for once?"

Eric stared at him blankly. "What?"

"I'm concluding the team meeting, and here you are doing gay shit with your pal."

"I wasn't… I was asking him—"

"Leave it," Mathias said. "Just leave it."

Kayvin swelled with anger and self-importance. "No, go ahead. I'm curious what he has to say that's more important than my speech."

"Nothing…" Eric muttered.

"Then fucking listen to what I'm saying."

Eric rolled his eyes in a way that implied he knew more about football than Kayvin, which he definitely did, and Kayvin looked like he wanted to charge at him, so Mathias stepped in front of him.

---

1. "On the moon". (French)

"What?" Kayvin gave him a look of disgust. "Are you fucking him, too?"

Mathias's stomach lurched. His fingers came to grip the insides of his pockets. *Think of mom*, he thought. *Think of mom. Or don't, actually. Don't think of mom.* Knowing her, she would have already flattened Kayvin to the ground and stepped on his balls.

"Come on…" Unlike Mathias and his mom, Eric displayed an impressive well of patience. "You know Mathias is just my friend."

Kayvin chortled. "Yeah, sure, I haven't heard that one before."

At the very least, he walked away. Eric stared after him until he was out of earshot then picked up his bottle with a downcast expression.

"Don't mind him."

He offered some water to Mathias who refused with a wave of his hand. "What's wrong with this guy, seriously?"

"He doesn't like me."

"Obviously. But why? Is it really because you're… you know…"

"With Zak?" Eric finished his sentence with a half-smile. "Yeah, there's some of that. Some other stuff, too. Old grudges. I don't let it get to me." Seeing Mathias's unconvinced expression, he set off with a grin and added, "He's just jealous because my boyfriend's got the deadliest ass around here, and he can't even get a girlfriend because of his temper."

Mathias didn't know how to answer that, so he just followed his friend in silence.

"A girl!" Eric was roaring, all flushed. "How hard is it to get a girl? I can do it with my eyes closed." He stopped in the middle of the field. "And so could you, with those sexy eyes—"

"Stop it."

"And you're really fit, too."

Mathias's eyes widened. "Don't tell me you've been watching me?"

Eric laughed. "Nah, of course not, but you always wear these tight long-sleeve jerseys during practice, and anyone can see you've got a nice body. I bet you're hard all over… Look at these babies—"

"Don't touch them."

"Buddy, you're not my type."

"Still, let go of them."

"Fine." Eric pouted but released Mathias's arms. "Anyway, why do you think the girls are waiting after every practice nowadays? It's not for me. I mean, not anymore. And it's not for Kayvin; he's scary now. They're all coming for you."

"What about Xavier?" Mathias had to admit the guy was handsome, well-built, and taller than himself.

Eric laughed. "Xavier has already dated them all except Elodie."

So, there was such a thing as preferring idiots, Mathias noted ruthlessly, before his thoughts drifted toward Alberto. He was in no position to judge anyone. The other day, he got a handjob from a demon. Now he wanted another.

Outside the pitch, a group of girls had once again gathered to praise them for kicking a ball around in the cold. Mathias had no interest in that, so he headed toward the gymnasium and left Eric behind to receive the compliments.

Elodie called his name, forcing him to pause. She was handing him a bottle of water. Behind her, her friends, Joy and Melissa, exchanged a knowing smile. Mathias accepted the water, a bit surprised, and he felt Kayvin's seething eyes on the back of his neck. Elodie purposefully avoided looking at him, which, for some reason, inspired him to knock into Mathias on his way inside.

It seemed that Mathias was as good as Alberto at making friends, and, just like him, he couldn't care less. He got inside, showered, and got changed, trying his best not to worry too much about what he should do next, but despite his efforts, two questions kept spinning around in his head. One: what the hell happened the other day? And two: will it happen again?

Only with great effort did Mathias manage to force his attention back to the real world. Sitting next to him on a bench and fumbling with his shoes, Eric was going on and on about a tennis ball he'd lost during the summer. He was convinced Xavier took it.

"No, I didn't!"

"I saw you play with it."

"Everyone was playing with it." Xavier was admiring his reflection in the mirror while talking to Eric. "Mother always says people shouldn't leave their stuff hanging around for everybody to steal."

Eric groaned and forcefully shoved his foot into his sneaker. "Who would steal a tennis ball? It makes no sense!"

"It's just a tennis ball," Charles-Henry said mildly. "Can't you get another?"

"I don't want another!" Eric whined. "I'd drawn little eyes on it so it would feel cute all the time, and it's the first thing of mine Zak ever touched…" Ignoring Mathias's grimace, he glanced over his shoulder hopefully. "Kayvin, did you take my ball?"

The other snickered. "I don't need to take your balls. You've dropped them on your own."

Mathias noted how daring Kayvin was becoming, taking confidence in the fact that Eric wouldn't react. To prove his point, his friend gave a nervous laugh and dropped the subject, but Kayvin went after him, a malicious glint in his eyes.

"Have you looked in your boy toy's mouth?"

Eric's face darkened. "Okay, got it, that's enough." He stood up. So did Mathias. "Zak isn't my boy toy. He's my boyfriend, and I love him."

Silence as thick as the steam coming in from the showers filled the room. Kayvin and Eric faced each other, sizing each other up.

"You used to love me, too," Eric said at last.

Kayvin's eyes bulged. "What?"

"Not the same love, but—"

"Fuck off, Eric. Don't make me sound like a—" He was approaching Eric fast, only to be stopped by Mathias again. "You again? So, what's with you, huh? You just showed up out of nowhere, and now you're best friends?"

Eric smiled. "That's right!"

Kayvin rounded on Mathias, who merely blinked, and scoffed. "Maybe you like having a so-called friend who pretends to be normal and steals all the girls, only to end up being another co—"

"I don't know what gave you the impression I was listening," Mathias cut in, "but just to be clear, I don't give a fuck."

Kayvin was just as tall as him, with deep-set brown eyes full of self-righteous anger that no one but a good shrink would have any chance at taking apart. Mathias wasn't afraid of him, and Kayvin could feel it. It took some time, but he stepped away with a crooked grin.

"All right. Let's get out of here."

After an impatient look at Xavier, who was struggling to put his jeans on, he took Steph and a couple of his other loyal friends and left the changing rooms.

"Three strikes in one day," Xavier said, looking worried. "Kayvin's gonna be mad at you now."

Mathias punched his dirty jersey into his bag. "If he's got a problem with me, he can come to see me anytime."

"He didn't use to be like this," Eric said with some sadness.

"Trust me," Mathias said, putting on his jacket. "That guy only understands dominance. He's not interested in friendship."

Xavier turned to stare at the door from which Kayvin had left with a puzzled expression.

"You're probably right," Eric said, "but don't get into a fight with him, please. You know I can't have your back on this one."

Mathias had other things on his mind than that douchebag anyway. He spent his lunch break trying not to throw looks around, searching for a certain face. After some time, he gave up, left Eric in the welcoming arms of Zak, and went for a walk. But chance, God, or the Devil himself put him on this path because he hadn't walked two paces when he found Alberto in a deserted corridor, standing in front of the infirmary with his hand on the doorknob. His movements paused when he saw Mathias.

"Feeling sick?"

Mathias really did wander this way to ask for painkillers for his wrist, but this random encounter had cut the wind out of him. He scanned around for passersby and found none, and his skin started buzzing.

"She's not here," Alberto said.

"What, you know her schedule?"

Alberto pushed the door open with the heel of his foot. Inside, the nurse's office was plunged in darkness. Mathias could see she wasn't here, but he had forgotten all about her already. He stepped inside, waited a few seconds, and welcomed the sound of the door as it creaked closed.

Now they were alone in the room, the only light source coming from the emergency exit sign above the door. Alberto stood under it, tall, quiet, and dangerous.

"Do you know when she'll be back?" Mathias wished his voice sounded steadier.

Alberto's lips curled. "Not today."

Mathias had already moved in front of him. He admired in silence the way the shard of cold light fell upon his face, accentuating the high cheekbones, the straight nose, and the cupid bow of his lip.

"That thing, the other day..." Alberto said quietly.

Mathias was glad he brought it up first. Now he could come up with all kinds of excuses.

It was a mistake.

It will never happen again.

Now, come closer and bend your neck a little so I can catch your lips.

"That thing the other day, what?"

Alberto was very still against the door, but he was not tense. Alberto was never tense. He was indifferent. He lowered his head just an inch and whispered, "Did you like it?"

Mathias swallowed. He'd heard the mythological tales about vile temptresses to stay away from, but it was the first time he stood before somebody and felt he was facing a supernatural creature.

Will it happen again?

He already knew his answer to the question.

"You know I liked it," he told the emergency sign above.

The truth was, he'd never been so turned on in his entire life. If he hadn't been so mortified, he'd have been stunned by how much he came that day. So, yeah, he guessed he had liked it, probably just as much as he hated the memory of it; how he reacted, the way he ran out of the room like a flustered boy. And Mathias hated that Alberto acted like he couldn't care less, even though all of it was entirely *his* fault.

"And you..." Mathias coughed lightly. "Did you like it?"

The bastard shrugged.

Mathias bit the inside of his cheek. "Right. Get away from the door."

He was obeyed immediately; Mathias hesitated, his hand hovering above the handle. Alberto spoke before he could seize it.

"Why did you tell him my name was Alfred?"

I panicked. "I don't know."

"But Alfred? Really?"

Mathias's hand left the handle and came to rest on the wall near Alberto. He vaguely registered the pain from his earlier fall. In fact, everything else that happened today seemed completely irrelevant to him right now.

"I should call you Alfredo from now on."

Alberto's brow knitted in distaste. "Not if you want me to answer, you won't." When Mathias abruptly pressed him against the door, he swallowed, his eyes glinting. "What?"

"Nothing."

Mathias brought their lips together. Alberto was stiff at first, his hands flat against the door. Then, he relaxed and opened himself up. Mathias knew it was a bad idea to give in the moment their tongues intertwined.

Alberto's lips *were* poisonous. There was no way anyone could kiss him, really kiss him, and not want to take things further from there. Even when he stood at a distance, when those infamous lips parted, his gaze fixed on a distant cloud, the windows of the cafeteria, or the wrought iron school gate… Even then, something about him screamed *I don't care, and there's nothing you can do about it*, and it was the hottest thing in the world.

At times, Mathias felt so bewitched that he really was convinced Alberto was, in fact, a demon. Sent from Hell to tempt him. His mom believed in God, and he never used to care about these things until she died, and, suddenly, he had really, *really* wanted to believe in Heaven. But if there was a Heaven, there was a Hell, and from the depths of Hell came Alberto Gazza and his fucking lips. Tempting him, corrupting him, guiding him to the place he was always predestined to call home: the deepest darkness, the only source of light being the fire Alberto lit in his groin.

Eventually, they parted. A disheveled Alberto looked down at him, igniting all sorts of forbidden feelings within Mathias. "I want to touch you," he said, his voice raspy.

You really shouldn't.

"You should," Mathias said.

Alberto's lip disappeared between his teeth, and Mathias imagined biting on it until he begged for mercy. He felt him slide his hands into the pockets of his hoodie and pull him closer. A weird gesture.

"You don't want to touch me?" he purred right into Mathias's ear.

Red flags flooded Mathias's vision. "No."

After a brief pause, Alberto released him. Embarrassed, Mathias stepped away.

One minute they were making out in the dark, and the next, light was pouring in from the corridor, and Alberto was slinking outside, leaving Mathias squinting in discomfort.

It was better this way, he kept repeating to himself on his way back to class. It was better this way. He shoved his hands in his pockets, his fingertips grazing against something left in there. It was Alberto's number, neatly written on a piece of paper. Mathias turned the thing in his hands several times, seriously thinking of tossing it, but who was he kidding anyway? The paper did end up in the trash, but not before he'd stored the number safely in his phone.

At dinner that night, his dad had waited until Mathias's sister had left the dining table, pushed his glasses up his nose, and said, while trying to meet his eyes, "Your friend, Alfred…"

Mathias kept his eyes on his plate. "He's not my friend."

"Your Spanish homework partner, then."

Now he looked up. "What about him?"

It's not like he hadn't expected his dad *not* to say something. He was sober that day; he must have noticed Alberto was just as gorgeous as a certain woman. So, yes, Mathias was expecting his father to poke around, ask questions, and maybe even ask, "*Isn't his name Alberto?*"

"Will he come back?" he asked instead.

There, there it was, the reason why his tornado of a mother

married his soft-spoken, reserved father. Because of his unpredictable streak.

"Why are you asking me this?" Mathias asked, sweating.

"Why are you defensive?"

"I'm not!"

"I'm just asking if he'll come around again, that's all." His dad picked up his glass of wine with a sigh. "So… will he?"

Mathias almost regretted the time when his father wasn't speaking anymore.

"Yes," he said, hanging his head in shame.

"Good," his dad said. "In life, you'll need all the friends you can get."

After dinner, Mathias went straight to the gym to throw his fists at a punching bag. He worked out until rivers of sweat ran down his back and he felt like passing out. He worked himself so hard, his knees were shaking when he climbed the stairs back to his apartment, ready to drop.

Still, he couldn't sleep.

His cheeks were burning when he slid his hand into his boxer briefs. However much he resented him, it was still Alberto's face he conjured in his mind when he brought himself over the edge.

The next morning, Mathias dragged his exhausted body to Colette, and at the gate, he found the figure of the Devil, taller than everyone else by at least a head, and they made eye contact.

Alberto's full lips parted. He was cold and self-assured, and though he would never speak up, his narrowed eyes seemed to say, *"I know what we did to each other,"* and his expression dared him to do it again.

And Mathias thought, *Chances of surviving the school year? Down to 50%.*

16

SPANISH HOMEWORK

DESPITE MATHIAS'S insistence in inviting him over for Spanish homework, Alberto would say he didn't come here to learn a new language. And yet, that's exactly what he was doing.

He was learning how to seduce Mathias, which words would earn him a frown, which ones a glare, which ones a kiss. He was learning what he liked, what he hated, what oddities were making him who he was.

To his delight, Mathias remained somewhat of a mystery. That was partly because he was made of nothing but contradictions. For example, the first time Alberto returned to his flat, invited through a curt text message the day after their meeting at the infirmary, he learned Mathias could only do homework while playing music and that he hated it when Alberto got too near his hi-fi.

Mathias hated the sound of *Las Ketchup* even more — as anyone should — but for some reason, it was featured on this homemade playlist he listened to. *All. The. Time.* Alberto tensed every time a track ended, hoping the next one to play would be the cursed Spanish song. If it was, then he would make sure to stand in front of the hi-fi so that Mathias would have to manhandle him to slam his hand on the "next" button. There used to be a remote, but Alberto slipped it under Mathias's mattress when he wasn't looking. Then, he denied ever seeing it. Mathias would scowl and grumble "sorry", and Alberto would make a wounded face that would sometimes make the other flush to his ears.

Overall, their *Spanish homework sessions* consisted of Alberto doing real school assignments while Mathias would peer outside — with binoculars! — to prove to him their parents really knew each other. Alberto had long stopped caring about this nonsense and was spending most of his time swinging on the desk chair, imagining what Mathias looked like under his clothes. After a while, the latter would inevitably lose patience, stick the binoculars into Alberto's hands, and do his own homework.

Alberto started believing Mathias felt safer looking into the binoculars than at him, and he found it cute, but Mathias didn't find Alberto cute at all.

Whatever Alberto did or said, it was always wrong.

Whatever Alberto did or said, it always ended the same.

Mathias would say "You're doing it wrong!", get pissed off, then kiss him.

Mathias would say "Move!", push him aside, then kiss him.

Mathias would shout "Get out!", change his mind, then kiss him.

For days, they met to do their *Spanish homework*. Alberto still had no idea whether or not their parents knew each other, but he knew how coarse Mathias's carpet felt because he'd been pushed down on it twice already.

He had never seen Mathias's dick per se, but he held it enough times to know it wasn't small nor was it too large. It felt just right in his hand.

He knew some of Garbage's songs by heart; Mathias favoured them beyond everything else. But Bloodhound Gang songs could bring rare smiles to his face, helping Alberto realise there might be a raunchy fourteen-year-old kid living somewhere inside this angry boy.

And now, he knew Mathias wanted to be a chef. Alberto once asked him about the book on his desk, and he learned Mathias planned to enter an esteemed culinary school after graduating.

"Are you good with your hands?" Alberto had asked.

"Very," Mathias had replied, at first oblivious to his jest. Then, it hit him, and he'd shot him a black look.

It didn't matter. They ended up kissing anyway. Then, Mathias had asked him, "Do you like food?"

"Meh," Alberto had replied.

"As I thought… Dead inside." And then he'd recaptured his lips.

Time went by, and Mathias still knew nothing of him. The only other thing he ever asked him was if he was good at school. "No, not really," Alberto had said.

"What a surprise," Mathias had replied.

"What a dick."

Alberto may have let that one break free. Oops.

Mathias got all mad, but then he proceeded to lay him on the bed and kiss him until his lips went numb, so it was okay.

Every day, they met. Every time, they kissed. Twice, Alberto got Mathias off. True to himself, Mathias refused to look at him while it happened, and he never offered to return the favour. For four perfect days, it lasted.

Then, Alberto ruined it all.

It was Saturday. Mathias insisted on having Alberto over when the latter told him his mother took the car to get a haircut. He was staring into the binoculars at the pavement below. He looked nervous. Feverish. In any case, he was sexy as hell, with his sinewy wrists poking through his rolled-up sleeves and his eyes so bright, they looked like ambers…

Alberto was watching him once again, tracing the outline of his body with a burning gaze, imagining how Mathias's hands would feel on him, how his eyes would look as he came. Though he was pretending to write something in his notebook, in truth, he only drew a few doodles, and, after a second look, they all looked like dicks.

It had been two hours of this crap, and there was no kiss in sight. Alberto had met people dedicated to their lies, but this one was beyond belief. He gave a loud sigh when yet another Garbage song started playing through the hi-fi speakers.

"I should have known you were gay the moment I found out you liked Garbage."

Mathias didn't bother turning around. "Think wisely about what you're about to say next."

His eyes narrowing, Alberto tapped the tip of his pen against the sketch of a particularly large dick he'd just drawn.

Mathias, Mathias, Mathias... Whenever Alberto suggested to him that he liked dick because... well... his actions *somehow* implied that he did, Mathias would shut down, any other expression replaced by a scowl. He would tell Alberto to shut up, and no kiss would follow. But after so much time spent fooling around, Alberto felt a little daring and a little too confident. He thought to himself, if only he could push him over the edge, make Mathias face it, maybe he'd get rewarded with more than kisses.

"*Boy... Girl... Boy... Girl...*" He leaned toward Mathias. "Have you made your choice?"

"Shut up." Mathias didn't look up from the binoculars, but he didn't sound furious. He sounded way too focused on the stupid pavement below. Alberto sucked on his own lip and stretched out his foot to rub against Mathias's shin.

"Don't!" Mathias snapped. "I'm not in the mood."

Frustrated, Alberto tossed his pencil at him. "What a gay thing to say."

Mathias caught it with one hand, his eyes glowing with anger, and he threw the pencil back with twice as much force. Alberto, not bothering to defend himself, let it strike right into his forehead. Immediately, Mathias flung his binoculars aside and knelt by his side.

"Are you okay?"

Alberto felt victory close at hand. He tried to pull Mathias by the neck for a kiss, but he dodged.

"Stop."

Alberto stared at him, confused. "If you really aren't in the mood, then what the hell are we doing here?"

Mathias held his gaze but didn't answer.

"All right. This is boring. I'm leaving."

Leaving his homework and his dick doodles on the desk,

Alberto got up and picked up his bag. His hand was on the door-knob when Mathias called out, "Don't."

He slowly turned around. "What?"

"You— You can't go. My sister will see you."

Ah. Mathias's infamous sister. The whole week, Mathias had been shaking every time it was time for Alberto to leave. He would first exit the bedroom, make sure she either wasn't home or she was safe in her room, then he would basically drag Alberto outside like the dirty mistress he was. Alberto was tempted to go knock on her door right now to see if she even existed at all, considering Mathias's history of making stuff up. But what he had really wanted to hear was "Don't go", and this was close enough.

He sat back at the desk and put his chin in his hand, not caring that his elbow was crumpling his book report for Paquin.

"You don't want your sister to meet me?"

Mathias let out a derisive laugh. "That's right."

"Why not?"

"Take a wild guess."

Alberto tried, but he couldn't understand why. The only thing he could think of was that Mathias was worried his sister would like him too much.

Alberto didn't have to pretend like the hypocrites out there. He knew how good looking he was; people wouldn't shut up about it. It's not like pretending otherwise would help his case. Girls, in particular, adored him. The more he ignored them, the more they liked him, too. But he didn't want girls. He wanted the savage little werewolf who was half-sitting on the chest of drawers by the window, fingers curled around his binoculars, scowling down at the pavement.

"Don't worry, Mathias," he said, taunting. "I don't mind being your little secret."

His remark was met with a glare. "You're not. You're nothing."

He sure knew his way around flirting. Alberto couldn't even imagine him dating a girl with his gruff manners and the way he couldn't help saying *shut up* all the time. In fact, he couldn't imagine Mathias with a girl at all.

But the way Mathias's dick would feel in his mouth? *That* he could imagine, and he was doing it daily. He was doing it presently while trying not to hiss at the discomfort building up inside his jeans.

"Anyway," Alberto said, "I won't tell if you won't."

"You won't?" Mathias asked.

"You think I want everybody to know about this?"

Mathias was silent for a while before he grunted, rubbing his nose. "Why not? What's wrong about me?"

Alberto knew an opening when he saw one. For years, all sorts of people had tried all sorts of things to coax and woo him. He only had to replicate.

"Nothing's wrong about you," he said, lowering his voice. "Just the way you treat me."

"The way I treat you?"

"The way you push me around." Alberto looked up, deliberately. "The fact that I want you to."

Mathias rose again, his eyes lit up. But it wasn't with anger anymore. Alberto had won. They would do no more homework today.

"You're so weird," Mathias said when he had him in his grasp.

Alberto didn't bother replying. He let Mathias move him across the room toward the bed, huffing and puffing, his brow wrinkled. Alberto wondered what he was going to do this time. Put a bag over his face or something like that? But to his infinite surprise, and though the hand that touched him shook, Mathias grabbed hold of his crotch.

Alberto blinked. "Hello."

Mathias's voice lowered to a whisper, "How come you're like this already?"

"Like what?"

"… Like this." He gave a squeeze, and Alberto chuckled.

"Why?" Mathias insisted.

"I don't know. You're all pissed off. It's hot."

Mathias studied his face. "So, you're some sort of freak?"

Alberto shrugged. Mathias narrowed his eyes, but thinking Alberto was a freak didn't make him remove his hand. His other gripped the back of his head to pull him down for a kiss.

Alberto really enjoyed kissing Mathias, the frantic and so sensual way their tongues intertwined, like they really craved each other. Obviously, with such stimulation, Alberto could only get harder, and just as he was about to say, *Hey, let's do something about this*, Mathias released him and turned his back to him. Alberto stared after him helplessly. What was he supposed to do now?

"So… what do you want exactly?" Alberto asked coldly.

"Hm… Let's see… Oh, right. I want you to shut up."

"Nice." Alberto smoothed the sides of his kimono. "And people call me an arsehole."

Mathias ignored his jab and pointed at the desk. "Homework."

Uh-uh. Screw that. Alberto crossed his arms over his chest. "Boring."

"Then… go to the window."

"No."

Mathias whipped around, eyes blazing, and Alberto couldn't help snorting. Mathias grabbed his sleeve, roughly dragged him toward the window, and handed him the binoculars.

"Get to work."

Alberto sighed, bitterly disappointed, and only did as he was told because Mathias was really sexy when he was domineering. He was about to sit on the chair left by the window, but he was stopped by Mathias's hand.

"No. Stand."

"Seriously?"

"Yes."

Alberto gave him a look that implied, *Have you met me? Everyone knows I can't stay upright for more than ten minutes at a time*, but Mathias ruthlessly forced him to face the window.

"Eyes on the street. Don't turn around."

"What the f—?"

He felt Mathias's hands on him and froze. No way, there was no way he was about to…

But yes. He really was doing it. The buttons of Alberto's trousers popped open one by one, then Mathias just yanked his trousers down.

"You're skinny," he said after a pause.

"Of course I am." Alberto shivered a bit under his gaze. He used his hand to steady himself against the window and pretended to look into the binoculars at the street below, mumbling, "I don't know what you expected."

As for him, he expected hands to touch him, pull down his briefs, maybe pinch his arse or even slap it, or Mathias to simply push him and take him against the window. He was fine with all of it, really, but he didn't expect that nothing would happen and that he'd just stand around like a fool for half a minute. Alberto started to feel really skinny now and really frustrated. He tentatively twisted his neck to check whether Mathias looked disgusted by the sight of him, but he was snapped at.

"What the fuck did I say?"

Alberto sighed. "Eyes on the street."

"And?"

"… Don't turn around."

Two warm hands finally gripped his hips.

"Right. See anything?"

Alberto noticed he sounded a little hoarse. "Just boring, boring pedestrians."

Mathias scoffed. "The way you say *pedestrian*. Like it's a crime."

"Mm." Alberto didn't bother saying more.

"You wanna know what I think?" Mathias's voice came low in his ear just as his fingertips slipped into the band of Alberto's underwear.

As long as Mathias's hands kept touching him, Alberto would have listened to anything he had to say, including reading the phonebook aloud.

"Yes…" he murmured, and a shiver ran through him when Mathias's hands slid into his briefs to cup his cheeks.

"Sometimes, I think you're the Devil."

Alberto's chin jerked slightly, but Mathias's hand had found its way around his dick, and he no longer wanted to talk. Though he refused to look at him and forced him to turn his back the whole time, Mathias still got him off in the same way Alberto did for him all these times.

Finally, they were going somewhere.

17

OUT OF SIGHT

At first, it was a little awkward. Mathias didn't dare look in Alberto's eyes. Even after it was cleaned up, he could only stare at the spot on the wall where Alberto had shot his load.

Alberto didn't seem to find any awkwardness in the situation. He tossed the towel in the laundry basket and laid himself flat on his back on the bed, his fast-cooling gaze fixed on the ceiling.

Mathias couldn't stop staring at his own hand, like what he just did was unfathomable. After a whole week of messing around with that creature, he'd promised himself to take it easy today. Not only did their lips touch, but Mathias had grabbed Alberto's cock, too. He could still feel it throbbing in his hand. How good it felt, knowing he was all-powerful, that, if he wanted, he could have that demon mewling under him, tame at last.

Just thinking about it…

He felt himself twitch in his boxers.

Stretched on the bed, Alberto was watching him through half-closed lids. Whatever Eric or Zak said, Mathias was convinced Alberto was no stranger to these practices. For someone who claimed he didn't date, he was way too chill about this, way too sure of himself. He must have had lovers. He may even have other lovers now. Mathias wanted to ask, but he had a feeling it wouldn't serve any purpose, and he decided it was none of his business anyway.

Alberto slowly extended his hand toward him. "Give me a cigarette instead of looking at me."

"I'm out."

"No, you're not."

"I'm out." Mathias grabbed his wrist and pulled him to his feet.

Alberto shuddered when their skin made contact and yanked himself free. Mathias suddenly recalled that movie he watched with his mom, *Lady and the Tramp*. He couldn't remember anything besides the title, but he definitely felt like a tramp every time he stood close to Alberto.

Instead of recoiling or stepping back, Alberto pushed his luck and, diving his fingers into Mathias's front pocket, retrieved a crumpled pack of Marlboro.

"Help yourself, why don't you?"

"Thank you."

Alberto slipped the smoke between his dangerous lips, and Mathias plucked it out and put it back in his pocket.

"What the hell...?" His crude words clashed with the mild tone of his voice.

"I told you. You can't smoke in here." Mathias tightened his grip on his wrist. Damn it. They were so close. His blood was boiling just looking at that face. He lowered his voice. "If you're so desperate to put something in your mouth, I've got a better idea for you."

Whatever Mathias had expected, it wasn't that: Alberto burst out a laugh, his whole face transforming. Mathias's mouth fell open.

"Okay," Alberto said.

"Huh? What?"

"*O-kay*," he repeated, and he sunk to his knees, his long fingers already on Mathias's belt.

Mathias almost said, *I was joking, I was joking*, but, suddenly, it didn't matter what he wanted to say. Alberto was on his knees, laughing at his joke, and Mathias was too stunned to react.

154

I was only joking, he kept repeating to himself while Alberto worked to free him from his jeans.

I was only joking, not remembering the joke, not remembering what was funny to begin with.

And Mathias thought, *Phew. I'm in serious trouble.*

Alberto paused when he was faced with his cock. He'd held it before, but it was the first time they were facing each other. Mathias fought the urge to run away; he buried his hands in his pockets.

"What? You've never seen one up close before?"

Holding his gaze with a lifted eyebrow, Alberto gave Mathias his answer. To his dismay, his pulse quickened. "Have you seen many?"

"Do you really want to know?"

"… No."

With a last taunting look, Alberto lowered his head, and Mathias felt himself melt away.

So, Alberto wasn't the high-prized virgin the others thought him to be. Turned out he had plenty of lovers behind everybody's back, and he got to play aloof and unattainable behind the gates of Colette. Mathias was probably just one of many. But still… to hear it from his mouth was unpleasant all the same.

But why? It's not like Mathias had plans for them or anything. This was *fine*. In fact, this was already too much. Way too much. So much, in fact, that he should maybe stop right no—

"Fuck!"

He tried to push Alberto's face away, but that mad bastard stuck to his dick like a starved stray to a milk bottle, and he swallowed all he had to give with a low hum that instantly burned itself in Mathias's memory. His knees buckled, and he had to support himself on Alberto's shoulders.

"I'm sorry," he panted, his cheeks burning.

"Why are you sorry?"

"I didn't have time to warn you."

"Warn me of what?"

Mathias didn't like to see him so smug. His face also flushed, Alberto wiped his mouth with two fingers and a mocking glint in his eye. He had never looked so beautiful, and yet, Mathias had never felt so strongly the need to get him out of his life. He turned away and hurriedly tucked himself back in. Alberto couldn't take a hint to shut his mouth, however. He spoke in a languid voice behind his back.

"I've never met a guy like you before."

Mathias hesitated then faced him again. "A guy like me?"

"You know. The angry closeted homosexual. I used to see them in movies, and I was like, no way, these guys can't possibly exist. That's too far-fetched."

Mathias's eyes fell on his mother's Garbage poster. He could feel her own teasing eyes on him again, hear her laughter, feel her hands messing with his hair.

"Watch it," he said in a cool tone.

"Am I wrong, then? Are you straight? Do you know how long it took me to get you off?"

"I don't know how you could have counted, considering how happy you were with my cock in your mouth." He approached Alberto, who fell back onto the bed. "What? You deny you liked it?"

"No, I don't. I *loved* it. You know why? Because I'm gay." He tilted his head back and laughed.

Mathias looked at him, his heart in his throat. "Do you find me funny?"

"It's a bit funny, honestly."

Mathias failed to understand the joke. He dug his nails into his palms until the pain forced him to stop. Right then, to top it all, *that fucking song* started playing.

They both froze, their gazes flying toward the hi-fi then toward each other. Alberto's eyes glinted excitedly from all the fun he was having at Mathias's expense.

Mathias stepped to the side and reached out to press the "stop" button. Alberto let out another laugh.

"I had no idea I was so damn funny."

"Sorry."

But he wasn't sorry. He looked almost delirious, even as he noted the cold anger visible on Mathias's face.

156

"You don't find it funny? But look, it is! You want me. You want me so much you can't take your hands off me, but it's like you don't know what it means, right? It means you're g—"

"Get out."

There was a pause.

"What?"

"Get the fuck out." Mathias calmly pointed at the door.

This time, Alberto stopped laughing, and he glanced from the door to him and back with a gradually perplexed expression. Mathias went to open the door and gestured for him to get moving.

Alberto's lips tightened. "Fine," he muttered. He got up and gathered his belongings in silence. Mathias watched him, quieter than he'd been in a long time, knowing that this would soon be over.

"Coward," Alberto mumbled on his way out.

Mathias was about to slam the door in his face, when he heard an unmistakable girly voice speaking from the corridor.

"Alfred?… *You're* Alfred?"

Mathias knocked his own head against the door instead.

Mathias showed up at school the next Monday only to find out everyone in his social circle now knew his mom was dead. His chest tightened painfully when it occurred to him Eric told people when he'd explicitly asked him not to. But when his friend showed up late and flushed—tell-tale signs Zak slept over last night—he seemed as shocked as he was.

"Do you think it could have been Zak?" Mathias asked reluctantly.

"No! Does that even sound like Zak?" Eric replied in a pleading tone. "He would never. And I would never. You have to believe me."

Mathias didn't have to exert himself to believe Eric. It was written all over his face. So that just left Alberto… but, to his annoyance, and even though he got confirmation this weekend that he was a cold-hearted bastard, that betrayal felt even worse, almost as bad as if he'd raised a megaphone in the middle of the schoolyard and announced to the entire crowd that he'd spent the last couple of days with his hand down Mathias's boxers.

When Joy and Melissa rushed over to profess their deepest condolences, flinging their arms around his neck and hugging him to their chests, Mathias miserably stared at Eric, who stepped up for him.

"He knows, he knows. He's very grateful." Eric gently pried them away from Mathias's neck. "Now give him some air."

Mathias asked the girls, "Who told you my mom was dead?" If he could trace back the origin of the rumor, then—

"Kayvin," Melissa said immediately.

Joy gave her a pointed look. "He said not to repeat that."

"I don't care," Melissa said. "He can be a real piece of work, and he did this for a reason."

"What did I ever do to that asshole?" Mathias asked, confused.

Eric shrugged. "You're my friend?"

"Is it about the other day? Because I didn't let him get into your face?"

Joy laughed. "Kayvin's possessive."

"But he fucking hates Eric!"

"Hey!" Eric pouted. "Nobody hates me."

"It's not only about Eric," Melissa began, but Joy elbowed her in the ribs, and she huffed in pain.

So, that was it. Last week, Mathias put Kayvin in his place, and now this. Mathias fell onto a bench, at a loss for words.

"How does that guy even know about my mom…?"

Melissa chortled darkly. "Kayvin's dad is a senator. He can find whatever he wants about anyone. Kev probably asked him to run a background check on you. It wouldn't be difficult for him to find out about your mom."

"Do you know how insane that sounds?"

"Kayvin's dad is… something," Joy said with a grimace. "It's best you be careful with him now—"

"Fuck's sake!" Mathias sprung to his feet and walked away.

How fast things fall apart. He was really stupid to have forgotten, even for a minute. He had gone home Friday night with plans to make out with that slutty little giraffe all weekend, but it all turned to shit, and now, he was back to having all his friends going *aww* and *aaah*, their eyes filled with pity.

He'd managed to last three months before his secret was out. Now he was back to being the kid with the dead mom.

Cool. Amazing. Top-notch, really.

Oh, and he and the giraffe weren't in ~~speaking~~ kissing terms anymore. Cherry on top of the turd cake.

Mathias had a really bad week after that. He gave an excuse to his dad about how his Spanish homework buddy no longer needed assistance, and that was pretty much it.

Things were more complicated with his sister. She wasn't a fan of Alberto, so Mathias had tried his best to avoid letting the two of them meet, and that worked well enough for a while. After all, she was a busy kid. It was hard work to be the editor-in-chief of *The Colette Times*, especially when you had to make up drama to compensate for the fact nothing ever happened at school.

Elisa was tiny in stature, but the expanse of stars living in her dark eyes had shone with shock and outrage when she caught Alberto outside Mathias's bedroom, and she looked more frightening than Kayvin.

"Alfred? Seriously?" she asked. "He looks an awful lot like that guy from school, Alberto. You know, the sexist pig."

Alberto had looked down at her with contempt. "I'm not a pig."

"Shh…" Mathias silenced him.

"Whatever," Alberto said, and he'd slunk out without another word while Mathias was left to answer his sister's questions.

Elisa was half as insane as her mother and infuriatingly encouraged by her carefully selected entourage. In one word, she was unstoppable. She put him through a thorough interrogation, and Mathias had to lie to her for the first time in his life, but it was better to claim he and Alberto were just hanging out and hiding it from Eric than to admit to… well… anything else.

"Hanging out?" she'd asked. "Like… you're friends?"

"Something like that," Mathias had muttered.

Friends with Alberto. How ridiculous. No wonder that freak didn't have anyone at school. He was insufferable. Calling him a coward... Even if it were true, that wasn't something he wanted to hear.

"Eric would freak out if he knew," Elisa said.

"That's why you shouldn't tell anyone," Mathias said with a warning look. "Anyone, you hear me?"

"Fine!" she'd barked, glaring at him. "But how could you, of all people, become friends with him? I don't like it, and I don't like him."

Neither do I, Mathias had thought. *Neither do I.*

But losing Alberto proved more difficult than he'd thought, especially when some people's clueless attitudes weren't helping at all.

"Come on, sit on my lap."

"No."

"I won't do anything."

"I don't believe you."

"Come on..."

"I'm not gonna sit on your lap."

"That's not what you said this weekend."

"You fu— Eric! I'm a guy!"

"So? What do you think I am?"

"... Fine."

Zak reluctantly sat sideways on Eric's lap and let him leave a wet peck on his cheek.

"See? I didn't do anything."

"Mm."

"What?"

Eric gave a childish laugh when he saw his boyfriend's disgruntled expression. Zak plugged his mouth with his own, and seconds later, all that could be heard was the sound of their lips as they kissed meticulously in the middle of the playground.

Sitting on the same bench on either side of them and feeling pretty awkward, Mathias and Elodie accidentally crossed sights. She grimaced a smile, and he took a drag of his cigarette before getting pulled into a yawn. Elodie got up from her seat to stand in front of him.

"You look tired. Been busy lately?"

He could say that. He hadn't spoken to Alberto since he'd kicked him out of his apartment almost a week ago. The wet kissing sounds coming from his right side did nothing to help with the memories of what he used to do with him before he got rid of him. You'd think he'd be able to sleep a whole lot better now, but life was never so simple, was it?

"You wanna go for a walk?" Mathias said.

Elodie's pretty face brightened. "Sure!"

"Just wanted to get away from them," Mathias said when they'd walked a safe distance away.

"Yeah, they're… pretty intense."

He slipped her a few glances as they walked. She was tall for a girl, and she was athletic, with long blond hair and almond-shaped eyes. She was the most popular girl at school. Mathias didn't know how any of this worked, but he had to admit, she was pretty charismatic.

He threw a look over his shoulder at the most popular boy at school, Eric. Van Bergen had interrupted his make out session with Zak, giving him such a scare that he'd fallen from the bench, and he was pointing his riding crop at him. Mathias returned his attention to Elodie with a shrug.

"What happened to you? You used to hang out all the time. I haven't seen you around in a while."

Elodie stopped in the middle of the playground and scanned her surroundings, her arms wrapped around herself.

"That's actually… embarrassing."

Mathias didn't want her to feel compelled to share something private, so he said nothing.

"It's Eric," she said.

"Eric? What did he do this time?"

"Nothing. It's just… being around him was too much. I couldn't stop having these feelings, so I thought it best to, you know, keep my distance."

Elodie had been Eric's girlfriend for some time. Some months, at least. Everyone knew how Eric broke up with her out of nowhere because he fell in love with Zak and wanted to pursue him. Elodie had even spent some time consoling him when Zak was wasting his time dating Alberto. She was a good person, but once Zak and Eric got together, she gradually made herself scarce. When Eric saw her today, he was ecstatic and almost forced her to take a seat next to him, otherwise, Mathias didn't think she'd have lingered.

"You still like him?"

"Not so much anymore," she said, staring at her feet. "But I have such good memories, it took me a while to let go. I know it's not good to do this. I need to move on." She glanced up at him. "Soon."

"Yeah." Mathias shrugged. "He's gay now."

"But he's not. He's bisexual."

"Right… You're right."

She chortled. "Eric never shagged like a closeted homosexual, that's for sure."

"All right." Mathias stretched his neck toward the front gate. "I don't need the details."

Why did he have to hear the words *closeted homosexual* twice in the course of one fucking week? Unbelievable. He was cursed or something.

He coughed lightly into his fist. "How would you know, anyway? Have you slept with a closeted homo before?"

Elodie laughed. She had a really nice laugh, matching her really nice voice. "No, or I don't think so, at least. I just imagine they kind of…"

"What?"

"I don't know…" She made a funny face. "Flip you over or something?"

Mathias briefly thought of flipping a certain someone over, and his fists clenched in his pockets. "Who knows…"

"I should ask Xavier," Elodie said.

"Why?"

She grinned. "He's got a thing for Alberto, doesn't he?"

"Does he? Really?" Mathias scratched his cheek. "Huh. I didn't know."

"Nah… it's just a joke. But…" She leaned in closer, and Mathias caught a whiff of her perfume. "Last year he was 'Kayvin this' and 'Kayvin that'. Now it's 'Alberto this' and 'Alberto that'."

Mathias dug his fists deeper into his pockets. "Everybody's always going on about that guy. What's so special about him?"

"He's kind of beautiful, isn't he? A shame he's so weird."

Mathias didn't know what to say, so he looked down at his shoes. Elodie took a step closer to him.

"Mathias, I wanted to say…" He glanced curiously at her, and she gave him a clipped smile. "I was really sorry to hear you had a really hard time and all—"

"What?"

"We've all heard about your mom."

And Mathias thought, *God, I don't want your pity. I don't want pity at all.* And he thought of Alberto, who didn't have an ounce of pity to spare, and his insides churned weirdly. Closing his eyes, he fantasized about feeling his lips against his own again, pulling them, biting them, forcing all sorts of sounds out of him, and suddenly, he had a headache.

"Anyway…" Elodie said after a moment. "If you ever wanted to, you know, hang out…"

"Hang out?"

"Here's my number. You can call me anytime."

Mathias took the piece of paper with a faint smile. He wished he could say yes and date the hottest girl at school—plus she was cool, and she smelled nice, and she said all the right things—but he was haunted by a certain pair of lips, and there was no escaping them.

What he wanted, *really wanted*, this sweet girl could never give to him. He wanted to taste evil again.

He thanked Elodie and marched toward the building, his face set.

PROVE IT

Alberto was having a bad day, one of those bad days in the middle of a bad week. Nothing interesting ever happened here, just life as it ever was: dull, boring, grey.

He could have slapped himself.

He did, actually. He had faced his monstrous appearance in the mirror and gave it two hard slaps with the flat of his hand. His arrogance and his stupidity had made him lose the only good thing in his life. If he could turn back time, if only he could turn back time, he wouldn't ever antagonise Mathias about being gay ever again.

Alas, he was too elated after having had his dick in his mouth. Alberto didn't have many aspirations in life, but sucking cock was definitely at the top of his list, and if Mathias would ever let him do that to him again, he'd show him how much he meant it, too.

Their relationship had progressed too fast in the course of one afternoon. Alberto lost himself to the delights of victory, and he had planted his flag in Mathias's territory only for it to be set on fire. He agreed with Mathias's anger. He went too far. He should never be allowed in his presence again. He might not be the Devil, but he'd spent too much of his life in evil company, only to have them affect him after all.

They didn't see each other for four and a half days. Not a look, not a word. Just as if they'd never met. Having tasted Mathias in all the best ways, how could he return to his dreary little life again? He even thought of apologising, of throwing himself at his feet, but, then again, that would have looked desperate. Mathias wasn't the only dick Alberto could have in his mouth, should he ever seek one. He just happened to be the one he wanted, that's all.

As a result, Alberto was in a sour mood all week, going to school and back with a dark scowl that would have impressed Mathias, if he'd ever bothered looking at him. In class, he fell asleep again. There was no point keeping his eyes open for anything any longer. Even the money he received from his last shooting, coupled with the promise of more work during the Christmas holidays, couldn't bring even the hint of a smile to his face. Between never seeing Stasia again or never being allowed in the presence of Mathias, it seemed his triumph was doomed to be tainted by failure anyway.

Alberto didn't really have a proper understanding of how different his existence had been these past weeks until he had to contend with his fangirls again. He realised he didn't have the patience to deal with them any longer.

He'd just finished snapping at them for the first time ever, telling them, not very nicely, to piss off, and shocking them into running in the opposite direction, when he was roughly grabbed, pulled into a classroom, and slammed against the wall.

Hey, must be Mathias.

Indeed, Mathias was looking at him, his eyes burning but also anxious, wondering how he'd be received. They were saying, *Long time no see. I hate you, maybe. I resent you, most likely. But I want you, and you want me.*

Alberto ignored the pain in his lower back. Relief mingled with delight and turned on the light inside him. He accidentally smiled. When Mathias saw this, he crashed lips-first into him.

How good it felt, how intense… and it was made even better in an empty classroom, with the distant chatter of the others on the other side of the wall. Alberto couldn't even make himself limp. He was all nerves. His hands had flown to hold Mathias's face in a fierce grip. He wanted to take control, but he hesitated to do so. To lose this feeling again for another week would be unacceptable, but at the same time, he felt desperate. School was the worst place — no, the *best* place — and if this kiss continued, he wouldn't be able to stop himself...

Sadly, Mathias pulled away. Saliva weaved a glinting thread between their mouths. Alberto stared at it in awe until Mathias wiped his lips with the back of his hand, tearing it.

"You look completely high." He sounded amused.

Alberto had lost the feeling in his legs. He was aroused. At school. He didn't even care. "I am high." He haughtily shook his head to rearrange his hair.

They must have fallen perfectly into place because Mathias stared hard. Then, he finally got closer, dug his fingers into Alberto's chest, and asked in a hoarse voice, "Am I your favourite drug?"

Alberto leaned down for another kiss, but he was denied. "You are now."

A half-lie, but it made Mathias lick his lower lip and press him deeper into the wall, eyes bright as smouldering embers.

The sight was enough to send a tremor rocking throughout Alberto. "What?" he asked hoarsely.

Mathias didn't reply nor did he break eye contact. He was searching for something on his face. An answer, perhaps.

Alberto spoke up, tentatively using his most sensual voice, "Do you think I'm sexy?" He even dared the impossible, slipping his hand up Mathias's chest, lightly hanging onto the side of his jacket.

Mathias finally blinked. He looked like he had found his answer and wasn't too impressed by it.

"I don't know," he said in a hushed tone.

Alberto felt a pang of apprehension and willed himself to ignore it. He slowly, very slowly, leaned into Mathias's space. "I think you're sexy."

That twitchy idiot Duvo, in charge of the Drama Club, had called him the worst actor in the group behind his back, but Alberto was really good at playing certain parts. He was once told with a face like his, his fate was sealed, that with the right guidance, he could bring the world to his feet. Alberto didn't care about the world, but he sure would have loved to see Mathias on his knees.

"Come to mine later," Mathias said.

In an instant, he was at the door. Alberto wanted to reach out to him with both hands but wisely kept them down.

"What time?"

"Don't be late," Mathias added aggressively. When Alberto arched an eyebrow, he nodded, looking satisfied. Then, he left.

Now alone in the classroom, Alberto noticed a timid ray of sunlight had pierced its way inside through the window, stopping right at his feet. He exhaled a long breath. This day wasn't so bad after all.

Mathias was scowling when he answered the door.

"You're late."

"You never gave me a time."

"I thought you'd come earlier. I texted you over an hour ago."

"But I had to have dinner with my mother," Alberto explained while straightening his sleeves. "She doesn't like it when I have my meals elsewhere."

Mathias pulled a face but fully opened the door for him. "Whatever. Come in, quickly. My dad and Ella have gone to the movies. An hour ago," he added resentfully.

Alberto fumbled with the buttons of his coat. "Which movie?"

"What?"

"Which movie?"

"Does it matter?"

"It could mean they'll be back in an hour or in two. Depends on the movie. Depends on what you want to do to me."

"What I...?" Mathias glowered at him and picked up the pace. "Just come."

Alberto followed Mathias down the corridor to his room. The door to his bedroom was left open, and inside, it was dark. The only source of light came from his computer, and Alberto noted he had been on Facebook. Mathias shut the door and immediately put his hands on him, pushed his coat off his shoulders, and gripped the hems of his sweater and T-shirt.

Alberto snorted. "We're not even wasting time with excuses now?"

"Do you mind?"

Alberto was surprised by his gentle tone. And frightened, somehow. He could return to a dynamic he liked by angering Mathias, but he could also lose more than an opportunity if he opened his mouth again.

"Whatever," he said, thinking it was safer.

Mathias pulled him down for a kiss, turning his mind blank, before he slid his hands under his sweater to grip his waist. Alberto felt himself turning soft between his hands.

Their kiss deepened and turned a little frantic, until Mathias suddenly pulled Alberto's sweater over his head. Alberto let him, at first, distracted by his burning kisses, but when Mathias tugged on his T-shirt, something flashed in Alberto's mind. They had never done this. Removing clothes. Skin against skin.

What if Mathias wanted to…

And Alberto realised he would give him whatever he wanted. Anything. Anything so that he could feel alive again and feel someone's breath on his neck in a good way. His heart gave a wild thump in his chest; he hoped Mathias's intentions were dirty.

Alberto let Mathias strip him of his clothes more or less clumsily and in silence. He felt nervous, but, mostly, he was excited. Alberto managed to get the other's T-shirt off, but not much else, and he barely caught a glimpse of a lean and sculpted torso before Mathias turned a little rougher and pushed him down.

Being flung onto the bed made Alberto see stars for a moment. He squeezed his eyes shut and breathed hard, and when he reopened them, his trousers were gone and Mathias was on top of him, kissing him. He didn't need his eyesight, or even his full brain capacity, to enjoy this. This was a language they were fluent in. Their tongues did all the silent talking for a minute until Alberto felt Mathias's impatience digging into his hip. He let out a laugh.

Mathias jerked his head back. "Are you seriously laughing at me again?"

Fuck. Alberto put his hand over his eyes. "I'm not. I'm just…"

"What? What?"

So susceptible… Alberto fretfully directed Mathias's hand toward his remaining layer of clothing. "Hard."

Mathias glanced down, his face serious. He peeled himself off Alberto and looked back up, a gleam of determination in his eyes. Then, he gripped Alberto's underwear with both hands.

"Prove it." He gave a sharp tug.

Once Alberto was bare in front of Mathias, he found it unacceptable that the latter wasn't. He found he didn't want him to stare at his tool anyway, thinking it might scare him away, like, *oh no, his dick*! Mathias had touched it, but, of course, he'd never looked at it. Better safe than sorry. All in all, he easily convinced himself that it had nothing to do with being self-conscious at all.

So, before Mathias, wide-eyed, was even done appraising *it*, Alberto had trapped him between his legs and was zipping his jeans open. He expected to be pushed away, but, between bruising kisses, Mathias let him slip down his clothes without complaint.

That was it, then. Mathias wanted to do things to him. Possibly even with him. For once, Alberto was grateful that he wasn't one to discharge at a mere touch because the sight of Mathias's silhouette as he got up to kick off his clothes made him feel a bit overloaded.

Then, the two of them were naked together.

That feeling when Mathias laid his burning body on top of him made Alberto curl onto himself like a boy and even make a pitiful sound. To conceal his turmoil, he bit down on Mathias's shoulder, and he received a grunt of pain and a nip back on his neck.

"You're biting now?" Mathias said, gripping his hair and giving a ruthless yank.

"You do it to me all the time." Alberto wanted to do the same, but Mathias's hair was barely more than fuzz. He gripped his arms instead. They were so hard. Iron under smooth olive skin. Fists attached to arms like that could kill. Alberto shook all over in trepidation.

"I can do whatever I want," Mathias whispered by his ear, tightening his grip on his hair.

Goosebumps of pleasure flared all across Alberto's skin. "So can I," he breathed.

Mathias nipped his bottom lip. "You can shut up, for once."

Lust rushed to Alberto's head when he reached down to grope Mathias's arse cheeks and press their bodies together. They accidentally rubbed against each other's hard-ons and cursed at the same time.

His forehead glistening with sweat, Mathias bit into his neck again. With a low chuckle, Alberto jerked his hips forward.

You missed me, didn't you? He could think it, but he wouldn't dare say it.

Mathias's eyes narrowed. He seemed to have read his thoughts. "Fuck you."

"F—ah!" A broken sound ripped from Alberto's throat when his hair was almost torn from his scalp. He snarled and writhed under him. "Fuck you, too!"

Those words started something.

Mathias's eyes seemed to glow in the dark. He pushed himself between Alberto's legs, tight enough that there wasn't a sliver of space left between them. "Who's laughing now?" he purred, grinding their dicks together.

Alberto lost his mind. He thought, after this, he'd never know sleep again. His heart was pounding when Mathias turned him over.

That evening, the two of them went all the way.

19

I HAVE A LOVER

I HAVE A LOVER, Mathias repeated to himself, gazing at the white clouds outside the window instead of at his notebook. *I have a lover, and no one needs to know.*

Every time he closed his eyes, he replayed what had happened last night. His lips. *Alberto's* lips. They knew the secret of life. They brought him freedom. Now he had conquered more than them. His neck, his chest, his cheeks… He had explored them, tasted them, and kneaded them like dough between his hands.

They were lovers now. They had to be. They'd never been naked together before last night. Small stuff was over. Alberto was the most beautiful creature in the world. A demon, for sure, but he was his last night. Slipping under the sheets with him, skin against skin, watching his knuckles turn white, it felt like slaying dragons. Mathias felt godlike. In the bedroom, at least, Alberto was pliable, docile even, and his to command.

This morning, when Alberto walked past the school gate alone, as usual, Mathias noted a trio of his groupies staring after him with the same desire he had read in his eyes when he was inside him. *Inside him.* Mathias said nothing, showed nothing, but all the while, internally chanting, *He's mine. He is mine. I've possessed every inch of his body last night, and he begged me. He begged* me.

And so, Mathias had charged straight into that trio of girls.

They parted like the Red Sea to make way for him, the real champion who fucked their idol last ni—

Thump.

Something struck and bounced against his forehead, tearing him from his daydream. Eric had thrown his eraser at him. Standing a few feet away, the Economics teacher was watching him with an impatient expression.

"Mathias, are you with us?"

No, Mathias thought, even as he nodded. No, he was, and would be for the rest of the day, pressed into the crook of Alberto's neck, counting his cries.

"Oh, look! It's Alberto! Look! Oh my God! He's so hot!"

Faced with Xavier's outburst, Eric let out a bright laugh, something that sounded so ridiculously childish that Mathias had to smile despite himself. Next to him, Kayvin was not smiling. He was looking from Alberto's airbrushed face to Xavier's flushed cheeks, and he looked pissed off.

Outside the metro station near Xavier's second home in Neuilly (yes, that's right), where they were headed for another one of his frequent parties, they'd stumbled upon Alberto's face on a bus stop. He was posing for a clothing brand named *Occult*. Mathias made sure not to look at him until everyone had moved on, chastising Xavier for his man-crush on Alberto. Then, he tossed a look over his shoulder, and his heart sighed. Alberto's cold gaze seemed to follow him wherever he went.

In the picture, he looked older, refined, and definitely unattainable. A stunning girl was clinging to his neck, staring into the side of his face with longing, but Alberto had eyes only for the camera. It was as if he knew Mathias would be watching, only to fall into his trap.

Mathias didn't know the brand Alberto was posing for, and he probably couldn't afford it anyway, but he thought he should go and check it out for himself, see what it was worth.

"Zak just texted me!" Eric burst out, stopping everyone in the middle of the crosswalk, as if the interruption had come from the

Queen of England. He read the message with a tense face then cackled gleefully. "Ehehe… He's just finished class, and he's on his way!"

"You're letting him come to Neuilly alone?" Charles-Henry asked, clearly teasing him, but the color drained out of Eric's face.

"I hope he'll be safe! What if someone attacks him? Or worse… hits on him?" He gasped. "Maybe I should go back and get him."

Ignoring the cars honking angrily all around them, he turned around in the middle of the crosswalk. Mathias ignored his ramblings and dragged him to the sidewalk.

"I'm sure Zak can manage without you, just like he's done for the past sixteen years."

"Almost seventeen now, next month," Eric noted, coming back to Earth. "I'm planning a party. You better be coming."

"All right."

"Don't worry about Zak-Zak," Xavier said with a wave of his hand. "He'll probably come with Alberto."

Eric wrinkled his nose. "Alberto is coming to your party?"

"I think so! He's so funny! At first, he said no, that he didn't know how to take the metro."

"He's lying," Eric said darkly. "Zak said Alberto's mother has her own chauffeur. Technically, he shouldn't even bother coming to school by public transport, but he always does."

"Maybe he likes trains?" Charles-Henry said. "Where does he live?"

"No clue," Eric said, "but he takes Line 10 to go home. Westward."

"Why are we talking about that fucker again?" Kayvin scowled. Without Steph and his other goons, he was pretty subdued today. He added, mumbling, "Who cares where he lives…?"

"He lives in Boulogne," Xavier said.

"How the hell do you know that?" Eric asked. "Even Zak doesn't know that."

Xavier's exaggerated shrug caught Mathias's attention. "I just know. Anyway, I offered to pick him up for the party. After all, it's a short drive from Boulogne to my dad's house. He said no, but then I managed to convince him to come anyway."

"How?" Mathias couldn't help asking.

Xavier flashed them a grin. "I have ways of making him come."

Eric started giggling inexplicably; Mathias glared at him until he stopped.

"Can we stop talking about him for a second?" Kayvin muttered.

"Are you afraid Alberto's going to steal your thunder again?" Charles-Henry joked, grinning.

Kayvin didn't smile back. "Me? Afraid of that guy? Even if girls like him at first, they all change their tunes the moment they try to strike up a conversation. He has literally nothing to say."

They grew silent as they arrived at Xavier's house, a modern construction beyond a high black gate with a tidy lawn, a fountain, and a covered pool.

Alberto may not have been good at conversation, Mathias ruminated as he walked past the pool, but there was one place where that didn't matter and was even encouraged, and it was in the bedroom. If Alberto could still talk, that meant Mathias wasn't doing his job properly anyway.

With a beer bottle in his hand that was now too warm for consumption, Mathias stood at Eric's side in silence, letting him do all the conversation. He felt febrile ever since he was told Alberto was coming tonight, and he found himself perspiring under his layers of clothing.

Why the overreaction? It's not like it was the first time he had ever had sex, and judging from his behavior last night, it clearly wasn't Alberto's first time either, whatever he may have said about his dating habits, or lack thereof.

Perhaps he felt a bit overheated because it was the first time he had sex and remembered all of it? No, that wasn't it exactly, but he'd definitely remember this one for a while, possibly forever, because it was the first time he actually understood what the fuss was about. Before that, he really believed having sex was overrated, and people were making up rumors about how good it felt to encourage procreation or some shit like that. They talked about it all the time. Sex was great. Sex was mind-blowing. Sex was *e-ve-ry-thing.* Mathias thought differently.

Sex was *fine.* Whatever.

He'd always been like a panda. He could be placed in a giant cage with the hottest female specimen around, but he'd direct all his attention on chewing his bamboo stick in the corner, and it would be difficult to draw his focus elsewhere. After all, bamboo was useful. Having sex wasn't.

Fair enough, when they were kissing and touching last night, and Mathias had felt him so hard against himself, he had to confess he was a bit unsettled, but when he flipped Alberto over and ended up pressed between his plump ass cheeks, he somehow knew exactly what he had to do.

Now, as opposite as the other times in his life, he had only one wish: to do it again as soon as possible. Since he'd found out Alberto was coming, the thought of kissing him, of touching him, of taking him apart again was making his palms sweat in anticipation.

Mathias wanted to tell the world, *Did you know? Alberto's hips are so narrow, his trousers slide down his thighs like slow-cooked meat falls off the bone. His skin is cool to the touch, and his arms hold no strength at all. Did you know? Fat tears hang from his eyelashes like precious pearls when he's being fucked, and his voice grows hoarse from all his pointless begging.*

Alberto arrived with Zak just as Mathias was crawling out of a pit of his own making. Eric jumped him the moment they came in.

"Did you have fun on the metro with Zak? Hm?" He pawed at his boyfriend, apparently checking for wounds. "Kept him safe?"

Alberto rolled his eyes. "Safe from what? Do you know who lives in Neuilly?"

"Did you keep him safe or what?"

"Yes, Eric. I made sure to hold his hand the whole time."

Eric turned brick red. "You—"

"Come on." Zak gave him a reproachful look. "We weren't even on the same metro. Alberto was right behind me."

"Oh." Eric calmed down. "You were right behind him?"

Alberto nodded with a fake smile. "Best view of Zak is from behind."

Mathias had to hold Eric back with both arms while Alberto slunk away.

Ignoring his boyfriend's antics, Zak watched Alberto turn the corner with a smile. "Did you see that? He's talkative today."

Eric wrinkled his nose. "I sure wish he'd talk less."

Mathias silently agreed in his heart.

He tried his best not to feel envious of his friends' intimacy, the way they kept touching each other, whether it was Zak sliding his fingers through Eric's hair as they talked or Eric pressing soft little kisses to Zak's cheek every two sentences. He kept his distance, interacting with them only when they included him in their conversations.

Xavier was hopping from group of people to group of people. It seemed that, once again, he'd invited the whole school, but his house could withstand it. It was massive, comprised of dozens of rooms including three living spaces and an indoor pool Mathias had declined to check out when offered to. Everywhere, there were people. Mathias spotted Elodie and her friends, Joy and Melissa. She waved at him with her signature crooked smile, and he waved back, his throat constricting when he spotted Alberto walking right behind her back.

When he turned back to Eric and Zak, a girl had appeared out of nowhere, perched on uncomfortable-looking shoes. Holding a glass of Champagne in one hand and the bottle in another, she had the strangest lips Mathias had ever seen. They were puffed up, like some sort of fish. Mathias felt it rude to stare at them, but it was hard not to. She'd lathered them in ruby-red lipstick that she'd smear on the rim of her glass every time she took a sip.

Eric and Zak had also noticed her, and even as Zak was looking at her suspiciously—he thought every girl was after his boyfriend, even though Mathias knew every girl was after *his* lover—Eric was grinning at her as if she were about to become his new best friend.

"You're Eric, right?" she asked, surprising Mathias.

Perhaps she really was after him, and Zak's eyebrows seemed to agree with him.

"Yes! That's right!"

"The American football player." Pouty-Lips's gaze glided toward Zak, and she sniffed. "And his boyfriend."

"Yes! That's Zak!" Eric nodded excitedly.

Mathias inwardly sighed, and Pouty-Lips's eyes narrowed.

"Zak? Is that it?"

Zak raised his hand in salute. "Yep."

"Where are you from?"

There was a brief pause before Zak flashed her a smile. "I'm French. Where are you from?"

She took a large swig of Champagne. "You don't look French."

Zak's smile froze while Eric let out a nervous laugh.

"I'm French," the girl went on. "My parents are French. My grandparents are also French. So on and on and on. Pure nobility. My family tree dates back to the seventeen hundreds."

"Wow…" Zak said with a lack of enthusiasm that reminded Mathias of Alberto. In fact, Mathias could have bet Zak was impersonating him at the moment. "Impressive."

"Where does your family tree take you?" She insisted. "Baghdad? Dubai? Jakarta?"

As Eric's expression darkened, Zak gave the girl an unimpressed look. "All wrong."

"Oh?" She blinked at him. "So you came to France through one of ours?"

"One of ours what?"

"Our colonies!"

Zak's eyebrows knitted, threatening a storm.

Mathias thought he'd step in before that girl ended up flat on her ass across the room. "And where did they hide?" he asked.

She turned up her nose at him, her pouty lips pursed impatiently. "What?"

"During the Revolution. Where did your family hide? How come they didn't get their heads chopped off?"

As Eric nodded eagerly, Zak tilted his head, waiting for her response. She blinked and stammered, "That's not… That's…"

Xavier, who just happened to be walking by, heard the conversation and stopped in his tracks. "Scotland!" he said, happily slapping his hand on Mathias's shoulder. "They hid in Scotland for a few years."

"Are you guys related?" Zak asked, his brow still furrowed.

"Yes! Gwen's my cousin."

He flashed her a grin that she didn't return. Instead, she chugged down an entire glass of Champagne.

"And Xavier's my cousin," she muttered.

She didn't seem too pleased with people knowing about that, and she started throwing anxious looks around. She finally took notice of Mathias and staggered back. "Damn... where do they make them like you?"

"Excuse me?"

"Where are you from?"

"None of your business."

She laughed. "All right."

Xavier, who couldn't read social cues, nudged Mathias with his elbow. "Matt is half-Venezuelan. Isn't that cool?"

Gwen pulled a face. "Vene-what? Where the hell is that?"

"It's somewhere in South America?" Xavier didn't sound too sure.

"Ah! That explains his temper."

Xavier thought her remark was hilarious, so he broke into a laugh that no one else joined. Mathias, who usually liked to blame his Venezuelan mother for ~~everything~~ his temper, kept quiet and smiled, knowing if she were here today, this poor girl would have definitely been kicked so hard in the rear, she would have reached Caracas before the party was over.

Gwen wasn't as clueless as Xavier, and one look at Mathias's face inspired her to scan around the room, possibly in hope of finding someone else to annoy to death. Then her mouth fell open. "Holy shit, is that Albertino?" Flushing excitedly, she turned to Xavier. "You weren't lying; you really do know him!"

Xavier spun around, perplexed. "Who's Albertino?"

His cousin clicked her fingers in front of his nose. "Here, here, look. That's not Albertino over there? That tall, handsome freak?"

Xavier, as well as everyone else, followed the direction she was pointing in.

"Oh, you mean Alberto," Eric said.

"Yes, him!"

"I told you I know him!" Xavier puffed out his chest. "He's my guy!"

Gwen looked dubitative. So did Eric. Zak hid his face in his drinking cup, but the knitted eyebrows could tell legion. As for Mathias, he didn't believe Xavier at all.

"Is he single right now?" Gwen asked.

Mathias's stomach jumped right into his throat, choking him. Which was good, because part of him wanted to open his mouth and not to say pleasantries.

"Uh…" Xavier hesitated. "Why?"

"Because…" Gwen said, "he's a sex machine."

Zak burst out laughing into his cup, splattering Eric, who blinked at him in shock before joining in on the laughter.

"Sorry," he told Gwen. "You must have him confused with someone else."

"Uh-uh." She shook her head. "That's Alberto Gazza."

Zak became really serious, looking just as Mathias would have if he could have shown any reaction. "You know Alberto? How?"

Gwen emptied the rest of the bottle of Champagne into her glass. "Through Stasia, of course."

"Who's Stasia?"

She laughed. "Only his sister."

"Wait, what?" Zak's eyes turned as round as dinner plates. "Alberto never told me he had a sister."

"Okay, fine, she's not really his sister, but her dad and his mum are married, and they live together."

"And she told you that he…"

"All the time! Stasia told me he was insane. A total freak. Boning her right under their parents' noses."

"Right." Eric looked disgusted. "I'm not sure I'm comfortable with this information."

"I don't believe you," Zak mumbled, and Mathias tried hard not to nod.

"Then don't," Gwen said haughtily, "but I'm telling the truth. They live in Boulogne, in that horror on Schuman, next to the football stadium. I've known him for years. We used to chase him around the pool." She gulped down her Champagne and rubbed her nose resentfully. "He wasn't all that, then, trust me."

"You've known him for years?" Zak asked, his eyes bright. "Like, as a *kid?*"

Gwen made a face. "Yes! He was already a model, I think? I remember Stasia showed us some giant pictures of him they had stashed in the basement. They had brought them over from London."

"Alberto lived in London?" Zak sounded flabbergasted, as if Alberto never sharing any of this with him was like some sort of great betrayal. Eric's expression grew from amused to concerned before Mathias's eyes.

"He couldn't speak a word of French," Gwen went on, "so we were teaching him only terrible stuff, and his mother lost it. She's a frigid cow, but she's always acting like she's some sort of queen. I don't know why she got so mad; we were just having a bit of fun. Anyway, she said she'd homeschool Alberto because he couldn't learn French, but I can see she sent him to Colette in the end."

Gwen glanced at Xavier who'd been listening with a slack jaw the entire time. "I saw him at one of your parties some time ago, and he pretended not to know me. Too bad. He's clearly passed the age to be chased around the pool." Noticing her bottle of Champagne was empty, her shoulders slumped. "I'm not lying, you know. I used to be best friends with Stasia. She's a bitch, and I hate her now, but whatever she said, I believe her, because she always has her way."

Muttering to herself, Gwen staggered toward the kitchen, catching the attention of Kayvin, who granted her an appreciative look. Xavier followed after her with a blank expression, as if the whole conversation had gone completely over his head.

"I still don't believe it," Zak mumbled, clinging to Eric's sleeve.

Eric met Mathias's eyes and shrugged. "I don't know. Anything's possible with that guy."

Mathias agreed. He agreed. In fact, he should have known.

After all, Alberto claimed he didn't date, claimed Zak was his first boyfriend, but last night, it was clear he knew what he was doing.

Did you know? Alberto is a liar.

Perhaps he did girls on the side.

His own stepsister, too. Why not?

He was a freak; he said so himself.

Mathias understood at the right moment that he had been acting like a kid all day, and so he checked himself. Who was Alberto beyond the confines of his bedroom? It didn't matter. It shouldn't matter.

It *wouldn't* matter.

No, fucking was enough.

Fucking was *fine*, until it'd get boring, and then, they'd part ways.

20

THE KILL

OF ALL THE secrets Alberto had to keep, Mathias was his all-time favourite. Clad in different clothes that somehow always looked the same, in different moods but always with the same scowl, Mathias was so hot, he made Alberto look like a pile of rubbish. If they were to stand next to each other, anyone would see.

But, of course, they'd never stand next to each other; that was the whole point. And they probably wouldn't enjoy each other so much if they acted in the open. Sneaking around in the dark, that was fun.

Alberto, persistently deprived of fun, had never had such a good time before, and he had no intention of letting this thing go. Withstanding the freezing temperatures in Xavier's impeccable garden, cigarette hanging from his lips, surrounded but alone, he was weighing his options.

Some girls came to talk to him, interrupting his thoughts. He exchanged a few words, knowing it would please Xavier, who would reward him later, but, in truth, Xavier didn't need to buy his favour any longer. He just had to mention Eric and his friends were coming, and Alberto knew that meant Mathias would stalk the corridors of the villa all werewolf-like. He just had to be patient before he'd get to feel his hands on him again, and Mathias's hands… weren't they something…? Rough and tender at the same time, just like the dirty words he'd whispered into his ear last night.

Alberto felt lightheaded, but he knew better than to trust any of what happened, so he wisely kept his mouth shut and his hands to himself all day, waiting for Mathias to find him again. He was hoping it would happen soon. Then, he'd work out a way to ensnare him, put him on a tight leash. He would make himself obtainable while keeping his distance, just as he did last night when they fell back onto the mattress out of breath, and Mathias's brow started wrinkling in apprehension.

Alberto got the hell out as soon as possible before things turned sour, but not before he said, *Thank you*, as casually as possible. It worked. Mathias had stared at him with a slightly baffled expression and watched him put his clothes on quietly, but at least he wasn't mad, and, despite having had his dick up in Alberto's arse, he absolutely didn't seem as traumatised as when Alberto had suggested that he might be homosexual.

"I'll see you later?" Alberto had ventured, his hand on the handle — Mathias had gone as far as walking him to the front door!

"Are you okay?" he'd asked, eyebrows still risen in astonishment.

Alberto couldn't help rolling his eyes. Mathias wasn't much of a talker, but once he'd found his words, he wasn't afraid to repeat them.

"Yes!" Alberto said for the thirtieth time. "Why wouldn't I be?" Then, he'd left, and he did not allow himself to utter any sound of pain even as his arse slammed onto the taxi's back seat. Mathias was not a gentle lover. Or maybe he could be. Alberto did not want him to be.

No, the only problem with Mathias is that he didn't like him, and if things kept happening between them, the more time they'd spend together, the less he'd be impressed with Alberto's unremarkable personality.

No, to get what he wanted, Alberto would have to make use of that part of him he'd always resented: his physical appearance. Finally, he'd get to put his so-called irresistibility to the test. Finally, he'd be able to use it for his own benefit instead of letting others use it for theirs.

Little by little, the other smokers left the garden until Alberto was the only one left under the beam of light cast by the timid moon. Then, a shadow in the shape of Mathias approached. Alberto used the excuse of the cold to justify the incredible shudder that rocked his body, but it had nothing to do with the temperatures outside and everything to do with the way Mathias was looking at him.

"What are you doing here alone in the cold?"

"I'm not alone." Alberto pointed out the small groups of people gathered at different corners of the garden, some doing drugs, some doing each other, who knows? It was dark in the back. "What are you doing here?" He added under his breath, "They'll see us speaking together."

"Give me a cigarette, then. That'll give me an excuse."

"And what's the real purpose of your visit?" Alberto handed over his pack of smokes with a quirked eyebrow.

Mathias helped himself to a cigarette, and Alberto, nervous, took another. He lit up and took a long drag. Mathias stared at his face for a long time, until Alberto lost patience and blew smoke right in his face.

"What?"

Mathias's gaze flickered. "You wanna make out?"

Straight to the point.

Alberto pretended to hesitate, to think it through. "Sure."

Mathias expertly turned on his heel, hands in his pockets, a picture of nonchalance, and he strolled toward the house with Alberto in tow. They passed Joy and her blonde friend, Odile, on the way. Mathias acknowledged them with a nod and a faint smile; Alberto didn't spare them a glance. When Joy began to speak, Alberto pretended he didn't hear her and closed the door in her face.

They opened a door at the back of a summer kitchen and found themselves in a long, narrow pantry with doors to each side. Alberto wasn't sure it was the best place to hide, being so close to a kitchen and having two different points of entry, but at least they could use the excuse of looking for something to drink if they were discovered. There were probably a million better places to hide in this large house, but they didn't know the layout, so they had to make do. Mathias had a crazed look that implied they were out of time to find a better spot anyway.

Indeed, Alberto was quickly spun around and pushed against a cramped worktop, his arms accidentally knocking over a bottle of olive oil, before they were grabbed by Mathias and twisted behind his back. Lips fell upon his neck, warm and soft, and his mouth was claimed the moment he turned his head.

Mathias got very handsy as if after what happened last night, he didn't have to pretend not to desire him anymore. Alberto lost himself to his touch and the intoxicating scent of his skin, fresh and earthy at the same time. His mind raced back to their entanglements of last night, the weight of Mathias on his back, the sound he made when he came inside him. Soon, his whole body was itching from want, and after a bit of enduring in silence, a pitiful sound escaped his lips. Mathias reacted by lifting him up high enough to shove him onto the worktop before sliding his tongue into his mouth, triggering sparks of pleasure like fireworks shooting along his spine.

Alberto knew himself, and he could sense, not without fear, that he was about to lose his mind. One moment of inattention like this could cost them both too much. Before it came to this, he pushed Mathias away.

"Stop, stop."

Mathias obeyed but looked at him through unfocused eyes. "Why?"

"You know why." Smoothing the sleeves of his jacket, Alberto attempted to conceal the tremor in his voice. "You don't know how to make out. You're going straight for the kill."

Mathias dipped his head and snorted into his neck. Alberto shoved him.

"Disgusting."

He had to. What he said was true. It had become such that every time Mathias had taken Alberto's lips, it had ended in orgasm for at least one of them. One week apart, and Mathias was like a wild beast last night. Not that Alberto complained, but right now, they both wanted to do it too much to be careful, and it was too dangerous.

These few days without him had been hell. He would not risk losing this again, especially now that Mathias had proven himself to be just as perverted as Alberto had hoped. If Mathias wanted to stay in a dark, dark closet with him, then Alberto would help him keep that door locked, and he'd also swallow the damned key.

Mathias looked sickly. He was probably drunk. "Come to my place later," he said, his eyes glinting.

Alberto slid down from the worktop with a shake of his head. "Can't. I have work tomorrow."

"Tomorrow is Saturday."

"That's why I have to work tomorrow."

Immediately, Mathias's expression turned morose. He caught Alberto's waist and forced him to face him. "Hey."

Alberto played hard to get. "Stop it. We'll get caught."

Mathias grabbed his chin and bore his eyes into his. "Tell me it's not true."

"What?"

"Just tell me it's not true."

Alberto smirked. "Fine. It's not true."

"Who's Stasia?"

Alberto stopped smirking. "What?"

"There's a girl here, and she says she knows you through a girl called Stasia, that this Stasia's your stepsister and that you two are lovers."

Alberto laughed. He could see his outburst surprised Mathias, who released his chin then his waist.

"That duplicitous bitch," Alberto said.

Mathias frowned. "I gather it's not true, then."

True? Stasia was the last person on Earth Alberto would sleep with, and even if she and he were the last people on Earth, he would still choose death over sleeping with her.

Alberto tugged on the strings of Mathias's hoodie. "She's a girl. I don't do girls."

"Really?"

186

Alberto laughed in his face. "Why would I lie about this?"

Mathias got away from Alberto then abruptly lunged at him and captured his lips again. Amused, Alberto held a finger between them.

"Back off."

Mathias obliged with a grunt, and at that moment, Xavier, followed by Eric, burst into the pantry, freezing them both on the spot.

"Hey, Matt! Do you have a spare fag by any chance?" Noticing Alberto, Xavier laughed stupidly. "I guess you do!" He laughed even louder. "Sorry, man, couldn't resist."

Alberto shook his head. "You're so funny, Xavier. It's a good thing you're rich."

"Aww, thanks! You're funny too, Alberto!"

Xavier, still laughing, didn't mind his retort. Neither did he notice the tension in Alberto's eyes despite his blank expression or Mathias's flushed neck when he gave him a cigarette and dashed out through the other door without a word.

But then, Alberto felt some eyes on him, and he saw Eric was hovering by the door, staring.

"What?" he asked.

Eric shrugged. "What are you doing?"

"I'm going home." Alberto pushed past him, eager to get away from them.

"Wait, what?" Xavier pulled his head out of the fridge. "You can't go, wait!"

Alberto raised his hand in goodbye and left the room before Xavier could catch him. He didn't feel like being squashed to death by that big oaf. Mathias would have been a different affair, but they'd already barely made it out of there. Another second and Xavier and Eric would have discovered them making out.

What would Mathias have done, then? It was probably best not to know. But Alberto could bet his arse that, if discovered, Mathias would never lay his hands on him again.

The house was quiet when he returned. His mother and Dimitri were still out, so Alberto smoked a well-deserved cigarette on the terrace while he still could. The garden stretching at his feet, eerily quiet, somewhat gloomy, filled him with a sense of safety. He loved the peace and—

"Albertino!"

Alberto's heart stopped. He choked on cigarette smoke and went into a fit of coughing.

Stealthy as a cougar, Stasia walked up to him, squeezed him and pinched him the way he hated. He tried to wriggle out of her way, almost dropping his cigarette. She laughed viciously.

"Leave me alone, Stasia."

"I'll tell your mother," she said, pointing at the cigarette.

"I'll tell your father, then."

"Tell him what?" She stole his smoke, inhaled deeply, and sighed in pleasure as she exhaled.

"That you're a bitch," Alberto muttered.

Stasia giggled. "I'll just tell him you're a bigger bitch."

"Okay."

"I'll tell him you tried to force yourself on me."

Alberto's heart stopped again. "What?"

"I'm just kidding, silly."

She pounced on him again. He wrestled her hand away from his buttock.

"Stop."

"Stop what?"

"Stop touching me." He scooted as far away from her as possible. "Imagine if I were doing the same to you."

"Oh, come on. I've always wondered what you were worth in bed."

She gave the cigarette back only when there was nothing left to smoke. Alberto buried the butt into the nearest flower pot with a sigh.

"You'd be disappointed, I think."

"For once, I believe you. You're so dull... Good sex requires creativity, you know." She tried to kiss his cheek, and he barely had time to dodge. "Don't be like that, Albertino, I'm only joking." She cast him a charming smile, one that she'd perfected over the years. "I have a new boyfriend."

Alberto's heart lurched hopefully. "You do?"

"Yes. His name is Ludwig, and he's a German aristocrat. How about that?"

Alberto thought of that girl who knew Stasia — and himself — whom Mathias had met, and he wondered what her name was. "Good, good for you."

"So, I'm not going to need a dog after all," Stasia said.

"Yes… Good for you."

"Your ass is safe for the time being."

He jerked out of her reach. "Stasia…"

"God, you're so easy to bully!" She grabbed his arm and shook him. "Fight back a little!"

Alberto wrenched himself free, knocking his elbow against the balustrade. He winced in pain. "Men don't fight with girls."

"Oh, calling yourself a man now?" Stasia burst out a laugh. "You're not a man. And can I give you a piece of advice, Albertino? Stop mistaking girls for innocent and delicate things. If you're not more careful, they'll fuck you over." Her eyes narrowed. "Ask your mum if she's not a fucking shark. Dug her teeth into my daddy fast enough."

The familiar sound of the opening front gate forced her lips shut. Her precious daddy was returning with Alberto's mother. Stasia made a disappointed noise. Playtime was over.

After making sure he didn't dare open his mouth to defend his mother, which would have made things worse, she flicked Alberto and went off.

Alberto returned to school with a plan. A half-arsed plan, maybe, but he was never really smart, and he wasn't about to become smarter now that Mathias had laid waste to him so nicely. Pretending not to know him when he knew what he could do to him seemed near impossible. Alberto had only two thoughts in his head, and they were, "*When can we do this again?*" and "*Can he do it harder next time?*"

Alberto thought about talking to Mathias all morning, and, at lunch, he became grateful for Eric's relationship with Zak. He just had to pretend to ask a question about some stupid Maths equation while Zak and Eric were huddled together at a table with Mathias looking like a third wheel next to them.

Mathias had started kicking his leg nervously every time Alberto made eye contact with him, and he usually clung tightly to the pockets of his hoodie whenever Alberto got too near. Today was no exception. His knuckles turned white around his pen, and he was struggling to focus on whatever late homework he was doing.

Zak answered Alberto's fake question, then Eric made a face and said something in his ear. They excused themselves and left. Alberto hummed as he drew closer. "Wow. It seems Eric really does hate me."

Mathias stared, and his forehead creased. "What do you want? The cafeteria's full of people."

Alberto gracefully fell onto the chair opposite him, making him jump.

"Don't!"

"What?" Alberto smirked. "People know I never stand if I can help it."

"What do you want?"

"I want to play a game."

Mathias looked to the left and to the right. Then, he swallowed. "What sort of game?"

Alberto smacked his lips. He loved the way Mathias's eyes flew to them and stayed there.

"The lavatories by the library. Last stall on the left. I've left you a message. If you can complete the chorus, I'll give you a treat."

Mathias threw another look over his shoulder before leaning closer. "What sort of treat do I get?"

That was easy.

"Anything you want." He stood up slowly. "No take-backs."

"No take-backs?"

Alberto crossed his arms over his chest. "But only if you get it right."

21

THE GAME

MATHIAS WENT to the suggested men's room on the ground floor immediately after lunch, and after skipping through a series of stupid graffiti, he found it.

There, scribbled in black ink under a bad drawing of a penis and the engraved letters M&M, was the first line of the chorus of "The Ballad of Chasey Lain."

Mathias rubbed his finger over the lyrics, thinking, *Pff, too easy.* Unplugging the marker, briefly enjoying the smell of it, he wondered, with some worry, if the reward would match the task. He wrote back immediately, snickering as he did so, but instead of the name Chasey, he wrote the letters "A.G."

He ran away from the place with a smile, and during the next break, he and Alberto exchanged an imperceptible nod as they passed each other in the corridor. Mathias watched with a certain anticipation as Alberto sucked in his lower lip, and he already fantasized about his treat.

Soon after, he got a text with a place and a time. *Infirmary, five p.m.*

Usually, they met at Mathias's, so he was curious when he went over there after class. At this time, the corridors were packed, but the nurse's office was locked. Just when Mathias was about to send him a rude text, scolding Alberto for wasting his time, the latter opened the door and roughly pulled him inside. Ignoring Mathias's shock, he locked the door behind them.

"You wrote my name?" he asked, leaning against the door. "*My name?*" It seemed he'd found Mathias's answer. "I had to use another marker to cover the initials. Are you crazy?"

Mathias snorted. "Come on, it was fun. Your initials rhyme with Chasey."

Alberto cursed under his breath, but his expression soon relaxed. He flattened his palms against the door, and Mathias felt like pinioning them there and kissing him until his legs turned soft.

"Concerning the lyrics," Alberto said, "you've got your facts wrong."

"How so? Oh, right. You did have my dick last week."

Alberto's eyes narrowed. "But you got the lyrics right. Did you google them?"

"What? No!" Mathias scoffed. "I just have a better memory than you."

"Everyone's memory is better than mine."

"So you admit it."

Alberto didn't answer. Mathias let him off and sat on the edge of the nurse's desk. "So, my treat?"

Leaving his spot against the door, Alberto fished something out of his pocket and dangled it in front of Mathias, who stared at it, perplexed.

"What's this?"

Alberto blinked impatiently. "Guess."

"A key? That's my reward, a goddamn key?"

"That's right."

"Didn't you say 'no take-backs'?" Mathias eyed the key in Alberto's palm with dislike. "What could it open that I haven't gotten into already?"

Alberto's eyebrows shot up. "Wow."

Mathias was pleased. He grabbed the key, feeling its warmth from being nested in Alberto's hand for some time. "So, what is this shit?"

"This shit?" Alberto took the key back and hid it behind his back.

"Come on…"

"This shit is a key to this office. The nurse, Sana, is only here three days a week. The other days, she's not here, but I am."

"Oh…" Understanding dawned on Mathias. "So that's where you disappear to all the time."

"Have you… been looking for me?"

"Don't flatter yourself." Mathias grumbled. "Everyone has noticed your fan club searching the corridors for you, weeping like Italian widows."

"Let them weep." Alberto impassively shook the key before his eyes. "Do you want it or not?"

Mathias opened his hand to receive his reward. Alberto leaned forward dangerously.

"Now, do you want to play doctor?"

"Nope," Mathias said to thwart him, but he was tempted. He gripped Alberto's chin when he tried to kiss him and pushed it away. He loved it when he didn't complain. "How did you get the key?"

"This?" Alberto stepped back. "I come here all the time. Sana's cool; she lets me stay here, and she makes me a note. One day, she left her keys lying around, so I secretly made a copy before I gave them back."

"Why do you lock yourself up in here? Because of the girls?"

"You and your questions…" Alberto let out a bored sigh. "So, your reward?"

"Wasn't this my reward?"

"No. Only giving you a key… What would be in it for me? I gave it to you so you can hide here and do things with me."

"I see…"

Mathias knew what things Alberto was talking about. He thought about all the people going back and forth behind that very door while he could have him pressed up against the nurse's desk.

"So… what do you want?" Alberto perked up. "I could do you."

Mathias flinched, and his hands subconsciously flew to his back. "You stay away from me!"

His reaction was met with a dry laugh. "I was joking. What do you want?"

"I don't know. Can I get anything?"

"Of course. Well, unless it's something that I can't give."

You already gave me everything, Mathias thought despite himself.

He didn't know what he wanted or what to ask for, and he wasn't sure he was brazen enough to actually have sex with Alberto at school, at *this* school, with this fucking headmaster looming around. Yet Alberto was here, staring at him with a provocative expression. *No take-backs*, Mathias kept thinking. *No take-backs.*

"Why are you suddenly so shy?" Alberto asked, teasing.

"I'm thinking."

"You weren't thinking so much the other day." Alberto leaned back against the wall, his arms folded over his chest.

"What, is there a problem?" Mathias watched him with mounting scorn. "If you didn't like it, you could have said something. You didn't say anything."

"But I did. I said something."

Mathias froze. He replayed the scene as fast as he could in his brain, but he didn't remember. Did Alberto really try to stop him?

"You… you did?"

The fear his expression betrayed did not move Alberto. His cold eyes swooped down on Mathias like the wings of a bird of prey.

"I said then the same thing I'd say now if you were to do it again."

Mathias swallowed. "What? What would you say?"

Alberto approached, catlike, dangerous. He leaned into Mathias's space, lips grazing his ear.

"Harder."

Mathias clenched his fist and heard his knuckles pop.

"There's a party at Joy's on Friday night," Mathias said a few minutes later.

Alberto exhaled another sigh as he fastened his pants. "So?"

"So, will you be there or what?"

"You'd need a miracle to see me at one of Joy's parties."

"Why?"

"Joy? Seriously?"

That again. Alberto really seemed to hate every girl in the vicinity. Maybe what Elisa said had some truth to it. Maybe he really was sexist.

"Is it true what my sister says? That you hate women?"

Alberto smirked. "Your sister would say anything because she hates me."

"Why would she hate you?"

"I called her out for being obsessed with Zak."

"My sister isn't obsessed with Zak."

Alberto's smirk deepened. "If she were any more obsessed with Zak, she'd be called Eric."

Mathias held up his hand. "All right. Enough." He'd have to deal later with the problem between these two. Right now, his mind was more agreeably engaged. "About Friday—"

"I'm not going to Joy's party. Thanks."

For once, Mathias was in a good enough mood to go along with his bullshit. "What is it, hm?" He pulled Alberto against him and tried to kiss his nape. "Are we too good for parties?"

Alberto wriggled away impatiently. "Exactly."

"Not even tempted by free beer or pizza?"

His disgusted expression was enough of an answer. Amused, Mathias slid his hands all over him and lowered his voice to a whisper, "What is it? Your body's a temple or something like that?"

Alberto spun around and hooked his arms around his neck. "That's right," he said languidly. "My body's a temple." He brought their lips together, making Mathias forget all about having a conversation. "Mathias…" he whispered. "Care to worship this temple?"

Mathias repressed a shiver. "What do you have in mind?"

Alberto dropped to his knees in front of him. Without a word, he expertly zipped his jeans open. Mathias grabbed his hands to stop him.

"Shit! There are people out there!"

"You better do it fast, then." Alberto freed him, embarrassingly half-hard already, from the confines of his boxers. "Make your offerings, Mathias. I'm *wide* open."

Mathias's cock twitched and grew harder. He frowned at it in disbelief. *Little traitor.* Alberto saw that and glanced up, smirking. This demon would be the death of him.

"You really talk too much."

Mathias didn't wait for an answer; he grabbed a chunk of Alberto's hair and just shoved himself in there. Alberto's eyes welled up, finally showing some life. Gripping Mathias's thighs for support, he laughed around his cock, and Mathias thought:

Chance of finishing the school year unscathed? Program error. Results unavailable at this time.

All week, Alberto had left little tidbits of saucy songs lying around school, and Mathias had finished his lines and went to collect his rewards; sometimes in Sana's office, sometimes directly in the men's room by the library. They'd started by meeting twice a week, and now it was constant, between classes, at lunch times whenever he could escape Eric... Mathias had become so familiar with Alberto's body, he could pinpoint the precise location of his moles and which ones were his favorites. And, yes, they still met at his place in the evenings for their *Spanish homework*, but in truth, behind that locked door, it was a whole different set of skills they were practicing.

And Mathias was discovering things about that dark creature, like how quickly he could fall asleep after an orgasm. Mathias usually let him snooze for a spell before rousing him and sending him on his way. But little by little, he'd let him sleep a bit longer, and then a bit longer, thinking, one day, he wouldn't wake him at all. Rather, he would wait for morning and see for himself what he was made of in the early hours of the day.

The only problem was Elisa. She hated Alberto. She'd come prepared, too, in all her insanity. She wrote reports—including testimonies of his alleged cruel behavior toward members of the opposite sex—and hid notes all over the apartment informing him of all the times he called her paper a rag. She would also corner him outside the bathroom to ask questions like, "Are you still friends with him?" and "What would Eric say?" or "Do you know what he did to Zak?" which made Mathias realize maybe Alberto was telling the truth about her obsession with Eric's boyfriend.

"You're gonna get caught!" Elisa had threatened the night before. "You're gonna get caught, and Eric won't speak to you again!" She'd clung to his leg outside the kitchen. "Mathias, *por favor*, be careful! You've been so much happier since meeting Eric. Do you really want to lose him over Alberto?"

What would happen if she found out what they were actually doing together? Mathias would rather not think about it, but he did agree with her about one thing: they were gonna get caught.

He was frantic at times, running from secret meeting to secret meeting, his blood pounding in his ears. They were gonna get caught like in the movies, the movies he thought he'd watched once but couldn't remember. They'd get caught with their hands in each other's boxers or they'd get caught with his dick inside Alberto's mouth, right when he was about to pop, and then—ah shit, now he was turned on.

Mathias readjusted the bulge in his trousers before he exited the gymnasium's bathroom, and, of course, that dumb dog, Eric, was waiting for him. Since when had he begun calling his best friend a dumb dog? Mathias swallowed the lump in his throat and cast Eric a smile, and they hurried together out on the field for morning practice.

Ninety minutes later, back in the changing rooms, Eric was in a great mood after an excellent session.

"Matt was on fire. C.H., did you see his last save?"

Charles-Henry laughed good-heartedly. "Yes, I was there. Kayvin didn't like being stopped so easily, though."

"Who cares?" Eric gave a light shrug. "Matt, listen, listen. You've been great all week, really good. Did you change your diet or something? If you did, could you tell me what you did so I can copy it? I have to get better to make sure I become a football super-star…" He approached, his face threateningly close to Mathias's. "Matt, buddy, are you with me?"

Mathias startled. "Superstar? Sure, I'm with you."

He'd been too busy recalling the sight of Alberto's limbs all twisted up last night to care about Eric's ramblings.

"What's going on with you?" his friend asked suspiciously.

Mathias's chest tightened painfully. He knew, he *knew* he had to put a stop to this as soon as possible before irreparable damage was done. But not tonight. Absolutely not tonight. And probably not tomorrow, with his father gone for the weekend and his sister at a sleepover...

"So, what?" Eric insisted. "You don't want to tell me?"

"Tell you... what?"

"What's going on with you?" He giggled. "Is it a girl? You'd tell me if you had a girl, right? Right?"

"Why? Why would I tell you?"

"Because we're best friends!" Eric pouted. "I tell you everything about me and Zak, don't I?" He approached him with his arms stretched out, about to hug him.

Mathias shoved him away. "You're telling me too much! I don't even want to hear it!"

Charles-Henry started and gave Eric a pointed look, but Mathias's friend broke into a nervous laugh. "It's not like that, C.H., don't listen to him."

"Why are you asking me that anyway?"

"Because if you didn't make changes in your diet, then something else happened. Something that has made you... better at your job."

Good to know that all his pent-up horniness made him better at springing after a ball. Hurray. Mathias let out a sigh. He wished he could tell Eric about Alberto, but what was the point? It would cause everyone a whole lot of heartache for nothing. But perhaps... perhaps he could tell him about... someone else.

His throat hurting from the effort, Mathias took a chance and spoke up. "Did you ever hook up with someone who was like... driving you crazy and made you feel like... like you wished you'd never... met her?"

"You mean like sending death threats to my mom and leaving period stuff in my mailbox after I broke up with her?" Eric asked.

Mathias's eyebrows shot up. "What the fuck?"

"No?"

"No! Christ… I meant more like… You know you shouldn't bother with her, but you also can't stop… boning her. That it's, like, driving you slowly crazy how much you want to put your hands on her."

"Oh, that! Well—"

"Except…"

"What?"

She's a he, and I fucking hate him. Oh, and so do you.

"Nothing, nothing. You get the gist."

Eric smiled. "Seems like you have a lot on your plate."

Mathias couldn't reply. His jaw suddenly felt wired shut.

"That's okay," Eric said. "You can tell me. I know all sorts of stuff. I mean, just wait until you find out you're in love with another guy out of nowhere!" He broke into a fit of laughing.

Mathias closed his fists on his lap. "That's just dumb."

"It happened to me," Eric said, looking hurt. "Are you saying what happened to me was dumb?"

"I'm not saying anything."

Charles-Henry approached them, already dressed in his usual clothes. "Who is she? She must be tough. I know I wouldn't like to be Mathias's girl."

Mathias gave him a wary look. "Why not?"

Charles-Henry hesitated, but after a quick look at Eric, who nodded, he said, "You look like you want to punch people in the face most of the time. It mustn't be very agreeable for them." He slammed the door of his locker shut. "Even… scary?"

"Pff, I treat my girls really well," Mathias said, adding rather defensively, "You don't know shit."

But he knew this wasn't true. First, what girls? His only ever girlfriend constantly complained about his negligence. As for treating people well, didn't he have Alberto pressed against the wall last night, his fingers buried into his mouth until he cried out?

But it wasn't a cry of pain Alberto let out in the dark, it was something else entirely, the memory of which made Mathias's skin flare with goosebumps. They were fucked up. They were so fucked up.

"Don't worry," Eric said once Charles-Henry had stepped away. "I don't find you that scary, personally." He laid a warm hand on Mathias's shoulder. "I'm sure you'll figure it out with this girl. As long as she knows you're just having fun, and it's nothing serious, you can keep messing around with her. Doesn't mean you have to marry her or anything, but you have to let her know you're not looking for something serious." Eric squeezed his shoulder gently. "So, how was I? Did I help?"

Mathias slapped his hand away with a sigh. "Yeah, thanks."

Forget it. Eric was something that Mathias wasn't. How could he possibly help? And, apparently, C.H. saw him as some sort of asshole who terrorized his girlfriends.

Since his mother left him, he'd never really had anyone to talk to. Mathias once again bore the brunt of her loss. He wondered what was the most fucked-up thing about all this: the fact that he absolutely couldn't resist putting his hands on Alberto or the fact that that cold-blooded monster was the only one he felt relatively close to.

Long after Eric had abandoned him to catch Zak before his next class, Mathias remained on his bench, thinking of what he should do next. Just then, the door to the changing rooms opened, forcing him out of his thoughts.

"I'm almost done," he said.

"Are you?"

Recognizing that voice, Mathias leapt from his seat.

22

HORNETS

ALBERTO WATCHED as Mathias stood between the goalposts in the Colette colours, originally white and blue. The foul weather had turned grass to muck, and his uniform was splattered with mud. Like a boxer, he was dancing on his feet, and he squared his shoulders when he spotted Kayvin fast approaching him with the ball, Eric on his tail. Kayvin took the shot with skill, with confidence. There was a loud thump as it connected with Mathias's gloves. Right there, on his knees, he looked magnificent. He rose up, lifted the ball in salute, and Kayvin turned away, his face dark. Eric joined Mathias, and he broke into a silly dance. To Alberto's surprise, Mathias playfully clapped in rhythm, joining in his dance then his laughter.

Alberto exhaled a large cloud of smoke as he watched the scene, concealed behind the gymnasium's billboard by the entrance gate. Mathias looked so happy whenever Alberto wasn't around. How wonderful. How sickening, too. Alberto wished he could tear his gaze away, but there was nothing he could do. Mathias was too handsome. Mathias was too sexy. *Mathias knew how to fuck.* In short, Mathias was everything.

To be fair, Alberto assumed his opinion was subjective. After all, a different person — a healthier person, maybe — might not have appreciated rough hands upon their skin. Alberto was the sort that liked to be tossed around and devoured like prey. Not that he knew that for sure before, but, nowadays, he couldn't deny how consumed he was by desire every time Mathias put his hands on him. The harder the grip, the better the outcome, and that boy just went for it. He wasn't shy, and, thank goodness, he wasn't wary either. If the first time, he had annoyingly pulled out at the first sign of tears, he had been spectacular ever since that small matter had been resolved.

Alberto would have never thought sex could feel so good, but before he met Mathias, he hadn't really associated anything with the words good, or brilliant, or *ohgodfuckyes*.

"What do you know..." he murmured to himself.

"What was that?"

Alberto froze, and he turned to see Charles-Something in his football uniform, staring at him all wide-eyed. Caught in the act of spying on Mathias like a fangirl, Alberto was so mortified, he crushed the cigarette he was holding in his fist and only dumped it when he felt it burn into his skin.

Charles-Something readjusted his bag over his shoulder with a smile. "I'm late this morning. Did you..." He hesitated. "Want me to let you in so you can watch?"

Alberto blinked. "I wasn't watching."

"What were you doing, then?"

"Smoking."

Charles-Something looked down at the crumpled cigarette at his feet. "Okay."

A shiver ran down Alberto's spine. If this guy spoke to Mathias, he would absolutely get ditched. There was already the matter of his sister, who happened to be that little witch from the paper, and now this. Alberto should never have used this unexpected free period — their teacher was sick — to come ogle at Mathias.

If people knew about them... If people knew, then there would be nothing to know, since Mathias would break off Alberto's carefully woven leash and disappear forever.

"So..." Alberto said, hating himself for not remembering Charles's full name. "How are you?"

"I'm good, thanks." The corners of his mouth turned down. "I'm not with Nadia anymore."

Who was Nadia again? He had no idea. Alberto nodded — for show.

"But anyway…" Charles hesitated. "Are you sure you don't want to come in? It looked like you were waiting for something."

Alberto shook his head. Charles pushed past the gate before stopping and turning around, his expression twisted. "Just… don't let Kayvin see you. He doesn't like you very much."

"Why?"

"You know…" He looked embarrassed. "Just don't let him see you, okay?"

That was weird. Alberto had spent two and a half weeks in close quarters with Kayvin last summer, even sharing the same bedroom, and they never had a problem before. But since he knew him to have a vicious streak, he was grateful for the heads-up.

"Thank you," he said.

"See you around tomorrow night, then?"

Confused, Alberto didn't reply, and Charles briefly waved before disappearing into the building. Staring at the closed door, Alberto exhaled a long breath. He had been busted, but at least he'd managed to catch a glimpse of Mathias covered in grime. He dragged his feet back toward the gate, his mind lost in thought, his brow furrowed.

"Charles-Henry!" he suddenly blurted out.

Charles-Henry. That was his name. Because he'd been so nice, Alberto would try his best to remember this time. He paused in front of the gate, knowing nothing interesting would be waiting for him at Colette except a nap in Sana's office.

A nap was nice.

A nap was always nice.

But Mathias was better.

He turned on his heel and retraced his steps toward the building.

Alberto hid in a corner, a skill he wished he'd never had to learn, but now that he could put it to good use, he admitted to being grateful for it after all. When practice was over, he fought against a series of yawns, almost regretting not taking a nap in Sana's office, until he had made sure every member of the team had left the changing rooms, including the annoying Eric. From the way that fool ran over Charles-Henry and Xavier to get out of the building, he had found out that Zak had a free period and was waiting back at Colette.

Mathias looked dumbfounded when Alberto showed up on his turf. Alberto was surprised about himself, too, but he didn't show it.

"So, this is where the magic happens?"

"What the fuck are you doing here?"

Alberto gave him a quick once-over. "You look clean," he noted with disappointment.

"You shouldn't be here!"

Mathias grabbed his wrist and dragged him roughly toward the showers, away from the door.

"You're insane. Someone could have seen you."

Alberto put his index finger on his chin. "Mm, no. I made sure I counted everybody."

"You could have missed one. You don't know shit about football. How many players are on the team?"

"With or without substitutes?"

Mathias froze. "What?"

Alberto shrugged. "There are twenty-two players on the Colette team. Eleven good ones, eleven seat-fillers."

Mathias huffed angrily, but on his face was the same expression that usually ended with Alberto on all fours. Perhaps the danger of being found here was also too tempting.

And, as predicted, not a minute later, Alberto stood with one cheek pressed against the shower tiles with his hands all over him.

When it was done, Mathias stared in awe at the proof of their shame, and Alberto couldn't help laughing. He felt dizzy, both from his position and from his own release, but also from having gotten away with it without angering him. He took Mathias's towel to wipe himself off as well as the wall, and he tossed it back to him.

"At least I didn't leave any evidence," Mathias muttered, dropping the towel into his open duffle bag with a grimace.

"*I* got rid of the evidence, you mean."

That small retort earned him a sudden, hungry kiss, a kiss Alberto hoped allowed Mathias to taste himself on him.

"Fucking's fine," Mathias whispered, releasing his lips.

"What?"

"Us. Fucking. It's fine, right?" He gave him a searching look. "Until it gets boring."

Alberto's heart thumped. "I guess? Yeah… Whatever."

Mathias smacked their lips together again.

Still lightheaded from his orgasm, Alberto let him do as he pleased, even allowing him to grope him shamelessly. He looked up; his gaze found the neon lights overhead, casting their hideous light and buzzing like hornets. Alberto started to feel uncomfortable; he sucked in a breath. When Mathias was done gnawing at his lips, he proceeded to rain soft kisses down Alberto's neck and along his jawline. Alberto's shoulders tensed. With each kiss, the walls seemed to be shifting closer and closer. Sudden nausea filled the back of his throat, and he suddenly jerked his head, knocking the back of his skull against the shower tiles in the process.

Alberto felt Mathias's hand slip around his neck to cup his head. "Are you okay?"

Once the ants in his vision had cleared, Alberto stared at him in silence. Then, he wriggled out of his grip and started for the exit. Mathias followed him, clicking his tongue impatiently.

"No, by all means, smash your head against the tiles. Why do I care?"

Alberto waited for a second or two, then he turned to face him.

"Don't be boring already."

Mathias stopped in his tracks, surprise plain on his face. "What…?"

But Alberto was already out the door, knowing Mathias couldn't follow him out.

Coming here was a stupid thing to do. It had felt good, though, at first. He'd loved how his own cries of pleasure echoed off the walls and only seemed to egg Mathias on. He tried to remember how that felt, but it was too late. All that was left now was that horrid taste in his mouth and a burgeoning headache that he knew wouldn't get better. He knew himself and his limits. He had no choice but to go home.

The truth was… his body *was* a temple; his body was a prison from which there was no escape.

Alberto woke slowly the next morning. Daylight filtered through his drawn curtains and fell into patches here and there, and he wondered vaguely how long he'd slept. He took his time stretching while trying to get his thoughts together, and then he heard the voice by his ear.

"Wakey wakey, sleepyhead."

Alberto's blood turned to ice in his veins.

She was in his bed again.

With a groan, he scooted as far away from her as possible before turning over. Stasia was sitting under the covers, fully dressed, looking perfect. She always looked immaculate despite being a monster.

"Why aren't you at school?" she asked her manicure.

Alberto was wondering the same. "My alarm… My phone…"

"Yeah, I turned that off for you hours ago. It's twelve-thirty already." Stasia nudged him with her foot. "Last day of school before the Christmas break, and you spend it in bed?"

A feeling of helplessness spread throughout him. Alberto turned his back to her so he wouldn't say something bad.

"Where… where's Mum? Why didn't she wake me?"

"You seem to have forgotten she went away with my daddy; she won't be back before tonight." She giggled and added, "Funny how you cannot function without Mommy to drag you out of bed. Just like she can't function without my daddy doing the same for her. You're both complete wastes of space."

Leave Mamma alone, Alberto thought with anger. She had always shown nothing but kindness to her.

"Get out of my bed, Stasia."

"Let me think about it." There was a pause. "No."

She reached out to ruffle his hair. He tried to swat her, but she gripped a few strands and yanked mercilessly.

"Stop it." He sat against his headboard and held his head between his hands. "Please."

She only scooted closer. "Albertino, come on. Let's get it over with! The tension's unbearable, so let's just do it, all right?"

Stasia often spoke like this. Alberto knew she didn't really want to sleep with him, she just played around with the fact he was repulsed by her and usually recoiled in horror every time she approached him. This time, he snorted and turned over to admire her dumbfounded expression.

"That tension between us…" he said, "… it's not sexual, I promise you."

"It is, a little bit. Call it the thrill of the chase." Leaning over, she tried to kiss his cheek, but he jerked away.

Alberto thought of Mathias and the game they shared all week, of that Bloodhound Gang song he hadn't had time to play with yet. His courage — or his stupidity — rose, and before he could stop himself, he was quoting, his face set, "I hope you die."

It didn't take long. Stasia moved like lightning and landed a sharp slap on his face, one of her ugly rings smacking against his ear. Alberto almost passed out, his vision filling with black spots. Gritting his teeth, he slid down the headboard, buried his head in his pillow, and waited for the explosion of pain in his head to settle.

Stasia usually aimed for the back of his head because his pale skin marked ridiculously quickly, but in her anger, she'd fucked up, judging by the worried look she gave him as he clutched his burning cheek.

"You okay?"

He forced himself to sit up, his head still swimming. "Like you care."

"Of course I do, Albertino." She jumped on top of him and clawed at his wrist. "If you were nicer to me, I'd be nicer to you. Never occurred to you?"

Whatever. He'd tried everything, even knelt once, but she'd never stopped. He wasn't about to believe her this time.

Stasia pulled his hand away from his face. "Oh, fuck. Damn it."

Worried enough to stand the sight of her sitting on top of him, Alberto immediately stopped struggling. "How bad is it?"

"I don't know. A part of me thinks you look better now. Put a bit of color in your cheek, you know?"

She rolled aside, and he forced himself up to look in the mirror, his ear ringing unpleasantly. Stasia followed him and watched his reflection in the mirror. As expected, the whole left side of his face was glaringly red.

"I have a shoot on Monday, you evil skank."

She jammed her foot in his calf, ripping a curse from his lips.

"Don't look at me like that, Albertino. You deserved it. And what did you just call me? Do you wanna try that again, see what happens?"

Alberto was tempted, but in the end, he didn't.

"What *is* wrong with you?" he asked instead through clenched teeth.

She laughed, a vicious burst of glee he loathed so much he had come to flinch every time he heard girls shriek in laughter.

"Me? *Me?* Nothing. I'm just playing around with you. *You,* you're evil. I mean, really? Wishing for my death? Makes you sound like a total psycho, but, again, why am I surprised? You know what they say: like father, like son."

Alberto clung to the mirror, his eyes closed. "Which one of your parents is responsible for what you are?"

"Watch it or I'll do the other cheek."

But when Alberto turned around, the sight of him had Stasia spit in anger.

"Fuck you, Albertino. Now I have to go downstairs and get you some ice. You really like to get on my nerves."

Alberto stepped away from her. "Can you at least remove your rings next time?"

"No promises." She pointed her finger at his face. "And don't you dare get me in trouble. I'm going to Cuba with Ludwig tonight."

Downstairs, the bell rang, startling them both. Stasia wrenched her head toward the window, her blonde hair slashing through the air.

"Who the fuck is that? Are you expecting somebody?"

Alberto shook his head. A weird tremor rang through him, like maybe, *just maybe*, the gods were real. Maybe they heard his prayer when the pain flared across his cheek, and he had wished somebody, anybody, would come and get her and send her back to Hell where she came from.

Stasia squinted suspiciously at him. "Must be my delivery... I wasn't expecting it till tonight."

She left him alone in the middle of the bedroom, the bedsheets a mess, the curtains still drawn. Alberto flew to the window first and almost tore them open. None of what had just happened filled him with as much dread as what he was feeling now, watching the figure of Mathias following Stasia across the lawn.

Mathias, who was alone with Stasia. Mathias, who was coming to see him right now, and Alberto, whose red face looked like he'd just been slapped and was not fit to be seen. He didn't need to imagine how his hook-up would feel about touching him when he'd found out Alberto was getting pushed around by a girl.

Could he hide? Was there a point? What was she telling him as they were walking toward the house? Did he even stand a chance?

Alberto usually couldn't think fast at all, but Stasia's slap must have displaced his brain because he found himself surprisingly alert. He thought of throwing himself into bed and pretending he'd slept on his inflamed side, but he decided on something else.

Running into his bathroom, he opened the tub's two giant faucets with trembling hands. Water gushed out with great speed, quickly filling the air with steam. Alberto returned to his room, quickly tossed the comforter back into place to give the illusion of having made his bed, and let out a gasp when he saw Stasia had left her keys behind. He didn't hesitate. Finding the key to his bedroom on the ring, he pulled it out and flung it under the bed.

Alberto raced back to the bathroom and, quickly removing his clothes, he turned off the faucets and jumped into the tub. His mouth twisting from the pain, he submerged his entire body into the scalding water. When he emerged in a great splash, he heard Stasia's voice as she led Mathias into the bedroom. He pricked up his ears, a lump stuck in his throat.

"I don't know where he is. Doing weird things, as usual."

Of course she'd try to convince his guest that he was a weirdo.

Come to think of it, he *was* a weirdo. Stasia was dangerous even when she was just stating facts. *Please don't let her blab on*, he prayed, his blood thrumming in his ears. *Please, please, go away Stasia. If you go away, I'll let you bully me without complaint next time.* He hoped she could hear it.

Perhaps she did. She entered the bathroom, and, seeing him there with his flushed skin screaming in pain, she smirked, and that smirk also meant: if you want me to behave, then *you* better behave. Alberto held his breath.

"He's in here," she cooed.

Mathias gave her a weird look as she showed him inside. He was probably thinking "What sort of person invites a guest to a fucking bathroom when his pal is taking a bath? For fuck's sake, another goddamn freak!" and Alberto almost wept from relief at seeing his familiar pissed-off expression.

"I'll wait for you outside," Mathias said with a disgusted expression. He turned around, only stopping to glare at Stasia. "You're gonna stand here?"

She was tempted to say yes, obviously, and taking her eyes off Alberto's body in the tub, she whirled around, flashing him a charming smile.

"Where did you two meet again? I've known Alberto for years, and he's never brought anyone home."

"I've brought myself. And I told you, we're in the same class."

"Literary, huh? *Hablas español?* Dutch maybe? *Italiano?* I speak five languages."

Alberto slid deeper into the tub with a sigh. Mathias cast Stasia a frosty look and didn't reply. She looked a tad vexed, but Alberto felt he could read Mathias at times, and right now, he wore an expression that screamed *"Bitch, congrats for being annoying in five fucking languages! I don't have time for you, you creep me out, watching your stepbrother take a bath, what the hell, so how about you fuck off nicely before I deck you straight into your bad nose job?"*

Or maybe Alberto was just reading too much into it. Either way, Mathias was here. Alberto felt himself begin to relax. He thought warmly of his bed and his plush pillows and wondered if, in a perfect world, he could lock Stasia in her studio forever, then have a nice little nap with Mathias, and maybe start living like a normal person.

When he opened his eyes, Mathias was standing over the tub, so he slowly emerged, the skin on his whole body now a bright, angry red.

"What the hell are you doing?" Mathias asked softly.

"Taking a bath," Alberto said in the same tone.

"Yeah, I can see that," he mumbled, his brows knitting. "But why is the water so hot? You look like you've been whipped or something."

"Have you ever seen anyone get whipped?"

"Fine, I haven't. Just get out of the water, okay?"

Alberto did not move. He extended his hand to touch Mathias's chin and took on his sexy voice. "What are you doing here?"

"I… ahem… I wanted to…" His expression shut down. "Doesn't even matter."

Alberto withdrew his hand. "And how did you get my address?"

"What's going on here?" Mathias cast him an outraged look. "There's a seriously weird vibe around here."

Alberto forced himself to shrug and pretend as if nothing were amiss. "Nothing. I fell asleep, my phone died while I slept, and I forgot to go to school."

"You forgot to go to school," Mathias said, disbelief plain on his face.

"Yes." It was not even untrue. Alberto was already slower than most in the morning, and waking up to find Stasia alone with him had removed all other preoccupations from his mind. "Hang on." He got up, splashing water everywhere.

"Watch it!"

Mathias whirled around abruptly, possibly afraid of finding himself face-to-face with Alberto's naked body. He grabbed a plush towel and tossed it at his face. Alberto tucked himself in it and struggled out of the bath. With a quick glance over his shoulder, he checked the door to the bathroom was closed before he wrapped his arms around Mathias.

"Are you fucking kidding me?" he barked. "You're wet!" But he didn't move either.

Alberto pressed his body into his back and heaved a sigh against his nape. He wanted to ask again why he came here, but Mathias spoke first.

"Why do you sleep so much?" He sounded angry. "You have cancer or something?"

Alberto chuckled against Mathias's skin, cooler than his own after the scalding bath. "Would I look this good if I had cancer?"

"You don't look *that* good."

Alberto didn't know what to say to that. He usually abhorred comments about his appearance, but now that Mathias didn't find him handsome, he found himself annoyed. He released Mathias and left the bathroom in silence.

Back in his room, he unwrapped the towel and let it fall softly to the floor before getting dressed in the outfit laid out for him. In the reflection of the mirror, he saw Mathias was watching, his expression sulky as usual, somewhat unreadable.

"Why did you come, Mathias?" Alberto adjusted his collar, his sleeves, and his hair in the mirror, being careful of looking elegant so that Mathias would find him attractive again. His face was the same shade as ripe tomatoes. He hated himself so much right now, he could slap himself. *Or maybe not.*

Then, Mathias took something out of his pocket. "Where did you get this?"

Alberto stared at Eric's tennis ball in silence.

23

THE VISIT

HE SHOULD HAVE BEEN NICER yesterday. He kept thinking about it. He was upset that Alberto acted as weird as he did every time they got each other off. One minute, he's all doughy between his hands, nice and soft, and the other, he's cracking his fucking skull against the tiles because Mathias dares to kiss him.

Fucking weirdo! He hated him so much!

But also…

Mathias should have been nicer.

And so, he kept thinking about it. He wished he was a nicer guy in general. A guy with a nice attitude, a nice partner, a nice cushy life, a not-so-dead mother, a dad who didn't drink so much and who remembers how to laugh again. But that's now how things worked. His mom was dead. So was every assumption he had about love. That, and the fact that grieving somehow made you crave dicks. And not just the penis type, but also the real 190 cm Italian dickhead type. The one who won't leave your head no matter how many times you hit a punching bag after school.

Joy tugged at his sleeve, pulling him into her conversation. "You're coming, right? You're coming to my party tonight?"

"Yeah, yeah." Mathias lightly shook his sleeve, but she only clung to him more, invoking the cold.

She was always around, her and her friend, Melissa. They

weren't in Mathias and Eric's class, but they were friends of Elodie, who hadn't been around in a while. They weren't bad girls, but they were a bit clingy and chatty, and Mathias usually tuned them out.

"Is Alberto coming?" Xavier asked out of nowhere.

Melissa, hearing this, pursed her lips and walked off. Joy released Mathias's sleeve and went after her, but not before she glared at Xavier.

"Can't stop him from coming," she said, "on account that he's gorgeous, but I didn't bother inviting him. He's such a wanker."

Zak, wrapped like a burrito in Eric's sweater and nestled into his arms, gave her a haughty look. "It's unlikely he'll come. He hasn't shown up for class yesterday or today."

Mathias closed his fist on his empty packet of cigarettes, crumpling it. He wanted to ask, but Xavier mercifully did it first.

"Is he sick, then?"

"I guess." Zak seemed hesitant to speak up, probably because Eric was around. "I heard him tell Mrs Paquin he's often sick."

Xavier spotted Kayvin glaring at him in the distance and grabbed his backpack. "I'll text him and offer to pick him up in my brother's Porsche. I'm sure he won't say no this time."

Mathias scoffed inwardly. Even if Alberto wasn't sick, he would say no. He didn't care about cars, about parties, about Xavier. The fact that Alberto was interested in Mathias's dick was already extraordinary enough.

Christ, he really should have been nicer yesterday. He should have. Why did he have to bring up the "fucking's fine" line, huh? Why was he so worried Ella would snitch on him? She wasn't going to tell the whole school. She'd never do that to him. Plus, she had no idea how close they actually were. As far as she knew, they were only homework buddies who shared a passion for vulgar songs.

He should have just told him to come over this weekend, but he chickened out, worried Alberto would laugh in his face. Mathias imagined his free time was mostly spent hanging out with his supermodel mates, all these other richer, smarter guys. His other lovers. He and Alberto, they already had Tuesdays and Thursdays, and now the infirmary and the funny rewards. Why would Alberto agree to see him on the weekends? But why not? Mathias was getting better and better at taking him apart, and Alberto was constantly begging for his dick. Maybe he'd love to spend the weekend with him. Maybe he wanted nothing more.

So, what happened since yesterday? Was he okay? Maybe he caught a cold from standing bare arse in the showers for too long. Maybe Mathias was too rough with him. Maybe he was simply heartbroken because Mathias had not invited him over this weekend. Ha! Imagine that for a sec.

"Elodie doesn't hang out with us anymore," Eric said in a sad tone, interrupting his thoughts.

"No," Zak replied with a small shrug, like he didn't think it was all that bad.

Mathias didn't mind Elodie. She was pretty chill, and she usually kept Joy in check. He wished she'd spend more time with them, in fact. He could use a normal, reasonable friend. A nice girl, not an eccentric bisexual or a supernatural freak.

"That's because she still fancies you," Mathias said after a short hesitation.

"She does?" Eric seemed surprised.

"Yeah."

Eric rested his chin on Zak's shoulder, a worried look on his face. "Do you think I did her a dirty?"

"You didn't, but she's smart enough to know to keep her distance from now on."

Zak nodded thoughtfully. "Maybe she should date someone else. That should help her move on, forget all about him. What about you, Mathias?"

Funny how amazingly fast that conversation took an unpleasant turn. Thanks, Zak!

"Me?" Mathias pulled a face. "Why me?"

"I don't know... You're good looking."

Eric narrowed his eyes. "Okay, you watch it."

"*You* watch it!" Zak's eyebrows drew together. "I'm just saying he's good looking."

"Not you, baby. I was talking to Matt."

These two idiots broke into a laugh that ended in another drawn-out kiss.

"Thank you," Mathias grumbled when they finally parted. "But no. I'm not interested."

"Why? You don't like her or—"

Eric cut in, "Are you saying my boy ain't cute?"

Mathias threw his empty pack of cigarettes at him. "Shut up, you psychopath."

While Eric wailed on and on about Mathias's cruelty, Zak ignored him and waited for Mathias to answer his question.

"I like her," Mathias said, "I mean, she's nice, but… I'm just not interested at the moment."

"Okay." Zak granted him a sweet smile. "I apologise for being presumptuous just now."

Mathias snorted, amused. "Okay, Mister Big Words, I forgive you."

If he talked weird like Zak, he would have said his tastes lie elsewhere. Definitely elsewhere, he reflected, thinking of a certain pair of lips.

When the bell rang, Zak and Eric parted reluctantly. Eric only stopped complaining about his terrible loss when he realized he could torment Mathias on their way to class instead.

"Matt."

"…"

"Matt, Mattou, Mathias… Matt!"

"*WHAT?*"

Eric rubbed the back of his head thoughtfully. "Is the reason you're not interested in dating related to what you said yesterday?"

"What are you talking about?"

"You said you met this girl who's driving you crazy."

Mathias was surprised he actually recalled. "I don't know. Maybe."

"Matt, are you saying you're in love?"

Mathias stopped in his tracks and shook his head hard enough to tear it from his spine. "No! I just have sex a lot."

Also stopping in the middle of the corridor, Eric observed his face then burst into a laugh. "Oh, so you're not in love, but you have a lot of sex. And… And I'm in love, but I don't have sex at all. Haha! Hahaha!" Eric's laughter gradually turned to sobs. "Haaa…"

Mathias looked around helplessly. "Christ…"

"Oh, don't mind me." Eric wiped his nose on his scarf. "I must be paying for mistakes made in my past life!"

Was there anyone in his life who wasn't a complete weirdo? Mathias wondered, stomping into the classroom. Clearly, Eric couldn't understand him. He had his own problems to contend with. At times, he looked so on edge, Mathias was kind of afraid he would ask for his assistance, you know, in that tone of his, "Heyyy best buddy, can you help me? Between friends!" or some shit like that.

Muttering under his breath, Mathias dropped his backpack onto his table, but Eric stopped him before he could sit down.

"So, that girl, what about her?" he asked, sniffling. "Do you really like her?"

The cold and his parting kiss with Zak had turned his cheeks bright pink, and the blue of his eyes stood out even more, highlighting the goodness of his soul.

"Nobody likes her," Mathias admitted reluctantly. "She's not a good person, I think."

"Oh. Is she Kayvin?"

"What? No!"

"Then you're golden!"

How was he supposed to talk to this motherfucker, really? Mathias gave up and took his seat. Eric sat in the next one and immediately leaned into his space.

"Does she like you?"

"I don't know, and I'm not sure I care, okay?" He just wanted to have sex with Alberto all the time. They didn't have to like each other for that, right? He took a deep breath. "… I don't know."

"Alright." Eric rested his chin in his hand. "I'm just saying, if you want to know if someone likes you, it's easy."

Mathias straightened up, his whole body standing to attention. Maybe Eric wasn't so useless after all. "How—" He lightly coughed in his fist. "How easy?"

Eric smugly leaned back in his chair. "You go see them unannounced. Their reaction will tell you everything you need to know. For example, when Zak participated in Van Bergen's kiddie race to see me, I did the only sensible thing—his words, not mine—and immediately kissed him! It was awesome. Wish you'd seen it."

Mathias tried not to roll his eyes. "I really feel like I was there, considering how many times you've told me that story."

"What can I say?" Eric asked, grinning. "I'm a grand gesture kinda guy."

Mathias had thought about it quite a lot already. Where did Alberto live? He never told him. He never even told Zak when they were dating, and God knows how close they were since Alberto never let anything out. Xavier seemed to know, which was surprising, for sure, but Mathias couldn't ask. He thought of what Xavier's cousin, Gwen, said at the party, that he lived in Boulogne. The horror on Schuman, near the football stadium, she'd said. Funny, for a guy who hated football, to be living by the Parc-des-Princes.

Mathias left school at lunchtime and hopped on the metro. He'd miss his afternoon class, but so what? When he had something in mind, he never really cared about the consequences. And right now, he really needed to make sure Alberto was fine, that his bare ass didn't catch a cold, and that he didn't find Mathias boring after all. So, no, there was no stopping him.

To Eric, he said, "Cover for me," and his friend shouted back, "What does that mean?" Mathias left it at that; he would be fine.

On the quiet, leafy, and definitely opulent Schuman Avenue, Mathias checked the name on every mailbox. An old lady walking her dog gave him a dark look, and he couldn't help lowering his eyes. She wasn't alone in thinking he didn't belong.

Eventually, he found it, a familiar name etched on a gleaming silver plate.

Ribakov - Gazza.

No surprise here, Alberto did live in a fucking mansion. The street was full of them. A high gate and a wall of trees hid the place from view, but by standing on the other side of the sidewalk, one could still catch a glimpse of some brightly colored monstrosity beyond.

Mathias pressed the button after a steadying breath, expecting some serving girl or even a dressed-up butler to open the door, but it was just some twenty-something girl who was gazing at him impatiently.

"What? What is it?"

He assumed she was the stepsister Gwen had mentioned, and a muscle twitched in his jaw. "I'm here to see Alberto."

The girl did a double-take, peering at him through washed-out blue eyes. "Who are you?"

"I'm his friend… from class."

"A…" She threw a look over her shoulder. "A friend, you said?"

Mathias nodded. It's not like he could just tell Alberto's stepsister, "I'm the guy who fucks him on Tuesdays and Thursdays. Who the fuck are you?"

Her face then split into a bright smile. "Oh, come on in! I'm so sorry. I thought you were the delivery guy." She opened the gate to let him in.

"That's alright," Mathias said, burying his hands in his pockets.

The girl had long bleached-blonde hair that looked expensive to maintain. She kept pushing a delicate strand behind her ear, revealing a perfect manicure.

"My name is Stasia," she said, with another charming smile. "Welcome to my house. And you are?"

If the other time he hadn't paid too much attention to her name when Gwen mentioned it, now it hit him. Stasia. Short for Anastasia. Alberto's safe word, the one they hadn't used yet. How weird was that…?

"Alex," Mathias said without thinking.

He didn't know why he lied. Perhaps due to his instinct, perhaps he was just nervous. He tried his best not to get intimidated by the model lawn, the giant pool, the perfect disposition of the plants in the garden, and the polished path that led to the house that looked more imposing as he got closer. It screamed of money like Xavier's, but in a more austere style, leaving him feeling a bit unsettled.

Mathias preferred to fix his attention on Stasia. She was dressed in clothes that probably cost his family's monthly rent, if not more. Her cheeks were flushed, perhaps from running to the gate, but the look in her eye was cool and confident.

Fine, she was rich, and Alberto thought of her name during sex. It really was strange, but, again, he was a fucking weirdo. But Mathias couldn't help thinking… she was a bit plain. Gwen must have been out of her mind. There was no way Alberto was doing this girl, no matter how fucked up he was. Plus, she didn't have a dick. Alberto really liked dicks. He had said and demonstrated it to Mathias enough times that he had learned to take that seriously.

The house was cold inside. By that, Mathias meant the furniture, the art, the general style… Everything was sparse and weirdly twisted, giving the house a chilly, empty feeling. A great marble staircase led to the rooms upstairs. As she led him up the stairs, Stasia talked and asked a lot of questions. A lot. Where was Mathias from, how did he meet Alberto? How well did he know him?

He's a weirdo, isn't he?

Yeah, Mathias said, non-committal.

You have no idea, she giggled.

Eager to see Alberto, Mathias asked *Where is everyone*, and she said, *Everyone? It's just us today*, and Mathias tuned her out.

He couldn't help wondering why Alberto would keep this place a secret. Sure, the house was kind of ugly, but it was still a mansion, and they had a giant pool! Even if the art on the walls was sort of creepy, there was nothing to be ashamed of, nothing that said *This is fucked up, let's never talk again*.

Mathias decided Alberto didn't like people knowing how much money he had, perhaps to avoid even more fangirls. Xavier could use his money and his baronet title to get the girls Alberto didn't want. The thought amused Mathias, and he almost sniggered in front of the girl. She didn't notice, and, still talking, she finally led him into a brightly lit room.

That's when things got weird.

Really, Mathias knew Alberto to be freakish, but this, this was something else entirely. Stasia entered what seemed to be Alberto's bedroom—and what a bedroom—and she straight up walked to the other side of the room, leaning against a doorway. "He's in here."

Mathias didn't know what he expected, but not that. When he approached, Stasia pushed him inside a large bathroom, and there, in the middle, Alberto was lying in some massive claw foot bathtub, completely naked. Submerged as he was in steaming water, his ice-cold grey eyes peering out of his flushed face really looked like a demon's.

Alberto didn't seem happy to see him, and Mathias felt like blaming the girl for that. *What kind of crazy weirdo would take a guest straight to the bathroom when the person they wanted to see was bathing? What was her fucking problem?*

"I'll wait for you outside," Mathias said, irritated. He started for the bedroom then stopped when he noticed she wasn't following. "You're gonna stand here?"

Stasia ignored his question and looked between the two of them. "Where did you two meet again? I've known Alberto for years, and he's never brought anyone home."

Mathias wondered why... His fists shook in his pockets. He gave her the same bullshit lie about being classmates, and the girl started blabbering on about her skills.

"I speak five languages," she boasted.

Mathias was tempted to ask her in which fucking language he would have to speak to get her to step out of Alberto's bathroom. And speaking of, that quiet Alberto sitting in the bath, looking like a plucked chicken, was really starting to freak him out, like he'd interrupted something between the two.

That's it. That's what it felt like. The whole vibe in this house was fucking weird.

Perhaps Gwen wasn't so wrong after all. Why else would this annoying girl be watching her stepbrother take a bath? Why else? He couldn't think of another explanation. Every bit and rumor he'd ever heard about Alberto started bouncing around in his head, and sickness rose up his throat. Oblivious to his internal struggle,

Alberto slowly slid under the water. Without any foam to preserve his modesty, Mathias could see his cock from here, and so could she. And she was smiling, as if this were perfectly normal.

Mercifully, she followed him into the bedroom when he stepped out, his heart pounding. He pretended to need a glass of water, and, though she hesitated, she left the room to get him a drink, and he slammed the door behind her.

Mathias was already halfway back to the bathroom to ask Alberto what the hell was going on when something caught his eye on the shelf before him.

24

TRUTH OR DARE

THEY WERE all staring at him as he stepped into the living room, perhaps because he'd invited himself to a party for the first time, and showed up in a designer suit. Perhaps because Joy couldn't believe he was treading on her parents' rug after twenty previous turned-down invitations. Or, perhaps because, despite Dina's best efforts — one bag of frozen peas and two bottles of Aloe Vera — his face still looked a bit too inflamed for his liking.

Alberto waited in silence for Joy's guests to finish staring and return to their drinks and their conversations. Joy, of course, didn't. Joy clung to him like glue, her socked feet gliding across her hardwood floors. She was beaming as she gave him the tour, stopping at her — unsurprisingly — tacky bedroom. And Alberto knew tacky; he lived in the ugliest house in Boulogne.

"I never thought I'd see you here," she said, her eyes glossy. She brushed her finger against the lapel of his jacket. "You dress really well, you know that?"

"I do, thank you."

Her expression crumpled. She didn't like his answer.

What could he say? He had never not been a model. Even as a kid, his mother always took it upon herself to style him, and she had very good taste. He knew it came off as arrogant to outwardly agree with vain compliments, so he usually stuck to a bland "thank you", but he liked to piss off Joy. She deserved to be thwarted at every opportunity.

"Where's your kitchen?" he asked.

Mathias would be in the kitchen. He was a kitchen guy. He cooked, for heaven's sake. He would be a chef one day, wearing a sexy black uniform, and he'd have Michelin stars. Alberto tried to avoid thinking of what he would have become by then.

He recalled the look Mathias gave him as he stood in the middle of his room, Eric's tennis ball in one hand, waiting for his response. Alberto kept thinking, *if you think I'm not good looking now, imagine your opinion of me when you see what I'm like inside.*

"Where did you get this?" Mathias had asked. Faced with Alberto's silence, he nodded slowly. "Is it Eric's? Why did you take it?"

Alberto was still trying to figure out that one and didn't know how to answer. Sometimes, there were no good explanations for the stupid things you did on a whim. Sometimes, the explanations were too embarrassing, even frightening. Alberto enjoyed scary things but only in horror movies.

Mathias had looked around his room, the ball squeezed tightly in his fist. Then, he'd asked in a tired tone, "You're not a good person, are you?"

Alberto couldn't say he was nor could he admit to being a monster either. But not being able to tell Mathias what he wanted to hear had weighed on his chest like a stone.

"Got it." Pocketing the tennis ball, Mathias had left without another word.

From his window, Alberto had watched him speed up toward the gate as though he couldn't get away fast enough, even ignoring Stasia's friendly little wave goodbye. His skin burning, his head buzzing, his dopamine depleted, Alberto had looked on with a hollow heart.

And that's why he was here tonight, following Joy across her flat, in the hope of convincing Mathias he might not be so bad after all.

There was so much to know about himself that would shed light on his singularities, if only he could say the words. But he couldn't. However, the tennis ball was different. This, at least, he could try to explain. Because after everything that had happened today, the real slap in the face had not been the one Stasia inflicted on him, but, rather, the look in Mathias's eyes when he concluded Alberto wasn't a good person.

Both arms wound around his own, Joy led him back to the living room. Alberto's breath caught when he saw that Mathias was not in the kitchen but sitting thigh to thigh with that Odile girl on the sofa, wearing his usual scowl, perhaps because Eric and Zak were making out right next to him.

"Those two…" Joy clicked her tongue. "Sorry. Must be hard for you."

Joy, for once, was showing some remarkable insight. Indeed, it was difficult. It had only been half a day since Alberto and Mathias parted, and he was already replacing him with another person? And worse, a girl?

"I… I…" he mumbled.

Joy gently squeezed his arm. "Don't worry, I'll take care of them." Releasing him, she tramped off toward the sofa. "You two, get a room!"

Zak and Eric separated with a popping sound. Eric gave Joy an aggrieved look, but she ignored him and flashed Alberto a thumbs up.

Of course she had been talking about them. How the hell would she have known about Mathias? But the latter, who'd heard her and noticed the following gesture, pierced Alberto with a murderous glare, while Zak and Eric resumed their inappropriate kissing.

Alberto knew about desire. He knew better than anyone here, and he could tell with one look that this girl sitting next to Mathias fancied him. He would have no choice but to make himself particularly unforgettable in bed next time or soon, Mathias and this pretty thing would be an item. Alberto was not ready to let go of the best thing in his life right now. He was willing to make efforts, even sacrifices.

Thankfully, Joy didn't particularly like seeing these two together either, and she asked Elodie — apparently Odile was *not* her name

— to help her convince the others to play a game. The girl accepted without enthusiasm and followed her to the other side of the room.

When Zak took Eric's hand and dragged him, seemingly in a trance, away from the sofa and out of the room, Kayvin made a loud comment about the *fags* finally leaving the room, so Alberto proudly laid his *fag* arse on the sofa next to Mathias, who snarled at him like the savage werewolf he was.

"Don't sit here!" He smelled like beer.

"You seem drunk."

"What if I am? Do you have a problem with that?"

"I don't."

Mathias grunted and faced away from him. Struggling to pluck a cigarette out of its pack with his fingers, he used his teeth instead with success and lit up without even a glance back. Alberto, who didn't mind keeping his mouth shut, sat wordlessly next to him for two minutes that felt like twenty until Mathias saved him, coughing up a cloud of smoke before breaking the silence.

"Why the hell are you dressed like that?"

Puzzled, Alberto examined his own appearance. "Like what?"

"Like you're going to some great party."

Alberto almost smiled at the gruff tone of his voice. "Isn't this a party?" He ran a hand through his hair to show off his cuff-links, noticing Mathias's eyes didn't leave him. "What about you? Why do you always wear the same thing, even at parties?"

"I like hoodies. They're comfortable." He gave his half-finished cigarette to Alberto, who took it as a sign he really was tipsy.

"Me too." Alberto noted the filter was moist and took a long drag. "They do a good job hiding my face."

"What's wrong with your face?" Mathias frowned at his own words then chugged down the rest of his beer.

Alberto's eyes fell on his lips, glossy from where a drop of beer lingered. "Do you want another?" he offered when Mathias wiped them harshly on his sleeve.

"Yes, please." He slipped him a dubious look. "Since when are you so helpful?"

Alberto said nothing, but he internally rolled his eyes. He

wanted to see Mathias's lips covered in a sheen of beer again; he wanted to lick it right off.

On the way to the kitchen, Alberto caught a glimpse of Eric and Zak making out in an office on the side. Zak's objectively nice arse kept scooting closer and closer to the edge of the desk until he elected to wrap his legs directly around Eric's waist. Theory confirmed: Zak had a little slut in him. The boyfriend was trying his best not to lose control, with one hand buried in Zak's hair and the other gripping the edge of the desk for dear life.

Alberto felt an unpleasant twinge he didn't understand and grew annoyed. Exiting the bathroom, Xavier saw them, too, and he whooped at the sight. Eric, without sparing him a glance, used his foot to shut the door.

Wanting to avoid Xavier, who was already calling after him, Alberto picked up the pace and found the kitchen on his own. Though beer smelled and tasted terrible, he took two from the fridge, one for Mathias and one for himself, so he wouldn't look conspicuous. Alas, Xavier cornered him anyway. That was the problem with being tall, people kept finding you. That, and the other thing he inherited from his mother: an appearance that attracted trouble. Hence, his thing for hoodies.

The beers turned warm in his hands as that grinning fool wasted his time with pointless questions, going as far as asking about the health of his mother.

"Don't worry about my mother," Alberto told him through narrowed eyes, slowly making his exit.

When he returned to Mathias, his heart sank to find him surrounded by several people, among them being Zak and Eric. Moreover, when he approached, beers in hands, a weird silence settled among them, giving Alberto the impression they had been talking about him.

Camille, short, attractive, and talented, was a writer and Zak's best friend. She was also respected enough by Joy to have been invited to this party. She recovered faster than everybody and said, "Guess what? I'm almost finished writing a new movie."

"A new movie?" Eric shoved Alberto aside and pulled at her sleeve. "A new movie?"

"Yes." Camille had the decency to throw his victim an apologising look. "Alberto, you should get a part, too!"

"Yes, you should!" Zak blurted out, sounding way too enthusiastic.

Now Alberto was certain they had been talking about him behind his back.

"Should I?" he asked with a fake smile.

"Yes!" Camille wrenched free from Eric's overexcited grasp. "Let's see… Which role would be best suited for your… talents?"

"What do you mean?"

"What are your strengths?"

"Oh." Alberto scratched the back of his head. "I play dead really well."

"But…" Camille said weakly, "There are no dead people in my movie. Do you think I should kill someone?"

Alberto gave a firm nod. "Yes. You should kill someone. And that someone should be me."

"Really…?"

"No one would see it coming. It would be like, a big surprise."

"No! You're too beautiful to be killed off!" Xavier had finally realised he had been left behind, and he reappeared, slapping both hands on Alberto's shoulders.

Zak and Eric glanced at him, then at each other, before Zak said solemnly, "Nonsense! The movie's a love story. No one should die in a good love story."

"You're no fun," Alberto muttered.

"Enough," Eric said, pulling his boyfriend to his chest. "You're upsetting Zak with your twisted jokes."

Zak's eyebrows shot up. "I'm, like, not upset, though?"

"And I say…" Alberto said, lifting his head up, "… if you can't kill me off, don't put me in it."

Overhearing him, Joy stomped toward their group with her group of friends in tow. "Why are you standing in a corner and talking about killing people at my party? Come play Truth or Dare instead." She cast Xavier a dark look. "Not you. You're banned since you peed in my mother's plants last time."

Spotting Camille slipping away toward the kitchen, Xavier

ignored Joy's words in profit of chasing after her flouncy — and unattainable — skirt. Joy stared after him resentfully. "I can't believe you dated that guy," she told Melissa in a superior tone.

Her best friend looked miffed, but she didn't say a word.

"Oh, but you're not anymore?" some tragic girl asked, a note of hope in her voice. "What happened?"

"He, ahem…" Melissa's eyes fell on Alberto.

What? What did he do this time? Surely, he wasn't responsible for Xavier's failures to please a girl, come on!

"Nothing," Melissa said. "He wasn't so much into me, that's all."

Kayvin let out a loud sigh. "Xavier's dumb as fuck, but he's not a bad boyfriend. You probably did something to annoy him."

The girls stared at each other, but no one said anything. Alberto took this opportunity to try to sneak away, but Joy caught his hand in a tight grip.

"You're staying, and you're playing Truth or Dare. So are you two—" She spun on her heel. "Where the hell are Eric and Zak?"

"Slipped away."

"To make out," Mathias added.

Alberto had seen them tiptoe their way to safety the moment Kayvin had opened his mouth. They were probably, as Mathias had said so strangely, hiding in some room or other and making out, while Alberto was forced to juggle with that rabble just to get one minute alone with him.

"Those fags," Kayvin muttered, only for Joy to point a finger at him.

"If you're insisting on using that word, I won't invite you to my parties ever again." She tugged on Alberto's hand. "Come on."

"I don't want to," he said faintly.

"Come on!"

"He says he doesn't want to!" Elodie intervened. "Leave him."

Despite Joy's irritated pout, the group started toward the sofas, leaving Alberto behind. Mathias, standing in the corner, made no movement to join them.

"Forget him," Kayvin said, slumping into the sofa. "He's just afraid of having to tell the truth."

"What truth, that he's soulless?" Joy said with a smirk. "We know."

Alberto shot her a look, and she turned away with flourish.

"Yeah, that, for example." Kayvin sneered and met Alberto's eyes. "And that you're all weird because your dad dropped you as a kid."

There was a silence, and everyone turned to Kayvin with incredulous looks.

"Just something I heard," he added, not the least bit uncomfortable. He even laughed at Alberto's bewildered expression. "Don't make this face! Xavier's cousin told us. That's all. Cheer up!"

Joy let out an impatient sigh. "Nobody cares. Let's play! Mathias, are you coming to—"

"No," Mathias said, and there was something in the tone of his voice that made her back off right away.

Receiving no support from Elodie or Melissa, Joy threw up her hands in defeat. "Fine... why don't you two get to know each other? You can mope together in a corner out of sight. At least you won't spoil our fun."

Mathias scoffed, and Elodie mouthed a *sorry* and gave him a little wave that he answered with a clipped smile. Alberto stepped in front of him to obscure her from his field of vision.

"Look, I got you a beer."

In fact, he couldn't believe his luck. Alone with Mathias, and with an excuse, he pushed the bottle into his hand, delighted at the opportunity to prove to him he could be quite nice and useful after all.

"Christ..." Mathias said, turning the bottle in his hand. "Did you put it in your pants or something? It's warm."

"You're welcome," Alberto mumbled.

Mathias slid down the wall and sat on the floor. Alberto reluctantly joined him in the corner. Mathias took a swig from his bottle, grimaced at the horrible taste of warm beer, and said:

"So... Truth or Dare?"

Alberto's mind went blank. He couldn't think of an answer at all and noted Mathias was experiencing the same. They chortled at the same time.

Alberto recovered first. "Looks like we're way past that."

"So past it."

"Where did our innocence go?"

Mathias gave a quiet chuckle. "My innocence died with my mom, I think. Where did yours go?"

The first or the second time? Alberto didn't know. A mix of both. Hiding at the bottom of the wardrobe or staring at a buzzing light overhead, whatever it was, at some point, something must have shifted in his brain. Damage was obviously done or Alberto wouldn't need to be roughed up to get off.

"Where did you go?"

Mathias's voice brought him back. Alberto replied, "Nowhere," in a flat tone.

"You're so fucking weird."

"Am I? I've never heard that one before."

The others had begun their game and forgotten all about them. Back in the kitchen, Xavier's guffaws resounded, followed by Eric's toddler-like explosion of laughter. Alberto shivered.

"What were they saying about me earlier?" he asked, noting with a start that Mathias had scooted closer.

"I thought you didn't care about what people said?"

Alberto didn't recall ever saying that. "What were they saying?" he insisted.

"I don't know. That you never come to parties, whatever." Mathias arched his brow. "Why did you come to this one?"

"Are we still playing Truth or Dare?"

"Yes. Let's just say you said *Truth*."

"No. I said *Dare*, actually."

"Fine." Mathias plunged his amber eyes into his. "I dare you to tell me the truth."

Alberto felt something unfold in the pit of his stomach. He could have kissed him right there, if only half the school wasn't gathered in this room. "O-kay," he murmured.

"Why do you go to Xavier's parties if you hate them?"

Alberto leaned closer to Mathias, close enough to make him

sweat, but not close enough that they would look suspicious. "The thing with Xavier… is that he pays me."

Mathias snorted in his beer. "Can you repeat that?"

"Xavier. Pays. Me."

"Bullshit." Mathias licked his lip. "You always do that."

"Always do what?"

"You talk a lot of shit. Your lies. They're too big. That's why no one believes you."

"It's true. It's true! Truth or Dare. He pays me."

Mathias laughed — Alberto felt like scooting even closer — and asked, "*Truth or Dare, Truth or Dare?*"

"Shouldn't it be my turn to ask?"

Mathias didn't reply.

"Fine," Alberto gave in. "*Truth.*"

"Did he pay you to come today?"

Alberto didn't want to admit it, but he also knew he'd have to make an effort, or he wouldn't get what he wanted tonight.

"He didn't. I came on my own."

"Why?"

"To explain."

Mathias furrowed his brow. Then, he sucked in a breath when he realized what this was about. "Explain, then. You better explain! You stole Eric's ball."

Alberto surrendered. "Technically, I found it."

"So you admit it."

"I do."

"Why?" Mathias's voice cracked, and his expression immediately turned sour.

"I can't do that here," Alberto said truthfully. "Too many people…"

Mathias zipped his lips shut. He looked around the room for a minute. Then, he said, "Come to mine."

"Now…? Isn't your family home?"

"My dad…" Mathias coughed lightly in his fist. "My dad's away all weekend, and my sister has a sleepover tonight."

"Oh."

"So… so…"

"I'll wait for you outside," Alberto said.

Mathias gave him a strange look, but it could have been the beer that gave his eyes an odd glint.

Alberto left, and no one tried to stop him. Outside, he lit up a smoke and poked at his own face. His ear had stopped ringing hours ago, and his cheek wasn't as tender. He had been right when he had carefully selected these clothes earlier. Mathias had to find him attractive again, or he wouldn't have invited him over.

Mathias came out, and their eyes met under the glow of the streetlight. Alberto felt again the same desire percolating under his skin. The first part of his plan, to lure Mathias to be alone with him, was done. He was close to getting what he wanted, and a fear of failure washed over him, cutting off his breath. His heart thumping, he followed after Mathias wordlessly and tried to reason with himself.

The second half of his plan was simple: all he had to do now was be really careful about whatever words would be coming out of his mouth.

25

THE FURNACE

IN THE ELEVATOR, Mathias pushed Alberto against the mirror, slipped his hands under his jacket, and felt the silky fabric of his shirt as he explored his mouth.

"Are you mad at me?" Alberto then asked out of nowhere.

Maybe not out of nowhere. Maybe Mathias had nipped his lip a little.

"I'm mad, yeah. I'm mad."

Mathias buried his nose in Alberto's shoulder, but the latter shoved him back. Mathias gave a dry laugh. He decided not to say a word before they'd be completely alone.

The apartment was dark and quiet. Mathias felt nervous for some reason. He had felt nervous all day. They went into his room, and he lit some of the lights, but not all of them. Enough that he could see Alberto, not enough that he could read his eyes. Not that he ever could anyway.

He thought of being a good host by removing Alberto's coat, but he got impatient and tossed it to the ground. Then, he did the same with his jacket, until Alberto backtracked into the bed and remained sitting there, glowering.

"What?" Mathias asked.

"You're mad at me."

Mathias went to drink some water after that. When he returned to the bedroom, feeling half-sober, he thought, maybe hoped, that he'd find Alberto asleep, but here he was, waiting, the tennis ball Mathias had left on the nightstand sitting on his lap.

"Why did you take it?" Mathias spoke in a commanding tone, somehow knowing and also dreading the answer.

"He was always playing with it; it annoyed me."

"Do you like him?"

"Do I like him?" His cold eyes glinting, Alberto got up, ball in hand, and gave a dark chuckle. "Dating someone like him would probably make me stick my head into a woodchipper."

"Then why—"

"He's so lively, isn't he? So bright, always so bright." Alberto abruptly turned away. "Insufferable."

Mathias watched him closely. "Do you hate him, then?"

"No, I don't hate him. But, yes…" His voice fell to a whisper. "It made me feel good to take something of his."

Something became clear in Mathias's mind, and his stomach turned. His worst fear was now confirmed: Alberto never liked Zak.

He took him from Eric just like he'd taken his stupid tennis ball. Because he found him insufferable, and because he could.

Such cruelty—such selfishness—was enough to make him recoil in disgust. Mathias could try all he wanted to look the other way, but the truth was, Alberto was as bad as people said. How much more proof would he need before he'd finally break ties with him?

"I despise you for what you did," Mathias hissed, his hands balling into fists.

Alberto cast his gaze down, and his lip twitched as though he wanted to smile. "If you like him so much, why don't you ask him out?"

A weird silence stretched between them, Mathias's mounting anger slithering painfully through his veins like a venom.

"What's going on between you and your sister?" he asked through gritted teeth.

"She's not my sister."

"Are you sleeping with her or not?"

Alberto burst into a cold laugh. "Are you seriously asking me that? I hate the bitch. I wish she'd die!"

That had the merit to make Mathias stop in his tracks. "You… You want her to die? Why?"

"Why? I don't know." Alberto looked away. "She's really annoying."

"You want to… Do you even hear yourself? Do you realize how fucked up you sound?" Mathias rubbed his hands over his face. "Jesus Christ, there is something really wrong with you."

Alberto's gaze hardened before his eyes.

"You know what you sound like?" Mathias continued. "A spoiled brat. You hate Eric, so, fuck it, let's hurt him. You hate your stepsister, so, fuck it, let's wish her dead. You can't wish people dead!" His voice broke. "They *do* fucking die!"

His body was shaking from the battle of emotions occurring within him. Meanwhile, Alberto was looking down at him, impassive.

"*You're* bratty when you drink. It makes me glad that I don't."

Mathias scoffed. "You don't drink, and you're still fucking annoying."

"Well, thank you."

"Always whining, even though you have everything." Mathias gave him a dark look. "Fucking grow up a little." He sucked in a breath, but he found that, between his anger, his confusion and his frustration, there was almost no air left in the room.

"I'm more of a grown-up than you are," Alberto said coolly.

"I seriously doubt that."

"Really? You want to compare notes? Real mature, indeed." Alberto stood in front of him, their height difference pressing down on Mathias.

"Step away from me."

Alberto snickered. "What are you going to do about it? Grown up, my arse. You can't even decide if you hate me or if you want to fuck me."

A switch was flipped in Mathias's brain. All of his rage and frustration spilled over, and he grabbed Alberto by his shirt. He wanted to yell at him, shake him, apologize, hug him, maybe; he couldn't know for sure. All he knew was that he needed to touch him, or he was pretty sure he'd implode.

They stumbled back into the bed. Mathias found his shoulders and pushed him down. Alberto made a meek sound when his back met the mattress, his expression twisted, and Mathias almost felt bad, but he mostly felt so much desire for him that there wasn't room for anything else. They shared a messy kiss, brutal, angry, needy, and Mathias wasn't sure whether he was the one shaking or if it was Alberto who was shivering under him. His mind a fog, he began tugging at his clothes and, to his shock, Alberto began resisting with all his might.

Usually, he enjoyed their games, even more so as they turned freaky. He was the one who liked being tossed around. Perhaps he really was scared this time.

Mathias suddenly recalled Charles-Henry's words. A familiar image of a long and large corridor flashed into his mind, filling his throat with bitterness, and he stopped moving altogether. Below him, Alberto's bullied lips pouted in defiance.

"Why are you fighting?" Mathias whispered.

Alberto pulled his face down and bit his nose. With a grunt of pain, Mathias grabbed his belt, and he started resisting again, so Mathias froze and leaned back, only for the other to sink his teeth into his jaw. It went like this for a while, until Mathias shoved him down.

"I'm confused."

"You don't say."

Completely at a loss, but now so hard it was actually painful, Mathias stared at the young man lying under him. "What do you want?"

Alberto murmured something in his ear before his head fell back onto the bed. After the initial shock, Mathias shook his head with a sigh.

"Fine," he grumbled. He gripped the buckle of Alberto's belt and yanked it open. "Have it your way."

But don't go complaining later, am I right? Alberto writhed and struggled all he wanted, and Mathias went along with it, or more accurately ignored him, until he lost patience and ripped his shirt open.

Buttons flew everywhere, raining down the carpet with muffled sounds, and that's when Alberto capitulated. Out of breath, he gazed up at Mathias with an awed expression and let his arms drop to the sides. Without a word, Mathias turned him over.

They didn't yet know how to make love, and neither of them particularly had any interest in learning at that point. Mathias was vicious that time. When he wasn't harsh enough, Alberto groaned and hissed and egged him on until he ramped up the aggression. Soon, the bedroom felt like a furnace, their bodies gliding against each other, slick with burning sweat.

"Oh, God," Alberto repeated over and over, and Mathias was thinking the same, his fist closed in Alberto's hair, and that's how they reached the peak and went over, both panting… and calling names… and trying to make sense of how anything so bad could feel so damn good.

When it was over, Alberto lay motionless amidst the crumpled sheets, looking like he'd just been chewed up and spat out by a wild animal, and Mathias sat on the edge of his own bed, his lust satiated and his heart full of unrest. The look he tossed over his shoulder gave him pause. Alberto's gaze, lost in a spot on the ceiling, was dazed and soft.

Mathias didn't think; he immediately turned around to catch his lips. Alberto raised a limp hand to stop him, his fingers tracing the length of Mathias's neck. He breathed a sigh into his mouth before he turned his head away. The softness was gone, replaced by the usual wall of ice. He pointed at his shirt on the floor.

"That thing cost over five hundred euros."

"What a rip-off," Mathias replied absently.

Their eyes met. Alberto's glare froze the perspiration on Mathias's back. "What am I going to wear to get home now?"

"I don't know. I'll lend you something."

Alberto smirked. "Do you have one of those T-shirts that say 'I'm with stupid'?"

Mathias gave him a warning look. Alberto parted his swollen, bitten lips. Despite his defiant attitude, he still looked like he'd been trampled. Mathias admired his work with a curled lip. He was glad he tore his fancy shirt, and he was even happier he tore into him the way he did and messed up his pretty face. He was getting really good at that.

Alberto reached behind himself to rub his back and made a pitiful noise. "I can't walk."

Even now, he sounded both amazed and bored with his realization. It was hard to explain, but he was unlike anyone Mathias had met before. Unbelievably weird. Mathias felt like telling him just that, and he also felt like kissing him all over his back and hugging him tightly against him. His fingertips hovered an inch from the pearly skin, and, in the end, they retreated in shame.

Alberto did attempt to get up, only to fall straight back into bed. Mathias's eyes widened. "Wait, you were serious?"

"You broke my arse; I can't walk anymore!"

They were both stunned into silence. It was the first time ever Alberto had raised his voice in Mathias's presence. The broken quality of it had the opposite effect of what he intended. Mathias willed his blood not to rush south, but it did anyway.

"Just... Just stay the night, okay?"

His suggestion was met with a dark glare. With his flushed cheeks, mussed-up hair, and the red patches Mathias's lips had left all over his pale skin, he looked truly divine.

"Come on," Mathias spoke gently. "Stay. It's not the end of the world."

Clearly exhausted, Alberto appeared tempted. "Maybe."

"Just tell your mom."

There, the light in his eyes changed. "I should... I should really go. She just got back from a trip. She's probably expecting me."

"Are you insane?" Mathias gripped the edge of the bed. "It's almost one in the morning! Who doesn't sleep at other people's places all the fucking time at our age? You think she won't get it? Even if I managed to throw your sorry ass into a car, what do you think she's gonna think the moment she sees you? You looked like you've been mauled by a pack of wolves."

Alberto arched his eyebrow. "And whose fault is that?"

"Whatever!" Mathias turned his back to him. "Just... text her. Tell her you're staying here. You'll look and feel better tomorrow."

Alberto was too tired not to see the merits of this plan, and after a sigh, he picked up his phone and typed—excruciatingly slowly—a text message. He got an answer in the form of a phone call, and he scratched his brow before answering.

Mathias knew one word of Italian—okay, maybe more—but only one to use in polite society, and that woman on the phone spoke freakishly fast, so even with his knowledge of Spanish, he understood nothing of their conversation. Alberto's mom sounded hysterical over the phone, *her poor baby was outdoors at night, oh noes,* and if she knew what Mathias just did to him, she'd lose her beautiful hair over this, and… he felt an awkward pang of regret about this, and suddenly, he couldn't look at the marks on Alberto's skin anymore.

After some negotiating on Alberto's part, he hung up and slammed face-first into the pillow. "Okay, all good," he said, his voice muffled. He turned his head to the side. "Just promise you won't feed me anything weird."

"I… uh… promise. Though…"

"Your cum's fine. It's low in calories."

"Okay."

Mathias looked at him. He had a twisted sense of humor, that's for sure… but at least he had one. And fucking hell, or whatever, he was snaking fully naked under the covers, and Mathias realized he could probably hold him for a while if he negotiated properly. Not that he had feelings for the guy. He just liked to cuddle after a fuck.

His pulse racing, he promptly wrapped his arm around him, only for Alberto to hiss at him like a murderous cat. "Back off!"

"What? Why?"

"I don't like being touched."

"I'd say you love being touched. Come here."

"Don't!" He shuddered under his touch, as if Mathias's hands were torture devices.

"Serious— Do you even know what we just did?"

"Yes." Alberto shook his hair away from his face. "It served its purpose. Good night," he said, turning away.

"Fine!" Mathias scooted away to a safe distance. "Fucking weirdo, you are."

"Yes, yes, whatever."

Mathias was disappointed. He had thoughts of spooning that bastard all night and now, all he'd get from letting that guy into his bed was a headache in the morning. Although... He realized with a start that he'd get to see Alberto asleep again, which happened not ten seconds after he stopped talking. Mathias walked over to his side of the bed. Alberto was lying on his side with his eyes closed, his long arm dangling off the bed. Mathias even crudely whistled straight into his ear, and he didn't even flinch.

Mathias went to shower, and when he returned with a bottle of water, Alberto was still sleeping on his side, but he was curled up like a cat with his hands under his chin, his lips parted. In this position, he looked somewhat younger. An uneasy feeling spread throughout Mathias's chest. Leaving the water on the nightstand within his reach, he pressed a tiny peck on his sharp cheekbone, returned to bed, and got as close to him as possible without touching him. Eventually, he fell asleep as well.

In the morning, Mathias woke with his lips against Alberto's neck and his arm around his waist. Since he could hear no complaint from him, Mathias allowed his hands to wander a little, his fingertips dancing across the fair skin of his side, his navel, and his collarbone. Feeling him tremble and sigh under his touch, Mathias dared press a kiss to his nape and was rewarded with the cutest sound.

So, there he was.

Morning-Alberto, curled up into a ball, could be unfurled with kisses.

Mathias's caresses became more insistent, and Alberto, consciously or not, pressed his body flush against his. Unseen by anyone, Mathias's cheeks grew hot. This version of Alberto was, by far, the best he'd ever encountered, quiet and sweet and ever so warm after lying for so long under the covers. He couldn't help pushing his luck. Mathias ran his hands all over Alberto until he plunged them into his soft dark hair, and, for the first time, he felt something that shouldn't be there.

"Do you have a scar?" he asked, tracing along the stretch of extra skin at the back of Alberto's skull. He heard a vague groan in response and couldn't help but joke, "Wait. Did your dad really drop you or—"

Alberto abruptly rolled over, and Mathias first thought he wanted to hit him. He didn't know why; Alberto had never raised a hand to him. Still, he was surprised by his sudden burst of energy, and he gripped both of his arms, but Alberto only looked at him through narrowed eyes.

"Worst pillow talk."

Coming from you, that's rich, Mathias thought, but Alberto was kissing him, his long fingers traveling dangerously south, so he decided to forgo the talking altogether and flipped them both over so he could lay on top of him. After suffering the onslaught of last night, the bed frame snapped under the strain. Mathias went *Merde!* and burst into a laugh. Quietly, Alberto put a finger in front of his mouth.

"What?" Mathias smiled at his reproachful expression. "We're alone, remember?"

"We're not alone," Alberto said.

Mathias's smile froze on his lips. "What?"

"We're not alone. I saw your sister last night."

Mathias's heart dropped like an anchor to the bottom of his stomach. "Are you sure?" he asked, sitting up.

Alberto blinked several times before he nodded. "Sure."

Mathias jumped off him and started putting on his clothes haphazardly. "That's not good, that's not good," he repeated under his breath. He helplessly threw Alberto his ruined shirt. "Wait here."

Elisa was in her room, at her desk, typing madly at her keyboard, no different from everyday Elisa, but when she saw him, her eyes immediately welled up.

"Why are you crying?" Mathias asked, putting his fist in front of his mouth.

"You know why!" Elisa couldn't meet his eyes. She typed even more furiously at her keyboard.

Was she disappointed in him? He would never be able to forgive himself if she were.

"Elisa…" Mathias stepped toward her. "What did you see?"

"Everything." She stopped typing and screwed her eyes shut. "The door wasn't closed."

"And you thought you'd just... watch?"

"Bitch, you were so loud!" She sent her chair swiveling with an angry kick and almost did a full circle. "It sounded like you were murdering someone in there!" She struggled to swing back to face Mathias and gave him that look of hers, 50% severe, 50% smug, 100% condescending.

"You weren't supposed to be home," Mathias said in a thin voice. "You were supposed to be at a sleepover—"

"I was, but it was kind of boring. Then, I had this idea about a *Naruto* fanfic, and I just had to come and write it down."

"In the middle of the night?"

"Pah!" She jerked her head. "How dare you tell me what I should or shouldn't do in the middle of the night? Who am I to deny Inspiration when it comes knocking on my door? At least what I write stays on paper. What you did to him...? That was real."

Mathias pinched the bridge of his nose with a sigh. "How did you get home?"

"My friend's mom." She dramatically filled her lungs with air. Then, she said through gritted teeth, "Your. Door. Was. Open!"

"I wasn't exactly expecting an audience!"

"Well, you got one anyway!"

They both fell silent. Mathias stopped a second to think about his predicament. He, a private guy, one who never talked much about anything and who had never brought a girl over to have sex with, was caught in the act by his fifteen-year-old sister, an aspiring journalist. He also inhaled a deep breath, half-hoping the air was poisoned, and he would die on the spot.

Elisa, already calmed down, gave him a long look. "Why were you hurting him?"

Hurting him? Didn't she understand what they were doing? Or... Fuck. Out of context, it probably did look like Mathias was bullying Alberto.

"It's not like that..." he began awkwardly.

"What's it like?"

That's what he likes, Mathias wanted to say, but he really didn't want to have this conversation with his baby sister. He said nothing, and Elisa's gaze, somewhat softened after his answer, turned fierce again.

"I wasn't hurting him!" Mathias said earnestly. "I mean… not really…"

Elisa shot a look toward the document open on her computer screen. "So, you're… you know…"

"You saw what you saw," he said, his voice set. "Why does it matter?"

Elisa shuddered visibly. "I'm trying to understand why you're… with him…"

With him. Him, him, him.

"I don't know, it just happened…"

"So, you were bored, and he just happened to be there—"

"I was— No!" Mathias swiped his hands over his face. He didn't want her to worry about this. He didn't want her to worry at all. "I don't know."

"Are you together?"

"No!" Mathias removed his hands. "No. It's not like that."

Mathias in a relationship, with Alberto, no less. What a joke that would be.

"I don't like him," Elisa muttered.

"Why?" Mathias asked, not meeting her eyes.

"He's weird. He's mean. He's trash! I don't want you to be with a guy like that."

"I'm not with him."

"You deserve better."

"I'm not with him!"

"Why would you let a guy like him use you?" She huffed. "Doesn't he have some baron of whatever to date?" She didn't bother lowering her voice, until now, when she added, "Can't you sleep with someone else?"

I wish! Mathias's heart cried out. *Don't you think I want that? Anyone else but him. But it doesn't work like that.*

"Look…" He let out a sigh. "Can you just… keep this to yourself?"

"Mathias…" Elisa gazed at him with a bewildered expression. "It's okay if you're gay. It's great to be gay, you know that, right? Zak's gay, and he's great."

The fact that she thought of Zak first amused Mathias enough that he snorted. Elisa didn't return his smile. She looked worried.

"Are you going to sleep with him again?"

Mathias scoffed, a pitiful thing.

Probably.

No, definitely.

Because before he'd found out his sister caught him in the act, Mathias was just thinking about how satisfied he was with himself that he'd convinced him to stay over. He had always wanted to find out if he was an asshole upon waking up or if there was a short window where he'd act like a normal human being. Having just found out it was the latter, he had wanted to enjoy that before breakfast.

"Just don't tell anyone," he said, turning away.

26

THE LAW OF THREE

Alberto decided to pretend not to have heard anything of Mathias and his sister's conversation. In truth, he quietly opened the door and tried his best to understand what they were talking about, but they spoke this horrible French, that language that is *never* pronounced the way it's written, making it impossible for him to learn. But with some effort, he did catch enough words to agree to finally address the problem of his reputation.

When Mathias returned to the bedroom, looking ten years older, and saw Alberto wearing one of his school football jerseys, he froze momentarily before closing the door behind him.

Alberto didn't know yet how Mathias would react to his sister catching them in the act. *And what an act.* Perhaps she'd need a therapist. Maybe she'd get her own Mathias instead. It worked pretty well for Alberto so far, and he really didn't want to lose that. But, if it had to happen today, if Mathias freaked out, then Alberto decided that whatever happened, he wouldn't lose his cool nor his dignity. He'd keep his head up, just like his mother. Mamma was beautiful even when she cried.

Mathias walked past him toward the wardrobe, his brow furrowed. "Why didn't you say anything last night?"

"About what?"

"About seeing my sister, you freak!"

Alberto put his suit jacket over Mathias's jersey with a shrug. "I wasn't sure she was real…" Mathias's frown deepened. "Then, this morning, when you were fondling me, I heard some movements, and I assumed she was home."

"I wasn't fondling—"

"You were definitely fondling me."

"Stop saying that word."

"What word should I use?"

Mathias blushed — *actually blushed* — making Alberto want to slap his own face for some reason. He stared at him, waiting. *Come on. Admit it. Admit that you are gay, and I'll admit I like you a bit.*

Mathias instead asked, "Can you walk now?"

"Yes."

"Good, that means you can help me change the sheets."

Alberto, who'd never once made his own bed, turned away to conceal a grimace. That's just what he needed, another chance to prove to Mathias he was utterly useless.

Mathias took clean sheets out of his wardrobe, dumped them on the bed, then lifted the mattress with one hand to inspect the frame. After shuffling some boards around for a minute, he dumped the mattress back into place.

"That will do for now, but I'm gonna need a new one."

"Do you need money for that?" Alberto offered hesitantly.

The look Mathias gave him made him regret his words. "Do you think I'm broke or something?"

Alberto hurriedly shook his head.

"Get your annoying ass over here," Mathias said, throwing a set of pillowcases at him.

Stuffing something into something else should be right up his alley, Alberto thought, forcing all of his attention to his task. He was a guy, after all. But he quickly realised, in that particular case, getting stuffed was easier than doing the stuffing. Mathias watched him struggle in silence, but his forehead was so creased, Alberto wasn't sure it wouldn't become permanent.

"How's your sister?" Alberto asked, in an attempt to distract him from his incompetence.

Mathias cringed and pulled the dirty sheets off the bed as if he wanted to murder them. "I don't want to ask what she's seen exactly, but I think we have scarred her forever. And believe me, she's tough."

"Why would she be scarred? It's not like we were doing something wrong."

"You go tell her that. She thinks I was hurting you." Mathias chewed on his lip. "I was… I was…"

Alberto dropped his half-stuffed pillowcase and approached him. He wanted to tell him he was brilliant last night, but the words got stuck in his throat.

"I should stop," Mathias was muttering while stretching the fitted sheet to its maximum. "I have to stop…"

No, absolutely not. It couldn't — it *wouldn't* — end like this. Not because of some pint-sized tabloid hack. In Alberto's mind, last night was a great success. It had been a rare instance in which one realises the person they were hoping was as weird as them proves themself to be just that. A precious instance as one realises they might not be alone after all. Not anymore.

Alberto would not let that go now.

"And then what?" Alberto ventured, knowing he was treading on thin ice. He seized the other end of the sheet and tried to fit it over the corner of the mattress. "You got caught. What are you going to do? Never do it again? I'm sorry to inform you, you like it too much."

"Shut up."

"You could return to having sex with girls, but what's so good about them? I can make you come just the same. Even better, judging from last night—"

Mathias flashed him with a warning look. "Shut your evil lips and make the bed."

But angering him was a better idea than revealing himself to be a pampered fool, Alberto thought, looking down at his own hands.

"Don't you think I'm better? You must, or you wouldn't come back for mo—"

"Okay, stop. Not like that!" Mathias tugged on the sheets so hard Alberto lost his balance and fell face forward on the bed. "Do you even make your own bed?"

248

There was a short silence. With a quick pulse, Alberto crumpled his end of the sheets between his hands. "You say I have evil lips, you say I have an annoying ass, but you clearly love fucking my mouth and my ass. You're confusing."

Mathias dropped the sheets altogether. "Stop talking or get out."

Alberto held his stare for the longest time. Mathias was good at not blinking. And his eyes, flashing with outrage, were so gorgeous, it took Alberto everything to keep up the act. But he did it. Haughtily tossing the sheets back to him, he grabbed his coat and showed himself out. The last thing he saw as he slammed the front door shut was Mathias's dumbfounded expression.

It was a very-pleased-with-himself Alberto who emerged from Mathias's building on a gorgeous Saturday morning. Glancing up toward the sky, Alberto lit up a cigarette and even raised a hand to the morning sun, and there was still a trace of a smile on his face when the sudden sound of a bike screeching to a halt drew his attention to the road. He tossed a disinterested look over his shoulder, and his stomach dropped.

There, in the middle of the road, with both hands clutched tightly around the handlebars of a shiny blue bike, stood a bewildered Eric.

Frozen into place, Alberto blinked helplessly and felt almost certain the bird splitting the sky overhead chirped a jolly *You're fucked!* as it flew away.

"What are you doing here?" Eric's voice was abnormally unsteady.

In an attempt to save himself, Alberto decided to say nothing. He adopted a cold expression, but he tightened his coat around him to cover Mathias's jersey, praying Eric wasn't really a dog, or he'd catch a familiar scent right away.

Eric's expression turned to shock when the front door opened to reveal a breathless Mathias. "Hey, you—" Spotting Eric too, he skidded to a halt, his eyes popping out of his sockets.

The three of them went awfully quiet.

Eric moved first and slowly lowered himself on the seat of his bike. Alberto couldn't help noticing his girly basket — of course it had to be the thing with the flowers, the birds, and the bees — was full of stuff, which meant he'd been up and about for a while already, when it was only nine-something in the morning and Alberto was in desperate need of a shower after the events of last night.

That was the thing Alberto had attempted to tell Mathias yesterday. Eric had a way of making you feel like a pile of steaming manure. He obviously didn't mean to make people feel like that, since he acted like he was everybody's best friend. Unless they were talking about him, of course. Alberto had never done anything to this guy, and Eric had treated him like a steaming pile of manure the whole summer anyway. It was difficult sometimes not to resent being hated for no reason. Alberto should have been used to it, his mother had warned him of such things, but he still resented Eric so much, he could almost taste it.

Eventually, Mathias found his balls and broke the silence, turning to Eric. "What are you doing here?" He then pretended to notice Alberto and curtly nodded at him. Alberto stuck to his style and didn't nod back.

Thank goodness, Eric seemed to be over his shock already. He pointed at something over his shoulder. "Zak and I went for a ride. I dropped him off at the bakery around the corner."

"The good bakery?"

"That one. We're getting *chouquettes*[1]! Well, he is. I won't be eating any, so I can get *Best Body* at the next Colette Awards. He's waiting in line right now. So I thought I'd drop by, see if you wanted to hang out."

Mathias scoffed. "On a Saturday morning?"

"Yeah! The day is so beautiful, and… we're getting *chouquettes!*"

Eric cracked a laugh. Then, he turned his gaze to Alberto. Just like Dimitri, Mrs Paquin, Dr Roland, and so many others, every ounce of warmth in his eyes extinguished at the mere sight of him.

Look, idiot, you weren't supposed to be here, Alberto thought.

What was wrong with these *bastardi* to leave the comfort of their

---

1. A small, round and objectively delicious sugar-coated puff pastry. Only worth buying by packets of ten.

250

bed to go for a ride on a Saturday morning? Couldn't they just shag all day like normal people? No, they had to drag themselves outside just to make his life difficult. Alberto always thought Zak was a sensible boy — besides his hopeless crush on him — but now he'd have to reconsider his opinion of him.

"You're clearly awake," Eric said, returning his gaze to Mathias, "Come on!"

Alberto decided to go all in and play the arsehole so that Eric would ask him to fuck off ASAP. "You live here?" he asked Mathias in his most condescending tone.

"Yeah, why?"

Mathias didn't have to be a good actor to look pissed off, so that was easy.

Eric chuckled darkly. "His Highness Alberto probably lives in a castle." He scrunched up his nose. "What are you doing so far from Versailles, by the way?"

Alberto used the excuse he had prepared while they were chit-chatting about baked goods.

"I was on my way to the museum. I just stopped to light a cigarette."

"The museum?" Eric smirked. "At nine a.m.?"

Mathias slid Alberto a murderous look, but Eric didn't seem to think it weird that he would be doing something so boring. In fact, he looked relieved.

"So, no *chouquettes* for you!" He sounded delighted not to have to invite him along.

"They're overrated anyway," Alberto said, vexed.

Eric's eyes narrowed. "*You're* overrated."

That was also true, so Alberto said nothing. They stared briefly at each other with as much contempt as they could muster, with Mathias looking back and forth between them like he was worried they'd start beating each other up.

"Goodbye, then," Alberto said.

He walked away with his head high, but when he turned the corner, he broke out in a cold sweat.

. . .

Upsetting things always happened in series of three. He knew, he knew, he knew. Alberto thought about it all the way back home. First it was Elisa, then Eric the same day, and if one followed the law of three, they'd be found out again, and the third time would be the last. *Third time...* He promptly pushed that thought out of his mind.

Mamma cornered him the moment he passed the front door. She started with, *"Where were you exactly?"* followed by, *"Who's your friend?"*

Then, her eye caught a glimpse of Mathias's jersey, and she gasped. "What are you wearing?"

And here she was, tugging at his coat, until she saw how wide his eyes were, and she stepped away, her lips pinched.

Dimitri walked by with a smirk. "Do you have a girlfriend, Alberto?"

Alberto didn't reply nor did he break eye contact with his mother, until she relented and turned away from him.

"Well..." she muttered, running her finger along the spotless furniture. "I hope you haven't forgotten about tonight."

Alberto, who naturally forgot everything unrelated to Mathias, cocked his eyebrow. "Tonight?"

"We're having guests over before leaving for Verbier." She spun on her heel, her eyes glossy. "Jean-Pierre will be there. He said he'd love to see you again."

I'm sure he would, Alberto thought vaguely, but he wouldn't be too difficult to avoid. And since Mamma hadn't figured out he was shagging a *commoner* and that she had agreed to leave him behind while she spent Christmas in Switzerland with Dimitri, Alberto decided he'd make an effort and be on his best behaviour tonight.

Though he nurtured no delusions about meeting Mathias during the two-week holidays, especially after what happened this morning, Alberto was relaxed for the first time in a long time. He and his mother cared little for Christmas. It was supposedly a family holiday, but his mother had nobody but him to call such, and most occasions had been spent in the company of her husband of the time and his loved-ones. Mamma was always the trophy-wife, inspiring awe and terror in the heart of mothers-in-law, but love, not so much. And Alberto was thoroughly ignored and usually irritated because he was not allowed to retire to bed early as he wished.

This year, he'd finally succeeded in avoiding that torment. Using the modelling jobs he had booked as an excuse, Alberto pleaded and begged for her to leave him behind, and encouraged by Dimitri, Mamma eventually capitulated. As for Stasia, she'd left for Cuba the day before, so Alberto would have the house to himself for a whole week.

If he were bold, he'd invite Mathias over and mess around with him in Dimitri's designer sheets. *If* he were bold, which he wasn't, and, in any case, Dina would also be staying to watch over the house and possibly over him, too.

Alberto joined Dimitri's party early and in a good mood, even sparing a few words here and there, taking comfort in knowing that tomorrow, he'd be alone, completely alone, as he always wanted to be. He was like that for a while until he recognised his good mood was merely latent anxiety. Since when had the thought of being alone for a whole week made him squirm and twitch in his tailored clothes? Since when?

He didn't have to think too much about it. The moment Jean-Pierre jumped him between the sushi bar and the Champagne fountain, he thought immediately of Mathias, and he knew.

"Alberto, look," Jean-Pierre began, stretching a hand toward him.

Alberto stepped back right into the corner of the table — seriously — and winced in pain. Just then, his phone beeped, giving him the excuse to ignore the old man.

"Don't be afraid," Jean-Pierre said. There was no trace of whisky on his breath this time. "I won't try to kiss you again."

Noticing with a start that the text was from Mathias, Alberto ignored him and opened the message.

> Eric hasn't noticed anything weird. That's unbelievable.

His teeth sinking into his lip, Alberto typed:

> You mean he's unbelievably thick.

"Can we talk?" Jean-Pierre said somewhere miles away. "Alone?"

Alberto reluctantly glanced up from his phone.

"Come on, please. Just for a minute."

After much cooing, Alberto agreed to follow Jean-Pierre to the library. The latter then started pacing around nervously, while Alberto remained standing by the open door, his gaze flickering between the old man and his phone.

"What happened the other night…" Jean-Pierre began. "… I'm sorry. I've been having a rough time lately, and drinking when you're having a rough time is the worst thing you could possibly do…"

Nodding absently, Alberto opened Mathias's answer.

> You kept your cool. You really did.

Was Mathias praising him? Was that some sort of new foreplay? In any case, it worked, because Alberto started shaking as he typed:

> What can I say? Being me has its benefits.

> Whatever. So I guess I'll see you next year, then? If you're going away.

> Not going away. You?

> Nope. Come by tomorrow?

Alberto answered to the positive and locked his phone with a racing heart.

"Anyway…" Jean-Pierre concluded. "I'm really sorry, and I hope you can forgive me." He suddenly pulled the wolf ring out of his pocket and handed it to Alberto. "I… I didn't know how else to say sorry."

Alberto stared at him blankly.

"I had a different size made for you. Please, take it." Jean-

Pierre laughed nervously. "And the next time some old man tries to kiss you, kick him in the balls, okay?"

Forcing his lip to stretch in a semblance of a smile, Alberto took the ring. *Of course he took it.* An ugly wolf-head ring with amber eyes just for him, and he didn't even have to kiss that creep? It's like he wasn't unlucky anymore.

Jean-Pierre looked relieved when he accepted the ring. "You know, it's worth a lot of money."

"So am I," Alberto replied absently.

Naturally, Mathias hated the ring.

"I don't want to be seen with you wearing that monstrosity," he said when they were rolling around on his bed the next evening.

"You don't want to be seen with me anyway," Alberto said, shrugging.

Mathias caught his hands and pinned them over his head. He tried to remove the ring by force, and Alberto struggled and faked a cry of pain. Mathias snorted before he landed a hard kiss on his lips.

"Fine, keep your ugly wolf. You have the worst taste."

"*No, sei tu che hai pessimi gusti²*."

"What?"

Alberto shoved his knee between Mathias's legs to get him going, but his phone beeped. Mathias gracefully freed his hands, but only because he needed his own to unbutton Alberto's shirt, who let him tend to him while he checked his messages. That's how he saw a text from Dina that instantly ruined his appetite for good things.

Stasia and Ludwig had broken up. The lucky man had escaped Stasia's death grip, and she came back to the house "in a state of distress", she wrote. She would be where Alberto would be, just the two of them, alone. Alberto felt like someone had punched him in the stomach. He rose abruptly, his forehead knocking into Mathias's chin.

---

2. "No, it's you who has the worst taste." (Italian)

There it was again. The law of three.

Winter

"After years of stillness,
the first tremor will feel earth-shattering."

Liars

27

SHAME

"WHAT THE?" Rolling onto his back, Mathias rubbed his chin with watery eyes. "What's the matter with you?"

"Sorry, I…" Alberto quietly dragged himself to the edge of the bed. "I…"

"What, what? Speak up, I can't hear you."

"Could I, maybe… stay over tonight?"

Alberto's words made Mathias bolt upright. "What?"

"Sorry, sorry." He waved his hand in his face. "It was a stupid idea. It's just that something came up… and I… and I…"

He started muttering words under his breath. Mathias wanted to tell Alberto to shut up and lay back on the bed so he could continue removing his shirt—instead of mumbling shit no one could hear.

"Sure," he said instead.

The surprise in Alberto's eyes looked genuine. "Really?"

Mathias produced a half-shrug. "My sister and my dad aren't even here. You can stay as long as you like."

Alberto's eyebrows drew together, making Mathias almost regret saying that.

"Thank you. I just need to get back home quickly to get some clothes."

"Get some clothes?" Mathias huffed. "It's going to take you

more than an hour just to get there and back!" He realized he didn't want Alberto to leave his side even for an hour and cursed inwardly.

The truth was, after that thing with Elisa, then Eric, Mathias didn't even think he'd see him again so soon. Now he was offering himself for another sighting of what his best friend called a "sleepy-cuddly" version of himself, meaning soft and warm and definitely open to snuggling under the blankets. Mathias couldn't wait to get his hands on him since they were cock-blocked yesterday; he forced himself not to rub them together like some cartoon villain.

"What am I supposed to do?" Alberto's languid voice brought Mathias back. "I have work tomorrow. I can't wear the same clothes twice in a row. I'd feel dirty."

Alberto was an enigma. He was always so well put together, *pristine*, even, for a guy who constantly asked Mathias to do the dirtiest things to him.

"Fine. I'll lend you some clothes."

"But…" He tilted his face toward him. "You're so short…"

"I'm not short! You're… unusually tall."

Alberto got up and started poking into Mathias's wardrobe. "I like the way you speak. *Unusually tall.*"

"I'm trying to choose my words more carefully since I know you."

"Why?"

"Because…" Mathias hesitated. "You're so posh."

"I'm not that posh."

"You're posher than me."

"*O-kay.*" Alberto faced him. "Anyway, I can't wear any of this. Too short, too much *not* my style, too *Mathias-messed-me-up-all-night-and-I-had-to-borrow-his-clothes* obvious."

"All night, huh?"

"A guy can hope, can't he?"

Mathias chortled. "Right. There's a store down the street. Can you make it there and buy yourself some clothes, perhaps?"

Alberto did a cute little nod, and Mathias knew he was in. He, however, didn't know what he was in for until he got inside the store. He had to bury his hands so deep into his pockets, he thought he'd punch holes through them.

There were three employees in sight inside: two girls and one guy. Sure, it was quiet at the time, but still. None of them were working because they were all staring at Alberto as he browsed through the articles, looking bored. Wondering why they were doing this, Mathias studied him from the heel of his Converses to the top of his head, and he quickly figured it out.

When Alberto caught him staring, he smirked that way he did when Mathias shot his load without meaning to, so he got pissed off, and he had to pretend he wasn't by asking in a fake-ass tone, "Why are they doing this?"

So obvious.

"Mmmmh…" Alberto took his time, toying with him. "Either one of us is incredibly sexy, and they can't help themselves…" Mathias kicked the heel of his shoe. "… or they have a picture of me in the back."

"They have a picture of you in the back," Mathias repeated nervously. "Like… what sort of picture?"

You never knew with that guy. Judging from some of the stuff he pulled when they were alone together, if Mathias didn't know Alberto to be seventeen, he could have believed he did porn on the side.

Alberto seemed like he had read his thoughts and cocked his head. "A picture of me… wearing their clothes?"

"Why?"

He fluttered his eyelids. "My, my, Mathias, don't you know I'm a model?"

Mathias turned around abruptly, his gaze flying in every direction. They were in one of those popular chains that had a terrible reputation for abusing workers, bunnies, and the environment, but where everybody ended up shopping anyway. And they did have some pretty decent clothes for men—the ones Alberto was inspecting right now, for example. He pointed his long, demonic finger at the picture right behind the cash registers, and the young man standing there beamed at him. Alberto managed to curl the corner of his lip in a way that wasn't snide. "See?

Right over there. So, that must be why they're staring. That picture."

"Or both," Mathias grumbled.

"What?"

"Nothing."

Alberto gave him a look, a burning look, to be honest, made of dark and lustful promises. Mathias took out his phone to check the time. Alberto shook a few hangers under his nose with a pale hand.

"Anything you like?" that asshole asked, articulating every syllable.

Mathias cleared his throat with difficulty.

"Just pick something and let's leave. This whole thing's starting to look... domestic."

"You really know how to ruin the mood, don't you?"

"Oh, shut up."

As he waited for Alberto to make his selection, Mathias was wondering what he should do tonight. More precisely, what he could cook for him. He had no idea what Alberto ate in general, what he liked, what he didn't, if he drank coffee or tea... He wondered if he'd prefer a French or an Italian type of breakfast—was there any difference?—or if he really was subsiding solely on a diet of cum as he had claimed last week.

Alberto picked an ensemble from the front of the shop with one quick glance at the sizes and brought them to the cash registers. He saluted the employee in English and in a bored tone that contrasted with the flirty one he'd just used with Mathias.

"You bought the same ones as the picture!" the clerk said, all flustered.

Alberto glanced at Mathias, who shook his head, and he told the young man, "When you know something works, why change it?"

A shiver trickled down Mathias's spine. That was just it. He was right. He and him... they worked. The way their bodies moved and interlocked together... Mathias thought he should probably feed him rat poison tonight, get rid of him before damage was done.

"Sounds right!" the clerk said. "I could even use my company discount for you if you want."

Alberto silently took his card out of his wallet.

"Why would you do that?" Mathias gruffly asked.

"You know…" The young man blushed. "Since he worked so hard for it."

"Thank you," Alberto said. "That won't be necessary."

"Are you sure? I'd really like to—"

"Thank you."

Despite the clear lack of interest denoted in his cool tone, Mathias caught the employee writing his number on the ticket, and his hands flexed in his pockets. This guy, he was gay, right? He had to be. And he was so obviously hoping to get rammed by Alberto's annoyingly long dick. *Well, surprise, dickhead! He's a raging bottom. A taker, not a giver. And he begs, too. Also, he's an asshole. Now step the hell back, and let* me *handle him.*

"I really…" Obviously-gay-clerk saw Mathias's expression and fell silent, not daring to finish his sentence. Mathias, in turn, dipped his head. What did he see on his face? Jealousy? Anger? Did he really have a face that terrified people?

But honestly… if Mathias couldn't even watch the scene, how could Alberto endure it? The constant staring, the flattering? Mathias couldn't help thinking of all the other guys who wanted him and the ones who most likely had him whenever they weren't together. But tonight… tonight he was his, and Mathias didn't like sharing.

He led the way toward the exit. "Let's go."

"Look at you being all possessive," Alberto said, lighting a cigarette once they were outside.

"Quit dreaming." Mathias plucked it from his fingers. "Now move your flat ass; I don't want to run into Eric again."

"I was joking." Alberto took his cigarette back with a glare. "And my arse isn't flat."

Oh, *now* he cared about the way he looked. Sly lying prick. Pretending not to give two shits about his appearance, but always double-checking himself in the mirror. Mathias had caught him a million times, and yet…

He tossed a look over his shoulder and made eye contact with the employee back inside the store. The young man was still staring, his chin resting in his hand. Mathias couldn't help it. He slammed his hand on Alberto's absolutely perfect ass.

"I know. Get moving."

Alberto exhaled a large puff of smoke. "Awfully domestic." He sounded bored, but Mathias noticed his eyes were almost glinting.

They made their way back, half-bantering, half-fighting, the usual. *No serious words shall ever past thy lips.* Something like that. The more time he spent with Alberto, the more pretentious Mathias felt himself becoming. It was as if the little nerd he used to be was begging to resurface. Feeling increasingly resentful, he kept his eyes on Alberto, the way he lifted his hand to his mouth to smoke, the way he always kept his eyes on the ground. Mathias knew that once he stopped, Alberto would invariably lift his head toward the sky or lose his gaze to a distant horizon, but while walking, he was always careful, as if he'd trained himself not to be distracted while going from place to place. Mysterious, elusive Alberto. He didn't even notice how Mathias had fallen behind just for the sake of watching him, and he barely glanced at him when he caught up.

They had almost made it to his apartment building. Alberto was gone elsewhere, his shopping bag swinging from one hand, his cigarette in the other, and Mathias was forcing himself to keep that languid pace, when a look ahead made him jump out of his skin.

Half a hundred meters ahead, typing on her phone and walking straight toward them, was their schoolmate, Joy.

Alberto hadn't caught sight of her yet, but Mathias, wanting to leave nothing to chance, spotted an open gate on his left. Without a second thought, he brutally shoved Alberto out of sight. Ignoring his churning stomach, he forced his expression to look neutral and kept walking at a controlled pace until he came face-to-face with the girl.

"Howdy howdy!" Joy said with a gleaming smile.

Mathias was pretty certain he'd heard Alberto crash into something when he hurled him to the side, but he was hoping—*seriously hoping*—first, that he would stay put and not say a word, and second, that he didn't seriously hurt himself. Or, you know, the other way around. Joy knew them both, and she knew they weren't friends. To meet them together like that would be too suspicious. And after the whole Eric debacle yesterday, it wouldn't be long before people started to make wild assumptions about their relationship. Even maybe wild enough to be the fucking truth.

"Hey…" Joy said, her perfected smile freezing on the edges. "Are you alone?" She stretched on her toes to look over his shoulder.

"Yeah, why?"

"Nothing. I thought… I'm seeing people now."

"Where are you going?" If she kept walking down that road, she might spot Alberto standing weirdly to the side wherever he left him. That couldn't happen.

"Home."

"Oh, you live around here?"

"You literally just went to a party at my place?" She looked vexed as fuck.

"Sorry, sorry. My head's all over the place."

Her expression immediately softened. "That's okay, I don't mind. And you could…" she hesitated. "I mean, do you want to come with?"

"With?"

"With me? To my place?"

Mathias's eyes widened. What? No! What he wanted was for her to leave so he could return to Alberto and hopefully not get murdered by him.

"Can't do. Homework."

"Homework, right." She sounded upset for some reason Mathias couldn't understand. He felt a bead of sweat sashay down his spine, and he gritted his teeth.

"I'll call you later, all right?"

"Really?" She brightened up. "I'd like that!"

Yeah, sure, whatever. His heart in his throat, Mathias pretended to walk up the street until she was out of sight, then he turned around and raced back toward his building. What he saw when he reached the gate made his jaw drop.

QUEER

IN HIS HASTE, Mathias hadn't bothered checking where exactly he was shoving Alberto, as long as it was out of sight, but it just so happened that the gate led to the waste bin room belonging to the adjoining building. And Alberto was still where he landed, ass deep in a pile of trash bags, his bags in one hand, cigarette still burning in the other, waiting.

"*Pollito*…[1]" Mathias murmured. Seeing Alberto so quiet and obedient, only mildly staring at him, his chest tightened, and he didn't know how to act. "Alberto, I…" He went to him and extended his hand. "I'm…"

Alberto took his offered hand and rose clumsily to his feet.

"I'm so sorry," Mathias managed at last. "Are you angry?" He attempted to wipe away the dirt that was stuck to his pants.

Alberto slowly put his bag down and twisted his neck to check the state of his derriere. "Now I really need to change my clothes."

"I'll lend you some for tonight. No one will see you in them but me."

"Okay."

"Fuck." Mathias pushed his hands into his pockets. "I'm really sorry. I— I owe you one, okay?"

---

1. Spanish pet name: literally translates to "Little chicken."

"Okay." Alberto sounded strangely dazed.

They returned to the apartment in silence. Mathias couldn't believe he did that to him. To another human being. What if he had fallen onto some broken glass? He wanted to slap himself across the face.

They went inside. Alberto stomped straight toward the bedroom, and Mathias hovered behind uncertainly. If Alberto had reacted with outrage, shouted insults at him, even told him to fuck off and left... all of it would have been fine... but his passive attitude made Mathias's actions look almost criminal.

Alberto was standing in the middle of the room when Mathias joined him. He closed the door after himself, fighting down a furious urge to wrap his arms around him and apologize to the crook of his neck.

"I'm sorry," he said, feeling like a broken record. He hurried forward to take his coat and hang it on the peg on the door. It was such a nice coat, and, mercifully, it was barely soiled. But his pants... they were fucked.

"I think I fell into someone's leftovers," Alberto said without emotion.

His heart sinking, Mathias approached his hands, wanting to do something, anything, but the sound of Alberto's cold laughter stopped him in his tracks.

"You want to help me out of these, too?"

"Sorry. I'll find you some clothes." He went to the wardrobe, almost turned around, hesitated, and clutched his fists. "Do you need underwear, too?"

"Do I?"

His voice was low, teasing. Mathias anxiously kept his eyes away while he removed his pants. Alberto scoffed behind him.

"What? You can't look at me anymore? What's wrong with you?"

"Nothing," Mathias grumbled.

"Then check my arse for me, please."

Mathias threw a quick look over his shoulder.

"Looks good— I mean, looks clean."

"*Perfetto.*"

Alberto then pulled his sweater over his head and stood almost naked in the middle of the room, his pale skin stark against his dark briefs, his eyes fixed on Mathias. And Mathias stared back, his heart thumping, not knowing what to do. Eventually, he thought to ask, "Are you okay?" hearing the tension in his own voice.

"I'm a little cold." Compared to him, Alberto's voice was like a gentle whisper.

"Oh."

"And you're a little weird. I mean... weirder than usual."

Mathias was struggling with his guilt, with his lust. He shook his head. "Sorry."

Alberto blinked patiently while Mathias stared to his heart's content, his desire rising with each breath.

Why? Why did it have to be him? And why did Mathias feel so bad about earlier? Of course he was meant to feel bad. If it were a girl... but Mathias knew full well he'd have never shoved a poor girl into a waste bin area. He'd never have shoved a girl, period. He could complain about Alberto being a selfish, cold-hearted, and freakish monster all he wanted, but Alberto wouldn't have pushed him aside at the sight of some random schoolmate. No, Mathias was in the wrong. He knew it, he felt it, and, yet, it didn't alleviate the way he felt right now looking at Alberto's almost bare body. His shame was never as powerful as his yearning. Not when it came to this guy.

"So... these clothes...?"

Mathias jumped. "Yeah, yeah." He tossed him the first oversized sweater he found. Alberto dutifully began sticking his long arms into the sleeves until Mathias closed the distance between them and tore it from his grasp. "Forget it."

Their eyes met.

There. Right there. Alberto's lip twitched as though he'd been hoping just for that. Mathias almost lost his mind at the sight.

Half an hour later, Alberto was no longer cold—despite being naked—and he was getting sleepy already, lying on his side on the bed. Mathias tossed the cover over them and hesitantly reached down to cup a perfectly round cheek, knowing Alberto would probably reject him again. But this time, he didn't. He let Mathias put his hand there, even let him stroke his thumb across his fair skin, and it was good he had his back to him, or he would have seen how wide Mathias's eyes were at that moment.

"See?" he mumbled. "My arse isn't flat."

Mathias scooted closer. "Are you still going on about that?"

"Just establishing facts."

"Your ass is perfect, and you know it." Mathias pressed a kiss to his shoulder blade.

Alberto let out a satisfied sigh. After a pause, Mathias's hand slid up to rest on his thin waist.

"Thank you for letting me stay," Alberto whispered.

It wasn't even nine p.m., but he was already about to give in to sleep. What a weird creature he was, sleeping most of the time, talking bullshit the rest of the time. But, sometimes, he could be sort of sweet. Rarely, rarely, but Mathias remembered his expression when he was in the middle of the trash, all quiet, waiting for him to return, and his chest hurt when he thought about it. Wasn't his expression familiar? It was…

A long and wide corridor suddenly flashed behind his eyelids, threatening to ruin everything. Mathias screwed his eyes shut until it went away.

"Are we doing it again already?" Alberto asked.

"No, why?"

"You're squeezing me."

"Oh, shit, sorry." Mathias relaxed his hold on his waist. "Sorry, sorry."

It was silent and peaceful in the room for a moment. Mathias enjoyed this position very much, his hand warm on Alberto's waist, his lips half-buried into his soft dark hair. Alberto had curled into a ball again, and Mathias thought him long asleep, so he was surprised to hear him talk after a while.

"Who was it?"

"Who?"

"The girl. Outside your building."

"Ah. Joy, it was Joy."

Alberto removed his hand from his waist and didn't speak again. Cute time was over, apparently. But Mathias was a regular eighteen-year-old with anger issues, and there was no way he'd fall asleep at nine p.m., even on Sunday.

He turned and squirmed around in bed, his throat and his chest burning, until Alberto hissed, "Stop it!"

"Sorry if I don't want to sleep."

"I can't have sex right now. I need to sleep."

"I never said we should have sex! God, you're so annoying!"

Alberto threw a dark look over his shoulder. "Then what do you want?"

How nasty he could be sometimes. It was like a giant wall had been erected between them when two minutes ago, he had the most vulnerable part of Mathias tucked away into his mouth.

If he was waiting for signs that Alberto felt human emotions or started acting like a normal human being to start a conversation, he'd have to wait a long fucking time. Might as well go with it. With any luck, it would start a fight, and he knew what to do when they started fighting.

"Hey."

No reaction. Mathias thought about whistling, but he thought it a bit rude, so he pinched his asscheek instead.

"Alberto."

A pair of cool gray eyes glanced briefly at him from over his shoulder. *Fuck this guy!* Mathias hated him. He bit on his tongue to strengthen his resolve.

"Hey, so… do your parents know you're gay?"

Alberto slowly rolled on his back and stretched on the bed, clearly uninterested in the question, so Mathias grabbed his wrist and held it in a tight grip to get his attention, and perhaps a little more than that.

"Hm?" He wriggled his wrist in a half-assed attempt to free himself. "Why? You want to ask them for my hand already?" Mathias responded by pulling him closer. Alberto sighed. "Maybe. Maybe not. I haven't said anything."

"But… they have doubts or suspicions of something, right? They must have at least some suspicion."

"Why?" Alberto's voice was raspy from sleep. "Do you think I look gay?"

Mathias felt himself blush. "I don't know."

Alberto puffed out a laugh. "Do you think you—" He stopped himself abruptly. "I... I don't know exactly. My mother has always been surrounded by queers, and she's been alluding to it a lot lately. Her husband... never mind him."

Mathias hesitated. "What about your father?"

"He..." Alberto's brow creased. "He knew way before I did."

"How so?"

"He just knew." Alberto made an impatient gesture, and Mathias tugged on his wrist until they were nose to nose. Alberto looked into his face for a brief moment before lowering his gaze. "Predictably queer," he muttered.

"What?"

"He knew."

Mathias didn't understand. "Then how come... you didn't know?"

Alberto freed himself and spread out on the bed. "I was young, I was homeschooled, and I didn't care about those things."

"You were homeschooled?"

"Mm. I didn't really meet people my own age until much later. The first time I went to school and saw all the other kids, I had a fit." He let out a dry laugh.

That bad, huh? Considering how Alberto acted around him, he didn't want to know what the sight of so many boys did to him.

"But..."

"But what?" Alberto lazily rolled to the side, his eyelids drooping. That fucker thought he could escape him by sleeping. Mathias rolled him over and held him under him.

"Do you think you were born like that or... you know...?"

"Know what?"

"If people thought you were gay when you were a kid, for whatever reason, maybe it made you gay."

Alberto snorted. "Nothing made me gay. I'm just... gay." His expression gradually turned incredulous. "Wait, are you serious? Do you think people can make you gay by just saying you are?"

"No!" Mathias wriggled impatiently. "But... maybe by spending too much time with gay people or, you know, if some-

thing bad happens to you—something really bad—then maybe…
it changes you that way."

"This is ridiculous," Alberto said, and his eyes turned frightfully
cold. "I was born gay. That's how it is. Everything else is… I don't
know… Church propaganda or some rubbish like that."

Mathias swallowed. "Why not? I saw this documentary on the
cable once, and they were saying—"

"Oh, no." Alberto shoved his knee between Mathias's legs,
cutting off his breath. "You shouldn't watch homophobic docu-
mentaries on TV. You should watch me instead."

"What good does that—"

He rubbed his knee against his crotch. "You like this?"

Mathias stifled a groan and jumped off the bed. Alberto, who
never had an ounce of energy to spare unless it was to beg for
more, didn't let him escape and pulled him right back into bed.

"If yes, gay. If no, not gay." He got up and stood between his
legs, leaning over him. "There. I helped you. Pay me."

Mathias had to push him away or he'd find out how aroused he
was by the mere sight of him standing there and saying *Pay me*, but
Alberto knelt down at the same time. He almost sent his foot flying
into his jaw and cursed.

"Get up, get up!"

Alberto pouted. "Now that I'm on my knees, you want me to
get up?"

In truth, Mathias wanted to let him do whatever he wanted. It
would end up just the same as always anyway, but he knew he
couldn't. If he let Alberto take charge, there was no way of
knowing what would happen down the road. A crash, most likely. A
casualty, for sure.

Mathias sprung up and tossed him on the bed like he was nothing. He still gave him what he wanted, but with the certainty he
had been in charge the whole time.

Another ten minutes later, Alberto looked nothing like a
polished supermodel, but he was weirdly even more attractive.
They lay side by side on the bed, and Mathias finally felt sleepy
himself, but now that he had received confirmation that there was
a short window between the moment Alberto came and the

moment he returned to his cold-hearted self where he was… more manageable, he thought perhaps they could talk some more. And perhaps Alberto wouldn't even remember the next morning. He snuggled up to his ear to whisper as quietly as possible, "How did you find out, anyway?"

A faint voice replied, "What now?"

"You. That you were gay. How did that happen?"

He half-feared Alberto would laugh and say something like *Why do you want to know? Feeling like coming out?* That sort of shit, but no. Alberto opened his eyes and fixed them on the ceiling.

"I…" He hesitated, then flashed a fake smile. "I watched porn."

Mathias looked at him in disbelief. "Seriously?"

"Yes." He hid his face in his hands, muffling his voice. "Watched straight porn, then gay porn. One did nothing, the other did… it. There. I knew I was gay."

"No great romance, then? You didn't meet anyone who… who made you feel different, and—"

"Pff." Alberto mocked. "You spend too much time with Eric."

His comment wounded Mathias, somehow. "Poor Zak," he mumbled, his thoughts fluttering briefly to some dark place.

"Hm?"

"Nothing."

Alberto yawned and made himself comfortable on the bed. "You never watch porn, Mathias?"

"Not really."

His answer made Alberto blink in surprise. "Really?"

"Really."

"Why?"

"I find it depressing."

Alberto made a little noise that sounded like he was sort of agreeing with him, but not enough to care, and he turned his back to him.

Mathias had, in fact, watched gay porn before. Once at a party with his former friends, as a drunken joke, and again the day Alberto grabbed his dick for the first time. He checked it out that same night, but he didn't really enjoy it as much as he thought he would. He tried straight, he tried gay, and he disliked them both for different reasons, until he chanced upon a video where the bottom looked vaguely like Alberto. Then, he had a decent hard-on.

Perhaps he was only into Alberto, and he didn't know which was worse: being gay or being into Alberto. All Mathias aspired to, was a simple life filled with simple things. But no, he had to like cocks, and worse, he had to be obsessed about the one cock all his instincts told him to stay away from.

Oh, and his mom was still dead.

Beside him, Alberto was already asleep. Mathias observed the side of his face for a long time, resisted the urge to kiss it, and got up to make himself dinner.

29

DATING

DESPITE THE RUMOURS ABOUT HIM, Alberto did, in fact, consume food. Not exactly the same food as most people, but some food. He usually started the day with a smoothie packed with vegetables, fruits, grains, and added vitamins. For lunch, he preferred salads, and at dinner, he feasted on sweet potatoes or spinach and the like.

If his father called him *predictably queer* today, Alberto might have understood why. He thought about that with a bitter smile when he got up early the next day, starving. Though he would find it very cool, and in some way, romantic, he couldn't survive solely on Mathias's offerings. So, he slunk into the kitchen, hoping to find there some fruits or other sustenance, only to find himself face-to-face with the little sister.

Sitting at the kitchen table, she would have looked minuscule if those great black eyes of hers didn't shine with such intensity, they made Alberto feel small. So, he froze in the doorway, and they stared at each other for an interminable amount of time. Then, she let out a dramatic sigh, not unlike the one Zak used when Alberto took him to the Cognacq-Jay Museum on an especially hot day and he couldn't wait to get out.

"I guess it can't be helped," she said.

Alberto checked the time on his phone. It wasn't even eight a.m. "You weren't supposed to be home."

She shrugged. "I wasn't. I was dropped off earlier to get my books. There's coffee," she added, pointing at the counter behind her.

Earlier? Alberto bit back his retort and went to the coffee machine. He was glad he didn't have to make it; he wasn't sure he knew how to. Helping himself to a cup, he gingerly took a seat across from Elisa and her pile of binders and books. She scribbled nonsense in the margins of a glittery notebook for a while. Then, she looked up with a frown.

"You're not talking."

"Should I?"

"I was thinking we should at least make an effort."

Alberto tried to think of something to say. All he knew about this little girl was her annoying crush on Zak. "Why are you doing homework so early on a Monday morning? Aren't you supposed to…"

"To what?"

"… Have fun?"

Elisa chortled. "Yes, so, you see, my mom gave me this tip: get the most annoying tasks out of the way first, then you're free to move on to the good stuff."

"What's the good stuff? Ranking the teachers by their body odours or whatever stuff you're writing? *Ten ways Zak's hair looks adorable?*"

"You're just jealous because I never write about you," she said, her tone laced with contempt.

"Yes, that's it."

"But, no, it's not that. Though I *was* planning to rank the teachers in the next edition of the *Colette Candy Guide*. It's my duty to report, as editor-in-chief."

Alberto made a noncommittal sound.

"But this time," she continued, "I'm doing history homework about Ancient Rome, and I have to pick a specific subject about the daily life of Romans and all, but I don't care for it, so I can't think of anything."

That's because you're straight, Alberto thought. *Unlike me*—and *Zak*.

"How about fashion?"

She kicked her feet under the table. "I may be a girl, but I don't want to write about fashion! And anyway... everyone else will probably pick that, and then what? I have to think of what's most likely to impress the teacher. Ever heard of 'You play the player, not the card?'"

Very true. With an appreciative nod, Alberto leaned back in his chair. "Who do you have?"

"Racine."

"He's boring."

Elisa pouted. "Yes, yes, he's awful, but he's exigent."

"I mean, he likes boring stuff. Write your paper about something boring. Interesting, but boring."

"What do you mean?"

Alberto thought about it for a moment, then said, "Pots from Ancient Rome. There's even an exhibition about it nearby."

Elisa pulled a face. "Sounds *really* boring."

"And it is." Alberto picked up a bunch of grapes from the fruit bowl on the table with a half-smile. "Zak dumped me when I offered to take him there."

She sniggered. Her eyes lit up like a bonfire, not unlike her brother, but very much not like her brother, thank God.

"I think he was too bored with the prospect," he added. "What?" He had noticed Elisa looking at him with an incredulous expression.

"Nothing!" She blushed a little. "It's just, you're pretty straight-forward."

"What can I say... I'm a sucker for the truth."

"Not just the truth, apparently," she said, deadpan, making Alberto snort into his cup of coffee. She handed him a pile of paper napkins with a bored look. "Seriously though, for my history project..."

"It's legit," Alberto croaked, hitting his chest. "I went there. *Without* Zak."

"And how was it?"

"Great. Lots of pots... and... you know, things."

"Amazing."

Alberto nodded. "Go take a look. Racine will love it."

"Thank you," Elisa muttered, her forehead creased. She then got up and started spinning around in the kitchen.

She really was tiny. Her mess of black curls made her look like an overexcited little poodle. Alberto watched her, mildly intrigued.

"What are you doing?"

"Food, you know, food!"

"Food…"

"Aren't you supposed to give people food to say thank you? Mathias does it all the time." She glanced at him helplessly. "So… you want some eggs? I'm not good at cooking. My brother is, but I'm really not. But I can make eggs."

"No, thanks." Alberto stopped her before she caught on fire. "I don't like the way they're made."

Her eyebrows rose to her hairline. "Because they come from the chicken's butt?"

"Yeah, that's it." Alberto suppressed a laugh. "Butt stuff's just disgusting."

She looked even more bewildered after that.

"I'm okay with grapes," he said gently. "You can sit down."

She did, but she kept shooting glances in his direction as though he were some supernatural creature sitting uninvited at her table. Mathias used to look at him in a similar way before they started messing around. Alberto hoped she wouldn't start having any ideas about him.

"So you really spend a lot of time in museums?" she asked.

"Yes."

"You must be really educated, then."

"Not particularly."

"Then what's the point?"

And what, exactly, was the point of these questions? This inquisitive little girl was probably probing him to report back to her brother. Alberto didn't enjoy being interrogated, but Elisa being a threat to his relationship with Mathias, he agreed with her about the need to make an effort. He swallowed the last of his grapes and rested his chin on his hand.

"The thing about museums… is that nobody ever bothers you there."

"What do you mean?"

What, how, why? God, the Rodin children were relentless with their questions. Alberto tried his best not to roll his eyes.

"It's the safest place besides hospitals, but hospitals aren't as cool as museums, obviously."

"Are you worried about not being safe?" She sounded dubious. "How so? You're a guy, and you're tall. *Really* tall," she added with a hint of resentment.

"Honestly? I'm not worried about anything anymore."

Elisa gave him a searching look as she drummed her pen on top of her notebook. The more he looked at her, the more he noticed how similar she was to Zak. She even dressed somewhat like him. He wanted to comment on it, but she spoke first.

"Are you okay?"

The question startled him. "What?"

"Are you hurt?"

Alberto's throat abruptly tightened so much, he couldn't utter a word.

She sighed, out of patience. "Did my brother hurt you the other night?"

"Oh." The tension left his shoulders so fast, he felt lightheaded, and he even let out a laugh. "No, he didn't."

"It sounded bad."

"It really wasn't."

Elisa didn't seem convinced. "I don't like you with him."

Why? Alberto was tempted to ask, but he felt he knew the answer already.

"I don't think you're a good person," she added.

"Because I called you out for objectifying Zak?"

"I'm not objectifying Zak! See? You're super mean. And what's your problem with girls?"

"I don't have a problem with girls."

"Yeah, you do. It's pretty obvious. What? You haven't noticed how rude you are to us?"

Alberto stared at her. It finally hit him, how he'd never stopped a second to think about it. Perhaps he really was sexist. He didn't like being around girls, and he avoided women at all costs, save for his mother. Besides, he hated Stasia so much that his skin literally seethed upon seeing her.

He must have looked pitiful, because Elisa's face relaxed, and her eyes even held a glint of regret. "Look... My brother doesn't have many friends, and he wants to... hang out with you, so I'm not gonna give you a hard time, but..." She took a deep breath. "Just think about it for a second, okay?"

Alberto had almost stopped listening upon hearing that Mathias wanted to hang out with him. Thankfully, he also caught the rest, and he thought Elisa was actually not so bad. Perhaps they could learn to tolerate each other since they both cared about Mathias. Cared at least a little.

"Okay," he said softly.

"But let me warn you..." that tiny girl said, her voice suddenly shaking. "If you hurt him, I will go medieval on you. I'll rip you open and feed you your own black heart."

Alberto's heart thumped with a strange sense of anticipation.

"Mark my words," Elisa added, pointing a strangely ominous pen at him.

"Are you making friends again?"

Mathias cut their conversation short. He entered the kitchen in a sleeveless T-shirt, his sweatpants a little low on his hips, and Alberto's stomach leapt.

"No," Elisa said just when Alberto murmured, "Yes."

Alberto watched with a beating heart as Mathias walked past him to kiss his sister's forehead. He felt a sharp stab of jealousy when she wrapped her arms around his waist and briefly hugged him. Mathias then looked around his kitchen, his hands on his hips.

"Breakfast?" he offered, his eyes bright.

Alberto's lips tightened into a fine line.

Mathias had decided it was too much work to deal with these two. One was fifteen, the other was a spoiled demon. They were basically on the same level, except that their mother's blood ran through Elisa's veins, so she could be ruthless to protect her family.

Mathias didn't know if Alberto was capable of ruthlessness for the sake of anything but his own enjoyment.

He asked, "How come you're up before me?"

"Miracles do happen," Alberto mumbled.

Mathias wanted very much to believe in miracles, but this was the sort of miracle he didn't care for. He thought he'd get to rouse Alberto himself with his own special method, and instead, he woke up to an empty bed. Alberto kept proving himself the most uncooperative fucker on the planet. But of course, seeing him talking to his sister in an *awfully domestic* setting had put out the fire he felt at waking alone, so he said nothing.

Alberto got up abruptly. "I'm going to shower."

Before Mathias could protest, he had left the kitchen, leaving him to wonder what the hell he was up to. He glanced at Elisa with a startled expression. "Is he hungry, you think?"

She lifted her shoulder in a half-shrug. "He had like, fifteen grapes."

"That's not much."

"Shit, I offered eggs, but he said butt stuff is disgusting."

"He said that?" Mathias chuckled, helping himself to some coffee.

"If you want my opinion," Elisa said, dead serious, "he's full of shit, this one."

Yes, yes he was, but she hadn't seen him naked.

"And he's always talking about Zak," she added, relentless. "Bizarre, don't you think?"

Mathias put the coffee down. "What did he say exactly?"

Elisa rolled her eyes obnoxiously. "You know, I thought I could convince you to reconsider and come stay with us, but I see there's no need."

"Ella—"

"It doesn't matter, as long as you're not alone. But remember, Christmas Eve is on Friday. Dad won't let you spend it on your own. And... you can't rely on this one to keep you company."

Elisa started packing the mess on the table with a resolute expression. "I won't tell Dad a thing, but you should use this time to figure your shit out." She stretched on her toes to kiss his cheek. "Right?"

"I will," he grumbled.

"What was that?"

"I will!"

"Good. I have to go. It seems I have a date with Ancient Roman pots."

Sitting on the edge of his bed, Mathias had been waiting in the bedroom for ten minutes. Alberto returned from the bathroom smelling of his body wash, his hair damp, and he stopped right in front of the nightstand.

"Oh, look, gum."

"It's Eric's."

"Why do you have Eric's gum?"

"He left it here the other day."

"Hm." Alberto helped himself, slipping the entire stick into his mouth, and plopped on the bed. "*Tutti-frutti.*"

"You can't resist, can you?"

That earned him a teasing smirk. Mathias hesitated a moment, then scooted over to him. "Seriously… what's your deal?"

Alberto stretched leisurely next to him, his legs parted a little too wide for Mathias's sanity. "What's my deal…? You've already asked me that."

Mathias didn't recall and didn't care. His gaze lingered on Alberto's long neck. He imagined his hand around it and had to look away.

"Zak really was your first boyfriend?"

"Mm-hm."

"No one asked you out before?" Mathias received a pointed look. "So, you just refused all these times?"

"Mm-hm."

"How many people have you rejected?"

Alberto hummed thoughtfully. "Girls? Guys?"

"Guys."

"Lost count."

Mathias snorted. "And girls?"

"Lost count."

"Ass."

Alberto's expression turned playful. Mathias fought the urge to put his hand on his thigh. He just got out of the shower. He couldn't mess him up so fast, right? No, no, he had to focus.

"Why did you reject them?" he pressed on. "They weren't good enough for you?"

Alberto shrugged. "I never thought about it much."

Mathias's pulse quickened. He experienced an odd feeling of excitement. "And then you took Zak from Eric just because you hated him."

"No." Alberto worried his bottom lip with a frown. "No, I never said that."

"Then… why?"

He turned his face away. For once, Mathias wanted him to talk, but he was clamming up. Useless and unhelpful, as always. And Mathias was slowly but steadily starting to burn for want of answers, and for want of… something else. He forced himself to stay calm and get as many answers as he could from the beast while he was still in the mood.

"You liked him?"

"Who?"

"Zak!"

He was fucking with him, right?

Alberto took an unnerving amount of time to pop a bubble before he spoke. "Zak's nice."

"So you *did* like him?"

A response in the form of another half-shrug irritated him even further.

"Were you sad when he broke up with you?"

Alberto let out a sigh. "What are you asking me, Mathias?"

"Nothing, nothing." He frowned. "I don't know."

Perhaps he wanted to know if Alberto was capable of normal human emotions. Of liking someone, more precisely. Why? He wasn't certain. All he knew is that *he had to know.*

"Did you and Zak…" He lightly coughed in his fist. "You know… do stuff?"

What? He had every right to be curious. After all, why

shouldn't he be? Zak said nothing happened, but he also said Alberto might not be as gay as he claimed to be. And surprise! Alberto was the gayest man Mathias had ever met, and he'd met a few. But to his surprise, Alberto sniggered.

"What's so funny?"

"Do you think Eric would have let me live if I'd slept with Zak?"

It was Mathias's turn to chortle. "Yeah, I get it."

"I barely touched him. *Lo giuro su mia madre*[1]."

"*Te creo, pollito*[2]," Mathias replied absently. For once, he truly did believe him. Eric would have never shut up about it otherwise. Slowly, he reached out his thumb to Alberto's lip to stop him from biting it. When he realized what he'd just done, he abruptly drew his hand back. "Anyway… I…"

Alberto swiped his tongue over the spot he'd just touched. "What?"

"I wondered how it would have worked, between you two."

"What do you mean?"

"I mean… you would have…"

"What?" Alberto seemed amused.

"You know…" Mathias felt himself blush, and he grimaced. "Topped him?"

Alberto gave a laugh. "Now we'll never know."

Mathias snuck closer, wanting more details, wanting *more*. He rolled between Alberto's legs and pushed on his chest, forcing him to lie flat on his back.

"I want to know."

"Know what? No, I don't want to top Zak." Alberto paused, frowning. "And I sure don't want Zak to top me."

With a low hum of approval, Mathias snuck his hands under his shirt. He felt Alberto quiver from his touch, and a certain object below roused from its slumber.

"Why are you asking me this? Do you have a thing for Zak?"

---

1. I swear on my mother's life. (Italian)
2. "I believe you, 'little chicken'." (Spanish)

Alberto pushed Mathias's face away to look into his eyes. "You wouldn't be able to do to him the things you're doing to me."

Mathias enjoyed very much the sight of Alberto's flushed face and indignant eyes.

"Forget Zak. He's not for you."

"Fuck. You *do* still like him."

"No." Alberto shook his head, but he seemed disgruntled.

"You're a liar." The king of bullshit had reared his head again, but Mathias didn't mind so much. He wanted to know if Alberto was capable of feelings, and even though his liking of Zak was a surprise *and* an annoyance, it still was evidence. "Tell me the truth."

"What?"

Mathias slowly took hold of his wrists and pinned them above his head.

"Are you only interested in sex? Not in dating at all?"

"Why?" Alberto's eyes narrowed. "You want to make me an offer?"

His grip tightened around his wrists. "No."

Under him, Alberto's expression gradually turned dazed. He pressed his legs on either side of Mathias.

"Fucking's fine…" he said quietly.

"… Until it gets boring," Mathias finished, unsure why.

"Until it gets boring."

30

LOOK AWAY

MATHIAS, both wonderfully and tragically horny in the morning, dipped his head for a kiss.

"Don't," Alberto said against his lips. If he relented, he'd never get out of this bed. He wouldn't want to. Mathias rubbed against him anyway, testing his resolve. "Come on. I have work."

Mathias jerked back with round eyes. "You have to *work*?"

"Yes, right now."

His pupils blown within his amber eyes, Mathias pointed at the very obvious bulge in his sweatpants. "But look! Look at me!"

"I don't need to look," Alberto said, amused.

He'd felt it against his stomach, burning through his clothes, and still, he managed to get up. However much he wanted to take care of Mathias's little problem, he also wanted to get this done and earn his check; he wanted to move out of that house so badly, so he got up and smoothed his clothes while Mathias stared at him with his mouth agape.

In truth, Alberto felt sorry for him. After all of his efforts, he'd gotten what he wanted. Mathias was hooked and couldn't help himself, even though he originally didn't want to have anything to do with him. Alberto could sympathise with that.

What was happening to him now? Feeling sorry for someone who held so much power over him… that wasn't like him at all. That had to be because of Zak. Why always bring him up? Not only was Alberto sort of ashamed about what happened, but telling Mathias would be as good as telling Eric… and Eric thought the worst of him already.

Alberto quickly gathered his stuff and left the flat after that. Now he was worried about what Eric would think of him just because Mathias was lovely last night, letting him stay over and acting all possessive and hot.

Imagine how bad things would get if he were to fall for this closeted mess. And imagine what his mother would think, after a lifetime of warning him not to date anyone who couldn't meet their standards. Imagine how happy she'd be to see this angry boy with no family, money, or connections. Crap. Alberto felt giddy just thinking about it. That was half the problem, wasn't it? He wasn't a sane person, and he'd likely never be.

The photoshoot was happening in the basement studio of the photographer himself. There were a lot of people around, so Alberto relaxed, took a seat, and accepted a bottled water. He posted a picture of the set on Instagram, sent it to Mathias to antagonise him a little further, and sat quietly on a chair, thinking he was lucky to have escaped Stasia this once, but tonight, he'd face the same problem. That evil spawn had already told her father he hadn't slept at home, because Mamma sent a dozen texts, and he had to make up this crazy story about having forgotten to let her know he was invited to a party.

How many more times would he have to dress and undress in public and strike silly poses so that he could leave this place? How many weeks? How many months? Tonight, Stasia would be ruthless. He had the key to his room, but she could catch him before he'd get the chance to lock himself in. And then…

His phone beeped. Mathias had answered his text with one gruff line.

I'm still hard.

Alberto let out a laugh and replied:

I'll make it up to you.

When?

Whenever you want.

No take-backs?

No take-backs.

It was dark when they were finished. Josephine showered him with compliments, told him he seemed brighter today, asked about his brand of moisturiser. *It's Mathias's cum! 100% organic,* Alberto wanted to retort, but she was his agent, and she was pretty cool, considering, so he kindly answered the question, and since he didn't like giving away his time for free, he turned bold and asked if he could keep the necklace he modelled with the clothes, and he was told that he could. He was even told to keep the shirt he had on, the one that said *LOOK AWAY* and that he complimented when they asked him to put it on earlier.

While he was undressing, he removed the necklace and separated the lock from the chain, thinking perhaps he could ask Mathias to choke him using that bad boy, and he didn't understand at first when the makeup artist gasped in horror at the sight of him.

He hadn't noticed she was around, or he wouldn't have stripped in front of her. But now that she was staring at his body in underwear, he didn't understand why she looked so shocked.

"Baby," she said, her hand before her mouth, "what happened to you?"

Alberto twisted his neck to look down at himself. "I don't know, I mark easily."

The girl rushed toward him, her eyes full of concern. "Did someone do that to you?"

"Well, yes," he replied, almost smiling.

He had very pale skin and marked easily. If he was held down for a certain length of time, he was sure to find a clear handprint later on. So, naturally, he bore the physical signs of his passion with Mathias. And he thought he looked beautiful, personally. These marks were a map of his relationship with Mathias, the places they'd explored together, blindfolded, making their way through the dark, following only the feel of their skin and the sounds torn from their throats.

"This is not right, baby," she said.

Alberto let out an impatient sigh. Mathias was the only one who was good to him, but all she could see was that they played a little rough. For once in his life, he wasn't in any pain, and that's the time people finally decided to take a good look at him.

Admiring the love bites on his clavicle, he threw his new shirt over his head, muttering to his reflection, "My body, my temple, my fucking rules." And he left the young woman to ponder his words.

From the other side of the exit door, he could already feel the biting December cold, the promise of an unpleasant evening and night. With a steadying breath, he pushed the door open anyway and emerged from the studio to find Mathias waiting. His breath caught in his throat, and he stood there stupidly while Mathias scowled back, his hood over his head and his hands buried in his pockets.

"Took you long enough," he mumbled.

"I didn't know you were waiting."

And Alberto realised he was a big fat liar.

Do you like girls or do you like boys? The words thundered through his mind, almost bringing him to his knees. The first time he was asked, he hadn't known what to answer. The thought had never occurred to him.

And so, Alberto found out he was gay by watching porn. Nothing romantic about that. He'd paced around Martin's screening room for a while, biting his nails, his bare head feeling uncomfortably chilly. His mother's former husband had an impressive movie collection, including hundreds of horror classics she didn't want him to watch. Martin didn't mind and encouraged Alberto to do whatever he wanted, even giving him access to the locked bottom shelf, the one with the really dark stuff. That's how Alberto stumbled upon Martin's straight porn collection hidden in the back. After a short-lived attempt at watching it, he felt resigned and decided to find his own.

It took him only a minute on the internet to find out he liked men on men very much, their edges, hard lines, and low grunts, nothing like the exaggerated shrieking of women he personally found repulsive. And so, he started exploring, and just like horror movies, porn had different subgenres. Alberto liked when they were rough with each other, he didn't care why, he just liked watching the bottom's face as he took it, he liked imagining himself to be him. *Must feel nice,* he often thought when he was lying on his bed at night.

Of course, he never thought such things would happen to him in real life. He believed they were in the realm of movies. No one fucks that well, right? He thought fantasies were best kept private anyway. But the first time Mathias took him, it happened so, so fast, there wasn't any time to think. Alberto didn't want to anyway, he simply couldn't believe his luck, how things were developing between them. Yes, it was fucked up, and yes, it did hurt, but he didn't want it to stop. Like with many things in his life, he was still pushing on, hoping for that moment when the pain would make way to something better, something brighter. And with Mathias, it did.

Prevedibilmente un frocio[1]. And so, he was.

Alberto found out he was gay by watching porn. Mathias found out he was gay watching Alberto. That's what he was burning to say last night, throw it out there as a joke, but he knew Mathias had limits, a fragile constitution when it came to that subject, and Alberto would rather die than lose his presence in his life. So, this morning, when he told Elisa he wasn't worried anymore, it had been a big fat lie. Right now, he was looking at Mathias's handsome face, and he felt worried.

———

"How did you find me?"

———

1. Slur; literally translates to "predictably a faggot". (Italian)

Mathias held up his phone with a reproachful look. "You pin your location everywhere. What if some crazy stalker starts following you?"

"You mean, like you?"

"…"

There was a silence. Mathias felt self-conscious, picking him up like that, but he'd spent all day trying to figure out how he could see him again, and he wasn't good with words, so he thought he'd just go there, grab him, gauge his reaction, reassess, that sort of thing.

Look away—look away—look away, his T-shirt said.

As if anyone could.

The silence between them stretched, until they couldn't even look at one another. Mathias glowered at his own shoes while Alberto gazed up at Saint-Étienne-du-Mont as if it were the only interesting thing in the vicinity.

"What?" Mathias gave in first. "You've never seen a church before?"

"I've never seen this one before."

"This one?" Mathias strode back toward the old church. "How is that even possible?"

Alberto followed him with a blank look. "Am I supposed to know it?"

"We're literally five minutes from school. You've never explored this neighborhood?"

"Oh? I didn't notice. I guess I'm not very good at this."

Mathias scoffed. "You're not good at anything, apparently. Except pissing me off."

"Really?" Alberto teased. "Nothing at all?"

Fire crept to Mathias's cheeks. "Seriously, you have the memory of a goldfish."

"That's a myth, actually—"

"Oh, *that* you'd remember. Anything to contradict me."

Alberto's gaze softened. His expression went straight to Mathias's head, causing it to spin. "I'm not good with memories, that's true. I only remember the bad ones."

All well-dressed and made-up, his hair perfect, he really was a picture. Mathias thought, *Hell, to catch him now and own him, that'd be such a great feeling. Hey, look what I've got. You can't find a better one. Or another one, period. I've got the only specimen right there.* A wave of longing swept over him, forcing his hands to ball into fists.

Look away, look away… The message on his T-shirt felt like a dare. Mathias tried, but it was no use. After a quick look around, he obeyed the impulse, dragged Alberto by his sleeve into the alley on the side, and pressed him up against the wall. His cold hands sliding under the taunting shirt drew an interesting sound from him, and he pushed his hips into him just as he kissed him with urgency because *Fuck bad memories, let's make some good ones, some really good ones.* Alberto loosely flung his arms over his shoulders but really dove into that kiss and damn, wasn't he a good kisser, just the right amount of everything, sending sparks shooting up his spine and blood rushing down his cock. He was the sexiest thing in the world, and he was his right now.

Mathias realized that if they were to be discovered right now, they would be found happy. The thought pierced his chest with the violence of an arrow, forcing him to break apart, but Alberto went chasing after him, and accidentally or not, he pressed one, two, three soft kisses on his swollen lip, and accidentally or not, Mathias brought him close and laid his chin on his shoulder.

"Alberto…"

"Yes?" He waited for a beat, then repeated, "Yes?"

Mathias shut his eyes. "… Nothing. I was just thinking about Eric."

"Oh… Oh."

He was just thinking about what Eric had said in the changing rooms. He was just thinking "That's just dumb" repeatedly, and he felt angry suddenly. He leaned back and stared into Alberto's impassive face. "Do you have to go?"

"What do you mean?"

"Don't you have something to do tonight? Someone… someone to see?"

Alberto didn't reply. Mathias pressed his body against his. "If you stay tonight, I'll fuck you better than any of them."

"I don't doubt that," he replied, looking amused. "But what about your family?"

"They're away all week."

"Really?" He sounded surprised. "Why aren't you with them?"

Mathias bit his own tongue. "I'm not good around this time of year. It's… It's… just how it is. So, you'll stay?"

"Is it because of your dad?"

"What?"

"Your dad. Are you afraid of him?"

Mathias stepped back, bewildered. "What?"

"You know, because he's a drunk?"

"No…" He had no idea how Alberto caught up on his father's bad drinking habit by meeting him once briefly in a hallway. "No, it's not like that."

"He isn't mean to you?"

"What? No! Can you please stop talking, for once?"

Mathias was seething. How hard could it be to invite one demon to sleep over without everything going wrong, for fuck's sake!?

Alberto didn't look too impressed. "I'm literally the least talkative person in the world, and every time I say one word, you always tell me to shut up—"

"Because everything you say is always wrong!"

They held each other's gaze for a certain length of time. Then, Alberto slowly parted his lips, which pissed Mathias off some more.

"Do you want to make out, then—"

"Yes!" Mathias grabbed him before he could even dare produce a smile, held his face between his burning hands, and devoured his mouth until he was reduced to moans. Then, he asked, "So, will you stay tonight?"

Alberto studied him through glazed eyes. "Why?"

Goddamn it.

Because I need you, that's why. You fill that void I've had since my mommy died. How about that, fuckhead?

"Because I'm bored," Mathias said.

Alberto revealed a faint smile. "I should buy you dinner," he said out of nowhere.

For dinner, they had popcorn to go with the movie they went to watch. What movie? No idea. They made out the first fifteen minutes until someone shouted at them to get a room, so they took it to the restrooms. Then, they ran out of the cinema, shouting and fighting about some dumb shit Alberto said or didn't say, and they frantically kissed again behind the dumpsters of some restaurant. Alberto slipped his hand into Mathias's underwear and laughed at him; he was shoved aside, and Mathias told him he was a bad influence, vexing him. Then, they walked around the city for a long time, not talking to each other, not parting either, and Mathias was exhausted when they finally made it back to bed.

Ten minutes later, they were at it again. Mathias gave in first, his hands groping blindly in the dark, unsure if they wanted to stroke or to bruise. Alberto wanted to fight. In the end, he got what he wanted.

Mathias thought he was an addict. He didn't know what Alberto was thinking, and it was angering him. Everything was angering him. He was pissed off at Alberto for luring him in, he was pissed off right now just as he was inside him. He was so pissed off. Alberto kept pushing him, he kept giving in, and that pissed him off even more. He was pissed off at himself because he couldn't stop. He couldn't love, but he couldn't stop. He couldn't care, but he couldn't let go. There was nothing he could do, again, but watch helplessly as the ground caved open under his feet.

Again, he was useless even to his own self.

31

HIDE AND SEEK

"Let me go, I need to pee."

Mathias begrudgingly let him go. Two mornings wasted now. No matter how sneaky he thought he was this morning, gradually scooting closer to get his hands on the sleepy creature who could make the cutest noises, Alberto wriggled out of his grip.

Naturally, he never came back from his trip to the toilet. Instead, he returned a quarter of an hour later all showered, and Mathias watched him get dressed with resentment. He knew the window was closed, and he'd have to find an excuse to have him stay another night.

He got up with a sigh. "I'm getting you breakfast this morning. Real breakfast," he added when Alberto smirked a little too seductively.

"No need. I'll get breakfast at home."

Mathias glanced up abruptly. "Home?"

"Home, yes." Alberto hesitated. "I have to change clothes, don't I?"

"All right," Mathias resisted the urge to kiss his nape as he walked past him. "Just wait for me here."

Alberto frowned. "Wait? For…?"

"I'll go with you. I need to stretch my legs."

A glint of mischief briefly brightening his eye, Alberto slumped against him. The fact that he smelled of Mathias's soap felt as weird as it was comforting.

"Don't you need to stretch your arms as well?" he asked.

Mathias's gaze fell on his lips. "My arms?"

"You know… boxing."

Mathias realized with surprise that he hadn't felt the need to go over there. He got so mad at his punching bag on Friday after visiting Alberto at his place that the owner had felt compelled to ask him if everything was okay. Since then, he'd been strangely fine.

"I'd love to come and watch," Alberto said, his fingertips dancing across Mathias's chest.

If Alberto came with him, Mathias felt the others would *notice*.

"They're closed during the holidays," he lied, gently laying him over the bed.

"Mathias…" Alberto slipped his hands around his neck and didn't notice him shudder. "Do you want to punch my face sometimes?"

Mathias was about to kiss his decadent lips, but after hearing such bullshit, he could only frown. "No, I don't want to punch your face." He paused, then added, "Weirdo."

His weirdo squirmed under him. "Do you want to fuck my face instead?"

Mathias wasn't sure what to say. He stared down at that face, wishing he could kiss it without creating a storm.

"Maybe tonight," he mumbled.

"Maybe before that," Alberto mused.

The matter of finding an excuse to ask him to stay over was resolved. Mathias buried his nose in Alberto's neck, nipped his earlobe, and chuckled at his outraged groan. "So, you'll stay, then. And your mother won't mind?"

"She went to Switzerland for a week."

"She left?" Mathias gave him a baffled look. "She left you behind?"

"More like I begged her to stay behind."

"Why?"

"I have work here," he said faintly.

"But what about Christmas?"

"What about it?"

"It's a family affair, isn't it?"

Alberto ran his hand over Mathias's scalp. "We should go soon. Go and get ready." And he pushed him off him.

They rode the metro together. Alberto's long legs were problematic between the narrow seats, so Mathias let him push his knees between his own so he'd have more space and threw discouraging glares at any fucker who felt inspired to take the seat next to his.

"How did you find my address the other day?" Alberto suddenly asked between two stations.

Mathias smiled. "I'm a spy, remember?"

Alberto didn't insist, but he did look concerned and kept quiet until they got out at Boulogne-Jean Jaurès.

At the sight of the mansion's gate, Mathias couldn't help feeling nervous. The last time he went in, things got weird. And it's not like they'd fixed the problem anyway. Mathias still had a million questions, Alberto was still holding his answers for ransom, and he feared bringing up the same old shit might result in the same debacle, when so far they'd gotten along surprisingly well.

Alberto let Mathias in, then stopped in the middle of the path and listened hard, so Mathias did, too. The wind whooshed past the bare trees and cars honked in the distance, but beyond that, it was quiet.

"What's wrong?" Mathias asked, perplexed.

Alberto turned to him with a half-smile. "Nothing. Let's go inside."

There was no one inside when they entered the house, but Alberto trotted up quietly, on his toes, and waved at Mathias to follow him upstairs. While he picked clothes from the largest and most organized walk-in closet Mathias had ever seen, the latter looked around the room to pass the time.

Alberto's bedroom looked like a movie set. It was perfect in a calculated way, like it was trying to imply the person residing here was rich *and* had taste. Despite the darker nature of who it belonged to, it was all white and beige and *soft*. He had a vanity table with a mirror like a real prince, and the rug on the floor was the fluffiest and most appealing thing Mathias had ever seen. A modern iMac was turned off on the otherwise empty desk. Mathias spotted a large picture pinned to a corkscrew above the screen and was drawn to the elegant figure of Alberto's mother holding a toddler on a beach.

"Baby Alberto."

Alberto looked over his shoulder but said nothing.

"Were you a cool baby?" Mathias asked, teasing.

"What's a cool baby?"

"Like, doing cool stuff, you know... weird stuff."

Alberto dumped a pile of black clothes in a mess into a leather duffle bag and lifted his gaze to the ceiling as if he were trying to remember.

"I was screaming a lot, apparently."

Mathias laughed. "Lost that urge along the way, huh?"

Alberto hung his head, and Mathias thought he was blushing a little. He couldn't be sure because he saw something else on the wall and became excited.

"Hey! Is that your dad?"

Alberto didn't look at the picture Mathias was pointing at. "Yes."

Alberto's dad had a fierce amount of jet-black hair and a seductive smile. He was shorter and not as good looking as Mathias had imagined. Next to him, pale and skinny and with his great cat eyes appearing larger than his face, stood a very young Alberto.

"You had already covered the supermodel look."

"What do you mean?"

"That cold, cold look. Eric once said you might be a serial killer."

Alberto huffed. "*That* look is worth a lot of money."

Not as much as your beautiful face, Mathias thought, not without shame. He forced himself not to gawk at it as Alberto walked out of his bathroom and tossed what looked like *beauty products* into his bag.

"Wait here," Alberto said. "I need to shave." He left Mathias and locked himself in his bathroom. Then, he returned looking somehow even better and smelling delicious. Joining Mathias by the window, he stood close enough that their arms were brushing against each other's.

"All done."

"Nice pool," Mathias said, jerking his chin toward said pool down below.

Alberto glanced down without interest. "Lots of people have pools."

"Nothing ever seems to impress you."

"Not swimming pools, in any case."

"That's because you're so weird."

Alberto slid him an odd look, and Mathias let it go. He didn't come here to rattle him. Why did he come here, exactly? That was another million-dollar question.

"What's that thing over there?" he asked to save face, pointing at a narrow building at the very end of their manicured garden.

"That is where Stasia lives. We better not go over there."

"Why?"

"Come on." He turned away. "I'll show you something *really* weird."

Mathias quietly followed Alberto into another bedroom and stopped, awestruck, in the middle of the doorway. This space was more like a temple than a place of rest, decorated in shades of red and gold and blue. Shimmering threads lined the sublime throw that covered the largest bed Mathias had ever seen, and every item of furniture seemed to have been purchased at an exclusive antique store. But above all, the place reminded Mathias of the Sistine Chapel because of the aberrant fresco painted on the ceiling. Mathias instinctively got closer to Alberto, as if the opulence of the room might be harmful to normies like him.

"Okay, it's… a bit much, but what's so weird about it?"

"This."

Alberto pointed at one spot on the ceiling, and Mathias went into a fit of coughing.

"Is that you?" He approached the bed, his eyes riveted to the ceiling. "That's you, that—"

"Not me." Alberto shook his head with a laugh. "That's my mother."

"God, you could be twins."

Alberto gazed up at the painted face, so similar to his own. "My stepdad is so obsessed with her that he's painted her on the ceiling of her own bedroom."

"She *sleeps* here?"

"No. Strangely, she moved their stuff to another room when he showed her the finished product."

Mathias couldn't help laughing. "She doesn't look that much like you, you know. Once you take a closer look…"

"She looked exactly like that when she was young. When Dimitri met my mother at a party in London, he told her he'd been in love with her since the time he saw her face on the cover of *Vogue Italia*, when she was about my age. He'd loved her ever since. He's obsessed with her, worships her like a goddess. Isn't that really weird?"

Mathias couldn't agree more; his stomach churned unpleasantly. "So, he had her eighteen-year-old face painted on the ceiling and didn't notice she looked exactly like you?"

His question was met with such contempt that Mathias had to ask, "You and him, are you close?"

Alberto's eyes narrowed. "He's not my parent, you know. He's just my mother's latest conquest. I've known him for about three years, and we've barely exchanged ten words. He thinks I'm weird. I think he's… orange."

Mathias chuckled. "Orange." He grabbed Alberto's chin and kissed his puckered lips. "Thanks, this room is disgusting, I don't feel so self-conscious anymore."

"The rest of the house is also ridiculous. Only my room is fine, because my mother designed it for me."

"Ever played hide and seek here?"

Alberto's eyes widened. "Sort of… why?"

"Mom said the only use for these mansions with a million rooms is to have some banging hide and seek parties. That's how we spent the time whenever we got invited to some big house."

Mathias couldn't help smiling at the memory. "I'm shit at hiding. She always found me instantly."

Alberto studied his face for a while, then leaned into him seductively. "We could play hide and seek." His lips grazed Mathias's ear. "I hide. You seek."

"Really?" Anticipation made him a little giddy. "And if I find you? What's my reward? Do I get to mess you up in one of these fancy beds?"

Alberto nodded and pressed their lips together. Mathias kissed back hungrily, but he was pushed away.

"Go on, count to one hundred."

Mathias did. And he counted fast because he had no patience.

He immediately lost him.

He went from bedroom to bedroom, checked the tub in which he found him the other day, scratched his head as he walked up and down the corridor, and kept thinking it only took him sixty seconds to lose him.

How could he misplace a guy as tall as a baby giraffe? Mathias seethed as he raced down the stairs. Some instinct made him doubt he'd find Alberto in the kitchen, but he went anyway. There was a stout woman wearing a black apron there. He froze when he saw her by the kitchen island, holding a knife. She blinked patiently at him, as if she wasn't surprised to see him.

"*Bonjour*," he said nervously.

She saluted him back in Italian with a smile. Embarrassed, Mathias whirled around and opened the first door he found. Cold air assailed him, and he found cement steps leading to a dark basement. Mathias smirked. Of course that dark creature would be hiding down there, for certain. He turned on the light on his phone and went down, thinking Alberto wouldn't give him a scare. Mathias would. He would make him squeak, and then he would make him come. The usual.

The basement was immense and contained all sorts of shit, which surprised Mathias, who thought rich people should be more organized than their counterparts, but in fact, they just have bigger basements. And this one was ridiculous, with one bare room leading to another, until Mathias reached the coldest and the deepest one where some old boxes and wrapped up frames were left to gather dust in every corner.

There was no sight of Alberto. Mathias walked over to the very end of the room just in case, and a shadow caught his eye. He raised his phone to light his way up and what he saw made his heart stop.

Alberto was looking down at him.

And smiling.

His mouth dry, Mathias lifted his phone a little higher. It wasn't Alberto himself who had startled him, but the second of three giant portraits propped against the wall, watching over the rest of the room like three sentries. About two meters tall and half a meter[1] across, each piece represented Alberto aged no more than thirteen or fourteen, focusing on his angelic face. And on the one facing him, his eyes were soft, and he was smiling.

Something about the innocence of that smile almost brought Mathias to his knees. He staggered back. The youthful faces were suddenly pressing down on him, the haunting smile sucking the air out of the room, crushing him under its weight. His heart pounding, Mathias abandoned the search and raced back upstairs.

He knew that face, he knew that smile. That *innocence.* He used to be that kid with the large hopeful eyes, the timid optimism. He used to look just like this. And then, his mom died.

Mathias returned to the ugly temple/bedroom and fell back on the bed with his face in his hands. A small noise caught his ear, and he glanced up just in time to see Alberto slowly stepping out of the walk-in closet. Mathias stared, bewildered.

"You— You were in here the whole time?"

Alberto nodded.

"Damn, you really are as quiet as a cat." Mathias chortled. "And you didn't even bother leaving the room. A masterclass in not giving a fuck."

"Thank you," Alberto said with a little bow.

Mathias was relieved to see him again. "Aren't you a bit too old and a bit too gay to hide in the closet?" he joked, his voice hoarse.

---

1. 79 by 20 inches

"It's very effective. You didn't think to look in here at all. Where did you go?"

"Everywhere else, including the basement," Mathias said, beckoning him closer. "I don't know why I thought I'd find you down there."

Alberto sat next to him on the luscious bedspread. "Neither do I. I never go to the basement."

Mathias reached out and pulled him for a kiss, stalling for time. When he released him, his lips were swollen red. "Down there… there were three pictures." He searched Alberto's face for traces of that expression he found downstairs, the sweetness that crushed him, but it wasn't there. Whoever Alberto kept his smiles for, it wasn't for him.

———

"They're good," Mathias was saying. "Who… who took them?"

Alberto rubbed his cheek against his shoulder. "A genius."

"Like… a big shot? Someone fa—"

He never got to finish that sentence. Alberto slipped on top of him, sat astride his thighs, and gave him a toe-curling kiss.

"Why are they in your basement?" Mathias pushed on his chest, his gaze unfocused.

"Mum wanted to keep them." Alberto cocked an eyebrow. "Look at you. You liked them, didn't you?"

"Yeah, I kinda did. That boy… I mean, *you*, you were cute."

"And I'm not cute anymore?"

Mathias scowled at him. "You're the opposite of cute."

"That boy…" Alberto rolled his hips, dragging a grunt out of him. "Do you want to do things to him?"

Mathias's burst of laughter rang false. "He's a little young for me, don't you think?"

Alberto gazed into his face with his most sensual expression. Under him, Mathias changed colours, his face also turning serious. Alberto's jumper was pulled over his head in an impatient gesture.

"This one, however…" Mathias clamped his hands over his bare waist. "Damn you… you're so fine."

"Thank you." Alberto offered his lips for a kiss.

He meant it for once. He was full of *thank yous* when it came to this one. He trailed his hands all over Mathias just to feel his hard edges again. Desire rushed to his head and his cock; he bit Mathias's lip, who pushed him away, his face serious.

"In the pictures…"

"What?" Alberto asked impatiently.

"You're… different."

"I was young."

"Not that…" Mathias's cheeks darkened. "You were so… so… beautiful."

Alberto let out a laugh. "I know."

"*I know*," Mathias mimicked, unimpressed.

"*He* said it. The photographer. He said I'd bring the world to its feet."

A strange glow appeared in Mathias's eyes. "And did you?"

"Of course not."

"Really?" Mathias flicked his lower lip. "Are you so sure?"

Yes, Alberto was quite sure the only defeated one was himself. He merely blinked at Mathias. "I quit after this shoot." He joined their lips together to avoid more talking, but he was only half successful.

"You really don't care, do you?" Mathias asked immediately upon getting some air.

"What?"

Alberto struggled with his zipper before he pulled the whole thing, hoodie, sweater and all, over Mathias's head. The sight of his skin and his lean muscles made his pulse quicken. At times, Alberto wanted Mathias to devour him whole and leave nothing behind, nothing for the others to scavenge. It was such an enthralling feeling.

"Anyone with your… face would, I don't know… be proud," Mathias said with a curious expression. "Or at least…"

"Grateful?"

Alberto noted with faint amusement that Mathias didn't seem to consider him so arrogant anymore. The childish part of him buried inside raised a victorious fist.

"How can you not care at all?" Mathias asked. "It's confusing."

Alberto felt like apologising, then he realised it would sound preposterous, to say the least. All he could do was put a stop to a conversation he knew he wasn't able to have. He could take him in his mouth. It was a way of saying *I like you that much* and also, *now's the time to shut up.*

In truth, Alberto felt grateful — not for that face, not unless Mathias confessed he adored it, otherwise Alberto would keep resenting it — but he was grateful for Mathias's company, here in this detested house, and he was grateful that Mathias appreciated how cute he still was at the age of fourteen. Grateful enough to be filled with a desire to give him the best of him.

They started fooling around in the guest room until they both agreed the setting was distracting because of Mamma's face staring down at them, all godlike. So, Alberto took Mathias back to Stasia's former room, where they made a real mess of the bedsheets. Well, Alberto did when he purposefully wiped his face on the bedspread.

Mathias never made a mess of anything, except Alberto himself. He fell back on the bedsheet next to him and reached down to pet his thigh, but he withdrew his hand at the last moment. Alberto didn't know how he felt about this. He made sure their arms brushed faintly against each other's, and he enjoyed listening to Mathias's ragged breaths for a while. Despite the silence, he felt comfortable. Perhaps because of the knowledge he would once again dodge Stasia tonight. Perhaps because not only would he get to avoid her, but he was to spend another night in a bed with Mathias. The thought filled his chest with an unfamiliar warmth. A series of yawns assailed him, and when he had finally conquered the last one, he caught Mathias staring at him. "What's wrong?"

Mathias hesitated. "Look, I'm not complaining…"

"But?" Alberto frowned. "Spit it out."

"You didn't."

"Never do." He nudged him. "What is it?"

"It's nothing, really, it's—"

"Just say it."

"Fine. Your jaw… it clicks."

That's it? Alberto assumed Mathias would tell him his technique sucked or something. He had watched so much porn since the day he jerked Mathias off and realised he could have performed better. He was tirelessly working to improve his skills, so any criticism would have been quite vexing.

This was nothing. Took him long enough to realise, in fact. Alberto stretched and rose on his elbow. "You're right. It does."

"How come?"

Alberto chuckled and put his chin in his hand. "When I was a kid, I was punched in the face so hard that my jaw broke."

Mathias sat up with a nervous laugh. "You're fucking with me, right?"

"I was in a coma for nine days." Alberto put on an air of innocence. "Does that sound like bullshit to you?"

"It does," Mathias said in a dark tone. "Ninety percent of what you tell me is absolute bullshit."

Alberto chortled. "Try fifty."

"Fifty, my ass. There. I'm not listening to you anymore. Why do you always say creepy shit like that to people anyway?"

"To *people*?"

"Okay, to me. That's because you know it riles me up, don't you?"

Alberto glanced at Mathias's lips. "You *do* pull the best faces."

"All right." He shook his head and laid back on the bed.

Alberto watched his concerned expression, and he wanted to sigh. His jaw clicked. So what? He *was* in a coma for nine days. It was a miracle he was still alive, the doctor had told Mamma. He was a miraculous boy.

But not a good boy.

Never a good boy.

Next to him, Mathias still looked unsettled. It amused Alberto, and he laughed, so Mathias's face relaxed some more, but even then, a slight frown remained. Alberto was not stupid enough to start talking now. There would be no one left to fuck him if he started blabbering on about his past. Mathias would run. Alberto had a nice arse, but he wasn't worth that much trouble in the end.

No one was, really. So, he crawled over to Mathias and took his lips before they could ask another pointless question. Mathias let go of his frown, and Alberto let go of these thoughts, but his jaw, unfortunately, still clicked.

32

ANGELS & DEMONS

THE WEEK PASSED IN A BLUR. Every day was spent together, in various states of mind — and undress — sometimes on their own, sometimes with his sister Ella. Each day, both of them trod carefully, mindful, in Mathias's case, not to ruin the fragile understanding between them.

"You don't have anywhere else to go?" Mathias had asked Alberto two nights before, when his eyelids were heavy with sleep after they'd done it.

"No... here is fine."

Here was fine. *They* were fine.

That day, it was raining, and they were trapped inside, bored. Homework wouldn't do, so they were killing time on their phones until Alberto started squirming on the bed, struggling not to fall asleep, looking extra devilish. He even held a lollipop between his treacherous lips, courtesy of Mathias's sister. To be honest, he had harassed her for it, and she only relented after Mathias begged her to let him have it.

Mathias, never an innocent, wanted Alberto to have it. He had his eyes on him, following him motionlessly like a predator stalking its prey. He knew that at one point, he'd get to have him today. So, there he was, in a good mood, wasting time for the sake of it, because he had no fear of watching him slip away. They talked idly, exchanging vague comments about the weather and Mathias's impending mock-exams as he flicked through Alberto's modeling account on Instagram. Picture after picture of him looking his best made Mathias feel amused at first, then gradually puzzled, then irritated, until Alberto took notice and even tried to take his phone away.

"Are you still looking at this?"

Mathias lifted the phone out of reach. "Almost done."

Alberto waved his hand, looking bored. "Why bother looking at these when the real thing's right in front of you?"

Mathias felt out of breath, so he kicked his foot, and Alberto withdrew his hand.

"The pictures are okay." He lightly cleared his throat. "But why do they only dress you in black?"

"*They* don't." Alberto popped the glistening lollipop out of his mouth. "I only post the ones I like."

Mathias gave a small grunt as he shifted on the bed. "That's dumb."

"Why?"

"People can't see what you're worth in other colors. Like blue or white."

"No need for pictures." Alberto blinked slowly. "I can tell you I look amazing in blue. And in green. And in burgundy—"

"You're so pretentious." Mathias nudged him with his foot.

"—and the world isn't ready to see me wearing all white."

"Why's that?"

"I'm too adorable. Societies would collapse at the sight."

The way he pronounced the word *collapse* had Mathias clench his fists. "You're so—"

"So what?" Alberto dragged the lollipop across the tip of his tongue.

"Forget it."

"You don't believe me?"

"Of course I don't. You're the king of bullshit."

"I *have* done photoshoots in white."

Mathias sprung to attention despite himself. He forced his voice to sound indifferent, but he wasn't too sure of his success. "Really?"

Thank God Alberto had turned his head away and didn't notice his eagerness.

"Really."

"Do you have proof?"

"... No."

"How come?"

"I don't remember the name of the brand."

"You're joking."

"I'm not."

"Fucking hell." Mathias threw himself back against the headboard. "I've never met anyone with such a shit memory."

He had been looking forward to seeing an all-in-white Alberto. Now he was in a bad mood.

Alberto gave a taunting laugh. "That's such a shame. Isn't it?"

Mathias grunted.

"Now you'll never know how adorable I look in white."

"No one cares."

"Oh. That's too bad. And just when I realised something..."

"What?"

"Never mind. Since you don't care."

Mathias could have hurled him out the window. "What? Spit it out!"

"There's a simple way to find out."

"What is it?"

Alberto looked at him as if he were stupid. "Guess."

"No care," Mathias blurted out. He meant to say 'Don't care' but was thinking 'No time.' His stupid brain seemed to be lacking oxygen every time that creature was lying on his bed.

Unconcerned by all this, Alberto played with his lollipop, rolling it over in his mouth while looking at him. "Easy. Lend me some white clothes. I'll wear them for you."

Fuck. Mathias had momentarily forgotten he *did* have the real deal in front of him. A real supermodel. Or just a model. Whatever he was, he was offering to wear clothes for him. The moment he heard him say *for you*, he'd already started to feel stiff down there. With the lollipop and the tone of his voice, it was a damn miracle this little talk had not escalated into some dirty shit already.

He didn't even bother answering him; he went straight to the wardrobe and picked up whatever clothes he could use. When he tossed him a few items, Alberto snorted and gazed at him with his evil eyes.

"What?"

"Oh, I see what you like," he said, holding a pair of socks.

"You don't know what I like," Mathias replied, a bead of sweat trickling down his spine.

"No?" Alberto started undressing, and for some reason, Mathias felt compelled to turn around, which only caused more dry hilarity on the monster's side.

"You're embarrassed and can't look at me anymore."

"I don't have white pants. I don't have pants in your size anyway. Your legs are too long."

"But the socks, really?"

Mathias whirled around. "Fine! I want you to wear the fucking socks. Will you please wear the fucking socks?"

"Yes, yes, fine."

When Alberto was ready, he went "Ta-dah!" and Mathias only briefly hesitated before turning around.

Alberto stood in a simple combination of a T-shirt, football shorts, and football socks, which, on him, did nothing to make him look like an athlete and everything like he was up to no good in an impossibly filthy way. The T-shirt and the shorts were a size or two too large as well, which only added to the sinfulness of the picture.

"It's not bad," Mathias said, swallowing.

Alberto laid back on the bed. "Told you."

"But it's not so great either."

He sat back up. "What's that?"

Mathias shrugged. "Could be better." He tried not to smile at Alberto's vexed expression.

"Of course it could. I could have been in a suit. I could have been in jeans. Tsk, even a lab coat would have been better than this."

Priceless.

"You look a bit like a tennis player."

"What? What!"

Mathias couldn't help laughing. He mimed the swing of a racket. "Yeah, you look like a tennis player."

Alberto grimaced. "Disgusting."

"Come on. A cute tennis player."

Alberto paused. "How cute?"

"Cute, cute." Mathias didn't want to annoy him too much, or he might not want to fool around anymore. "All innocent and shit."

"Oh, like a cherub?" Alberto's eyes narrowed. "I see your kind!"

"A what?"

"A cherub. You know those weird baby angels?"

"Angels…"

"Yeah, angels. Those chubby babies who are, like, servants to God or something." Alberto pulled the socks higher up his calves. "Child labour if you ask me…"

Mathias suddenly got an idea and left Alberto to speak nonsense on the bed. He borrowed something from his sister's room and returned, all proud of his brilliant idea. Alberto saw the thing he carried in his hands and forgot all about child labor. He knelt on the bedspread with his arms crossed.

"*O-kay*, Mathias, two revelations in one afternoon. Are you trying to scar me for life?"

Mathias turned and turned the fluffy angel's wings in his hands, unsure of how to proceed to make Alberto wear them. He could coax him, offer him a reward of sorts, promise to go along with his next ridiculous scheme, or he could simply say "Put them on or get out" and proceed to hold his murderous gaze for a dozen seconds.

And that's precisely what he did.

"Arsehole," Alberto said, but he was almost smiling as he put on the wings. "Happy now?"

Mathias watched him mess around for a minute, striking all sorts of silly poses and using the lollipop to tease him. He briefly consulted with his own body and nodded. "Happy."

Alberto jumped off the bed and began to slowly circle around him. Mathias said nothing, enjoying the view, until Alberto came around and slung his arms around his neck. The sweet scent of candy reached Mathias's nostrils.

"You've got an angel kink."

"I don't have an angel kick."

"A *kink*. And you do. Look at you." Alberto pretended to flap his wings. "All flushed. Just *ripe*."

"Demon," Mathias mumbled, hating and loving the way Alberto's lips looked when he over-pronounced his *p*. "You talk way too much."

Alberto arched an eyebrow. "Oh, am I a demon now? I thought I was an angel." He proceeded to prove he was *not* an angel by leaving a wet trail on Mathias's cheek with the tip of his tongue.

"You…" Mathias's hands showed restraint, but his thoughts scattered. "You're a wolf in sheep's clothing."

"Hm?"

"You know. A demon pretending to be an angel."

"And you…" Alberto almost kissed his lips. Almost. "You're the opposite."

Suppressing a shiver, Mathias removed Alberto's arms from around his neck, who turned around with a shrug. "Look, don't be embarrassed. It's fine. Angels in football gear. Some people like much weirder stuff. You wouldn't believe it."

"Pff. I don't care."

But he couldn't help thinking, *Like what? Like what, Alberto? What do you do with these other people? Do you like it better with them? Do they make you beg and cry as I do?*

As Mathias struggled with his frustration, Alberto was running around the bedroom and flapping his wings. Mathias couldn't remember the last time he saw that much animation in his eyes. He stared, losing track of his surroundings, and he started thinking, *run, run around, little one. If I catch you, I'll rip you apart.*

Who was the wolf? Who was the wolf again? Mathias staggered forwards to seize him, and in doing so, he forced Alberto to backtrack. Suddenly, the demon was toppling over on top of his dresser.

Mathias had had that thing his whole life. That's where he kept his school supplies and old textbooks and such. It was just a piece of furniture, and he'd never really thought about it until the day

Alberto, wearing cheap angel wings, fell ass-first on top of it, his eyes round with shock.

Mathias grabbed him. He really grabbed him. He dug his fingertips into his flesh and pushed his tongue into his mouth without mercy. After a strangled noise of surprise that sent Mathias's head spinning, Alberto let out a throaty "*Fuck me*," and Mathias thought, *just about, just about*, while trying not to snap.

Alberto hooked his legs around him and pressed their bodies together. "What's gotten into you?"

Mathias shook his head and closed his eyes, feeling suddenly like he couldn't breathe at all. He gripped the first thing in his reach, Alex's binoculars, and pretended to inspect the street down below.

"Hey," Alberto panted, his eyes glowing with outrage, "Are you serious right now?"

"Thought I saw something." Mathias couldn't help snickering. "False alarm."

Out of nowhere, Alberto clutched his face and gave him a bruising kiss. Mathias had no choice but to drag him down and throw him onto the bed, but to his astonishment, Alberto pulled him down with him and rolled over to lay on top of him. Mathias scooted backwards toward the wall. The moment their eyes met, his heart jolted savagely, and a powerful wave of longing rippled through him. The force of it confused him; he tried to push Alberto away.

"Go. Go away."

"You dress me up like this, and then you want me to go away?" Alberto watched him retreat deeper into the bed until his back met the headboard. "Not gonna happen." With those words, he jumped and sat on top of him, trapping Mathias between his knees. Mathias wanted to shove him aside, but it was too late. The moment he felt Alberto against him, he turned both as hard as a rock and as soft as the drizzle outside.

Alberto knew he had won. He gave a little smirk. "Angel kink."

"I hate you," Mathias said, but he couldn't help laughing.

When they looked at each other then, they both seemed to realise something was different. Alberto on top. Never happened.

Mathias smiling. Never happened. But there was something else. They were so close, and if they were to fuck right now, they would see each other's faces, and that had never happened before. The idea filled him with excitement yet also with inexplicable fear.

Maybe he had overdone it today. Taken their games a little too far. He really should push him away now, call it a day, invoke the great excuse of piled-up homework. Maybe he shouldn't see him again this week. This year. Ever.

But then, Alberto pulled the lollipop from his mouth, and slowly rolling his hips, he hummed like this shit piece of candy was the best thing he'd ever tasted. Desire became stronger than fear, and suddenly Mathias wanted to tear off his clothes and take him in the middle of the bed with his socks on.

"Is it good?" he asked, his voice thick.

Smacking his lips, Alberto rolled his hips back before answering, sending a shiver rocking through him.

"It's good."

"Yeah?" Mathias's hands had already moved to his thighs. He pointed at the lollipop. "What does it taste like?"

"Coke!" Alberto said, bouncing up and down, causing Mathias to dig his fingers into his flesh. "I like the way it tastes. Even feels tingly, like the drink."

"Bullshit."

Alberto leaned closer. Cold grey eyes, vaguely shaped like a cat's, bore into his. "*No, sei tu. Sei il re delle stronzate.*[1]"

"*No comprendo,*[2]" Mathias croaked. "Give it here." He took the thing out of his mouth to plug his own, worried he might say something he'd regret later.

"*Bastardo.*"

"Hey!" Mathias laughed around the lollipop. "I got this one."

"Hot." Alberto hissed, then his gaze turned cold. "Give it back. It's mine."

Mathias had no intention of returning it, but the moment he removed it from his mouth to mock Alberto, the latter grabbed the

---

1. "No, it's you. You're the king of bullshit." (Italian)
2. "I don't understand." (Spanish)

stick and tugged it toward himself. Mathias resisted, and they went back and forth, until Alberto suddenly let go, and the lollipop flew across the room to stick itself to his expensive coat hanging on the door.

"Shit, sorry," Mathias said, thinking that thing was cursed. But Alberto didn't care. He was smirking.

"You've done it. Now there's nothing left for either of us."

"That's a shame."

"Although…" Alberto lowered his voice to a whisper. "There's still some on my lips." He swiped his tongue over said lips, then drew in a sharp breath when Mathias's fingers curled around his thighs before sliding under him as he brought their mouths together.

Something definitely felt different. Their kiss started slow and tender almost, as though they really were trying to taste each other. But maybe because Alberto rocked his hips once more, or because Mathias hummed into his mouth, it quickly grew out of control.

Mathias made short work of Alberto's wings, and they were tossed on the ground. The T-shirt followed, then his own, and suddenly, it was just Alberto in football shorts and football socks, grinding against him. Mathias broke away to look at him, his heart pounding so hard he thought it might blow up right inside his chest.

Fuck. Maybe that really was his thing after all.

At that precise moment, Mathias had never felt more like a man. Thoughts none too gentle bounced around in his head, turning his mind foggy. With one shaky hand, he scrabbled around for a condom in his nightstand drawer, and with the other, he kneaded his supermodel's ass, unwilling to part even for a second. Between messy kisses and with fumbling fingers, Alberto was opening his jeans. Mathias slipped his hand into his white shorts and swallowed his feeble moan. He thought he felt him *smile*; his own lip curled up.

And then, the doorbell rang.

Eyes flying to the door, they immediately parted. A series of excruciating noises blared out from the intercom in the hallway, as if the person ringing the bell was trying to play a tune.

"Ah!" Alberto put his hands over his ears. "What the hell is this?"

"No…" Mathias forced the lusty fog that had engulfed him to clear. "I don't have anything planned until… Fuck!" It *was* Friday already! "Fuck!"

Alberto screwed his eyes shut. "What is happening…?"

"It's Eric. He's coming for homework. I'd completely forgotten."

"That idiot! Does he have to ring the bell like that?"

"Y-Yes." In his panic, Mathias's voice cracked. "That's what he does. Come on, get dressed."

Alberto scowled briefly at the ceiling, but he didn't protest, despite Mathias's expectations. He rolled off the bed and began to put his clothes on. Mathias felt uneasy watching him do as he was told in silence, so he rushed to the intercom and yelled at Eric to stop ringing the door.

"Okay, but let me in, it's raining!"

"Just stop pressing that damn button!"

Mathias raced back to his bedroom. Alberto was already dressed. He threw a look over his shoulder, his beautiful face glowing even in the absence of light, and he asked, "What do I do?"

What do you do? What do I do? What do I do?

"Mathias? Where do I hide? There's only one door."

And Mathias thought about it for a split second. What would happen if he asked him to stay…? If he opened the door, let Eric in, and said, *That's Alberto, you know each other, we're just hanging out.* What then?

What a stupid question. Everything would be fucked, that's what would happen. Mathias had to be smarter than that.

"Come, quickly."

He led Alberto to the landing, hoping to let him take the stairs, but Eric, that maniac, was already climbing them. Mathias slammed the button to call the elevator, but that thing was God knows where and wouldn't make it on time, and all the time, Alberto was too tall and too quiet. And so, Mathias shamefully pushed him into the storeroom with the neighbour's stroller, his bike... and the garbage chute.

Right when he was closing the door on Alberto's expressionless face, grimacing at the bitter taste filling his mouth, Eric came onto the landing in a raincoat, wearing his backpack on his chest. He went to him, his hand stretched out as if he were about to shake it, but then he changed his mind and pulled Mathias close for a hug, or a kiss, who knows, since Mathias just shoved him away.

"Hey, Eric."

That was the second time in less than a week he had tossed Alberto into the trash. How the hell would he be able to look at himself in the mirror tonight?

"Hey!" Eric nudged him. "Did you notice anything weird?"

"Like what?" Mathias held his breath as Eric squinted at him.

"The intercom! Did you get it? I was trying to play 'Funky Town'!"

Mathias let out a relieved sigh, feeling a sudden rush of affection toward his friend. "You've watched *South Park* again."

"That towel really gets me!"

"I don't know what that means."

With a last look toward the storeroom, Mathias led Eric inside.

33

FAMILY TIES

MATHIAS FOCUSED on whatever his friend was saying just as well as Eric focused on anything whenever Zak was around, meaning *not at all.* Thank God they just had some documents to exchange and didn't have to write anything down, or Eric would have noticed something was off. The minutes dragged on while he explained how he had tackled his part of the economics project, and Mathias could only think of Alberto in the storeroom and couldn't help wondering what had happened to him after that.

At last, Eric got up, stretched to his maximum, then excused himself to use the bathroom just as Mathias's phone started ringing. He jumped on the device like a worried father in a kidnapping movie and clutched it close to his ear, his heart thumping.

It was his sister.

"Matt, I found Alb— I mean *Alfred* outside. You done with him?"

Mathias lurched forward and slammed his knee into the foot of the dining table. "Ah! Fuck! Fuck!"

"He says *fuck, fuck*—"

"Wait..." Mathias clutched his knee, tears pricking his eyes. "Tell him—"

"He says *fuck you, too.*"

"Fuck!" The pain in his knee was blinding.

His sister sighed on the other end of the line. "He says *fuck* again."

Mathias whimpered. "No! Listen. Do not let him go!"

There was a silence.

"He said he'd take me to a bar."

That freakish bastard. Mathias kicked the wall, and the pain reverberated in his wounded knee. "Fuck!"

"We'll meet you at the bar," she said, and she hung up.

Mathias dropped to his knees and didn't stop there. He lay on the cold floor and closed his eyes. Eric emerged from the bathroom and rushed to his side.

"Jiminy Cricket, Matt! What happened?"

Mathias let out a life-expiring groan.

Eric peeled him off the floor with a concerned look. "Is something wrong?" He bent down to brush nonexistent dust off his knees.

"It's Christmas Eve. I had forgotten."

"Huh?" Eric gave him a look of disbelief. "But nobody ever forgets Christmas. It's Christmas!"

"I was really busy."

Eric looked around the apartment with a quirked eyebrow. "M'kay... Imma leave you to it, then." He pulled a stunned Mathias into a *tutti-frutti*-smelling hug. "I'll see you at Xavier's brunch on Sunday."

"Oh, fuck! I had completely forgotten about that, too."

"You said you'd come, you have to come, or I'll be super sad. Everyone is coming." Eric added darkly, "Even Alberto, I heard."

Mathias forced his lips to stretch into a smile. "I'll be there."

"Great!" Eric wrenched the front door open. "I'll see you there, then! Merry Christmas, best buddy." And he left, humming to himself the melody of "Funky Town".

When Alberto returned, he was accompanied by Ella and, to Mathias's shock, their *dad*.

"Surprise!" Elisa cried, laughing. "You're so gullible! Alb... red didn't even take me to a bar!"

"I just couldn't let this poor kid spend Christmas on his own," Mathias's father said with a disapproving look.

This poor kid? *This poor kid?* No one knew what he was capable of. If Eric had not interrupted them, Mathias would be in serious fucking shit right now. *This poor kid* was a demonic creature carved from the pits of Hell and deserved to be put back in his place and—

"I brought you food," Alberto said gently, handing him a shopping bag.

"*Pollito*," Mathias choked out, feeling like slamming his fist directly into his own face. "You're back."

The confused look on Alberto's face was enough proof for him. He was in serious shit anyway.

"Why are you both here?" Mathias took his father to the side, leaving Alberto in Elisa's clutches.

"You want to stay home, that's fine, but we're going to keep you company. We're not gonna be apart on Christmas Eve."

"What about—"

"We'll spend the day with the family tomorrow. But, uh… is this one all right?" Dad sounded concerned. "Who leaves a kid behind at Christmas?"

Mathias wished he'd stop calling Alberto a kid. "He's fine, he's fine. He asked his mom to leave him behind. He has to work." Elisa pranced toward them and threw herself into her father's arms. Mathias checked Alberto was still out of earshot and added, "I've asked him twice already. He told me he doesn't care about Christmas."

"What a weirdo!" Elisa said with a giggle.

Dad ruffled her hair. "I'm not letting him spend Christmas Eve on his own. Isabella would kill me."

Mathias said nothing, knowing it was true. His mother had taken Christmas seriously.

Elisa grumbled, "That's what I said," and so it was decided. Alberto would spend Christmas Eve with them, but just to be safe, Mathias traipsed over to him and told him he could leave if he wanted.

"Do you want me to leave?" Alberto asked in his flat voice.

Mathias chose his words carefully. "They really want you to stay."

Alberto then pushed the bag of groceries into his arms and Mathias, with a sigh of relief, led him into his kitchen. "What do you usually eat at Christmas?"

"Oh…" Alberto stood in the middle of the kitchen with a perplexed expression. "I don't know."

"*You don't know?*"

"It's all catered." He hesitated. "I had a bad oyster once."

Mathias bit back a curse. "Well, here, we make our own food, then we eat it, like normal people. So, what do you like?"

Mathias opened the grocery bag Alberto gave him and recognized the ingredients for the chicken recipe they liked above all. No Venezuelan ingredients this year. Mom had had the terrible idea of dying around Christmas time, and since then, Mathias tended to choke up at the mere sight of a can of black beans. "Apparently, we're having chicken tonight. And… shrimps. And…" He glimpsed into the bag. "I see you were in charge of the veggies. But why so many cucumbers?"

Alberto shrugged. Mathias let it go because he looked adorable, so tall and useless in his kitchen. He could probably do whatever he wanted to him in here, but he decided not to think too much about it.

"And what do we have here?" He dipped into the bag again. "*Une bûche?*" He quirked an eyebrow. "You got us… cake?"

"Yes," Alberto said. "Your sister insisted, but I got to choose. "So, I took an ice-cream cake. Coffee flavoured. Your sister said okay because she likes coffee, too."

"She's like you, she drinks way too much of it." Mathias set up the ingredients in front of him and went to wash his hands. "Do you want to help me?"

Alberto lowered his head. "I don't know how to cook."

Mathias grinned. "You've never asked your maid to teach you?"

His words brought a look of shock to his face. "You know I have a maid?"

"Yep. Stumbled upon her the other day when we were… playing." Mathias recalled how their game degenerated in the pink bedroom and felt hot all over. "She seemed nice."

327

Alberto's expression relaxed. "She *is* nice. Her name's Dina. She's Italian, like me."

"I kinda figured you had a maid the moment I saw the size of your house."

"I just thought—"

"What?"

"I thought you'd be, you know…"

Mathias realized Alberto didn't want him to know because he thought he would give him shit about it. And his concern that Alberto may be frightened of him at times intensified, turning his stomach.

"That's okay. Sit down. Yes, here. You could slice the cucumbers, for example. That's easy."

Alberto gave a small nod. "Okay."

When Elisa entered the kitchen, her mouth fell open. Mathias was elbow-deep in flour, stretching the dough for his pasta, and Alberto sat at the other side of the table, cutting a cucumber into overly thin slices.

"What's that?" Elisa asked, approaching to inspect her brother's work. "You made pasta?"

"Yeah."

"You *made* pasta?" She frowned. "You made the dough yourself?"

"*Yes.*" Mathias gave her a warning look.

Her clever little eyes narrowed and fell on Alberto, his lower lip stuck between his teeth, dutifully slicing his cucumber.

"You never make pasta," she said with a sly smirk.

"That's not true." Mathias waved his knife. "I've made pasta before."

"Nah… I'd have remembered. You—"

Mathias stabbed the knife into the cutting board to shut her up. She did so with a cheeky grin. Alberto, fighting with a yawn, shot them a look.

"What's so special about making pasta?"

"Get back to your cucumber!" Mathias barked. He had begun to sweat. It seemed the water had finally reached boiling point.

"And why do you have him cut cucumbers?" Elisa went on. "Is

that a new recipe I've never heard of? What's the point if you're not going to use them?"

Alberto glanced up. "What?"

"Don't mind her, she's a demon." Mathias pushed his sister toward the door. "Out! Out! This is my kitchen."

"I'm hungry!" She whined, ogling the ingredients scattered across the countertop.

"She's always hungry, this one. She eats like a horse."

"But she's so tiny," Alberto said.

Elisa glared at him then tried to pilfer a shrimp. Mathias slapped her hand away. "Get some peanuts if you're hungry, but don't touch my shrimps."

She grunted and watched Mathias shelter the shrimps into the fridge with a begrudging look, then she stood on her toes to reach the snacks cabinet. Mathias put down his rolling pin to help her, but Alberto was faster.

"Don't try to woo me," she snarled, stretching her hand toward the peanuts. "I still think you're trash!"

Mathias's stomach dropped. He turned around to tell her not to say that to him, but the two were obviously having fun. Alberto was holding the peanuts way out of her reach, and she had already climbed over his back like a monkey to get them.

"You're not useless after all!" She squeaked, excited. "You're like a human ladder!"

To Mathias's shock, Alberto helped her down with a laugh. A dry sort of laugh, but a laugh, anyway.

"Write that on my tombstone," he said, laying the bag of peanuts on top of her head. "*Here lies Alberto. He was especially good at letting others climb on top of him.*"

Mathias broke into a coughing fit while Elisa split the bag open with a maniacal laugh. Now that she had her prize, she had no interest in sticking around. Worried Mathias might ask her to help out, she dashed out of the kitchen in an explosion of peanuts.

Alberto shook off the ones that had landed in his hair and glanced down at his pile of sliced cucumbers. "Are you seriously making me cut ingredients you won't use?"

The truth was, cucumbers were easy to slice, and Alberto was already so slow at it, it was clear he would be a burden if he attempted anything else, and Mathias didn't have the heart to tell him. He leaned across the table until they were nose to nose.

"We'll get to eat them if you want."

"We will?"

"Sure. They eat whatever I put on the table. They'll do the same with you, too."

Alberto's gaze unexpectedly softened. It really was Christmas, Mathias noted wordlessly.

On Christmas Eve, Alberto had expected to dine alone at home and be asleep by nine with all his doors locked, and that sounded like a great night to him, honestly.

Instead, he sat at the end of Cyril Rodin's table, sandwiched between a constipated-looking Mathias and his sister who couldn't help throwing weird looks at him, probably hoping her dad would understand what sort of arrangement they had here.

He came across the Rodins right as he was escaping Mathias's building after being interrupted by Eric. Cyril called him Alfred and asked him his plans for Christmas Eve, and Alberto was either too dumb or too horny to lie, so he told the truth. Mathias's dad was horrified that anyone could spend the *Réveillon* alone. Elisa, standing close to her father, was listening with a pompous look, but since he directed her toward the Pots of Ancient Rome exhibition, she was mostly civil with him. Yesterday, she even gave him a lollipop.

Alberto was afraid of being dragged back inside because Eric was still up there. If he weren't who he was, he might even have panicked. So, he gingerly offered to help Cyril shop for food, and the Rodins took him to the supermarket.

He didn't tell them he didn't know much about food, including how to shop for ingredients. He usually went for anything fibrous and with enough plant-based proteins not to die, and that was the extent of his palate. So, he seized the most appealing veggies and piled them up into a basket, hoping for the best.

Mathias's father was determined, going from aisle to aisle like, "My son loves to cook, so we must get him stuff to play with. He'll be all pent-up if he doesn't get what he wants."

It took Alberto everything not to snigger.

At dinner, he watched as Cyril tried his best not to drink his wine too fast when he clearly wanted to. In fact, everyone was making an effort. Cyril refused to give in to his coping mechanism, Elisa tried her best to be civil toward Alberto despite thinking he was *trash*, and Mathias's refusal to make eye contact with the family photographs on display across the room were clear indicators that his mother had probably passed away right around the holidays. And yet, he'd cooked everyone a sumptuous meal. These people were taking care of each other. That's what families were supposed to do, in theory.

To Alberto, family meant *Mamma*.

Sitting among the Rodins, Alberto felt her absence deeply. The thought of her away with yet another man instead of safely home with him brought a pang of jealousy to his heart. Then, he recalled that she had begged him to reconsider, even offering to cancel the whole trip, and he was the one who insisted on solitude.

Solitude was all he ever wanted, or so he thought, until earlier today when he was easily convinced to spend Christmas Eve with strangers.

Cyril caught Alberto gazing into his glass of Bordeaux. "I drink too much," he said with a clipped smile.

Mathias shot him a nervous glance.

"It's the truth," Cyril admitted. "What about you, Alfred? What's your vice?"

Caught off guard at being asked a direct — and meaningful — question, Alberto opened his mouth, but nothing came out. And speaking of vice, the man in front of him was free of it. His gaze held all the softness Alberto found in Mathias's eyes after he'd messed him up, which he insisted on interpreting as gratefulness. Cyril Rodin was shy and probably thought himself very plain. This man had never hurt anyone but himself.

Alberto couldn't be unhelpful and sardonic as he liked to be with other people. He couldn't say, *Monsieur Rodin, in truth, I'm addicted to sucking your son's gorgeous, gorgeous dick. Merry Christmas!* And so his mouth hung open, and he could feel Mathias gradually tense next to him, knowing full well what was on his mind, meaning his *gorgeous, gorgeous dick*, so Alberto swallowed — he was very good at swallowing — and blurted out, "I'm a vegetarian."

That's when the little shit that was Mathias's sister exploded in laughter, and Mathias jumped to his feet, shouting, "Fuck!"

Cyril was mortified, and immediately removed the plate of chicken that was in front of him, muttering, "That's why he didn't touch the shrimps," and Elisa roared, "Unleash the cucumbers!" and they both tore toward the kitchen while Mathias stood in front of Alberto, looking flabbergasted.

"I'm sorry," Alberto said weakly.

"Huh?" Mathias shook his head. "No, it's me. I can't believe I never noticed. Didn't you say you had a bad oyster once?"

"I did. Before I became a vegetarian."

"Why didn't you say anything earlier?"

Alberto told the truth. "I didn't want to be a bother."

For some reason, his answer seemed to put weight on Mathias's shoulders, but he smiled and said, "That's fine. The pasta is vegetarian."

"I'm really sorry."

"I get it," Mathias said with a curt nod. "No meat for you until tonight." And just as his dad and sister were remerging from the kitchen, he flashed him a playful wink.

Relief flooded throughout Alberto, and when Cyril put down the new dishes on the table, he thanked him with his best attempt at a smile. Mathias's father took his seat back and said, "My wife was a vegetarian."

Elisa acquiesced solemnly.

Alberto met Mathias's eyes, who lowered his head. "She was very annoying," he grumbled.

But it only made his relatives laugh.

"The worst!" Elisa said proudly, and she downed her glass of Champomy[1] as quickly as a literary prize winner.

---

1. Sparkling apple juice fermented and preserved in the traditional method of

They loved each other, these people, grieving from the absence of what Alberto assumed was the bonfire that brought the rest of them together. That woman was long dead, and still, Alberto could feel her warmth. Like Mathias, he avoided looking at the pictures on the wall for fear of being dragged into the abyss.

Alberto dined on a salad including delicious cucumbers *sliced by himself* and Mathias's homemade spinach and ricotta ravioli. He'd watched him roll these delicate ravioli between his fingers, and Alberto knew, oh god, he knew better than anyone what else these fingers could do. He enjoyed every bite as though it had really come out of Mathias, and maybe that's why he looked a little pleased with himself sitting at that table. For dessert, he had a slice of the ice-cream cake, which made Elisa act silly as though she were drunk on Champomy, and Alberto, amused, thought the whole thing really had not only started to look, but also *feel,* awfully domestic.

After dinner, Cyril and Elisa stayed in the living room to watch *Die Hard* — the only Christmas movie in their opinion — and Mathias took Alberto back to his room and started unwrapping him like a Christmas present.

"Your mum died around Christmas time, didn't she?"

Mathias pulled his jacket off and answered to the crook of his neck. "Yes."

"I'm sorry."

"At least I had a happy childhood," he said, leaning back. "Not everyone can say the same. I can still remember when Elisa was born… and I held my baby sister…" His voice grew thick. "God, we were happy. We were so happy, and we didn't know how much time we had."

Instinct told Alberto to move faster than he was accustomed to. He pressed their bodies together in the middle of the dimly-lit bedroom and found Mathias's lips, but their kiss felt too needy for his taste, and he broke away abruptly.

Champagne AND presented in a Champagne-style bottle. This beverage is much adored by children and fancy little sh*ts.

"What about you?" Mathias said, searching for his eyes. "Were you a happy child?"

Alberto couldn't help laughing under his breath. "Uh, *no.*"

His reply earned him a perplexed frown. "Are you saying you were always... gloomy, like this?"

"I'm not sure," Alberto said truthfully. He wanted Mathias to remove the rest of his clothes so they could get down to business, but the other did nothing but stare at him, so Alberto removed his own shirt, and Mathias caught his wrist as he was tossing it in the back.

"Alberto... where's your dad?"

"Italy." Alberto pulled Mathias's shirt over his head. "Where else would he be?"

Mathias's eyes narrowed. "Is he alive?"

"Yes."

"Do you miss him?"

Alberto took a moment longer before he answered "... Yes." Before Mathias could ask another question, he zipped open his jeans, tugged them down to his ankles, and slowly sunk to his knees.

There. No more talking.

Mathias received his Christmas present with the usual gratefulness, expressing it by fucking him senseless, his head buried in a pillow to swallow all of his noises. Neither of them attempted to look into the other's eyes. No one would dare, after today. And this day, which had felt to him like a bizarre truce, was finally over.

All but worn out, Alberto shivered ostensibly on his side of the bed. Mathias pulled the comforter over their naked bodies. "You're always so cold," he whispered.

"Am I?" Alberto asked, his voice sleepy. "I don't feel it."

Mathias grabbed him by the waist and pulled him against him before sliding his hand down to cup his bare arsecheek. A wave of pleasure swept across his body, causing goosebumps to erupt all over his skin. Mathias noticed him shuddering; he removed his hand and scooted away.

"Sorry, forgot," he muttered.

Alberto struggled to repress the cry that wanted to break free.

Whatever meek sound he'd make was sure to disgust Mathias forever, but he kept thinking the words as he missed the touch of his hands.

I'm a little cold, he wanted so badly to say.

I'm a little cold, a little cold…

He fell asleep clutching his chest, hoping for some warmth, finding none.

34

INTERLUDE

When Alberto worked on two other shoots that week, Mathias went to pick him up afterwards as if it was a normal thing, just like their Bloodhound Gang game that was just between the two of them. Mathias and Alberto had listened to that band so many times during that week, they now knew their songs by heart.

Alberto favoured the one about *Dads and Pussies* — a weird choice — and liked sharing the lyrics with Mathias, but they could never finish it. The first time because Mathias couldn't resist the way Alberto said *pussy*, so he had to push him against the wardrobe to plug his mouth with something. They tried again the next day but went only as far as *Matthew McConaughey*. After that, Mathias lost it when Alberto, brandishing his toothbrush, shouted *surge protector!* A laugh turned into a kiss that turned into something else... Alberto never raised his voice unless he was having a *very, very* good time, usually when Mathias was a bit rough with him. In any case, they didn't even make it to bed that day, but jerked each other off right there on the floor.

Good times.

Alberto never said he wanted to go home. Mathias never asked him to. It seemed they were both killing time until night came and they could finally fall back into bed under the cover of the dark. No questions asked. No bad answers.

They were fine, Mathias thought. And he knew in the back of his head he had gotten used to this strange creature. He had gotten used to his weirdness, his sleep pattern, and his constant lack of appetite, but mostly, he had gotten used to his presence by his side in the dead of the night.

After an intense night spent in his empty apartment, Mathias woke up late, wishing Alberto's mom would've stayed in Switzerland for another week. Because today, right after Xavier's stupid Christmas brunch, Alberto would have to return home to her side.

Alberto was curled against him, his back against his chest and his ass pressed nicely against his fast-stiffening cock. Mathias silently thanked the gods he didn't believe in for finding him like that. Or perhaps he should just thank the fact that it was cold last night. He quietly buried his nose in his hair, inhaled his scent, and slowly, slowly started rocking his hips to entice him.

A whole week they had spent together, and Mathias had never had the chance to reunite with Morning-Alberto. Each day, the creature escaped him to go to the bathroom, and each time, he returned showered and "ready to start the day." Desperate, Mathias had even thought of setting his bathroom on fire, but he agreed that sounded a little drastic.

On the third strategic roll of his hips, his erection slipped between Alberto's cheeks, and Mathias almost let a sound loose. Next to him, the creature stirred. Mathias held his breath.

"Mm…" Sleepy Alberto sounded like a disturbed kitten. Mathias repeated his earlier thrust, and the demon coiled against him and *moaned*.

Mathias almost came.

With great focus, he did it again, and again, and again, and Alberto finally reached behind him with a hand, warm from hours in bed. It found its way to Mathias's thigh and squeezed it gently.

"Hi…" Mathias said.

Alberto slowly opened his eyes. To Mathias's consternation, the first word that came out of his lips wasn't *more* but, "Xavier…"

A thunderbolt striking him over the head would have had less effect. All the blood that had eagerly rushed south flooded right back into Mathias's cheeks. He didn't even move but asked in a hoarse voice, "… Xavier?"

Alberto hummed and rolled onto his back. He met Mathias's furious glare and pressed his finger between his eyebrows.

"We have to get ready for Xavier's brunch."

"Oh."

Mathias felt really stupid at times. He buried his nose in Alberto's neck and rocked his hips into his side again. "Wanna play first?"

Alberto wriggled away. "Too tired."

Too tired. Keeping his disappointment to himself, Mathias sat up.

"Say, you really don't have cancer, do you?"

Alberto also sat up. "What? Why?"

"You sleep too much, and sometimes, you also look on the brink of death." Mathias flicked his lips, the annoying things that caused him not to sleep at night. Alberto slapped his hand away with a grimace. "And I know it's not because you're a vegetarian."

"Oh?" He dodged his attempt at a kiss. "Is that because you're personally watching over my protein intake?"

Mathias chuckled. "You're so filthy." After a pause, he added, "My mom was a vegetarian, and she could have kicked your ass."

"I don't doubt that." Alberto ran a hand through his hair. Mathias felt the inexplicable urge to tear out a good chunk of it. "Anyone can kick my arse, to be honest."

Not while I'm here, no they can't. Mathias furrowed his brow.

"Your sister could probably do it," Alberto continued. "What? Why are you looking at me like that?"

"Like what?"

"Like you want to hurt me."

"I *do* want to hurt you."

Alberto tilted his head. "Don't make promises you can't keep."

"Who says I can't keep them?" Mathias flattened him into the mattress and bit into his neck. He felt Alberto's dry laughter reverberate through his throat.

"No, no, no, no!" He pushed him away. "Come on, we have to

get ready. You know I can't deprive poor Xavier of my company. He's desperately in love with me."

"Oh, yes, that's true." Mathias rolled his eyes. "He's paying you to come, right?"

Alberto got up with a quirked eyebrow. "Sometimes…"

"Lies… Lies!"

"If you say so."

"Come on. You expect me to believe this? Xavier pays you? You don't need money, you're rich!"

Avoiding his attempt at dragging him back to bed, Alberto went to his bag and picked up a black outfit from the pile of other black outfits packed in there.

"First, I am not, in fact, rich. I barely own anything. Second, he doesn't give me money. He gives me stuff like opera tickets and such. My mother loves those."

Mathias gave him a long, suspicious look. "Your mom can afford opera tickets."

"It's really not the same." Alberto waved his pile of clothes in front of Mathias. "Bathroom."

"Right." Between that and the fact that Xavier's name was the first thing on Alberto's mind this morning, Mathias already felt irritated.

Alberto paused by the door and asked, taunting, "Should we arrive together?"

The question was innocent enough, a jest, coming from a weirdo, but Mathias felt the weight of it, and it made his stomach drop. "Don't be stupid," he muttered, getting up.

Don't be stupid.

They did arrive together. Sort of. Mathias wanted to jump into a metro, and Alberto waved briefly at him before getting into a cab.

"Only princesses take cabs," Mathias mocked.

Alberto retorted, "Now you know why they're so tired all the time."

His cheeks burning, Mathias shut his big mouth. Alberto then invited him in.

"Princesses don't travel alone. Get in."

Mathias didn't want to take the metro and stare at ugly faces when he could be cozying up with a sexy Italian freak in the back-seat of a cab, so he got in, and they spent the whole time pretending to be innocent in front of the driver while secretly groping each other when he wasn't looking.

In front of Xavier's gate, they stood a little to the side to make sure no one would see them arrive together. Alberto was chewing another one of Eric's gum sticks. Worried it could look suspicious, Mathias told him to spit it out, but that bastard wouldn't, so he had to stick his fingers into his mouth and retrieve it himself. Alberto didn't mind; he let Mathias explore his mouth and seize the gum without blinking. Then, he licked his lips while hanging onto Mathias's jacket.

"Give me a kiss."

"Not here, come on."

"*You* come on. I *need* to make out with you before I go, or I'll think about it the whole time."

"Nah. Won't take the risk." Mathias shook himself free. "Just hold it in! I'll make out with you later."

Alberto stepped back. "I'm going home later, remember?"

Mathias ignored that sentence, burying his hands in his pockets. "Whatever." He turned his back to Alberto and left him pouting in the middle of the street.

He should have kissed him; he thought about it so many times afterward. He should have kissed him. Why, why didn't he kiss him that time?

Sprawled over the sofas around the marble indoor pool was the same old crowd, faces Mathias didn't care about, and some, like Elodie, he liked.

"Mathias!" Joy rushed toward him with open arms.

Eric was sitting in the back in a stupid sweater with some big cat curled in his side. That was Zak, in an equally dumb sweater. Mathias hurried toward them before Joy could get him. She didn't like to be around Zak and Eric. Truthfully, few people did. They had a tendency of reminding you that your life was shit compared to theirs. Mathias didn't mind so much now. He'd gotten used to it.

Alberto arrived shortly after. Mathias had seen him dressed and yet, when he arrived, he was still amazed by how good this guy could make clothes look. He'd probably make a garbage bag look like *couture*.

Mathias mentally shook his head. He had to stop associating the two. That wouldn't end well.

"Cool, right?" Xavier asked with a smile, holding on to Alberto's shoulder and dragging him toward the pool. "Right?" He kept touching him and grinning at him, which pissed Mathias off for some reason. "Does anyone want to swim?"

Rich people often have terrible taste, and Xavier's house was particularly bad, but this room took the prize, really. The brownish marble was disgusting, but the insides of the pool were even more so; they were a sickly green, which made the whole thing look like either a pool of absinthe, or poison, if there was any difference. Alberto, indifferent to Xavier's pawing, couldn't tear his gaze away from it, and Mathias thought perhaps he had a thing for absinthe or poison — probably the latter, knowing him.

Mathias grabbed a beer from an ice-filled Champagne bucket and went to Eric's side. Zak looked terribly limp, so Eric left him in his chair and got up to give Mathias a bone-crushing hug. Xavier patted a lounge chair next to his own and called Alberto. "Come sit with me."

The *girafon*[1] slid him a look colder than Mathias's beer. "No."

Mathias's lips stretched into a smile. *Unhelpful prick.* He never raised his voice but always refused to cooperate without being cooed the right way. The right way was usually to twist his arm, literally. As he murmured against his ear that one time, after Joy's party, *"If you want it, you'll have to fight me for it."* Just like when photographing his face, Alberto didn't mind giving it up, but never for free. To each their own fucked-up fantasies. Mathias wasn't one to judge. His own fantasy? Unattainable, emotionally cold demonic freaks like Alberto.

It was a pretty uneventful, boring event, to be honest, and Mathias missed the warmth of his own home. Zak was useless because his Christmas had been an exhausting family reunion. Eric was the opposite, too much energy, and without his boyfriend as a

---

1. Alternate name for 'baby giraffe' (French)

buffer, Mathias had no choice but to suffer through his retelling of each minute spent with Zak in the past week. As for Alberto, he stood awkwardly around, not eating, drinking, or even talking, and dealing with Xavier's inexplicable over-friendliness with a mildness that was bordering on excruciating.

Mathias felt like dragging him away to finally make this brunch a thing to remember, and he was just about to, when that pouty-lipped girl from last time, Gwen, strolled in with Kayvin—of all people—and stopped in front of their group with a smirk.

"Oh look! If it isn't *America's Next Top Model!*"

Apparently confused by her sarcastic tone, Eric didn't know whether he should smile or not. "Me?"

"Yes, you."

Kayvin snickered. "And look who's behind him. *Italia's Next Bottom Model.*"

Eric's expression darkened, while Alberto puffed out a laugh.

"Why are you laughing?" Eric asked, frowning. "He's insulting us."

While Alberto shrugged, Xavier scratched his cheek awkwardly. "What are you saying? Alberto's not even a bottom. Don't— Don't be rude."

As Zak started and gave Alberto a long puzzled look, Kayvin glanced at Xavier with a bewildered expression, and Mathias chugged down his beer for something to do. Alberto, for whom the word *bottom* wasn't even close to describing, stood still behind Eric, the faint hint of a smile stretching his lip.

"Hey, Alberto," Gwen said in a sing-song voice.

He vaguely glanced at her. "Hello."

She looked scandalized. "Seriously? You're really gonna do me like that? Pretending you don't know me? That's rude."

Everyone around the pool turned silent.

Alberto gave her a blank look. "I don't know you."

"Oops!" Eric giggled. "Seems he really doesn't know you."

More easily irritated by his cousin than by Xavier himself, Alberto spun on his heel and began to walk away. Mathias noted Gwen looked furious, but she was still smiling. She seemed to struggle with something, then she suddenly blurted out, "Hey, Britney!"

Everyone saw how Alberto froze, but no one paid more attention than Mathias. With slow steps that testified to his reluctance, Alberto retraced his steps, stopping in front of Gwen.

"Do you remember me now?" she asked with a satisfied smirk.

Everyone waited with bated breath. After a dozen seconds, Alberto's lips parted. "… Gwen?"

"Duh!" Instead of brightening, her face turned ashen. "Wait… so you really didn't remember me this whole time?"

Whether he did or not, Mathias wasn't so sure. Alberto was perfectly capable of feigning ignorance. For instance, no one here knew Mathias was inside him last night. And no one knew the sounds Alberto made when Mathias was inside him last night. To everyone here, they appeared nothing but mere acquaintances, while in fact they were… in any case, Mathias found his fingertips trembling every time that monster drew closer, while Alberto faced Gwen, looking as cool as ever.

"What happened to your lips?" he asked, squinting. "You look like you made out with a steamroller."

Eric snorted, and Zak quietly scolded him. The color drained from Gwen's face, but before she could retort, Alberto had already slunk out of the room.

"What a bitch!" she said, vexed.

My words exactly, Mathias thought while looking at her. Xavier let out a nervous laugh and urged people to grab a drink and have some fun, but Mathias couldn't help noticing the mean glint in Gwen's eye. She downed a glass of Champagne and looked around the crowd with a wide smile.

"You're all in Alberto's class?"

"We're all in the same school," Elodie replied, somewhat impatiently.

"You know he's a model, right?"

"Yes…"

"So what?" Zak was no longer limp, sitting upright on his lounge chair with one of his murderous scowls. Behind him, Eric gave a faint nod.

Gwen ignored him and withdrew a DVD box from her hand-bag. "My friend works for the production company that did the last *Occult* campaign."

Xavier snapped his fingers excitedly. "Yes! Yes! We saw the poster at a bus stop, like… two minutes from here!"

"Poster?" Gwen let out a derisive laugh. "I've got the movie!"

"The movie?!"

Joy and Melissa sprung up. In less than a second, most people went from uninterested to circling Gwen, who seemed to relish the attention.

"Yes, the movie." She handed the DVD to Kayvin and pointed at the screen on the other side of the pool. "Go put it on." She slapped his ass to send him on his way.

What a perfect couple, Mathias couldn't help thinking.

"There was a movie?" Xavier sounded crestfallen. "He never told me."

His cousin shushed him. "The movie was made for their store in Tokyo." She turned to Kayvin impatiently. "Is it on or what?"

His cheeks grew red immediately. "Just give me a second!"

Elodie went to stand at Mathias's side. "I'm not sure we should watch this."

Gwen ostensibly rolled her eyes at her. "Then don't watch, why should I care?"

"Come on!" Joy bounced on the balls of her feet. "I want to watch it."

Mathias stood quietly among the lounge chairs between Zak, Eric, and a muttering Elodie. He didn't know whether he should watch or not. He didn't even know whether he wanted to. But despite his reservations, when Kayvin pressed the play button, some fast-beat rock song started shaking the walls around them. He couldn't help but stare.

The frantically edited black-and-white footage showed Alberto standing in the middle of the blindingly white studio in rock star clothes while heaps of gorgeous girls in nymph-like attire threw themselves at him.

Mathias watched. In fact, he couldn't tear his gaze away. He watched as their greedy hands clasped around his arms, his neck, gripped his clothes, tried to tear them off him. He watched as Alberto stood perfectly still, looking into the lens without expression. He watched as he was pushed and shoved and spun around, as he was all but devoured by this hungry crowd.

And the more he watched, the more Mathias's chest tightened.

35

LOVE WITHOUT LIES

WHEN THE VIDEO was over and started playing again, Gwen flashed proud smiles around, and noting Alberto standing alone by the water, she let out a gleeful laugh.

"There he is!"

Alberto had evidently heard the music and had returned to the swimming pool when Mathias wasn't looking. Just like in the video, he looked unaffected by whatever was going on. "How did you get this?"

"Asked an old friend. Don't you know?" Gwen pulled a face. "Models have no privacy."

"Why should I care?" he asked with a shrug. "I got paid really well for this."

She waited and waited for another reaction, but apart from an imperceptible glance in Mathias's direction, Alberto showed nothing. The others, however, eagerly congratulated him, showering him with compliments about how cool he looked. Kayvin, realizing no one was making fun of Alberto but drooling over him instead, quickly ejected the DVD from the player just as the models had managed to tear Alberto's jacket off his shoulders, revealing a ripped tank top that made Mathias's knees grow weak.

Gwen advanced on him, furious that her little stunt didn't go as she expected. Mathias couldn't fathom why she thought people would make fun of him. The only one who looked personally affected by the video was Eric, who kept throwing worried glances around.

"Britney wasn't so arrogant when we were chasing him around the pool," Gwen blurted out when everybody—except Xavier— had calmed down. That idiot wasn't aware that Kayvin had already recovered the film, and he was prodding the TV in a futile attempt to save the footage.

Melissa's eyebrows drew together. "Why do you call him Britney all the time?"

"That's…" Gwen enjoyed the attention so much, her cheeks took on a glow. "It's simple." She glanced back at Alberto to gauge a reaction. He met her gaze coldly, but Mathias noticed he was blinking faster than usual. "My friend Stasia said that once, Albertino—"

"Alberto," Xavier corrected.

"That once, *Alberto*'s hair…" Gwen reprised him with a glare. "… was as long as… yours!" She pointed at Mathias with a bejew- eled nail.

"Mind-fucking-blowing," Zak said.

"Why did you do it?" Gwen ignored him, her attention fixed on Alberto. "Tell them why you did it."

He pursed his lips. "I don't know what you're talking about."

"Oh, come on." Out of nowhere, Gwen reached her hand up toward Alberto's face. "Is it true you have a scar up there? Stasia said—"

Alberto recoiled and almost stepped backwards into the pool. Xavier lunged toward him, and Alberto, glaring, used his hand to stop him, but he didn't pay attention to who stood next to him, and before anyone could move, Kayvin had flung him into the pool with a flick of his hand.

The poisonous-looking water swallowed Alberto with a splash. Melissa gasped, Joy screamed, Zak lifted his hands to his cheeks, and Gwen burst out laughing.

Mathias's feet were cemented to the ground. He knew he should move, and yet he couldn't even will himself to. He couldn't feel anything at all, like his body didn't belong to him anymore. He stood there, frozen, until the wave of disgust submerging him made him feel like retching. His fist closed around his beer tighter and tighter until he was sure it would explode in his grip. But it didn't. In fact, nothing happened at all until Alberto resurfaced, and then people finally seemed to wake from their trance. To Mathias's surprise, Eric was quick to move, but he was beaten by Xavier.

"Alberto."

Xavier held out his hand, the expression in his eyes a far cry from the dumb look Mathias was accustomed to. And to his shock, Alberto took it. They silently held each other's gaze as Xavier helped him up the stairs. He then led him, shivering, out of the room. Three times, he threw angry glares at Kayvin over his shoulder. Alberto didn't look back once.

"But what the hell is their relationship?" Zak cried out helplessly.

What a great question, Mathias thought, reflecting on how a simple thing like Xavier putting his hand on the small of Alberto's back had him seething with jealousy.

"You really outdid yourself this time," Eric said quietly.

Mathias whirled around. Eric was looking at Kayvin, who met his stare, defiant.

"What is it? The last punch wasn't enough? You want another?"

Eric blinked, unfazed, and turned his attention back to Zak. Mathias wished Eric wasn't a professional football player and could punch Kayvin straight to the bottom of this shit pool, but he knew it wouldn't happen anyway. For weeks, no, months, Mathias had heard Kayvin take jabs at Eric, and his friend took it like the champ he was because that's who he was, a fucking champ. Mathias was no champ; he was a piece of shit. If he had been there the last time, Kayvin wouldn't be talking like this right now; he would have no teeth left anyway.

And yet… And yet, right now, he couldn't move, even after what he'd done to Alberto. His mouth felt like paper; he put his beer down.

"Whatever, Kayvin," Eric said, sounding tired. "You and I are done." He held onto Zak's hand, and they started walking away.

Gwen, that awful girl, not knowing when to stop, picked up her phone and snapped a picture of them. The loud sound of the camera made Eric stop halfway to the door. This time, when he turned around, he looked genuinely angry.

"What are you doing?"

"Nothing," she said, but she took another picture just as Zak clung to his arm.

"Seriously?" There was fear on Eric's face.

Zak charged back toward Gwen with a set jaw. "Give me your phone."

"No, baby." She waved her finger under his nose. "Your boyfriend might be famous one day. These can come in handy."

"No!" Zak tried to grab the phone from her hands. Kayvin was about to intervene, but Xavier walked in and called out his name, looking furious. He had caught sight of the scene and was rushing over.

"What the hell are you doing?" he asked his cousin.

She looked slightly embarrassed. It was enough even for Xavier to understand her intentions. "You wouldn't," he said, sounding shocked. "Give me your phone."

"No."

"Give it!"

Xavier managed to wrestle the phone from her hands, and he tossed it straight into the water, astounding everyone. Gwen screeched, but Kayvin was so surprised, he could only stare at his friend dumbly.

"What the hell is wrong with you today?" Xavier poked his cousin in the chest. He turned to Kayvin, his eyes flashing. "And you... Why would you push him into the pool?"

Kayvin tried to laugh it off. "You did it to me this summer, and I didn't cry like a girl about it."

Gwen gave a fervent nod. "Don't worry, Xavier. We did it to him all the time when he was younger. You saw his face. He's used to it."

Mathias finally glanced up, close to telling her to go fuck herself, but Eric spoke first. "You're a meanie..." he said quietly.

"A *meanie*?" She laughed. "What are you, twelve? What is that supposed to mean?"

It means you're a bitch, Mathias thought. And he almost blurted it out.

"It means you're a bitch!" Zak shouted, trying to charge at her. Eric effortlessly held him back.

"What the hell?" Gwen clutched her chest, her eyes instantly brimming with tears. "Why are you so aggressive? He's gonna dump you when he goes to Lyon, anyway."

There was a brief silence, which Melissa broke by anxiously muttering, "Oh, oh…"

Zak's face turned white from shock. "What did you say now?"

"What? He didn't tell you?" Gwen took a dramatic breath. "He's been sold off to Lyon. Bye-bye, Paris. Bye-bye… you. What's your name again?"

Mathias's stomach plummeted. He staggered backwards and almost fell ass-first onto a lounge chair.

Eric turned to Xavier. "Did you tell her?"

A suspicious-looking blush crept up Xavier's neck, and he grumbled something incoherent.

Zak threw his hands up. "I need some air. Some actual air." Eric made to follow him, but he was stopped with a glare. "*Air.*"

"Thanks, well done." Eric faced Gwen and Kayvin, his face flushed. "I really wish you hadn't done that."

Kayvin puffed out a laugh. "I don't take orders from you anymore. You lost your privileges when you started sucking dicks."

Gwen whooped, grabbed a bottle of Champagne, and poured herself a drink. Joy and Melissa both exhaled sighs and left the room after that. Elodie followed, adding, "You're the biggest asshole I've ever met," and the rest of the crowd followed after them with their heads down.

Mathias had literally dug a hole through his pockets and was wondering how he could possibly fix that. Gwen, seemingly satisfied with all the chaos she created, took Kayvin by the hand and also left the room, leaving Eric and Mathias alone together.

Eric dropped onto the nearest chaise-longue. "What a fucking brunch!" He glanced up at Mathias. "You look pale, Matt. Have a seat."

Mathias didn't move. "You've been sold to Lyon?" The look on his friend's face gave him his answer.

"Yeah, a bit."

This time, Mathias took the seat next to him. "You have or you haven't?"

"Yes. It's true."

"And you haven't told Zak?!"

Or me.

But Eric started waving his hands frantically in front of his face. "What? No! Of course he knows. If I've learned any lesson from my troubles with Zak, it's *don't lie*."

"And Xavier?"

"He was with me when I got the call, so... yeah. He knows. And he can't shut his mouth, apparently... I shouldn't have said a thing!"

So, it was just me, then.

"No, you shouldn't have," Mathias said resentfully.

"I was about to tell you too, you know."

"... Sure."

Eric was annoying and too loud anyway. Mathias would enter culinary school, and Eric would go on to become a famous footballer, and it was fine. It was *fine*. It's not like he had cancer or anything. It didn't matter where he lived. Didn't matter at all. It was *fine*.

Mathias forced his voice to sound normal. "What are... ahem... What are you going to do with Zak?"

Eric slowly drew his knees up to his chin. "Hopefully all sorts of things..."

"What? No, I meant—"

"I know what you meant. I'm just kind of hoping he'll go along with what I want."

"What you want?" Mathias's heart leapt anxiously. "And that's..."

"Long distance doesn't work, Matt." Eric hung his head. "Everybody told me."

"Oh…"

"So, I don't think I have a choice…" He looked up abruptly, his eyes bright. "I gotta move in with him!"

Mathias didn't expect that and blinked several times.

"Take an apartment in Paris…" Eric said, taking a flyer for a real estate agency out of his pocket. "Near the station, right here…" He pointed at a spot on the flyer near Gare de Lyon. "…and I'll come back whenever I can. I've calculated, it's only two hours away. Then every minute we have, we'd spend together. I thought about it. I thought about it a lot!" He bit the nail of his thumb anxiously. "I'm just hoping he's thought about it, too. He keeps telling me he's too young for, like… everything." Eric let out an anguished sound. "God, Gwen is such a meanie. I think she made him mad, reminding him of my transfer like that. And I can't believe Kayvin, either. What he did to Alberto? He's getting worse and worse."

The thought of Alberto all drenched and miserable somewhere in this house made Mathias want to ditch Eric to find him, so he pushed it away and patted his friend's back. "Those two are both shitheads; they deserve each other."

Eric pouted with a determined frown. "Sucking dicks… sucking dicks… For his information, I have never, *ever* sucked a dick in my entire life!"

"Yeah, but… not from lack of wanting."

"Huh?"

"You want to do it, right?"

"Oh, yeah. I want to. Definitely, definitely!" Eric dropped the dejected act and sprung to his feet. "I want one specifically. I hope I get it soon." He started dancing in place. "Soon, soon, soon, soon!"

Mathias couldn't help pulling a disgusted face, and Eric gave a frustrated groan.

"Matt, not you!" He fell back onto his chair. "You know some people still talk to me like I haven't noticed Zak isn't a girl? I've noticed! I've noticed! He has a penis—"

"No p-word, please."

"*Pe-nis*! And I want it, Matt! I want it, I want it, I… want… it!"

Mathias waited patiently for Eric to stop shaking him. "You're obsessed."

"What do you mean *obsessed*? I love him, and I know a few tricks to make him feel good, so it's pretty straightforward to me. You've never gone down on your girl… friend?"

"Let's not talk about my sex life. You really wouldn't like it." Mathias realized he had started to sound like Alberto.

"Let's talk about it just a little bit."

"What? Why?"

"I'm… you know…" Eric said, blushing, "… a pervert. I'm a pervert, so I need to know."

Mathias gave him a bewildered look. "… What?"

"What about that girl-person you were telling me about? Didn't you say you had sex with her a lot?"

He looked so serious. Mathias wasn't used to seeing him look like this unless:

A: He was about to shoot a penalty.

B: Zak had asked him to focus, and so he did with every inch of his life.

In other words, he was taking this talk very seriously, and it made Mathias feel a little weird inside.

"We…" He flinched under his friend's earnest expression. "Yes. We've done pretty much everything there is to do."

"Ah-ah!" Eric grinned, triumphant. "See? You're going down on her, too."

"Well, actually… no. I'm not doing that."

"Oh." Eric wrinkled his nose. "But is she going down on you?"

"Yeah. But it's different. She likes it."

"Yeah? Then you're lucky! Lots of girls don't like doing it, especially if you can't be bothered to reciprocate."

There was a hint of judgment in his voice. Of course Eric was the sort to reciprocate everything when he wasn't the one initiating it. He was the sort not to worry about a thing, the sort that went *Oh, look! There's a dick in my face, ah great, I always wanted to see one up close, thanks, buddy!* Mathias wasn't like that. He wasn't particularly a fan of genitals, or at least, he didn't spend much time thinking about them. Eric and Alberto probably did. Come to think of it, the only things Mathias had ever seen Alberto put in his mouth beside his dick were cigarettes, plastic straws, and XXL lollipops. The real problem was not to get him near his cock, but away from it.

"She's... she's really into stuff like that, so..."

Eric scratched the back of his head with a grimace of sorts. "And you're not? You don't like it?"

"I haven't thought much about it."

Lies. All lies. *Lies, lies, lies, lies, lies.*

"If you loved her, you'd do it." Eric shrugged, but his expression was still serious. "No questions asked. You don't even think in those cases. You'd take that dick and just... gobble it all up!"

"What...? Never mind." It seemed Eric had returned his thoughts to Zak again. Once that happened, there was no talking sense back into him for a while. Mathias turned his head away with a scowl. "You seem very confident for a guy who's not getting any."

Eric clutched his chest, the rims of his eyes already red. "Oh, come on! I'm being such a good friend, and you stab me in the heart like that."

But then, Zak made an appearance, his arms full of snacks. Eric's expression transformed before Mathias's eyes, and he couldn't help staring at it in wonder. He realized with a pang of sadness that no one would ever make that face whenever he entered a room. No one would ever care for him that way. He wasn't deserving of such love. He thought of Alberto, and his throat constricted.

Zak was no idiot. He saw Eric's face, and he knew he was loved. His cheeks darkened, and he kept a controlled pace, but Mathias could see it was taking him everything not to run.

Mathias didn't wait for them to fall into each other's arms. He got up and walked out of there. Where was Alberto now? How long could it take to dry himself off? He needed to see him now. He needed to find him.

With a racing heart, Mathias left the party and made his way upstairs.

36

CAREFREE

XAVIER LED ALBERTO silently up one staircase after another. He was dripping water, and the fat drops fell to the carpeted stairs with a *tap tap, tap tap, tap tap*. Alberto shivered, and Xavier's hand tightened around his arm. He hadn't even noticed he was holding him.

"So, are you a fan of Britney, then? Is that the story?"

"What?"

"Britney. The singer."

"Oh." Alberto sniffed. "You could say she's an inspiration."

"I like Britney, too. She's cool."

Alberto didn't reply.

They went to the very top of the house. Xavier opened the door to a smaller bedroom at the far end of a narrow corridor. Inside, dark furniture and vintage wallpaper gave the place a gothic atmosphere, and Alberto immediately felt at ease. He fell onto the black-and-white bedspread with relief.

Xavier went to a linen cupboard on the side and retrieved some towels. "I don't understand my cousin, sometimes. I'll talk to her, try to make her apologise."

"No, thank you."

"But you deserve——"

"Thank you, but no." Alberto took the towels from his hands. "I just want to be left alone."

Alberto wanted nothing to do with Stasia's friends. Gwen was one of the harpies who kept chasing him around the house and would toss him in the pool when he first arrived from London in bad shape. She may have been botoxed out of recognition, but now he'd never forget her face again. She *knew* things about him, and now, she was hanging out with this crowd. Worse, she was related to Xavier, who was with Eric every day. Eric, who was with *Mathias* every day.

God, he was so unlucky, he could weep, sometimes.

He unbuttoned his trousers and lifted his drenched jumper over his head with mechanical motions. Xavier stared with his vacant eyes. Then, he suddenly sprung forward.

"Wow! Don't—"

"What?"

"Don't get undressed in front of me!"

Alberto glared at him. "Then leave."

"I can't. I need to put your clothes in the dryer in the next room."

"I can do that myself."

"Do you know how to use one?"

"Do *you*?"

"Of course. I fall into the pool sometimes, too."

Alberto stared at him. "Really?"

Xavier grinned. "I'm just clumsy."

Since he'd been kind enough to get him out of the pool, Alberto didn't want to make fun of him, so he stood there a bit awkwardly.

"I'm gonna pop downstairs for a minute, then, okay?" Xavier pointed at the door. "Give you some time to dry off. Make yourself comfortable. I'll be right back."

Alberto watched him leave, and he immediately discarded his clothes, thinking of the *Oɔcult* video everyone had seen minutes ago. Despite the drama that followed, it'd turned out quite all right. When Alberto told the production he wouldn't remove his clothes, not even for a raise, they were quite unhappy, but the client was determined to keep him, so they adjusted the campaign, giving him a tank top to wear under his biker jacket. That choice may have accidentally made the whole thing look better. The way the girls pulled at his jacket, revealing the torn top underneath, made them look far more desperate. Almost as feral as Mathias on a Friday night.

Alberto finished towelling himself dry, wrapped himself in the largest towel, and went into the next room to toss his clothes in the dryer. Thankfully, this old thing only had two buttons, which probably explained why guys like Xavier and him could use it. Then, he went back to the bedroom and lay down on the bed with a sigh.

When Xavier returned, he looked both restless and concerned. "How are you doing?"

"Just tired," Alberto said.

"You can sleep here. No one ever comes to this room. You'll be fine."

"I don't want to sleep here, but thank you."

Xavier approached him slowly and put a pile of clothes on the bed. "Brought you some of my clothes, so you don't get cold while waiting." He turned his back to him.

Alberto immediately put on the soft sweater and even softer sweatpants. They smelled nice and clean. "Thank you," he said, grateful. He shook his hair back into place.

"Wow."

"What?"

Xavier was staring at him. "Nothing. Just… You look good in my clothes."

Alberto held his gaze but didn't reply. Xavier let out a laugh and gingerly sat on the edge of the bed. "So… is your house nicer than mine?"

"I don't…" Alberto hesitated. "I don't understand the question."

"Forget it." Xavier waved his hand and scooted closer. "But you were having a good time before this… stuff happened?"

"No, not really."

"Ah. Because of Zak?"

"Zak? Why because of Zak?"

"Because he broke up with you for Eric."

Alberto put his head in his hands. "No. I'm fine."

"Because they're happy, you know."

"Seems like it."

"Make a good couple and all."

"Look… I don't want to talk about Zak."

"All right. But if you're sad—"

"I'm not sad. I don't want to talk about Zak!"

Alberto knew he must have looked frightening, with his grey irises sometimes appearing a little too cold despite not being able to do anything about them, but Xavier climbed in bed next to him and went as far as hugging him and laying his head on his shoulder. Alberto, too surprised at his impertinence to react, only blinked dumbly.

"You can't fool me…" Xavier said. "I can see right through your bullshit."

"What bullshit?"

"You're a good person."

"I never said I wasn't."

There was a brief silence.

"Oh. Right. But…"

"But what?"

"Nothing. Nothing. It's all good. You're my friend."

Alberto huffed, exasperated. "No, I'm not!"

"Doesn't matter…" Xavier buried his nose in his neck, astounding him. "I'm yours."

His cluelessness drew a laugh out of him. "Do you know how gay that sounds?"

"I don't care." Xavier gave a light shrug and kept nuzzling his face against his shoulder. And a slow, irrepressible urge to be naughty rose within Alberto. He suddenly rolled over and pressed him down into the lush bedding.

"Is that what you want? Hm?" He used his sexiest voice. "A little piece of Alberto?"

Xavier's eyes grew the size of the moon. "I d-don't know…"

Alberto went as far as lightly rubbing their noses together. "Well… would you like to find out?"

To his surprise, Xavier replied with a hesitant nod. "Y-Yes?"

Alberto was amused by him, and so he thought *Why the hell not.*

It was nothing to him. So, he bent his head down and covered Xavier's lips with his own.

Under him, Xavier's breath hitched, and his fingers curled around Alberto's shoulders. Alberto had only intended to tease him a little, but when Xavier opened his mouth, a feeling like gratitude overtook him, and he went with it, pushing his tongue inside and kissing him with something akin to affection. They snogged for what felt like a long time, in a room that was dead quiet, save for the sound of their lips, before Xavier gently pushed him away, his expression blank.

"Sorry," he whispered.

Alberto feigned surprise. "Oh, no. Really?"

"Really. I guess I'm not gay."

He looked so puzzled that Alberto had to suppress a laugh. "You're breaking my heart."

Xavier gripped his shoulders. "Really?"

"… No."

But he wasn't upset in the least. He jumped off the bed with a happy expression. "Can I tell everyone? Girls are gonna be all over me after this!"

Alberto shook his head. "No! Not only will that make you look gay, but I'll deny it, which will make you look gay *and* desperate."

"Good point, good point." Xavier patted himself all over, his cheeks red, so red that Alberto started doubting his previous statement. He gripped the door handle and gave Alberto a weird military salute. "You're a good friend, Alberto."

"I'm really not."

Xavier guffawed and almost tore the handle off the door. "Anyway, Gwen and Kayvin are gone, and Joy found Mother's *Hits from the Eighties* compilation and put it on in the blue living room, so come back downstairs if you want. We're gonna have some fun!"

He left. Dumbfounded at first, Alberto slowly stretched his long limbs and finally allowed himself to laugh, but the moment his lips stretched, his thoughts flew toward Mathias, and his stomach knotted.

He returned downstairs shortly after, his clothes warm and smelling funny from their short trip into the pool, following the sound of eighties pop music, and found the whole gang in the De Dampierre's blue — an understatement — living room. Drinks were flowing, and the atmosphere felt a little electric, the special way it goes when people let loose after a tense situation.

Alberto was the one who had been thrown into the water, and he should feel like letting loose, too, but all he wanted was to find Mathias. His gaze swept over the room, checking every corner for him, but he found him nowhere. It seemed he'd left already.

Perhaps he'd had enough of this. Enough of him. After all, he stayed eerily quiet while all of this happened. And it was okay. Mathias had enough on his plate, and Alberto wasn't the kind of person worth saving anyway. They had a good time this week, but not many conversations. Every time Alberto started speaking, Mathias would kiss him silent, and he felt grateful in a way. The less he said, the more he was desirable. And to be desired by Mathias was a beautiful thing.

With Mathias gone and no one to flirt with, Alberto didn't know how to have fun, so he sat on an empty sofa, picked up a can of coke to pretend he was normal, and soon, Joy was clinging to his hand and urging him to come dancing because "You see, you can't stay alone like that all the time, people want to spend time with you, blah blah blah." He thought if that daft witch hadn't started the rumour that he was soulless and dead inside, maybe he'd have more friends, maybe even cool, dumb ones, but had she ever stopped to think about that? Alberto gazed into her eyes and saw she didn't spend much time thinking, and maybe she read his mind, because she gave up with an annoyed *tsk*.

Xavier was ecstatic, and Alberto wondered if it was because they kissed and he didn't like it or if it was because they kissed and he did. There was no way to know with the airhead ones. They could keep secrets; their eyes told nothing. At some point, Elodie sat next to Alberto and sighed, saying, "I want what they have," to no one in particular, and Alberto followed her gaze toward Eric and Zak, who were not exactly dancing, but sort of swaying on their feet while gazing in each other's eyes with foolish smiles. He felt that nasty urge to get up and tell them that they were a stupid, stupid couple, but he said nothing and showed even less, and when he turned his head back, Elodie was gone.

His head was hurting now. He never liked swimming pools.

"Alberto." Xavier was suddenly in front of him. "Alberto, I'm playing this one just for you."

"… What?"

It took him a few seconds, but he found his way back to the living room and recognised the song instantly.

Sarà perché ti amo.

It wasn't a great song, but it was a fun song. And more importantly, it was Mamma's song.

The musical notes triggered something in his brain, and suddenly, he could smell it: the briny scent of the sea through the open windows of the villa. Lengths of linen, colourful belts, sweet-tasting lip-balm, and the lustre of her hair. Broken waves hitting the rocks, Mamma panting, curled up on the living room's tiles.

Alberto had always been envious of other people's carefreeness. Even when he was a kid, catching through the same windows the unbridled laughter of children running across the beach gave him the certitude he had never enjoyed nor would he ever attain insouciance of his own.

He watched Xavier and the others sing and twirl around amidst shrieks of laughter, and his heart gradually hoisted itself up into his throat.

Carefree. The song was like an anchor, and in one second, he found himself at the bottom of a much, much darker pool, where only his mother's hand could reach to pull him out.

Unseen by anybody, Alberto found his coat and escaped outside.

Mamma's favourite song couldn't be shared with anyone else, just like their cries for help were never heard by anyone, and so their dance shouldn't be seen by anyone else either. Alberto took a few steps and filled his lungs with air. The ants cleared, and he instantly felt better. From the outside, he threw a look back at them through the window.

Carefree.

Xavier's street was quieter than a tomb. Alberto walked with his coat open. The gnarled hand of the cold gripped his chest in a tight vice. He wished Mathias was still around. He wished he'd dig his fingers into his flesh as he liked to do. He wanted Mathias to make him cry and make him forget all about this shit party, about Zak and Eric and the love they had for each other, how they were dancing together to this song, of all songs, to *this* song.

What's so funny? he wanted to ask their open, smiling mouths. *What's so funny?*

Then, he saw Mathias standing at a bus stop, and a low, startling laugh rolled out of his chest, and he picked up the pace.

"Hey, hey!" He stopped in front of him. "Why did you leave?"

Mathias puffed out a nicotine cloud and allowed Alberto to steal his cigarette. "This thing was even worse than I thought it would be."

"Tell me about it." Alberto glanced up at the bus sign. "Were you waiting for me?"

"Why would I be waiting for you?"

Right. Of course. But then why was he waiting for the bus instead of taking the tube? Alberto didn't dare ask this pointless question. He shivered and wished he had gloves for once.

Mathias gave him a strange look while chewing the inside of his cheek.

"What?"

He brought the sides of Alberto's coat together and started buttoning it up. "What were you doing up there with Xavier?"

He knew, didn't he? He knew. Didn't matter how. Didn't matter at all. Alberto met his eyes. "Making out," he said breathlessly. "I think he'd been dying to try it for a while."

A flash of genuine surprise lit Mathias's eyes, but his expression quickly turned into a cold sneer. "Cool. Did he like it?"

"Not as much as he thought he would, clearly."

"And you? Don't roll your eyes." He removed his beanie and slipped it over Alberto's damp hair with a grim expression. "Did you like it or not?"

A little confused, Alberto took a moment before answering. "All right. Yes. I think so."

Mathias chortled. "Xavier, really?"

"What? Xavier's handsome, and he kisses surprisingly well." Alberto took a drag of his cigarette. "Doesn't follow me around like some creep."

Mathias's face grew gradually flushed, but it could have been from the cold. "Then go with Xavier as well, the fuck I care."

"You're so easily riled up. So easy." Alberto tried to take his arm and was strongly rebuffed.

"Don't touch me."

Alberto knew Mathias was angry. He could hope all he wanted that this was jealousy, but his sharpened instinct told him it was nothing but possessiveness. He also knew from the glow in his eyes that if they were to go back to his place right now, Mathias wouldn't be able to resist him, and they'd have nasty sex, the sort that he'd need more than a few minutes to recover from, the sort that felt like he was being ripped apart. Then, he'd return home to see Mamma, Dimitri, and the others, knowing he'd been fucked inside out like the whore that he was — that he'd always been — and he got almost hard at the thought.

He leaned in, forced Mathias to accept the weight of his body on his own, pushed him up against the window of the bus stop. He ran his hands across Mathias's chest and whispered in his ear words only a whore would know. Mathias trembled against him, from rage or cold or lust, who gives a fuck, and Alberto, still high from his big plunge, realised if they returned together, he would be okay. Everything would be okay.

He repeated that thought over and over again in the cab that drove them to Mathias's, his skin itching in anticipation, that maybe this time, Mathias might actually fuck him to death. Wouldn't that be grand? He glanced at his lover's handsome face scowling at the window, thinking, *If he breaks me, splits me in half, or tears me apart, so be it.*

Go on, baby. Send me off in a pool of your cum.
Hit me like a high-speed train.
Then give me a hug.

37

MAINSTREAM

MATHIAS KNEW he was a bit of a freak. He loved it when Alberto cried. He would usually try his best to make him weep so he could kiss his tears away during that brief window after they'd just come, before Alberto became annoying again. He'd kiss the corner of his eyes and the peak of his cheekbones, then he would catch his lips, and their kiss would taste of salt and a bit of grief, too.

This time, Mathias grieved more than usual. He grieved because he'd fallen deeper into the same old pit, because he couldn't recognize himself at times, and he worried about his sister's words.

As for Alberto... Mathias would never know for sure what went down in his head. He hung to his neck in the middle of his bedroom, quiet as Mathias stripped him without ceremony. He pressed his lips to his neck, to his cheek. Mathias pushed him away.

"Don't kiss me."

"Why? Because I kissed Xavier?" Mathias didn't answer, but he didn't stop undressing Alberto either. "Are you mad? Are you mad that I kissed him?"

"No." Mathias removed Alberto's belt in one sweeping motion. It slashed the air like a whip. "I always knew you were a slut."

Alberto let out an audible laugh. Mathias couldn't see his face and regretted it. He wanted to twist him around, but Alberto ground his ass against his cock, freezing him on the spot.

"I *am* a slut," he purred.

That you are, Mathias thought with anger, with desire. He tugged down his clothes to his knees.

"How many others?" he asked, pulling Alberto against his chest. He grazed his thumb against a certain spot, and Alberto gasped and arched his back. "How many have been here but me?"

"Three more," Alberto confessed with a cruel smirk.

Mathias pushed him down. He didn't even bother undressing him completely. He wanted him *now*, wanted to possess him and not think about Xavier's lips on his. Conversation was futile. Confessions, worthless. Whatever Alberto's answer, Mathias would not desire him any less. He was burning for him. Nothing could relieve that ache but to taste his skin again.

He'd never be loved by him, and he didn't want to, but at least he could make him cry. Alberto would never make him cry, unless they were talking about the sounds Mathias usually made when he climaxed inside him, so that day, when the time came, he gritted his teeth not to let out a sound; his vision swam, he felt his eyes pricking, and he collapsed on top of Alberto. Under him, the demon huffed, his fingers curled around the sheets.

Mathias slowly rolled away from him, his hand over his eyes. He really wished he'd never gone to this fucking party.

Alberto lay there by his side, spent, not making a sound. Mathias noticed his ass cheeks were almost as red as the bedsheets, and he felt even worse.

He thought of Eric for some reason. Of Eric's face when Zak entered the room, of his face when he said he was going to leave. He thought of Gwen, of Kayvin. Of the girls in the video. He thought of Mom, and though he was sitting down, he felt like he was falling. He covered Alberto with the comforter.

"Hey," he called softly. "When do you have to leave?"

"Yes."

Mathias almost smiled. "I said *when*."

Alberto faced him, a few delicate strands of hair sticking to his forehead, a single gray eye peering at him, dazed and soft.

"Soon." He gathered himself and made his way to the shower with unsteady steps.

Mathias forced himself up and got dressed. He thought of making the bed, but he didn't want to. He straightened the comforter and sat against the headboard. Alberto returned ten minutes later dressed in fresh clothes, his hair wet, and fell face-first onto the mattress.

"Are you okay?"

Alberto said nothing.

Mathias insisted. "Hey, look at me." Still no response. Mathias pinched his buttock. "Why are you so slow? It's your ass I fucked, not your brain."

Alberto finally chuckled, his head buried in the pillow. "You fucked me silly."

"You're okay, then?"

He finally turned over. "More than okay."

A weight lifted off Mathias's shoulders. He was so relieved, he pulled him to his side and almost stopped breathing entirely when Alberto remained curled against him instead of hissing like a bullied cat. Pushing his luck, he ran his hand through his damp hair, and his fingers grazed that spot again. Gwen's words returned to him in a flash.

"Why do you have a scar?"

Alberto scoffed. "My dad dropped me as a kid."

"Bull… shit. Bullshit. Have you ever heard that word? Stop saying bullshit! Say something else! Tell me what you think of me, for instance! Tell me why you kissed Xavier. Tell me if it was to punish me. Was it? Was it?"

He didn't say any of that.

"I'm sorry," he heard himself say instead.

Alberto glanced up. "Why?"

Sorry for not lifting a finger when some douchebag threw you into a pool. I had my pride to consider before your wellbeing. By the way, sorry I got carried away just now and treated your ass like my personal venting machine. At least he could apologize for *that*.

"Just now, that was a bit—"

"Awesome?"

"What?"

"Mm." Alberto pressed himself against him. "We— You're getting so good at this."

Mathias wasn't sure about that, but Alberto looked all cute and sleepy, so he said nothing.

"Mathias…?"

"Hm?"

"Where did you learn to fuck like that?"

Cute and sleepy, my ass! He was still a shameless slut through and through. Mathias's fingertips twitched, and he buried them in the mess of soft black hair.

"Where? *Where?* I don't know."

"You don't know?"

"Don't know."

With you. Where else? Mathias would have never grabbed a girl by the hair. Even if she'd wanted to, he wouldn't have been able to do it. Even if she'd begged, he wouldn't have wanted to anyway. Mathias tried to recall the best sex he'd ever had before Alberto, but all he could think of was… Alberto.

"Tell me…" Alberto whispered below him, laying his head on his chest.

"What?"

"Were there others before me?"

Mathias grunted. "What? You thought I was some kind of virgin?"

"I meant other boys."

"… No." He didn't want Alberto to probe too much, or he'd realize he was freaking out the first time they slept together because he was afraid Alberto would laugh in his face.

"Tell me about your girls, then."

"Uh… Why?"

It's like he was getting revenge for Mathias's heated little interview earlier. *Three more. Three more.* Should Mathias count Xavier as one of them? Should he? He looked down and was met with two languid eyes that melted all other thoughts away.

"Okay." Mathias relented, gently scraping his scalp. "The thing is… I don't know if I told you this, but when I was a kid, I was a bit different."

"You were?" Alberto shifted a little closer.

"Yeah. Front row, top grades, glasses, the whole kit. I was a bit of a nerd, like Zak. Anyway, you wouldn't have recognized me." Alberto pouted, and Mathias poked the tip of his nose playfully. "I only had one friend, Daphnée, since we were seven. And I wasn't what you'd call popular at all. Didn't matter to me. I had my family, and I had Daphnée. Life was good. Then, one day, Daphnée comes over, says she's in love with me, and she wants us to date." Mathias paused, struggling to revisit the scene. All he could remember was how his stomach flipped when she said they couldn't be friends anymore. "So, yeah, we dated. Then, my mom got sick. In less than a year, she was gone. I remember Daphnée at the funeral looking at me with those immense eyes when I couldn't stop…" He cleared his throat. "… 'cause that insane woman had to make life difficult for everyone until the last second, and she wanted that shit song to play while she got lowered down." Mathias realized he wasn't making any sense, and he had begun pulling Alberto's soft hair. He relaxed his hold. "Daphnée probably thought it'd be cruel to ditch the guy whose mom just died. Six more months she held on."

"So, she was your first?" Alberto asked.

"Yeah. We were together a long time." Too fucking long, in his opinion.

"Was it good?"

Mathias hesitated. "I don't think so."

"You don't… think so?"

"If it had been good, I'd remember. But I don't."

There was his life before his mom passed away. Then after. It reminded him of those prisms that separate colors. Light passes through, and on the other side, you see a pretty rainbow. Except it was the opposite for him. He used to be that dumb rainbow, and he was forced back into blankness when she died.

"Strangely enough… I remember my first kiss."

"Really? With Daphnée?"

"No… it was someone else. Someone unimportant. It's just… I

remember." He made himself more comfortable, his fingertips absently dragging across Alberto's scalp. "I was thirteen. We were on holiday at the beach. Mom and Ella were burying Dad in the sand, and this girl came to me and asked if she could kiss me."

"How was it?" Alberto asked, his voice falling to a whisper. He was steadily slipping into that mode that made Mathias feel stupid about him.

"It was… nice."

Mathias recalled her yellow dress, her long black hair, her brown feet dug in the sand. The way she stood on her toes to reach him, the clumsy pressure of her wet lips against his own. How his heart beat at the time. How he thought, *Ah? Okay.*

Then, he compared it to how he felt every time his tongue slipped into Alberto's mouth, the way his stomach curled when he forced a pleasant note out of him, how greedy his hands turned at the sight of his bare skin. He shifted on the bed.

"Yeah, it was nice," he repeated blankly. "Anyway. When Daphnée broke up with me, our friendship really was over, so I hung out with these new guys in high school. We hit the bars who'd have us or crash parties here and there… and then, being the boy with the dead mom makes you weirdly popular, and all the girls are suddenly into you." Alberto wrinkled his nose. Mathias didn't want to ask why. "Drank a lot of booze, slept with girls, messed up that year in high school, had to repeat it, stopped drinking, stopped sleeping around, got my shit more or less together."

All these faceless girls. Never once did he feel with them the way he just did with Alberto. And never once did he fantasize about them before or after the act. *Shook* at the mere memory of their bellybutton or their collarbones. In fact, never once did he touch any of them sober, and he never contacted them again.

Would it have been different if these hookups had been with guys instead? He couldn't know for sure, as the opportunity never arose. Surrounded by straights, he didn't have the luxury to think much about it. When the bars closed, and his consciousness slipped away, he was often persuaded to follow a girl home; his conquests were always a conclusion—a consequence, really—of a night out, a futile attempt to feel that feeling again, to prove to himself that he could love… or care… about anyone unrelated to him by blood.

But it never worked; he never cared. And in the end, he just felt worse and worse and worse, until he felt nothing at all. The hard truth was that his capacity for love had died with his mother.

"My… my mom," he said, pulling Alberto close. "Her death. It defines me. It made me who I am. And so, with you… I keep thinking…"

"Thinking what?"

Mathias bit his tongue until the pain made his eyes well up. "Thinking I'm doing the same with you… using you because you're around."

Alberto was silent for a beat, as if he were pondering his words. Then, he blinked and whispered, "You can have my body. Everybody else does. I don't mind."

Mathias did not like the sound of that. At all. He felt his insides contract into a tight ball and wanted to purge it all. *Stop hiding. Let it out.*

But there was no point. Mathias had just plowed into him with the ferocity of a beast, and still, Alberto looked unruffled. Nothing he could do would ever reach him.

"I'm not gonna ask you the same question," he said, collecting himself. "Your first. I don't need to know." He felt, no, he *knew* he wouldn't like the answer.

Alberto's lip curled. "Even If I told you, you wouldn't believe me."

He was probably right about that. Lowering his head, Mathias found Alberto's lips, and he managed to kiss him without getting pushed away.

"Your first kiss, then. Do you remember it?" he ventured, leaning back.

Alberto inhaled then exhaled, his eyelids fluttering closed. Perhaps he thought the conversation was beneath him.

"Yes." He snuggled against him, puzzling him. He was halfway gone, and Mathias tried not to smile, but he also felt hopeful that sleepy Alberto would tell the truth for once instead of messing around like he usually did.

"What about it?"

"What about what?"

Mathias chuckled. "How was it? How old were you?"

"Oh…" Alberto blinked slowly. "I was fourteen."

Mathias wasn't surprised that Zak wasn't his first kiss, but he was surprised that it didn't happen sooner. With his looks, Alberto must have been popular since… forever.

"Fourteen…"

"Mm."

"And did you like it?"

"Not particularly."

"*Not particularly?*" Mathias repeated, incredulous.

Alberto conceded a half-shrug. "Just waited for it to be over, really."

"Fuck." Mathias snorted. "I forgot *nothing* ever gets you. I can imagine that poor little guy's face. You probably broke his heart." He felt a sharp twinge of jealousy when Alberto's lip lifted into a taunting smirk.

"Third time's the charm."

"What's that supposed to mean?"

"Nothing."

Mathias twisted his neck to look into his eyes. "What was it? He wasn't good enough for you? Or… she?" He froze. "Wait, was it a she?"

"He."

"Oh." For some reason, he felt relieved. "You've never kissed a girl?"

Alberto picked at the comforter with his eyes down. "Not really."

His voice was flat as always, like he wasn't interested in this conversation and was just humoring him, while Mathias wanted to know everything, but he didn't know how to ask. The moment Alberto got bored, he would start spouting crazy shit to throw him off, and it would work. Mathias gave up. "Not *really*. Not *particularly*. You're not saying anything. It's just bland words."

Alberto stared at him. "Words mean nothing."

"They don't?"

"Actions are what's important."

"Words are important, too," Mathias muttered, just as he smothered the desire to tell him how good he looked just now.

"Whatever." Alberto closed his eyes.

Actions, not words. *Actions*, not words. Mathias gave in to his urges, slid down, and straight up claimed Alberto's lips without bothering to ask. The following grip around his arms told him he'd made the right decision, so he forced Alberto's mouth open with his tongue and kissed him until he turned as soft as dough under him. Then, he stuck his hand between his legs.

"Do you have time?"

"I don't." He sounded irritated, and Mathias recognized the flash of desire in his eye.

"You don't have time." Another brief kiss challenged that thought.

"I want to, but I don't have t—"

Mathias cut him off when he tightened his grip, and he enjoyed watching the surprise on his face. Before Alberto could add another word, Mathias had unbuttoned his trousers and slipped his hand inside.

When his warm fist closed on him, Alberto let out a quiet gasp, so quiet, Mathias would have missed it if he wasn't so close, he felt his breath on his cheek. He brought their lips together again as his hand worked in swift motions. Alberto returned the kiss with a frown. Mathias understood why. In all their times together, they'd never done anything so intimate. The last time they came close was when Alberto wore those wings, and they almost fucked like normal people until Eric interrupted them. They carefully avoided finding themselves in that same position since, never being so close that they could count each other's eyelashes.

Until now.

The thrill of the sight burned the back of Mathias's throat. He proceeded aggressively, and he wrapped his other hand around Alberto's throat before he was even asked to do so. He didn't apply pressure, however, opting to kiss him instead.

Defiance, annoyance, and maybe something like alarm brightened Alberto's eyes. "You're too close."

Mathias didn't care. He wanted to see it, the exact moment he would come apart, how he'd look then. He'd never had the chance to see it before. Now it felt like the most important thing in the world. Alberto groaned and shook his head in protest, but his grip on his shoulders intensified, and Mathias knew he'd find marks under his shirt tomorrow. He didn't mind. He felt dizzy, drunk almost. Then, Alberto inadvertently let out a meek sound.

"That's it," Mathias whispered against his warm, parted lips. "Good boy."

Alberto turned his face to the side. He seemed pissed off, but Mathias felt him grow harder in his hand, and he rejoiced even more.

It didn't take long, considering, and it required no act of violence on Mathias's part. Alberto surrendered in his hand, but at the last second, he flung his arms over his face, denying him the sight he'd been hoping for.

Equally amused and disappointed, Mathias laid himself on top of Alberto's body. He dropped his head on his shoulder, feeling his chest rising and falling rapidly under him, his fingers twitching around his arms.

Clench, unclench… Clench, unclench… Clench…

Whatever happened between them, Alberto would never truly belong to him, and that was just the thing to make him come back for more. Mathias had a penchant for clinging to the ghosts of people, those who couldn't reach back.

Right now, it didn't matter that much.

Right now, it almost felt like a victory.

Not to Alberto, however. The moment he felt Mathias's lips graze his earlobe, he pushed him away. "Get off me."

Mathias rolled onto his back and stretched. Alberto moved fast, grabbed a tissue from the box on the nightstand, and cleaned himself up as best he could. Mathias lazily reached for him, and Alberto slapped his hand away with gritted teeth, causing him to laugh. Throwing the box of tissues at Mathias's face, he swiped a hand through his messed-up hair with a cold expression. Mathias said nothing, nor could he wipe the smug smile off his face. He knew Alberto was only mad at him for doing something so… *pedestrian*. Mainstream. He would get over it.

"Alberto."

"What!"

"What are you doing?"

"I told you I had to go."

"No, you said you didn't have time."

"Same thing."

"Same thing? You came in, like, one minute."

Alberto retrieved the box of tissues and threw it right back at Mathias's head. With a laugh, Mathias grabbed his wrist and yanked him down. Alberto fell forward, and before he knew it, Mathias had caught his neck and slammed their lips together. When he relaxed his grip, Alberto leaned back, but it wasn't just his lips that looked red and swollen. The rims of his eyes were, too.

"What's wrong?"

"Nothing."

He looked vexed and wounded, as if Mathias didn't give him a handjob but a slap in the face. Mathias sat up. He originally wanted to ask him his plans for the next few days, but now he didn't dare. "Are you sure?"

"Yep. See you later."

Watching him leave with a quirked eyebrow, Mathias knew Alberto wasn't really angry. He was annoyed, surprised, maybe. He would definitely get over it.

Mathias, on the other hand, wouldn't be so lucky.

38

STONE COLD FACES

HE WAS GONE.

Just like that time they played hide and seek at his house, it took Mathias no more than one stupid mistake to lose him. One attempt to look into his eyes, to be a little bit more than the asshole who held him down in bed, and he had disappeared.

And just like that time they were playing, Mathias knew he was probably just where he left him. Just being Alberto, doing Alberto things, doing other people, most likely. Doing Xavier? Possibly. And he realized he couldn't stand it.

Mathias would lie awake in bed at night, trapped between the memory of his lips, longing burning a hole through his stomach. Alberto had turned into a cancerous tumor. Alberto was poison. Alberto was the devil. *Alberto, Alberto, Alberto.* How many people had lain in bed just like him, invoking his name in hope of conjuring him to their side? And how many would there be after him? He was thinking about it and punching his pillow, and then he would get angry at himself.

After him *what?* They were nothing to each other, had nothing in common, apart from the fact they were both so fucked up, so unlovable that it brought them together in the first place. Mathias had known from the start that this couldn't go on, and yet, he'd lain awake at night, drinking the same poison, feeling the same tumor growing over his organs, repeating the same name over and over again.

Days without news had forced him to start lurking after his Instagram updates, where he'd only posted a museum still here and there. Mathias refused to break the silence, refused to admit defeat, but he also burned inside from wondering if he'd done it, if Alberto had moved on, replaced him with someone better, less *pedestrian*, who'd do as he was asked in bed and wouldn't bother him with stupid clichés later.

The last morning before school was to resume, Mathias woke with a heavy heart once again. The first thing he did was seize his phone and open Instagram. Then, he sat, scrolling and refreshing, scrolling and refreshing for over an hour. Only tearing himself away long enough to cook breakfast for his family and seek comfort from a cold shower, he returned to the app as soon as possible. Scrolling and refreshing, scrolling and refreshing… he was getting increasingly mad at himself, mad for waiting for something to happen, when he knew nothing would happen, when he knew that—

With a gasp, Mathias bolted upright on his bed.

There it was. *Finally*. An update.

The square picture showed the wide-eyed, curly-haired sculpture of a man's head behind a protective glass case or window. It looked like those Roman or Greek ones everyone knows, but he could never name them. There was no comment, only a tag for an address. A museum in Boulogne.

Who went to the museum on the second of January…? On a Sunday morning, no less? Alberto was probably the only fool in there. When he zoomed on the picture, something caught Mathias's eye. The statue appeared to be located in… public toilets. Who else but Alberto would find that stuff interesting? Fine arts in *lavatories*. Of course he'd love this. If he could, he'd probably open that case and "worship" the statue himself, dry hump its marble thighs. If he could, he'd do that. Nothing *pedestrian* about that.

Without even realizing he was doing it, he'd typed the address of the museum in his browser. Shortly after, Mathias texted:

That place wasn't far away. Mathias could get there in no time. Alberto would probably want to have sex in a museum. Alberto *deserved* to have sex in a museum. Mathias would give him what he deserved and reclaim the number one spot of guys Alberto wanted to fuck, the only position he willingly admitted he was afraid to no longer occupy.

Thirty-something minutes later, he stood in the dreamlike gallery on his toes, overwhelmed by the size of the place, the blinding brightness, the stone-cold faces of the displayed statues. And there, in the middle of the silent, empty gallery, sat a lone Alberto.

Mathias was about to call his name, but he couldn't find his voice. Alberto cut such a pitiful figure, slumped on that bench, looking too dark and too pale at once, a blotch of black ink splashed in the middle of all this white canvas. Either lost in contemplation at the pieces on the wall facing him or having fallen asleep with his eyes open, if Mathias hadn't known Alberto to never touch weed, he'd have made fun of him for smoking too much and spacing out.

Right now, however, he didn't feel like mocking him. In fact, he felt too self-conscious for his liking. He was wondering what the hell he was doing here, following around someone who hadn't contacted him in a week. But looking at that quiet person sitting on that bench all alone made his heart ache. Alberto looked so gentle when he was like this. Maybe it was the way he sat, the tips of his Converse touching, or the way his cardigan had slid off his shoulder, revealing a patch of white skin where his T-shirt ended. Or maybe it was that sleepy look on his face. Either way, Mathias found it impossible to call him a demon this time.

He strolled over to him, and since Alberto didn't notice him hover behind him, he simply sunk onto the bench next to him. Alberto finally looked up, and his face turned ashen.

"Mathias?"

He played it cool. "Who else?"

Alberto looked like he had seen a ghost. Mathias had never

seen him so surprised. He didn't know whether he should feel amused or vexed.

"What are you doing here?"

You, if I can, Mathias thought, pinching his lips. "Are you alone?" he asked instead.

Alberto nodded. His gaze flickered around the room before falling upon Mathias again, unsure. "Did you come to see some art?"

Mathias, staring at Alberto's face, realized he really did, but he couldn't confess to that. "Yeah, sure."

"Really?" Alberto's eyes widened some more.

Mathias shook his head. "Are you high? I texted you half an hour ago."

"Did you?" Alberto furrowed his brow. "I didn't expect you to come."

"I know, but I'm here anyway."

"Okay."

A shiver shook him from head to toe. It occurred to Mathias that he was not wearing a coat.

"Did you leave your coat in the cloakroom?"

"What?"

"You're shivering."

"Oh." Alberto glanced down at himself. "I must have left it at home."

With a derisive snort, Mathias patted his hand, only to find it frozen. He cursed under his breath. What was wrong with this one? He could never do anything like normal people. So annoying.

All the same, Mathias removed his jacket first, then his thick black hoodie. When he dumped it on Alberto's shoulders, he was met with a weird glance, one that reminded Mathias of how he looked back there in that pile of trash, quiet but also dumbstruck, as if he wasn't really expecting Mathias to return for him. Warmth spread throughout his chest, and he lightly coughed in his fist.

Once his own jacket was back on his shoulders, Mathias noticed Alberto hadn't moved. With an impatient sigh, he roughly forced Alberto's arms into the hoodie's sleeves since that idiot didn't seem interested in doing it himself. Perhaps he was uneasy about wearing his clothes. Mathias gently smoothed the fabric over his chest.

"Don't worry," he said. "No one will know it's mine." Alberto shuddered then. Mathias thought he was still cold. "Look at you, seriously… Who forgets their coat in winter?"

Alberto smiled a little at that, producing a half-shrug that looked a bit helpless, and Mathias found himself wanting to kiss that face, stroke that hair, bring some color to those pale cheeks. He boldly leaned forward and breathed a few words in Alberto's ear.

"You're so weird."

Mathias couldn't see Alberto's face, but his feet jiggled as he listened.

"I'm glad to see you," he said softly.

Mathias tried to ignore the way his heart bounced in his ribcage. "Really?"

"Come on." He slowly got to his feet. "Let's see some art together."

Mathias had no interest in these statues or art in general, especially when Alberto was moving in front of him, but he followed him anyway. At first, he tried to engage in small talk, but Alberto didn't seem interested. In fact, he didn't seem completely awake yet. His gaze was unfocused, and his constant yawning reminded Mathias of their first meetings before they started sleeping together. After the fiasco of the other day, he wouldn't dare ask if everything was okay. He could blame it on not wanting to upset him further, but in truth, he was just worried Alberto would tell him he found him as boring now as he did when they first met. So, he was thinking if what he had to do to get his interest back was to look at modern art, then they'd look at modern art, and Mathias would even pretend he was having a good time.

Alberto pulled up the zipper of Mathias's hoodie to his neck and wrapped his arms around himself, apparently appreciating its warmth. Mathias watched him go from statue to statue with mixed feelings, his hands twitching in his pockets. He did attempt to draw his attention towards the sculptures, but evidently, as with every time he was near Alberto, his dirty mind returned to one thing, bringing fire to his cheeks.

"What are you staring at?" Alberto asked after a long yawn.

Mathias scratched his head with a perplexed expression. "Why do statues always have small dicks?"

Alberto didn't laugh, but his eyes narrowed playfully. "If all you can focus on are their dicks, I'm not taking you to Rome ever."

Mathias tried not to feel agitated at the thought of Alberto wanting to travel *home* with him.

"You've never even thought about it?" He smirked. "*You?*"

"What, me? Am I such a pervert in your eyes?" Alberto asked.

Mathias scoffed, and this time, Alberto did smirk, even if only a little.

"There are several theories."

"See?" Mathias grinned. "I knew you'd know about it!"

"Of course I wondered why their dicks are so small. They look so perfect otherwise."

"So? Were they like, really small back then? Compared to us?"

Alberto chuckled. "Look at you, dick-shaming your ancestors."

"What?" Mathias cocked his chin arrogantly, but he was confident his dick looked nothing like the flaccid pinkie displayed in front of him.

"Why would they be?" Alberto went on. "Anyway, there's no proof of that. Apparently, the philosophy at the time was that smart people used their brains instead of their dicks, so by depicting small dicks, it implied the guy was... intellectually superior, a real man of the time. There is art of the same time depicting men with huge cocks, but it's vulgar art, like porn."

"There was porn back then?"

"I'm not sure if there was ever a time without porn, honestly."

"Of course you'd wonder that."

Alberto stuck out the tip of his tongue, and Mathias's hands shook in his pockets with the memory of that crafty tongue inside his mouth or around his—

"So! Ahem... tiny cock equals top dog, and huge cock means dumb dog, is that right?"

"Something like that."

"By your people's standards, then, you must be really dumb."

"First, *bastardo*, I'm Italian, not Greek. Second…" Alberto bit into his lip. "You must be pretty dumb yourself."

"But not, in fact… as dumb as you."

That early January morning, countless works of art soundlessly witnessed Mathias and Alberto argue about the length and girth of their genitals in the middle of the deserted galleries. That was, until Mathias proposed to settle the matter of who was *smartest* in the museum's bathroom, where he found out with surprise that they did, in fact, keep more art back there in alcoves behind glass cases. But that wasn't why he was here.

"You wanna take a seat?" Mathias asked while locking the door.

When he had set off to find the bathroom, Alberto shuffled after him with a blank look, not saying anything but pointing out the way, but now he turned to him with a quirked eyebrow.

"Why?"

"Let's see it."

Alberto gave a small laugh. Under this faint and pallid light, Mathias noticed the dark circles under his eyes. Lack of sleep during the holidays… Why should it be? His brow furrowed, he nudged Alberto toward the sink and urged him to sit up there.

"You… you really want to measure it?" Alberto did as he was told, looking adorably thick for once. "Don't tell me you carry around a ruler."

Mathias kissed him to shut him up and bit into his plump lower lip, loving the weak sound he was rewarded with. Mathias had no intention of measuring anything. He only wanted to drag Alberto back here so he could prove something to him. Still kissing him, he pulled open the buttons of his jeans, only for Alberto to tense under him.

"What are you doing?"

Mathias abruptly slipped his hand inside his pants. "I've got you now. Literally in my hands." He closed his fist around his cock. "Afraid?"

Alberto gave a dry laugh and leaned into his touch. "You think I'm afraid of pain?"

"You should be. Do you even know what pain is?"

"What?" He rolled his eyes. "Getting punched in the face?"

"Losing someone you love. *That* is pain."

Alberto turned silent. Mathias pinned him with his most domineering stare, roughly pulled him closer to the edge of the sink, and started to kneel. When he understood his intentions, Alberto's eyes widened and glowed eerily.

He had every reason to be surprised. They had done plenty of stuff together, and neither of them was afraid to get dirty when it came down to it, but Mathias had never put his face that close to his cock before. His heart thumping, he hesitated briefly as he held it in his hand, but he knew what he'd come here for. The moment Mathias took him in his mouth, Alberto exhaled a shaky breath and laid his back against the wall.

This should be good, Mathias thought as he attended to him with a zeal he believed he'd never demonstrated before. They might even remember this one. Nothing too *pedestrian* about this. Surely, he was marking points, but to his growing despair, it soon became apparent that something wasn't working. Mathias exerted himself, but five minutes later, Alberto was still soft in his mouth and staring at the ceiling with an awkward expression. Mathias thought with shame he was probably bad at it, but he couldn't understand why. He was doing exactly what Alberto did to him, and he wasn't lacking in enthusiasm. A dull pain started spreading throughout more than his knees. After another minute, he gave up, glanced up anxiously at those eyes he hadn't seen in a while. They stared at each other for a long time.

"I'm glad to see you," Alberto said in a weak tone.

The look on his face proved he didn't mean it, and Mathias's heart sunk to its stomach.

Alberto said "sorry" as he tucked himself back in.

.

YOU HAVE REACHED THE END OF PART ONE

After spending the Christmas holidays together, Mathias and Alberto return to school disenchanted, and convinced of the other's indifference… until they both end up in detention and decide to skip school together, consequences be damned. But as they are inexorably pulled toward each other, their personal demons are working their hardest to keep them apart. *Forever.*

Is love even enough?

Find out in the upcoming

He Looks So Fine: Part Two.

Release date: September 12, 2024

Bonus

DISCOVER THE FIRST CHAPTER OF PART TWO.

TOMORROW

TOMORROW WAS ALBERTO'S BIRTHDAY. On Monday night, it was on everybody's lips. "Look at him." "Look at the birthday boy." "Turning eighteen at last?"

How old are you, Alberto?

"Third time's the charm," he told a faded agent, and she said, "Wonderful, wonderful." No one ever listened.

Of course, now that he'd turn eighteen, a new chapter of his life was to begin. Adulthood, at last. Now, he'd get to look forward to that long, empty rail track stretching ahead of him. Him and Mamma against the world, as always.

Alberto snuck away from the cocktail party occurring in his living room and took refuge in the kitchen with Dina.

"I got you a gift," she said, putting a small package in his hand. They exchanged a brief hug.

Dina wasn't very talkative, but she was really kind. Sometimes, she would let Alberto sit at the kitchen island to do his homework. They would watch hoity-toity period dramas together, and Stasia could do nothing about it because Dina always kept an eye on her knives.

He opened the box, his lip curling. "Is this what we talked about two weeks ago?"

She nodded. "I was glad when you finally asked. It was about time. You know what I always say: you never know what can happen tomorrow."

"True." Alberto clutched the small USB device in his hand. The label on it said 2GB. It wasn't much, but it should be enough.

Dina gently put her hand on his shoulder. "Be careful, angel."

Alberto murmured his thanks and turned to leave, but she added, "That boyfriend of yours… he's very nice-looking."

"He's not my boyfriend," he protested, but his cheeks burned at the thought.

It did not surprise Alberto that Dina knew he liked men. After all, you couldn't watch the same programs together without showing a little preference for one type or another. Alberto's tastes amused Dina. She once said a sign of emotional maturity was when one stopped drooling over the bad boy type. Clearly, Alberto wasn't there yet. For example, Mathias was exactly his thing.

Alas, after yesterday… Alberto felt nothing but regret over what happened at the museum. The first time Mathias knelt down before him, looking even more striking than Belmondo's sculptures, and Alberto couldn't even get it up. Indeed, he never got over the shock of seeing him here, of finding him at his worst. Every word Alberto uttered yesterday had been at gunpoint, the weapon held at his temple by his very own hand.

If only Mathias hadn't attempted to look into his eyes, that time after Xavier's brunch. If only he'd turned him over like he always did, then Alberto wouldn't have fallen apart like a fragile house of cards. Too many things had happened in one afternoon, too many memories itching to resurface, too many doors to keep watch over and ensure they remained locked. An impossible endeavour with Mathias's burning eyes peering straight into his soul.

When Alberto woke up the next morning, he was eighteen years old, and when he returned from his shower, his outfit for the day was missing. Stasia was standing in the doorway, holding his clothes and laughing at his clueless expression. He chased after her around the first floor in his bathrobe. She ran into her former bedroom and stood in front of the closet.

"Happy birthday, Albertino."

He waved his hand impatiently. "Give it back."

"I will, if you kiss me."

He hesitated. If he did, she'd let him go faster, but if he gave in again, he'd feel bad about it all day. He did it anyway. Smacking his lips against her cold cheek, he either missed or was tricked, and he ended up kissing the corner of her mouth. She gave his clothes back with a laugh at his disgruntled face. Alberto returned to his bedroom and fell back on his bed with all his weight. "I swear, you're the worst thing that's ever happened to me."

"Don't lie, Britney," Stasia said in a falsely concerned tone. "What would your daddy say?"

Alberto clenched his fists until his nails pierced the skin of his palms. "Will you get out now?"

She folded her arms over her chest. "No."

"Stasia," he warned, and the steadiness of his voice surprised him.

"Uh-uh."

"Get out!"

Her pale-blue eyes turned as black as her soul. "You're raising your voice now?"

Alberto leaned as far away as he could. "Please… I'm going to be late."

"Huh, I know, silly. And I'm not moving. Your choice."

That harpy. Alberto shrugged his bathrobe off and quickly got dressed while she watched with a little smile. He held her gaze with as much contempt as he could muster; she giggled, and when he was struggling to jump into his trousers, she landed a slap on his arse that resounded throughout the bedroom.

"Oops!" She pouted. "Sorry."

She'd been on his case the entire week. Without a boyfriend to suffer her antics, it all fell on him. She had sensed him weaker than usual after he returned from Mathias's, and she immediately burrowed her way in and launched enough attacks that he became too tired to move. She'd been so relentless, he had to revert to his old habits, even giving up the thought of getting out of bed. Because of her, he didn't get to see Mathias. Because of her, he even turned into a limp-dick idiot who let the best thing that ever happened to him slip between his fingers. It was all because of her.

His throat burning, his body shaking, Alberto forced himself to draw a deep breath. He had money, he had an escape plan, and he had a future, somewhere, waiting for him. He wouldn't surrender to the darkest thoughts he sometimes had in his heart. He was eighteen now, and he was no longer a child for people to torment at will. Soon, he would be free…

"What are you doing?"

Alberto and Stasia both spun around with a start. Mamma stood in the doorway, holding a garment bag, looking impeccable in her white Prada dress. Her steely eyes, often cold to the world — but never to him — were fixed on Stasia.

"Wishing him a happy birthday." The Devil always reacted fast. Wrapping her arms around Alberto, she held him tight.

"You're sweet," Mamma said, her lip twitching.

Now that Stasia was satisfied she had ruined Alberto's morning, she quickly left for her Pilates lesson in her little Porsche, and Alberto was left to sit awkwardly next to Mamma on his bed.

"You worry me sometimes…" she said in a tired voice.

Alberto feigned innocence. "Why?"

"You and her. I feel like something is going on that I'm not aware of."

"No." Alberto shook his head. "We're just friends."

Mamma smelled divine; her floral perfume transported him back to the gilded mirror in the villa in Napoli, to the polished tiles, to the costume parties, their favourite dance…

Mamma caressed his cheek, breaking the spell. "You used to tell me things, once."

"I don't have anything to say."

It wasn't even a lie. Even if Alberto wanted to speak, he wouldn't know how to begin. Mamma waited for him to add something, and when he didn't, she opened the garment bag with a sigh.

"It's just an Armani."

Mamma cut the label from the fancy boutique the suit came

from with her brand new pair of scissors — gifted by Dimitri. The glint of the silver almost blinded him. Alberto blinked at the suit and admitted it was stunning. Obsidian black and perfectly tailored, he knew already how good he'd look in it, and he would have loved to flaunt it before Mathias. *Look at me, am I not a vision in this?* Something must have flickered in his eyes, because Mamma's expression turned mournful. She put the suit down and scooted to the edge of the bed, and with her long fingers, she brushed Alberto's hair back, the way she used to when he was little.

"Don't you like it?"

"I do. It's perfect."

"*You're* perfect."

Shame coiled around Alberto's stomach like a snake. He shook his head.

"You are so beautiful," Mamma insisted.

"You're beautiful, too."

She smiled. "Beauty is all the more striking when it's also coming from the inside."

Alberto wouldn't hear this. He sunk his teeth into his lip and turned away from her.

"*Tesoro*," she said softly, "do you like modelling?"

"It's okay."

"Do you understand what it means for people like us?"

He glanced back, but he didn't answer.

"Freedom," Mamma said, and there was life in her eyes. "When they found me, they liberated me. That's what this job can mean to you, too. Independence, travel, money, connections... Fame and glory, if you want them. All of this and more. You must understand that right now, you are living your best years."

"Your career was over at my age."

"Yes, but you... if you play your cards right..."

"I'll do it, Mamma, I'll do it. I'm doing it right now."

Alberto's mother gave him a searching look. "I can see you're doing it, but you seem to take no pleasure in it."

"It's just a job."

"*Just a job?*" Pain flashed in her eyes, making Alberto regret his words.

Mamma never concealed from him she grew up very poor on the outskirts of Parma. Her family dealt in blows, not embraces, and she spent her childhood in abject terror, avoiding hits not only from her parents but also her brothers. She only survived by playing her old VHS tape of *An Impudent Girl* over and over until it fell apart and dreaming, like its heroine, of leaving her dreary village behind and moving to Rome — or even better, Paris.

Accidentally named after a goddess, it soon became clear she also had the appearance of one. When a scout discovered her at the country fair, he took her away from her horrible life and propelled her to stardom just as she reached puberty. Her career was stellar, but it was to be a short one. Before her nineteenth birthday, with a newborn son to raise, she was removed from public life, her career never to start again.

"This job, as you call it, saved my life, and it gave me everything I could dream of." Mamma's voice was trembling. "And all I ever wanted was the same… for you."

"I know…"

"That's why I wanted you to start early—"

"I know."

"And I know I've made a mistake—"

"Mamma…"

"And I don't want to make that same mistake again." Her eyes shone with grief but also determination. "If you don't like it, if you don't want it, just tell me, and you won't have to do it again. You don't have to…" She ran her hand through his hair. "… to do such things, you don't have to go so far."

"I want to do it." He wanted the money, the independence. Fame and glory, he would leave those to the others. "For now."

"In that case…" Mamma brought him close and hugged him tight to her chest. "Happy birthday, my love."

He held her back. When he'd be free from Stasia, Mamma would hopefully follow him, and it would be just the two of them for the first time ever. He didn't need anybody else.

"I'm going to be late," he muttered, breaking away.

Mamma released him reluctantly. "You used to love it when we hugged."

"I was a child."

"You're still my baby."

Alberto looked away. "I know."

He took the suit and hung it in the walk-in closet. Mamma remained on the bed. "Alberto…" she called. "Where were you during the holidays?"

The fact that she used his name gave him pause. He pretended to adjust some hangers in the closet to avoid looking at her.

"With a friend."

"With a friend…" Mamma didn't sound convinced. "*Tesoro*, talk to me."

Alberto turned around and faced her. "There really isn't anything to say. Only that I had fun, and that I was safe. *Very* safe," he added at the sight of her narrowed eyes.

"And when am I going to meet your friend? At your birthday party, maybe?"

He let out a dry laugh. "That thing next week isn't my birthday party. It's another excuse for Dimitri to show off. It has nothing to do with me."

"You're being unfair." Mamma got up and handed him his backpack. "If you'd invite your friends, it would be about you."

He thanked her with a half-smile. "I'll think about it."

There it was. The first lie of the rest of his life.

Alberto glimpsed him when he walked past the school gates: Mathias in football gear. He appeared to be in a bad mood, very nice, very sexy. And his arse in those shorts… Alberto stared a little too long, only to meet Eric's incredulous frown. *It's my birthday, Lassie. Give me a break.*

When he took his seat in Paquin's class, Zak expressed his best wishes, grinning from ear to ear.

Alberto frowned at him. "How do you know it's my birthday?"

The grin vanished, replaced by a deep flush. "You must have told me?"

I told you nothing, Alberto thought with bitterness, but he forced a small smile. It was Zak, after all.

"Stalker," he said.

His jest wasn't interpreted as such. Zak seemed embarrassed, and he didn't look his way until Paquin kicked Alberto out for falling asleep again.

It seemed he was to make a habit of this after all. Alberto accepted his teacher's note for Van Bergen without a word and dragged himself to his office one slow step after another to stall for time. When he got there, he came upon Mathias's sister closing the door with a grimace.

"You don't want to go in there," she said.

"Not really, no," Alberto replied honestly.

If she was afraid to go in, then he wouldn't last a second. Everyone knew Van Bergen considered Elisa Rodin to be his favourite. Why else would he have given her carte blanche as well as her own office — seriously — to write and publish her paper?

"No, I mean, you don't…" She waved both her hands. "Never mind. Do you need him?"

"Sort of. Paquin kicked me out again."

"Oh yeah, I heard she does that." She pointed to the empty detention room next door. "You better wait for him in here."

"Thanks." He entered the classroom, dropped his backpack onto a table, then turned back to Elisa with a frown. "What the hell is this?"

Notes from some horrible song were coming from a portable CD player encased in a clear box on the lone teacher's desk. Elisa perched herself next to it and knocked on the case with a smile. "That's Cher!"

"I can hear that, but why?"

She flung her thumb over her shoulder. "His idea of torture, I assume? Those who end up in detention must listen to 'Believe' by Cher. On repeat."

Alberto gave a resigned sigh. "Save yourself, then. Shouldn't you be in class?"

"Nope. I'm on paper business."

"Of course." He awkwardly sat down on an opposite table, so he wouldn't tower over her so much, while Elisa watched him, her feet swinging back and forth.

"Haven't seen you in a while."

And after yesterday, you probably won't see me outside of school again, Alberto thought with a sinking heart. But he didn't want to make a big deal out of it in front of Elisa. She was press, after all. He was about to give her a dumb excuse, but his group of fangirls walked by the classroom and got excited at the sight of him.

"Hi, Alberto!" "You look nice today!" "Hope you had a nice Christmas!"

Elisa waited for them to be gone and turned to Alberto, her mouth agape. "Do they…"

"Every day."

"They don't mean anything bad, you know. They just find you irresistible."

Gorgeous enough to bring the world to its feet.

Alberto clung to the edges of the table. "I don't like that word."

"Why?"

"It makes it sound like… like it's my fault, somehow."

Elisa winced at the chorus of "Believe" before asking, "Why don't you put your foot down, tell them they make you uncomfortable? Kindly, of course, but—"

Alberto scoffed. "I did! It didn't work. And that's not really the problem."

"Then, what's the problem?"

"How is it on me to make them better people? Why does everyone assume it's my duty to tell all the crazies not to act on their urges? I'm not their parents or their therapists. Even if they can't take a hint from how uncomfortable I look, I shouldn't have to stop whatever I'm doing to teach them basic decency."

They'd never attempted to put themselves in his shoes, not even for a second. Or else why would they keep at it? Alberto had even resorted to hiding in the infirmary just to avoid feeling their eyes on him. How could he not resent them?

Elisa reflected on his words with a thoughtful expression. "It's weird. Everyone wants to be as good-looking as you, but you act like you don't like it, like it's a burden. It doesn't make any sense to most people. In fact, it makes us feel like you're faking it. And we… I mean, *people* don't like that false modesty stuff."

"Whatever," Alberto mumbled. "I don't need them to like me."

Except that was a lie. He did want one person to like him. Only one. The rest could get lost, along with all the others who made the simple act of looking at his own face a challenge.

"Bull... shit," Elisa said, in a perfect imitation of her brother. "Everybody needs people. You do, too. Why did you date Zak if you didn't need him?"

"You—"

"I've noticed," she added haughtily. "Zak has the most kissable face in the entire school, and I've never seen you do so much as pecking him on the cheek. So, either you wanted to hurt Eric, or..."

Alberto's eyes narrowed. "I wanted to hurt Eric."

"And this! This thing you do!"

"What?"

"I'm never sure whether you're telling the truth or you're just fucking with me."

Alberto couldn't help but laugh. "You are very foul-mouthed for a fifteen-year-old girl."

Elisa smirked. "You should have heard my mother. She even had a Sailor Moon outfit that said *Sailor Mouth*. It was a whole thing." She checked the time on the clock behind her and slid down the desk. "Alberto Gazza, I'm sorry I called you a sexist pig. I can see why you would feel a bit... harassed."

"Thanks..." Alberto blinked at her, at a loss for words. He tried to find something equally meaningful to say. "I'm sorry I said you were objectifying Zak. You're actually... nice."

"Yeah?" She beamed. "Nice?"

"Too bad Zak is in love with that *guy*, or he would have liked .you."

"Pff!" Elisa pranced toward the exit. "I gave Eric a hard time in my paper, and he reacted like a champ! He's great. And since he's great, I'm happy for Zak."

"I know," Alberto said. "Me too."

She stopped as she reached the doorway. "Should I send my brother to rescue you?"

Alberto's shoulders dropped. He wondered what would be

worse: Mathias never giving him another chance — as he feared right now — or him charging into the classroom, renewing his offer to go down on him, only for Alberto to get all limp on him again.

"I'll be okay," he muttered, but when she was gone, he looked around the room at all the empty tables, and his heart felt heavy in his chest. "I'm eighteen now."

Find more information at:

WWW.HELOOKSSOFINE.COM

·

My deepest thanks to Silvia and Monica for *everything* Italian.

A WORD OF THANKS

For having selected and read this book. I sincerely hope you have enjoyed it.

And if you did, would you please consider **leaving a review**? **It's an easy and sure way to support an indie author.**

I'm aware that your time is precious; writing a single line or using the star rating can truly make a difference.

Keep on reading if you want to get **free access to bonus content** about Alberto and Mathias, and many other Colette International freebies.

With Love,

Zelda

DISCOVER THE FREEBIES

Readers who join **The Reading Nook** get access to every bonus relating to Mathias and Alberto, such as:

Of Love & Violence, the book's soundtrack featuring Alberto favourite French electro tunes as well as Mathias's beloved Garbage — and of course, the dirty songs of Bloodhound Gang.

Members of *The Reading Nook* also benefit from several art commissions, short stories and extras a year, as well as **special launch prices** for ebooks.

Sign up and find more information at:

WWW.ZELDAFRENCH.COM

★

CHAPTER LIST

FALL

Arc One: Strangers

Arc Two: Lovers

WINTER

Arc Three: Liars

Chapters in **bold are written solely from Mathias's POV.*

ABOUT THE AUTHOR

ZELDA FRENCH LIVES IN LONDON, LIKES CATS, SWEARING, GOOD WINE AND ROCK MUSIC, AND REALLY ENJOYS ANGSTY STORIES WITH HAPPY ENDINGS.

YOU CAN FIND MORE INFORMATION AT:
WWW.ZELDAFRENCH.COM

amazon.com/author/zeldafrench

goodreads.com/zeldafrench

bookbub.com/authors/zelda-french

instagram.com/zelda_french

tiktok.com/@zeldafrench

CONTENT WARNINGS

For the reasons listed below, this story isn't intended for readers under the age of 18. In addition to profanity and underage drinking, the contents of the book **DEPICTS** ACTS OR **MENTIONS** ACTS OF:

Abuse (physical, mental, emotional, verbal, sexual), depression, harassment, homophobia, grieving, implied animal cruelty, racism, sexism, suicidal thoughts, violence, as well as sexual acts between a seventeen-year-old and an eighteen-year-old, which at times may make the reader uncomfortable.

TREAT YOURSELF WITH CARE AND PROCEED WITH CAUTION.

Printed in Great Britain
by Amazon

55877225R00229